WORST CASE SCENARIO

WORST CASE SCENARIO

LARRY ENMON

People sleep peaceably in their beds at night only because rough men stand ready to do violence on their behalf.

GEORGE ORWELL

ONE

Paul Evans stared out the passenger's window at the black desert racing by at seventy miles an hour. With no moon, the only illumination came from the SUV's headlights. This area of Interstate 40, between Santa Rosa and Clines Corners, was the loneliest stretch of the covert escort mission. All personnel from the Office of Secure Transportation voted it the most boring. Miles of endless, dark freeway with a featureless landscape on all sides. Of course, driving it on a Tuesday, in the middle of the night, what could he expect? Paul checked the time to confirm they were still on schedule. They should be at Sandia in less than two hours. This was the day he'd been looking forward to for weeks.

It was his wife's thirtieth birthday. She'd be up later, getting Katherine off to school. Paul planned to be home with the bouquet of roses by then. This was his last mission before their vacation. In just over two hours, he'd have ten days off. The last few months had been crazy. The higher tensions with China and Russia only increased the frequency of the missions. His wife had arranged for her parents to look after the kids for a week. Paul had reservations at a mountain cabin for him and his wife in Cloudcroft. With all the stresses of her job, his crazy travel schedule, and two small children, they both needed some private time together on a secluded mountain. He took a swallow of water from his bottle and turned to the back seat, searching the rear floorboard.

"Are there any cashews left?"

"I dropped them back there somewhere," Steve answered, turning to help search.

Paul waved him away. "I'll look—you just drive," Paul said before moving a ballistics vest and found them sitting on top of an M-4 assault rifle. "Got 'em."

"What in the hell do you suppose that is," Steve mumbled, leaning closer to the windshield.

Paul pulled open the bag and grabbed a handful of nuts as he directed his attention back to the front. He gazed in wonder at the strange spectacle. The horizon ahead glowed bright orange like an early sunrise, but from the west. Distances were hard to gauge in the desert at night, but he made it at less than ten miles. Paul popped a nut in his mouth before saying, "No idea—aliens?" he joked as the glow continued filling the night sky. He popped a couple of more nuts into his mouth, but a feeling of dread settled in his gut.

Steve grunted. "Well, this is New Mexico; anything's possible."

"Better call it in." Paul grabbed the mike to the encrypted radio. The eighteen-wheeler was only five miles behind and closing fast. If there was a road obstruction up ahead, it needed to be checked out before the eighteen-wheeler rolled up on it. "Convoy Commander, this is Scout."

The deep, slow, baritone voice answering had a sound of authority. "Scout, this is Convoy Commander—go ahead."

The laid-back Tennessee drawl made Paul grin. The commander had grown up in Oak Ridge. He'd never lose that down-home accent. Cornbread, field peas, and sweet iced tea defined him. Old guys never got excited. Besides, he'd been doing this job almost since Paul was born.

"Sir, we have an orange glow directly ahead of us that may be a fire. It appears to be on the primary route. Request permission to investigate."

A few seconds passed before the commander answered. "That's a roger, Scout. I haven't heard anything on the state police radio—we'll give 'em a call."

"Commander, we suggest you drop it down to fifty—repeat five zero miles an hour. We'll check it out and advise when we're on the scene."

"Copy that, Scout, we're shutting it back to five zero miles—call us when you have something."

Paul popped the rest of the nuts in his mouth and dusted his hands on his tactical pants. "Okay, kick this thing in the butt, and let's see what's up there." They had only minutes to determine the situation before the convoy would be on them. If there was an obstruction on the primary, a quick secondary route must be established and approved. The convoy could never be allowed to stop—*never*, except in specially secured areas.

Steve hit the gas and upped the speed to eighty-five. The orange glow took on a large eerie appearance. Paul grabbed the binoculars but couldn't make out anything except a larger version of what they were already seeing. The bizarre, glowing shadows in the dark desert sky danced like ghosts in the heavens. In five years working for DOE, Paul had seen nothing like it. A feeling of apprehension again crept through his stomach. Within the next few miles, it became clear; the light was a massive fire. Red and yellow flames rose a hundred feet in the air as their SUV approached the inferno. The blaze lit up the dark road with a light as bright as day. A New Mexico State Police car blocked the freeway about two hundred yards from the conflagration. The car's red and blue lights flashed with the wall of flames in the background. Flares and orange safety cones blocked the freeway and were laid out in a pattern that directed all traffic off to a gravel service road to the right. A state trooper waved Paul and Steve to the side of the freeway toward the gravel road with his flashlight.

"Let's talk to this guy," Paul said. There were no other vehicles on the freeway this time of night, so Steve slowed to a crawl and stopped a few feet from the officer. Paul lowered his window, and the growl of the fire became louder. A petrochemical smell wafted past his nostrils. "What's happened?" he shouted over the noise.

The trooper paced to their vehicle. He had a look of total exhaustion. With the window down, the heat warmed Paul's face. The officer's features came into view. He had a lot of Native American blood. He was short—barely 5'8", but with broad, muscular shoulders and a thick chest. His most notable feature was a thin scar across the bridge of his nose.

The trooper continued waving his flashlight toward the orange cones as he wiped sweat from his brow. "You'll have to get off here—freeway's closed."

Paul dug into his pocket and held up his federal agent credentials. "We're OST, escorting a special cargo to Sandia. What's going on?"

The officer's forehead wrinkled as he bent down to the passenger's window and examined the credentials with his flashlight. He handed them back and nodded. "Oh yeah, they told us at roll-call you might be coming through tonight." He turned and pointed to the fire. "Tanker truck flipped—just rolled up on it about five minutes ago. Waiting for some help."

Paul asked, "Any survivors?"

The trooper removed his cap and wiped his face with a handkerchief. Had to be at least ninety-five degrees out there.

The officer shook his head. "Don't know—haven't been able to get any closer than this—doesn't look good."

Paul had to make a decision and fast. The convoy would be there in minutes. He glanced at the GPS map before asking, "How far is Highway Three?"

The trooper leaned both hands on top of the vehicle while he spoke through the passenger window. His eyes narrowed before pointing straight toward the fire. "Highway Three exit is about two miles up the freeway."

Paul hated delays. Always came at the times he had plans he didn't want messed up. "How can we get there? Any chance of staying on the service road and making it through?"

The officer shook his head. "None—you'd cook, and so would your cargo." He nodded to the improvised exit he'd formed with the orange cones. "You could get off here on the service road. In about fifty yards, it'll intersect a gravel road that heads north. That's where I'm directing other traffic. In a few miles, you can take a left on another gravel road that intersects Highway Three. Just follow the signs—nothing to it."

Paul studied the blaze. "Fifty yards, huh. Will that put us too close to the fire?"

The trooper shook his head. "No, you'll be well away from it. I directed three vehicles there a couple of minutes ago—not many choices until we clear the freeway."

Steve checked the officer's directions on the vehicle's GPS. He tapped the screen. "Here it is." He leaned toward the trooper. "Will that road handle an eighteen-wheeler?"

The officer smiled. "Sure—no problem."

Paul fiddled with the knobs on the police scanner and encrypted car radio. "We haven't heard a word about this. Have you reported it?"

The trooper glanced at the radio on his belt. "I'm having trouble getting through to base from here—must be a dead zone or something, had to use my cell to call it in."

Paul looked at Steve, who gave him a quick nod and then back to the trooper. "Thanks for the info. I'm calling the other convoy vehicles. Wish we could stick around and help, but we have to scout ahead. When they get here, just direct them toward the gravel road—I'll make sure they know where to go. Don't bother trying to talk to them. They're ordered not to stop for anyone."

"Will do—good luck." The officer stepped back and gave a quick wave.

Steve backed up and drove across the tiny sliver of turf to access the freeway's service road, while Paul attempted to call the commander on the radio. After several tries, he realized his transmissions weren't going anywhere. "Great, now our radio's not working." He dialed the cell phone number for the commander and explained what he'd discovered.

"Yeah," the commander said, "we got through to the state police. They confirmed the fire—said they'd had several calls about it. I'll contact Albuquerque base and tell them we're deviating from the primary. We'll be right behind you, so get well out ahead of us and keep in touch. Let us know when you hit Highway Three."

The light from the fire was like a giant torch behind Paul and Steve as they drove down the lonely gravel road into the black night. Paul kept messing with the encrypted radio, switching channels and trying different encryption codes, attempting to bring it back online—nothing. He couldn't understand it. *Worked fine until they stopped to talk to the officer.* By the time they made the final left turn on the lonely, dark road toward Highway Three, they were deep in the boonies. The narrow stretch wove through thick trees and desert scrum on each side of the road. Only the glow of the burning tanker in the distance to their left gave them any light. The commander wouldn't like this—always hated tight areas with no visibility.

After about three miles, they came to a major road and a sign that read Highway Three. Paul let out a sigh of relief just as his phone rang —the Convoy Commander.

"Scout, we just made the turn onto the gravel road, and we're only a few miles behind you. This is the crappiest damn excuse for a road I've ever seen. How's it look up ahead?"

"You're clear to Highway Three, sir. We're turning on it now." Paul disconnected and looked at Steve. "Take a left here—we'll try and put a little distance between us. Want to make sure there are no more surprises—he sounds pissed." Paul calculated the time. He could still be home with the flowers before his daughter left for school if there were no other delays. Every time he planned a surprise for his family, something like this always came up.

Steve turned onto the hardtop just as the alert signal broke the silence. He and Paul looked at each other with the same thought—*the convoy was under attack.* The shrill beeping alarm and flashing red light on the SUV's console so distracted Paul that he grabbed the dead radio's mic. "Convoy Commander—this is Scout!"

"Forget it—it's still out," Steve yelled, making a U-turn and heading back down the dark, narrow road they'd just left.

"Hurry!" Paul punched buttons on his phone. The commander's cell rang five times—then went to voice mail. Paul grabbed the ballistics vest from the back seat and slipped it over his head. His hands shook as he reached for the M-4 and chambered a round.

Steve speed-tested their nerves racing to the rescue. The SUV fishtailed in the loose gravel, and Steve had to let off the accelerator. When he rounded the only curve in the road, they both spotted it at the same time. A white, three-quarter-ton, dually pickup truck with a large camper shell straddled the dark narrow road.

"Where did that come from?" Steve yelled, slamming hard on the brakes. Paul was pushed forward as the SUV skidded to a stop and blinding dust overtook them. They were enveloped in a thick white cloud as Paul reached for the door handle. Through the swirling dust around the front windshield, the outline of a man popped up from behind the hood of the blocking vehicle.

Paul squinted. *What tha…* The flash from the shoulder-fired rocket the man held lit up the night. Paul had always assumed before someone died, their last thoughts would be on friends or family. He was wrong. His was on the eighteen-wheeler they were escorting, filled with nuclear weapons, which was under attack.

TWO

Simon Murr squatted on the deserted beach rubbing a couple of coarse pebbles he'd picked up in his hand. A gentle sea breeze ruffled his hair and beard as he gazed at the cloudless sky filled with the dying stars of dawn. It was going to be another beautiful day. The night faded with each passing minute. Soon there would be too much light, and he would become obvious to the traffic on the coastal highway north of Beirut. He frowned and again scanned the beach and dark ocean before him, checking his watch for the last time. He stood, dropped the pebbles, and brushed off his hands. It was 5:05 AM—he'd already stayed past the agreed-upon time. This section of the Mediterranean near the Dog River was popular with early morning joggers. Simon must leave or risk discovery. He dialed his cell while staring at the fading moon. He was heartbroken it had not been successful. Two rings later, the voice answered.

"I'm ready, come now," Simon said and pocketed the phone. He took one last look back at the dark water. Leaving the man wasn't something he wanted to do—they'd become friends the last two weeks, but he could not compromise himself or his family by being seen. Something must have gone wrong. The guy might not even be alive anymore. If captured, would he talk? Probably—everyone talked sooner or later. Best to get out of there right now and establish an alibi.

The car with no headlights slowly moved along the deserted beach toward Simon. He gazed at the sixty-foot luxury yacht a mile offshore—its deck lights outlining its form. *Too bad they'd come so close.*

Simon walked toward the approaching car with his son behind the wheel. Water splashing from his rear caused Simon to turn just as the head and shoulders of someone, clad in a black wetsuit, emerged from the surf. *It was him—he'd made it.* The man tried standing but fell to his knees. He struggled to rise again but collapsed back into the shallow water. *He must be injured.*

The car pulled up just as Simon rushed into the water. He was a big man but moved with incredible speed through the wet sand and waves. The coolness of the morning ocean came as a shock as Simon waded to within arm's reach of the man. He lifted him with a strong hand. Slinging his arm around the fellow's waist, he half-carried him to the beach. The rescued man breathed heavily and allowed Simon to carry his weight.

"Are you hurt?"

The man shook his head. "No." He gasped for a breath. "I'm okay."

Simon wiggled his finger at the driver of the car. "Peter, the trunk —quickly."

The young driver released the trunk latch and leaped from the car to help his father remove the exhausted fellow's diving equipment. They tossed the rebreather in the trunk first, followed by the mask, fins, snorkel, and weight belt. Simon peeled the wetsuit off the man and threw it on top of the pile as he closed the truck. His eyes scanned the area, making sure no one had observed them.

Peter reached into the back seat and grabbed the clothes. He handed the guy a shirt, slacks, and jacket. The man dressed and finished toweling his hair before slipping into jogging shoes.

Simon jumped behind the wheel, the man dropped into the passenger's seat, and Peter in the back behind his father. With the headlights still off, the black Peugeot moved across the beach toward the coastal highway before the rising sun crested the horizon.

Simon turned to the man. "What happened? Did everything go all right?"

"It's okay; I just ditched the water scooter a little too soon. Wanted to make sure it sank in deep water," the man replied.

"How far out?"

"Couple hundred yards."

Simon's jaw dropped. "You swam two hundred yards against an outgoing tide? Bishop, you should be in the Olympics!"

Bishop didn't answer; he leaned against the headrest and closed his eyes.

Simon caught Peter's eye in the rearview mirror and smiled. They'd pulled it off—thank God. He again looked at Bishop. His breathing was normal now, and he seemed completely relaxed. He would miss him—he wasn't like other Americans who worked in the intelligence community. Simon took a right onto the highway and headed toward the condo in the Mar Mikhael neighborhood of East Beirut. At this hour, the drive took less than twenty minutes. As Simon turned down the street to his house, a call to prayer echoed through loudspeakers from a minaret the next street over. Simon opened his garage door with the remote and pulled inside. He mumbled, "We must hurry—we have no time to lose. It leaves in less than an hour."

All three scrambled into the condo and were greeted by the sweet smell of Ruth's fresh-baked bread. Bishop jumped in the shower and washed the salt from his hair and face—he was out in two minutes. The dark blue business suit, white dress shirt, and burgundy tie were already laid out on the bed. While he dried off, Simon brought in a prawn omelet, hot pita bread, and honey.

Bishop looked up and beamed. "My favorite."

Simon watched him alternate between dressing and eating. The athletic build supported his 190 pounds with ease. He wasn't a giant at a little over six feet, but the military bearing made him appear taller.

"I'm happy we could extend our hospitality to you," Simon said.

Bishop cinched his belt and took the last bite of omelet before tying his tie in a four-in-hand knot. He stepped back from the wall mirror, put on the suit jacket, and affixed the top button. He glanced at Simon. "Well?"

Simon posted his hands on his hips and made a point to sound optimistic when he said, "You look like a successful international businessman returning from a foreign trip. Now let's go."

They marched back into the living area, Bishop toting a small black, leather carry-on, with Simon leading the way. Simon would mail the rest of his belongings to an address in Canada in a couple of weeks. From there, it would be forwarded to an obscure post office box in Maryland.

Bishop hugged Simon's wife, Ruth. "Thank you. I'll miss you, and your cooking."

She stared at him through motherly, misted eyes. "God go with you, Troy." She softly touched his cheek and smiled.

Heading for the door, Peter shoved a to-go cup of hot French roast coffee into Bishop's hand.

Bishop smirked. "Thanks—keep practicing your backgammon. I may just show up one evening for another game."

Simon hustled him back into the garage and into the Peugeot. Bishop sat in the passenger seat sipping coffee while his host drove him toward the harbor.

Simon handed him an envelope. "Here is your ticket for the hydrofoil to Cypress."

Bishop studied it a moment before nodding.

Fishing another envelope from his pocket, Simon said, "This one is the airline ticket from Larnaca to Washington DC, via London."

Bishop placed both envelopes inside his jacket pocket.

Simon held out a Canadian passport with a business card peeking from the top. "Here is your passport in the name of Sedgwick Hartman."

Bishop made a face. "Who in the hell thinks up these names?"

Simon smiled, handing over the document. "Anyway, the visa stamp shows you've only been in Lebanon two days and not two weeks. The business card is from the Solidere Company. You had a meeting with one of their vice presidents yesterday. If called, the man will confirm it. There are also a couple of credit card receipts showing you bought him lunch yesterday and yourself dinner last night." Simon waved a paper toward him. "This is the receipt for your stay at the Le Royal Hotel Beirut. Also—here's your wallet with all your Canadian identification and a few Lebanese pounds and Canadian dollars."

Bishop tucked the passport, wallet, and hotel receipt inside his other pocket.

"You've thought of everything."

Simon flashed a toothy smile. "I'm paid well to think of everything."

———

Bishop forced his mind and body to relax. He wasn't out of danger yet, and exiting an assignment sometimes proved the trickiest… He smiled to himself, recalling the circumstances that brought him here.

CIA had received the initial information from the Mossad. Their question to the United States was short and to the point. *Do you want to handle it, or do you want us to take it?* Since the US wasn't too keen on another possible military dust-up between Israel and Lebanon, they passed it to the DOD Special Operations Command as a *Direct Action Request*. Someone made the call that a full Seal Team was overkill for this type of mission. Best handled by only two men. One with the training and experience to execute it, and the other as back-up and support.

Since it involved weapons of mass destruction and complete secrecy was a must, it got pushed over to P2OG. And that's how Bishop teamed up with Simon. The Israelis smuggled Bishop into Lebanon, and Simon met him and took care of the rest. Made him part of his family, housed him in a back bedroom, and provided logistics and intelligence on the target…

Simon is what's known in the intelligence community as an independent agent. He didn't care who he worked for as long as it was against the current government of Lebanon. He'd grown up there— born and raised a Lebanese Christian. All his family was Lebanese. He still remembered when Beirut was considered *The Paris of the Middle East*. Before the ugly civil war, before he lost so many loved ones in the fighting. He wanted to kick Hezbollah out and start rebuilding a new democratic Lebanon. Bring it back to its former glory. That could never happen as long as Hezbollah and their sponsor, Iran, held a grip on the country. Today, Simon worked for the Israelis. Perhaps next week the English, and next month the Americans or French.

According to the schedule, the seven o'clock hydrofoil had been boarding for twenty minutes as Bishop and Simon pulled into the harbor parking lot. Only ten more to go before departure. Bishop pulled his ticket from his jacket before opening the passenger door.

Simon's expression softened. "I'll say my goodbyes here—better for me."

Bishop stared at the bear of a man he had trusted with his life the last couple of weeks. The full, red beard and thick eyebrows did little to hide the cartoonishly large nose. His smile was always genuine and kind. Type of guy anybody would love hanging with. "Goodbye, my friend," Bishop said, "and thanks."

They shook hands, and Simon gave him a wink and grin. "I think we did some good today—how much time left?"

Bishop checked his Rolex Submariner—"Twelve minutes."

"Take care," Simon whispered before Bishop sprinted across the parking lot.

When Bishop entered the harbor terminal, he didn't like what he saw. It was as he'd feared—almost empty. No crowd to blend into. Everyone else had already boarded. The whole back wall was windows that looked out over the water. To his left was a walk-up food stand with a couple of people waiting for their orders. The smell of grilling lamb and freshly baked bread made his mouth water even though he'd just eaten. There were perhaps a half dozen passengers scattered in the fifty or so seats in the center. A couple dressed in traditional Arab attire eyed him as he scanned the passport control area to his right. He looked for the General Security Directorate agent that hung back, watching everyone that boarded. They closely monitored all resident aliens and foreign visitors in country. *Yup, there he was.* Had to be him. Short guy with black curly hair in a dark, cheap suit and bored expression. He leaned against the wall with the inbound and outbound schedules directly above his head. *Okay, Bishop, time to play it cool.*

"Good morning," Bishop said and handed his ticket to the lady at the boarding counter.

She smiled, folded the ticket, and tore it along its perforated edges before returning the second half to him. She motioned with her head toward passport control. "Safe travels, sir."

Bishop took a breath and stepped up to the uniformed immigration officer at the second counter, placing his fake Canadian passport in the guy's outstretched hand. The GSD agent casually pushed off the wall he'd been leaning against and strolled behind the immigration officer, looking over his shoulder at Bishop's passport.

Bishop's mouth went dry.

The immigration officer flipped through the passport to the last entry and stared at Bishop. One of those deadpan expressions that neither expresses curiosity or surprise. In his most monotone voice, he said, "Your purpose for traveling to Lebanon, sir?"

In an even, relaxed manner, Bishop said, "Business."

The officer didn't speak but kept eying him. The frown forming on his lips put Bishop on guard. He wasn't taking the bait. Old interrogation trick—use silence to get someone to talk more. No one needed to tell Bishop that talking more usually meant going to prison or being executed in his business. As the seconds ticked by, Bishop's stomach twisted when the immigration officer passed the passport over his shoulder to the GSD agent with a noncommittal shrug. The agent closely examined it and met Bishop's gaze with another question.

"What kind of business?"

"Had a meeting with an executive from the Solidere Company. My company sells electronics. Solidere wants to place a large order," Bishop said.

The agent slowly thumbed through the passport pages with a confused expression like he was examining the Rosetta Stone. After a moment, he said, "Your airline ticket please," and held out his hand.

Bishop handed over the ticket. The guy went over every line, taking his time. Bishop turned to the wall clock above the door. Only five minutes left before departure. *Come on… come on.* The noise of the hydrofoil completing its inflation only increased Bishop's anxiety. The agent nodded to the immigration officer before handing back the airline ticket to Bishop. The clomp of the officer stamping the passport, at last, brought a little mental relief. Bishop glanced out the terminal window. The crew was in the final stages of departure. They were about to cast off the docking lines.

Bishop accepted his passport and picked up his carry-on. Just as he took a step past the passport control desk, the GSD agent held up his hand and asked another question.

"If you're from Canada, why are you also flying to Washington?"

Guy was more on the ball than he looked. His brows folded into an intimidating stare. Bishop knew the game, played it enough times.

"Another meeting," Bishop answered.

If he didn't board right now, he would miss the departure, and this goon could interrogate him at leisure for hours.

"When are you going back to Canada?"

Bishop nodded to the door a few feet away. "Depends on whether I miss this connection."

"You never said who your meeting was with while you were here," the agent said.

Bishop released a breath—*time for the power play*. He took on the confidence of a real business executive handling a pesky bureaucrat on the verge of making him miss a vital travel connection. Bishop put on his annoyed expression and walked toward the door leading to the hydrofoil.

He passed the business card Simon gave him to the agent. "Sorry, but I must go." In a stern voice that allowed no room for argument, Bishop said, "Call Mr. Lemoyne if you wish; I'm sure he'll be happy to answer all your questions." Bishop held his breath as he passed through the door, but the agent didn't challenge him further.

As he walked on board, an attendant said, "Please take a seat; we're departing."

The hydrofoil rocked as it edged away from the dock, and Bishop held on to seats as he eased his way down the aisle. As he walked, he scanned the passengers. No one gave him any notice. That didn't mean anything. Foreign security types didn't give any notice until they moved in for an arrest. Someone touched his shoulder from behind, and Bishop froze.

"Sir, would you like tea, coffee, or orange juice?" the hostess asked.

Bishop relaxed his fist. "Nothing for me, thank you," he said, dropping into a seat on the starboard side in first class. He was exhausted. Being up all night was one thing, but a brisk two-hundred-yard swim and the stress of boarding had taken a toll on his physical reserves. He casually pulled up his sleeve and eyed the count-down timer on his watch. He glanced out the window as the timer read zero. A giant, orange fireball rose from the ocean—about a mile offshore to the west. As it slowly maneuvered through the harbor, the hydrofoil's noise blocked out the sound of the explosion. Passengers jumped to their feet, pointing and rushed to the starboard side windows, searching the distance ocean and speculating about what blew up.

While the hostess tried corralling the passengers, Bishop rested his head back on his seat and closed his eyes. It was a hundred and sixty-four kilometers to Cypress. If he was lucky, he could grab a two-and-a-half-hour nap—he needed it.

The crackle of passenger's voices echoing through the cabin as they continued speculating didn't faze Bishop in the least. A slow smile spread across his lips. It was two advanced special-purpose limpet mines with 4.4 pounds of RDX placed under the fuel tanks of a luxury yacht.

THREE

J. Thomas Fuller stood at the window and gazed into the darkened Rose Garden. For a crowd this size, the Oval Office was unusually quiet. It always amazed him that during early morning meetings, people spoke so softly. Almost like they were still asleep or afraid they might wake someone else up. Or perhaps they just had a quiet reverence for the Oval Office. By the afternoons and evening, the voices were higher, shriller, with a kind of excited expectation over the latest emergency. Fuller checked his watch, then turned and looked at the seven other people and thanked God the meeting wasn't in that god-awful situation room. He and the President detested the place—too cramped.

Since Fuller had called the meeting at this early hour, he was responsible for seeing it went off smoothly. This was a demanding crowd, and he didn't want the added distraction of people grumbling before the President arrived. The cart of juices, coffee, and breakfast pastries had just arrived, and the room was filled with the rich smell of freshly brewed java and yeasty baked goods. Fuller checked the time again. The president would be along directly. The Secretaries of State and Defense sat on opposite ends of the sofa, exchanging quiet pleasantries. The Director of National Intelligence had retreated to one corner of the office, and the FBI Director to another—both speaking in whispered tones on their cell phones. The Secretary of Homeland Security studied a briefing sheet. The Secretary of Energy and Chairman of the Joint Chiefs were mumbling to each other, a grim look plastered on their faces.

All the cliques of the National Security Council were firmly in place. Fuller's role as National Security Advisor went far above the usual duties of the office. He was also the president's friend and former college roommate. Fuller would still be at Princeton teaching International Studies had his old friend not been elected president. Sometimes Fuller wished he hadn't. He would have been much happier in academia than in this world of secrets. Giving lectures to young, open minds was always better than conducting top-secret briefings, even in the Oval Office. The Director of National Intelligence disconnected from the call and wrote something in a pocket notebook. He eyed Fuller from across the room and made a beeline for him.

"What did you tell him?"

Fuller shrugged. "Only that there was a nuclear emergency."

The fellow grunted and helped himself to a fresh cup of coffee. "He didn't ask what?"

Fuller hated people questioning him about the president's actions. "No, up late last night watching the playoffs. Wasn't expecting his first meeting to be at five o'clock this morning. Didn't sound so good on the phone."

The director nodded. "Well, this isn't the way any of us wanted to start the day."

"Good morning, ladies and gentlemen," the president said, walking into the room.

Everyone stood, and the president waved them down. "Please take your seats."

He had black circles under each eye, and his step wasn't quite as lively as most mornings. He wore dark blue suit pants, a white dress shirt with open collar, and an Oxford grey cardigan sweater.

The extra chairs Fuller ordered for the meeting were quickly filled. He poured the president a cup of coffee and set it on the desk.

"Thank you, Jeff," the president said and stifled a small yawn before sliding behind the executive desk. He took a quick sip and looked up at the group before addressing Fuller. "Is everyone here?"

Fuller cleared his throat. "No, sir, the vice president has been informed and is en route back from Asia. The Deputy National Security Advisor is traveling with him. The Chief of Staff is also returning from his fishing lodge. He should be here," Fuller glanced at his watch, "within the hour."

The president nodded. "Very well, let's begin—Mr. Fuller, what're the details." The president rocked back in the leather chair and took another sip of coffee. He tried keeping a neutral expression, but Fuller knew his old friend well enough to understand that the wrinkling around the man's eyes indicated he understood the seriousness of the meeting.

Everyone stared at Fuller—waiting to see how he would begin. He removed a piece of paper from his jacket, glancing at it for a moment before speaking.

"At 1:16 this morning, mountain time, the Albuquerque control center for the Department of Energy's Office of Secure Transportation received an emergency alert from one of its convoys."

When Fuller said Department of Energy, the Secretary of Energy's head slightly bowed. The Secretary was probably very much aware that neither he nor the FBI director were members of this elite club. The look on his face confirmed that since they were there, it did not bode well for either of them.

Fuller continued. "The alert was triggered by the Convoy Commander escorting a nuclear weapons shipment to Sandia National Laboratory." Fuller cleared his throat again. "Attempts to contact the convoy were unsuccessful." Fuller glanced toward the Secretary of Energy. He continued looking down. "New Mexico Highway Patrol dispatched several units to the convoy's last reported location based on the GPS signal before the alert."

Fuller paused, took a swallow of coffee, and studied the paper again before finishing. He walked closer to the President's desk, dropped the paper on it, and stared at the group. "Upon arrival, the patrol officers found complete carnage. The convoy had been attacked, and all personnel were casualties."

The President's brow pinched, and he leaned forward, carefully placing the coffee cup on the saucer. He stared at Fuller a moment before asking, "How many killed?"

Fuller looked to the Secretary of Energy. "Mr. Secretary?"

"All of them," the man blurted out, wringing his hands.

The President didn't speak but turned back to Fuller. "There were no survivors—no wounded?"

Fuller lowered his voice. "No, sir, it appears several were wounded and might have survived, but they were systematically executed." Fuller remained silent for a while, waiting for a response from the President—there was none. He could read the shock and disbelief in his friend better than anyone. Fuller again spoke, but in a lower tone. "The tractor-trailer carrying the warheads was breached, and six weapons were taken."

The President looked up. "Taken?"

"Yes, the vehicle was set on fire, but a preliminary inventory suggests at least six. We'll have a final count as soon as they can confirm it."

Fuller handed the President a navy-blue leather notebook with a golden Department of Energy emblem on the front. The President opened it and scanned its contents, his face a mask of disbelief. No one said a word. He closed the notebook and laid his hands on top.

He gawked at the Secretary of Energy. "It has always been my understanding from earlier briefings that what was just described is impossible."

Fuller felt a tinge of sympathy for the Secretary of Energy. The Office of Secure Transportation and the security of nuclear weapons in transit were his responsibility. The man had been the governor of a big oil state and a great supporter of the President early in his campaign. His loyalty was rewarded with the DOE Director's appointment. Probably wished he was still just a governor right about now. The man stood, subconsciously smoothing his tie, before speaking.

"Yes, sir, that's always been the view of DOE. The trailer is designed to deny unauthorized access for up to four hours. It was thought that with the additional protection afforded by the escort team, that would be sufficient time to summon help anywhere in the country."

The President frowned and stood. "Are you saying it took over four hours to get help to them?" His voice rose with each word, and his tone sounded accusatory.

The Secretary of Energy blanched. "No sir, it appears the theft was accomplished in less than half an hour."

The man was uncomfortable with his answer—a bead of sweat ran down his cheek.

The President glanced at Fuller a moment before leaning forward, placing both palms on the desk, and fixing his eyes on the Secretary of Energy. "I don't understand."

"Sir, apparently, the denial safeguards failed. We're attempting to determine the cause, but it's early in our investigation."

The President ran both hands down his face and regained his decorum before again taking his seat. He released a breath before saying, "Thank you, Bill. Okay, so I assume we're tracking these things with some kind of satellite surveillance or something." He looked around the room. "Where are we on this?"

The Secretary of Energy sat down, and the Chairman of the Joint Chiefs gave him a sorrowful look.

The Director of National Intelligence stood to address the President's question. "Attempts to track the devices have not been successful, sir."

The President pulled in a sharp breath. "Are you saying we have no idea what happened to them?"

"Not exactly. We believe the weapons have been relocated to a place which defies detection." The DNI shot a glance at Fuller before finishing. "The satellite on station last night, which would have detected and tracked the devices, was down for a reprogram. It was out of service from 1:00 AM until 3:00 AM mountain time. The replacement satellite seems to have malfunctioned, which knocked its coordinates off by several miles. Before we could bring the original one back online, the stolen devices were no longer detectable."

The President showed a hollow look. "So we have no idea?"

The Director of National Intelligence said, "That's correct, sir."

The President stood, turned, and stared into the Rose Garden, both hands in his pockets. The room was silent—people hesitant to even breathe.

The President turned and again faced the group. "Director Campbell, are you able to give us any good news?"

The FBI Director stood. "Sir, we have agents on the scene who are working with NEST and RAP teams from DOE. Joint Technical Operations Teams are working with us and Department of Defense to render safe the devices when they're recovered. We've established a command center at Kirtland Air Force Base in Albuquerque, and the Hostage Rescue Team is en route there now from Quantico."

The President sat back down, elbows on the desk, and interlaced his fingers in a praying fashion. "But do we know who is responsible? Are they international or domestic? Where are the weapons?" The President's voice rose with each question.

"We're attempting to discover those answers, but it'll take some time, sir."

"Thank you." The President looked up at Fuller. "What about the media?"

Fuller nodded. "The Press Secretary has been briefed—he's keeping the lid on the information—for now. How long it can be contained is anybody's guess. We've released information about a cargo hijacking of computers from a government eighteen-wheeler. Don't know how long that cover-story will hold up."

"Good," the President said.

Fuller hated seeing his friend like this. His shoulders slumped, and his whole face appeared to sag, leaving him with a washed-out expression. Looked like he'd just put in a sixteen-hour day.

"Is there anything else?" the President whispered, staring at the DOE notebook on his desk.

The room remained silent, each person staring at the others. Fuller looked the group over and said, "Thank you. That will be all."

The President stood before saying, "Leave no stone unturned. Find those damn things and whoever did this."

When the last person left and only he and Fuller remained, the President strolled to the credenza. He stared at the photos of his family but said nothing. He genially stroked one of the frames containing pictures of his children. After a moment, he reached for the decanter on the silver tray. Pausing, he examined the photos again before pouring the Claude Chatelier VSOP Cognac in his empty coffee cup.

Fuller walked to his side and placed a hand on his shoulder. "You okay?"

The President stared straight ahead, and a pained expression crossed his face. "I don't want this turned into a turf war over jurisdiction." He cut his stare at Fuller and released a breath. "Any agency that can contribute to the investigation should be given as much free reign as needed." His lips flattened before saying, "Maximum effort, understand?"

"I understand—I'll make sure it happens," Fuller quietly said.

The President's brow furrowed before asking, "What was that outfit in Dallas last year, working with Secret Service—when the bomb went off? The Proactive Operations something or other…"

Fuller smiled. "P2OG—Proactive Preemptive Operations Group?"

"Yes, that's it—let's make sure they send that Dallas team to work on this business."

"I'll see to it personally." Fuller looked at the half cup of cognac the President held and the photos on the credenza. "Since we don't know where the weapons are at present—may I suggest the First Lady and children spend a few days at Camp David—just until we get a better handle on it?"

The President appeared lost in thought—he nodded. "Good idea— I'll talk to her. Thanks, Jeff. I think that'll be all for now." The President walked back to his desk and fell into the chair, the cup still in hand. He opened the blue DOE notebook again and flipped a few pages. Fuller was at the door as the President said, "Jeff, too many systems and back-up systems failed simultaneously for this to be a coincidence."

Fuller stopped at the threshold, one hand on the door frame. "My thoughts exactly."

The President's shocked expression froze. He lifted the cup and downed the contents in one swallow. "Then that means…"

———

Daniel Piedmont stood with the other men and looked into the deep hole through the clear water at the six silver objects resting on the bottom. Piedmont shivered from the chill but was also excited. The cave was cold, as usual. All the men knew each other—life-long friends. They had swum in that spring-fed pool dozens of times. Each glanced at the one beside him. The interior of the cave was illuminated by intense overhead blue Halogen lights. The six fat cylinders resting in the bottom of the pool were bathed in the blue lights, giving the water a glow and sparkle. Another tingle of excitement rushed up Piedmont's spine. *They'd done it… they'd actually pulled it off.*

"What are the readings now?" McFadden asked.

Monk pushed his glasses back up on his nose before reading the meter. "Very low." He turned a dial and made an adjustment. "Yeah, very low."

Piedmont rubbed the thin scar across the bridge of his nose and said, "Stand back." He pressed the button on the remote that controlled the motor mounted on the cave floor. The grinding sound of the lead curtain slowly extending across the length of the pool vibrated off the thick stone walls. It stopped with a clang against the opposite side of the pool.

Piedmont said, "Recheck it."

Monk had assured them he could all but eliminate the radiation signature by locating the weapons deep underground and in water. The lead curtain was just a bit more insurance…

Monk glanced back to the Geiger counter and adjusted another dial before saying, "CPM almost non-existent."

"Go outside and check it at the entrance," Piedmont said.

Moments later, Monk returned. "The readings are so low you would have to be standing right outside to detect anything. No way an aircraft could pick up a rad signature from a flyover."

Piedmont said nothing for a moment. He mentally went over everything that was probably being discussed in Washington about now. He had to get back to headquarters before he got cut out of the loop. He needed to be the point man on this.

McFadden rolled an unlit cigar between his lips and stared at Piedmont before saying, "What's your call?"

Piedmont nodded. "It's good." He eyed the other two. "Okay, I have a plane to catch. I'll find out what the FBI knows."

Monk stared at the others. "I'm heading back to Sandia. Got a call from the lab. All leave's been canceled. They want everyone there today. Don't expect to see me until we do the drive."

The three walked to the entrance of the cave room where the guard stood. McFadden touched his shoulder. "Nobody's allowed in for any reason unless they're cleared by me first—understand?"

"Understood," the man said.

McFadden shook hands with him, then hugged Monk and Piedmont. His brow relaxed, and he showed the fatherly expression they both knew so well. "Boys, we've accomplished the hardest part. We'll lie low and wait. You two will know when we can proceed. Ball's in your hands now." McFadden smiled. "Don't fumble it."

FOUR

olonel Maxwell was a little confused. He had only been in the Pentagon twice, once for a briefing, once for a meeting. He stopped walking and looked at the email again to confirm the day and room number. *Yeah, today was Wednesday, but which way?* Standing at the elevator landing on the mezzanine level, he consulted the signs and decided he should turn left. This was the "A Ring." Since the office numbers went clockwise, that was the most logical choice. Dozens of uniformed officers and enlisted personnel marched past, all carrying briefcases or notebooks. He was relieved to see there were many Black officers like himself. Not near so many a decade ago.

A high-pitched voice from the right broke his concentration. "You look lost," the young ensign said. "Need some help?"

Maxwell looked up. "Think I've figured it out. Looks like I'm going your way."

He fell into step with her. She was tall and somewhat attractive, but her features were a little too sharp. The aquiline nose and square chin gave her a slightly masculine air. Her brown hair was twisted and pinned into a tight ball behind her head.

"First time here?" she asked. Her relaxed smile and laid-back manner put Maxwell at ease.

"No, but I've never worked here—this is my first day."

"Sharon Webber—I work in planning." She extended her hand.

"Gary Maxwell, happy to meet you."

They walked in silence for a few seconds.

"So, where do they have you working, Colonel?"

Maxwell wasn't used to junior officers being so gabby. His Marine uniform and rank insignia usually kept them at a distance—unless they needed something. With so many officers working in the building, perhaps the rules were different here. He'd play along until he figured it out. Starting a new assignment in a place like this was a double-edged sword. One step could make or break a promising career. Maxwell had made enough wrong steps. This was his new beginning, and he vowed not to screw it up.

"I'm General Cook's new deputy director," Maxwell replied.

Her head snapped in his direction, and the smile faded. "General Harry Cook?"

"Yes."

Maxwell remained perplexed as to why he was working for an army general. Hadn't been able to get a straight answer from his people, but a promotion's a promotion—about time, too…

She kept her eyes looking straight ahead, never again glancing in his direction. She increased her pace like she wanted to get away from him. Something had changed—the friendliness gone. *What did I say to piss her off?*

Without fanfare, she pointed to a door on the right, "That's General Cook's office—good luck, sir."

With no additional comment or goodbye, she kept walking, the click of her heels on the floor echoing as she disappeared into the crowded mass of uniforms.

Maxwell stared at the door. The rest of the offices had the name of the director and the director's title affixed—this had neither. Only the room number on the wall confirmed he was at the right place. He had one of those funny feelings. The kind that wasn't funny, but disturbing. His promotion was long overdue, and he'd jumped at the chance to work at the Pentagon. Perhaps he should have researched it a little better before accepting this assignment. He had, but the online Pentagon roster didn't even show a General Cook working there. Perhaps Cook, too, was new to the command.

Maxwell tried the door handle, but it wouldn't budge. From the intercom speaker, a female voice asked, "Colonel Maxwell?"

His head swiveled up, looking for a camera. "Yes."

"Come in."

A metallic click sounded from the door. Maxwell pushed it open, and the woman at the desk smiled as she stood.

"Good morning, I'm Mary Sweeney—General's Cook executive assistant."

She was middle-aged, slim, and had a pleasant smile.

"How do you do?" He nodded. "Gary Maxwell."

She didn't leave her desk or offer her hand, only a fleeting grin before saying, "The general's expecting you." She walked to the door to the left of her desk and gave three short knocks before sticking her head in. "Colonel Maxwell's here, sir." She glanced back and motioned to him. "The general will see you, now."

The man sitting behind the desk stood when Maxwell entered. Probably in his late 50s, the short gray hair made him look a little older. He was a couple of inches shorter than Maxwell's 5'11" and stockier. Wearing a business suit, he didn't look any different than most men his age walking around Washington.

"I'm Major General Harry Cook."

He shook Maxwell's hand. The firm grip was what Maxwell had expected, but the school principal's stare wasn't.

"Please have a seat."

Maxwell pulled in a slow breath. The office was well appointed, with the usual shadow box of medals and ribbons, photos of old comrades, a bookcase, and map of the world. The office being on one of the two underground levels of the Pentagon and the lack of windows gave the place a tomb-like feel. Goosebumps popped up on Maxwell's arms. There was tension in the air. It hung in the small office, ready to explode at any moment. Maxwell's gut rumbled as he attempted a smile. In his most confident voice, he said, "Thank you, sir."

Each man took their seat, and Cook lounged back in his chair. He wore a Masonic ring on his right hand. The diamond in the center caught the light as he folded his hands across his middle. His outgoing, friendly smile helped Maxwell to relax.

Cook lifted a brown folder from the desk. "I've been going over your service record, Colonel—very impressive."

"Thank you, sir."

"So you were in Desert Storm, eh?"

"Yes, sir, I was an intelligence staff assistant to General Boomer."

A thin smile crossed Cook's lips, and he nodded and leaned forward. "Tell me about the decision to keep the 2nd Marine Expeditionary Force afloat off the coast of Kuwait."

Maxwell winced, cleared his throat, and looked down at his lap before answering. He could tell where this was going. The suggestion to a senior officer that had dogged him his entire career. The thing that got him passed over for promotion a half dozen times as he advanced through the ranks at a snail's pace.

In a low, even voice Maxwell said, "General Schwarzkopf believed the force could better serve as a diversionary unit to pin down large numbers of Iraqi troops, as opposed to actually landing and taking part in the ground invasion."

Cook rested his elbows on the desk and interlaced his fingers. He raised his eyebrows and asked, "General Schwarzkopf, huh?"

"Yes, sir," Maxwell looked Cook in the eye and answered in his most convincing tone.

"Well, I heard it a different way, Colonel." Cook leaned back again. "I heard old Stormin' Norman was looking for a way to tie down a half dozen Iraqi infantry divisions in Kuwait City. I heard he asked for suggestions from the intel commands."

Maxwell's stomach churned. He squirmed as Cook continued.

"I heard some young hotshot Marine lieutenant had the audacity and balls to suggest to General Boomer leaving his fellow Marines sitting out of the fight on ships as a deception, and Boomer brought up the idea to Schwarzkopf—that's what I heard." Cook placed both hands on the desk, and his stare sliced deep into Maxwell.

Blood drained from Maxwell's face, and a chill eased down his back. He'd been the first child in his school to attend a military academy. He was one of only a dozen Black kids selected for the Annapolis class, but something he'd done years ago still dogged his career. He knew the decision was the right one, history had proved him correct, but the Corps never quite forgave him.

Maxwell lifted his chin and said, "Where did you hear a story like that, General?"

Cook kept a steady gaze. "I have my sources. Do you deny it?"

"No sir, I was the lieutenant. That suggestion is the reason I'm still only a colonel after so many years of service."

Cook smiled again. "So your brass punished you for thinking out of the box and leaving the troops at sea, huh?"

Maxwell's anger rose; he'd come here to report to his new boss and was being berated. He exhaled and dipped his chin. "Something like that, sir."

Cook's smile dissolved, and his expression hardened. "That's the reason you're here, colonel." Cook's eyes met his. "I could have had anybody in the whole damn military, and I chose you for that very reason."

Maxwell blinked and shifted in the chair. "I'm not sure I understand, sir."

"It's simple—you put the mission and men first—not the egos of your superiors. That's what I'm looking for in a deputy commander. Our mission dictates it."

Maxwell sat upright at the unexpected compliment. "Sir, I'm not sure what the mission is or even what your command is supposed to do. It's like it doesn't really exist."

Cook grinned. "At ease, Colonel—I'm about to tell you."

FIVE

The long flight from Cyprus had left Bishop bone tired. He'd slept part of the way—waking to eat a bite and go to the restroom. The weeks spent in Beirut putting the op together with the ever-present fear of discovery and arrest. Late-night surveillances and meetings, with little sleep, had taken a severe toll. Two weeks' annual leave awaited him.

He'd already made reservations at his favorite Bermuda guest house. His parents had been friends with the owners back in the day. Bishop spent a week with the old couple every year in their special guest room of the main house. His air miles insured a free flight, and the forecast looked great for wreck diving this fall. The weather during his last two visits had not allowed him to dive the wreck of the Cristobal Colon. But nothing would stop him next week—he was going. He and his dad had dived the wreck when he was a kid, and for reasons Bishop couldn't explain, he longed to dive it once more.

The Cristobal Colon is the largest of Bermuda's shipwrecks. The Spanish cruise liner was almost five hundred feet long and three decks high. In 1936, it sunk on one of Bermuda's North Shore reefs. Having spent most of his teen years in Bermuda, when his dad was assigned to the air naval base, Bishop still had fond memories and a host of old friends he looked forward to visiting. But one thing had eluded him the last twenty years. It was like Ahab's great white whale—the wreck of the Cristobal Colon. Every time he planned a dive trip there, something always came up—usually weather-related.

Bishop held the Pentagon photo ID with the embedded microchip to the scanner outside P2OG's door. A series of red numbers scrambled on the keypad, accompanied by the usual chirping sound. He input the six-digit code, and the door clicked open. It had been three weeks since Mary Sweeney had seen him, but she barely acknowledged his presence—that was her way.

"Hello, stranger, long time no see," she mumbled, hardly looking up from her typing.

"Hello, Mary." Bishop dropped onto the sofa across from her desk. "Miss me?"

Sweeney grunted but kept typing. "Too busy to miss anything except lunch the last couple of days."

Bishop lounged back into the soft leather cushions. "New diet plan, Sweeney?"

That made her look up, but all he got for his remark was the stink eye. "As I said, I've been busy," she nodded toward Cook's office, "he's been on the secure phone or in meetings for the last two days."

Bishop sat up on the sofa. "What's going on?"

"No idea. By the way, the general's got his new deputy commander in there right now. Said he'd call when he wanted you."

It wasn't uncommon to report directly to Cook after an assignment, but Bishop usually completed his after-action report first. The general preferred to learn the details before he did a face-to-face. Cook on the secure phone, in meetings for two days, and wishing to see him immediately meant something big must have happened. There were no news reports, but Bishop wasn't surprised. P2OG operated in the shadows. All of their ops were top secret and never got splayed across the front page—unless something went wrong. Probably just called him in to meet the new deputy commander.

Well, whatever train rolled off the tracks this time, another operator could handle it. Bishop's mind was firmly on cool night breezes, tree frogs, and scuba at his favorite wreck-diving island. He looked forward to hooking up with his childhood friend, Sean, drinking beer, and eating fresh seafood.

———

Cook held Maxwell's full attention. He experienced that old pucker factor he'd known in combat. Cook's tone and expression did nothing to alleviate Maxwell's anxiety.

"Colonel, in 2003, the President authorized the Protective Preemptive Operations Group, or P2OG, if you prefer. We started with a hundred people. Our mission was to carry out secret operations aimed at stimulating reactions from terrorists and states possessing weapons of mass destruction."

Cook averted his gaze to the desk a moment before saying, "This is a covert command. There are certain operations that must be done. The President's no fool. But he needs an outfit he can turn his back on and claim plausible deniability if necessary. Can't do that with CIA or NSA."

Maxwell had that disturbing feeling again; he didn't know what to say, so he said nothing. This was *President's Book of Secrets* stuff. Commands like this usually came to light from the *New York Times* or *Washington Post* in a scandalous leaked report and blazing headlines. Everyone associated with it ended up retiring early. Not what Maxwell wanted to hear his first day.

Cook waited for the information to sink in and continued. "Only the President and a half dozen others outside the outfit know exactly what we do. We report to the National Security Advisor, and he reports directly to the President."

"Where do we get our funding?" Maxwell asked, his mind whirling from information overload.

Cook pursed his lips. "Our budget's so small it can easily be hidden in a hundred Pentagon programs."

Maxwell studied the idea; sounded like a recipe for disaster. Iran-Contra and Ollie North were written all over this thing. "Sir." Maxwell leaned forward in the chair. "When you say stimulate reactions from terrorists, what does that mean?"

Cook pointed toward the outer reception area. "Your example's sitting right outside that door. I'm about to introduce you to one of our operators. Lieutenant Colonel Troy Bishop. All our people are highly specialized, with unique technical and intelligence skills. Bishop came to us from Delta. A few months ago, we got wind that Hezbollah desired to purchase enough highly enriched uranium to build a couple of small nukes." Cook exhaled. "God only knows what the intended targets were—probably Israeli."

"Where were they getting the stuff? Black market Russian?"

Cook shook his head. "They didn't have a supplier yet—they just wanted to purchase it—so we fixed them up. Through a covert agent, we furnished them an ounce of the best U-235 we had. When they were convinced we could provide them as much as they wanted, we set up an exchange—the money for the nuclear material. They showed up two days ago off the coast of Beirut. By coincidence, their yacht exploded, killing three of their top commanders in charge of the project." Cook eyed Maxwell. "Understand?"

The earlier tension again invaded the office, sucking up all the air.

"Bishop?" Maxwell asked.

Cook nodded. "Bishop. All the operators have what we refer to as *ultimate discretion.*"

Maxwell shifted in his chair again, his expression serious. "I assume that means…"

Cook picked up the phone and pushed a button. "Mary, send in Bishop, please."

After replacing the phone in its cradle, Cook's eyes squinted before saying, "It means what you think, Colonel; they kill people, terrorists."

Bishop greeted Maxwell with a handshake during Cook's introduction. They took their seats, and Maxwell studied the man. He looked worn down. Sagging shoulders and puffy sacks from lack of sleep under each eye. He wasn't in uniform either—they seemed optional around here. Wasn't a big guy, but he was powerful. Maxwell felt it from the handshake.

"That was a good piece of work in Lebanon. Any problems?" Cook asked.

"No, sir, went as planned," Bishop said.

Cook sat back in his executive chair. "Have you heard of the Office of Secure Transportation?"

Bishop's eyes narrowed a moment. "Aren't they the people who escort the nukes?"

"Correct, and they just let some get away from 'em."

A cold chill seeped into the room, and Maxwell shivered. *Good God, no!*

Bishop only stared at Cook, not uttering a sound. He didn't have to. Maxwell read the urgency in his eyes.

Cook thumbed through a stack of papers and pulled one out of the pile. He glanced at it a moment before saying, "Two days ago, one of their convoys got hit in New Mexico. All escort personnel and one state trooper were killed. Whoever did it got away with a half dozen physics packages from the W80 warhead." Cook dropped the paper back on the desk. His expression darkened. "About sixty times the nuclear yield of the Hiroshima bomb."

Maxwell cleared his throat and regained his composure before asking, "Isn't that what the navy uses on their cruise missiles?"

Cook nodded. "Right, and the air force as well." Cook crossed his legs. "So far, no luck tracking the things. Something screwy going on there. Anyway, there's an all-hands-on-deck call out, and we're sending you, Bishop."

"Me? I just got back from an op."

"I know, but the National Security Advisor said the President wants our team that was involved in that Dallas business last year. Since you were the only one from our shop in Dallas—you're our team."

Bishop asked, "Doesn't the FBI have primary jurisdiction in this?"

"They do, but several other agencies will be assisting as well. You'll carry 902nd credentials for this one." Cook turned to Maxwell. "We have no jurisdictional authority to act in country. When we work in the United States, our people carry identification from the 902nd Military Intelligence Group. This gives them authority to carry weapons and affords them federal agent status."

"Any idea who's involved?" Maxwell asked. He really couldn't believe something like this could have happened in the United States. Not a peep from any news service.

Cook's lips twisted before answering. "No, and that's what has National Security Advisor Fuller concerned. We've heard nothing in the way of demands, and with the borders locked down, Fuller thinks it's the worst possible scenario. Someone intends to light one off."

Bishop showed a kind of weary acceptance expression. The look that comes with knowing that no matter how tired you were or how much you'd just given, you were being asked for one more maximum effort for the team. Maxwell knew how he felt. The military wrings every drop from you and then twists just a little more.

Bishop stood, and his broad shoulders straightened a bit. "Will that be all, sir?"

Cook released a long exhale. "That's about it. Sorry to turn you around so soon. Just act as liaison and let the Bureau handle the nuke end of the investigation. They have hundreds of agents combing the area. I expect it won't be difficult to find one to talk to when you're ready. Mary got you reservations in Albuquerque, which wasn't easy considering the damn balloon festival's going on. She has your briefing packet, and Andy has something for you at the offsite." Cook's brow folded, and he eyed Bishop. "One more thing, don't trust the locals out there. It appears a state police vehicle was used as a distraction to lead the convoy into an ambush. Until we get a handle on that, better keep your own counsel."

"Thank you, sir." Bishop turned and extended his hand to Maxwell. His eyes had brightened, and the weary look faded. "Welcome aboard, Colonel."

Maxwell shook Bishop's hand, and he left the office. Having served his entire career in intel, Maxwell had worked with plenty of Special Forces, NSA, and CIA types. But you could always spot the professional direct-action operators. Always calm, didn't have a thing to prove, and had a career of acquired skills to accomplish any mission. These were the ones thriller novels and movies were about, the ones not discussed in polite conversation at Beltway dinner parties—the killers.

SIX

Newman Smith studied Clark McFadden relaxing in the leather chair behind the desk in his home office. Smith knew McFadden loved this room—always had. The office had the most commanding view of the valley of any place in McFadden's spacious mansion. The wall of windows made you feel like a bird, flying over the ranch far below. Or, in McFadden's case, like a king overseeing his kingdom from his castle.

McFadden rolled the bourbon around in the glass, admiring its rich amber color. His lips formed into a grin, and his eyes had that glint, before asking, "Where did you attend law school, Newman?"

Smith sighed. "You know perfectly well where I attended, Clark. You paid for it."

McFadden chuckled. "Yeah. Bet Yale never had a class on how to take over a country, huh?"

Smith sat his glass on the edge of the desk. He had never liked the crazy idea in the first place, but he'd been overruled. This was madness, or something worse. He cleared his throat. "Clark, when will we know for sure?"

McFadden shrugged, and his brow rose. "When Piedmont and Monk return to work, they'll confirm we're in the clear. Until then, we wait. Our best move is to stay hunkered down and behave normally." He stretched out and propped his cowboy boots on the desk. "Don't worry. There's no way it can be traced back to us. All the bases are covered."

Smith laid his hand over his abdomen to calm his nervous stomach. "Yes, well, that's what worries me." He was having digestive problems again. Stress always did that. *If only he could be as relaxed as the old man.*

McFadden grunted. "If they had any idea of our involvement, we'd already be behind bars. Sometimes you worry like an old grandma, Newman."

Smith took in a low, slow breath. *Worry like an old grandma.* That was McFadden's favorite line. He never seemed to worry, or if he did, never revealed it.

McFadden sat up and fished a cigar from the humidor, offering one to Smith.

Smith shook his head. *Oh, God, not another one of those awful, smelly things.*

McFadden finished lighting the cigar and waved his hand to the side. "Besides, if the feds knew anything, our sources would have given us a heads up by now."

That was the one thing that gave Smith a small amount of solace. They had spies in every major department and agency. Supervisors, who would be briefed before any raid or action could be mounted. The old man was right. Waiting was the only thing they could do at this point. Going by the estimates, if there wasn't a federal response against them within forty-eight hours, they were in the clear. Smith glanced at his watch—twelve more hours and counting.

———

The Protective Preemptive Operations Group, *P2OG*, was headquartered in the basement of the Pentagon. Only Cook, Maxwell, and Mary Sweeney worked there. The actual building housing the meat of the organization was well away from the hustle and bustle of downtown DC.

Bishop walked into the front lobby of the nondescript two-story building near an office park outside of McLean, Virginia. Bishop liked this location. The building was at the bottom of a steep hill, with a clearwater creek behind it. The heavily wooded area surrounding the building, with ivy growing up on both sides of the stream, looked like a shady, hidden resort. Hundreds drove past daily and never gave it a second look—perfect location for a highly classified DOD offsite. Only someone with a keen eye might spot the heavy security. Cameras bristled from every corner, bulletproof glass, and the whole thing encased in an electronic protective envelope which didn't allow eavesdropping from outside. One large Sensitive Compartmental Information Facility, *SCIF*.

Bishop waved at the receptionist behind the admissions desk, and the man released the electronic lock, allowing Bishop into the back offices. After checking his mail and phone messages, he marched into the Technical Operations Support Lab. The place was a lot of stainless steel and glass. Always had a weird odor, thanks to Andy's tinkering. He was nowhere in sight. Bishop looked around and found him in the corner, behind a tall shelf at a workbench, fooling with some electronic device. Looked like he'd butterflied whatever it was. The thing was spread across the cold metal table. The smell of solder hung richly in the air as Andy eyed the object with a critical expression.

"Hi, Andy." Bishop strolled deeper into the lab toward him.

Andy glanced up. "Just a minute." He went back, connecting wires to the mysterious object.

Bishop didn't want to spend any more time than necessary here. He was still tired and had packing and phone calls to make, but there was no use rushing Andy. Guy worked at his own pace and always alone in his laboratory. Bishop meandered around the corner of a line of shelves to where a transparent softball-size sphere rested on a metal base. It gave off a low hum, and there were small streaks of blue lightning inside. *Probably one of Andy's new toys.* Since the thing wasn't plugged in, Bishop reached to touch it. Just before his hand made contact with the sphere, an electric arch shot out, and a jolt of electricity raced up his arm. He jerked his hand back with a loud, "Ouch!"

"Hurts—doesn't it?" Andy stood behind him with a smirk.

Bishop massaged the offending hand. He'd fallen for another one of

Andy's practical jokes. The tall skinny kid was one of the civilians who worked for P2OG. He'd earned degrees in chemical and electrical engineering, as well as physics, at MIT before his parents kicked him out and told him to get a job. He was the only true nerd Bishop knew. Apparently, from his T-shirt, he had a new passion. The words "QUANTUM MECHANICS ROCKS" were printed on the front.

"You set me up," Bishop said, massaging feeling back into his fingers.

Andy waved his hand over the sphere, just out of reach of the arch. He grinned and looked over at Bishop. "I've warned you about fooling around with stuff in the lab. How long have you been back?"

Andy blinked a lot—it seemed to synchronize with his speaking. He often wore glasses but occasionally tried contacts. On the days he wore them, he blinked even more.

"Just got in last night," Bishop said.

Andy strolled to a battleship-grey metal workbench, extracted a key from his pocket, and unlocked the drawer. He had a mischievous expression.

"So, you're going after a nuke, huh?"

Andy liked to guess what the operators were up to. He wasn't cleared for the details of the information, but that didn't stop him from guessing. He was pretty good. Of course, he supplied the operators with specialized equipment. From his deep science background, it wasn't that hard to figure out what the assignments were.

"Why do you ask?"

"Because I was instructed to give you this." Andy removed the red box from the drawer and opened it. Inside was a watch with a silver face and black plastic band. It resembled a Casio G-Shock but slightly larger.

"A watch?" Bishop wasn't impressed.

Andy nodded and removed it from the case. He gingerly held it up, admiring it. "Not just a watch. It has all the standard sports watch features, but it can detect nukes."

Bishop's brow crinkled. "Explain." He leaned against the bench and crossed his arms.

There was excitement in Andy's eyes as he caressed the watch. He moved his index finger around the watch face. "It will vibrate when it comes into close proximity to uranium which has been enriched or plutonium which has undergone separation."

"So how close a proximity are we talking about?"

Andy shrugged, and his eyes drifted to the watch. "Depends on how strong the radiation source? It's very sensitive and expensive."

"That's what you say about all your stuff down here. How does it work?"

Andy touched a button on the bottom of the watch face. "Once it vibrates, push this. The face will blink blue if it's uranium and red if plutonium. It's locked into the memory at that point."

"What if I push it and there's no radiation source to pick up?"

"Then it'll just act as a backlight and show the time like any sports watch."

Bishop examined it. "Does it have a name?"

Andy grunted. "It's a complicated piece of hardware, Bishop, not a dog. The device name is so long you'd never remember it. Just call it the nuclear watch."

Some people took offense to Andy's condescending attitude and sharp wit. Bishop never did because he knew something Andy would never admit. The guy was a geek. Probably looked at the P2OG operators as misanthropes, having advanced just enough on the evolutionary scale to perform simple tasks but incapable of higher concepts.

Andy continued to reside in his parent's Maryland basement. His desk at the office was decorated with a model of the Starship Enterprise and dozens of miniature action figures from Avengers' movies. He once bragged to Bishop that he'd repainted all the action figures— took him a month working late into the night with tiny brushes and a magnifying glass. It took all of Bishop's control not to laugh out loud. He knew several staff sergeants and sergeants first class in Delta who would happily eat Andy for breakfast, then fight over his bones to pick their teeth. But there was no use sharing information like this with Andy. Kid still needed to be able to sleep.

"Okay, it's the nuclear watch. Anything else?"

"Yes, I want it back—actually, it's on loan from Lawrence Livermore. Fifty-seven thousand eight hundred and thirty-three dollars. This is its first field test."

"No problem."

Andy showed his *yeah, right* face. "That's what you say about all the expensive items you either break beyond repair or never return."

Bishop had his mouth open to contest Andy's assertion but never got the chance.

Andy said, "Let's do a phone swap."

Bishop handed over his cell phone, and Andy removed the sim card and inserted it into an identical phone. P2OG had rules about which cell you could use "in-country, and "out of country." Andy held out the clipboard for Bishop's signature. "Sign here for the watch and phone. Instructions for the watch are in the box."

Bishop scribbled a signature on the form as Andy walked back to his tinkering project.

"Is that it?"

Andy looked back over his shoulder. "What did you expect?"

Bishop nodded. Fair question. A wave of fatigue moved through him. He was still beat from the op and long flight. A good night's sleep in his own bed was what he needed. He opened the door to leave when Andy added his usual goodbye.

"Be careful, Bishop." Andy flashed a quick smile before turning back to his work. He mumbled, "Nukes are dangerous toys."

SEVEN

The next day, Bishop took an early flight to Albuquerque. The plane was only about three-quarters full, not bad for a Thursday morning. Boredom soon set in. He relaxed in the aisle seat and glanced at the passenger by the window—guy looked like Major Headly. Bishop smirked, recalling when they first met.

After graduating from West Point, Bishop was assigned as a second lieutenant with the 505 Infantry Regiment of the 82nd Airborne. After two years, he was promoted and transferred as a first lieutenant with the 75th Ranger Regiment. On the first day of training, he met a group of rugged, highly motivated professionals. It took almost sixteen weeks to finish Ranger school. Half of the class flunked.

Bishop was stationed with the rest of the regiment at Fort Benning, Georgia. As the war on terrorism heated up, Bishop decided to up the ante. He applied to Delta. The thought of serving in a unit that wasn't officially acknowledged by the government or military somehow appealed to him. He attended the Delta Selection Course in the fall of 1999. He endured weeks of backbreaking testing, both physical and mental, but nothing he hadn't encountered in Ranger training. This whole thing looked like a pushover until they did *The Long Walk*.

Bishop was in the best shape of his life. He had a good, strong set of legs and a determined will, but of course, so did every other soldier in his group. The way it worked was pretty straightforward. At the end of a hard week of testing, when the men were at their lowest physical strength, they were informed to prepare for the march the next day. Rumor had it at forty miles, but none of the instructors would say. After the first few weeks of testing, the original group had now been seriously whittled down to only the hard-core fanatics. According to the Delta instructors, there were rendezvous points along the march known as RVs. When you arrived at an RV, a Delta cadre member would give you further instructions, which would take you to the next RV. This sequence would continue until the march was completed.

The following morning at 0300 hours, the group began their walk across some of the worst terrain West Virginia had to offer. A long march over uneven ground was one thing, but carrying a seventy-pound rucksack that distance wasn't something anyone was used to. Bishop put all doubts aside and settled into a good pace. The surrounding hardwoods glowed with yellows, oranges, and reds with the rising sun as the trees shed their summer colors. The cool morning breeze was a blessing. In a few hours, the heat would make the going more challenging. Staying hydrated was vital—nothing sapped energy faster than dehydration. Each man marched alone. Alone with his thoughts and pain to keep him company. There was no one to encourage you, no one to help you, and only a still silence surrounded you. Bishop knocked off the first RV before daylight. A set of scales hung from a tree limb.

"Shuck that ruck and let's check it," the instructor said, pointing to the scales. Each soldier had been instructed to load their rucksack with seventy pounds before the exercise. There was a scale just like this one at the camp to check your load before the march began. No cadre confirmed how heavy you loaded your ruck. It was the honor system. Several soldiers who had light-loaded their rucks were dismissed from the course at that first RV. Bishop had loaded his with seventy-two pounds the day before, just to be sure. He filled his canteens, and the instructor gave him new directions and pointed him down the trail to the next RV.

As Bishop topped the tall hill, Major Headly waited with his arms crossed. He grinned as Bishop passed. Bishop had the feeling Headly never liked him. Major Headly had nothing but negative things to say to young Lieutenant Bishop from the first day. Few academy men found their way to Delta. NCOs make up the bulk of personnel with just a few officers to lead them. Headly probably just didn't like academy officers in *his* unit. Old heads ruled this elite outfit, and traditions were everything.

By the time Bishop arrived at RV number four, he was tired. As best he could tell from the sun, he'd marched close to ten hours. He'd taken a five or ten-minute break every hour, which renewed him for the next leg. His feet throbbed from the pounding. The doubts settled upon him. No one would say how far the march was or how much further he had to go, but there *was* a time limit. Everyone knew that, and it pushed the soldiers into a grueling pace that was almost impossible to sustain. The distance and time limit were the most closely guarded secrets. *Was he marching too slowly? Would he complete it in the time left? Was he marching too fast? Would he burn himself out before he got to the finish?* That was Delta's head game. Just being in good physical condition wasn't enough. The head game was the true enemy.

Bishop played with this mental puzzle until he reached RV number five. He was spent. His feet ached so much he wondered if he was doing them damage they might never recover from. Again, he was instructed to weigh his rucksack, and the cadre recorded the weight. They told him to refill his two canteens and gave him more instructions to find RV number six.

It was dark again. Bishop had marched all day. The coolness of the evening did little to relieve his anguish. Each step sent bolts of pain through his feet, up his legs, and across his back shoulders. Not knowing how far till the next RV dragged his spirit down. Between that and the pain, he had serious doubts about completing the march. *Christ, how much further? Had to have walked fifty miles by now!* Bishop's mind clouded, trying to calculate distance, time, and speed. The throbbing agony of his body and mental dullness from exhaustion forced him to concede he had reached the end of his physical abilities. That's when he stumbled upon RV six.

Two soldiers from his training group sat on their rucks on the side of the road, and Bishop's spirit soared. *That's it.* He'd completed the march. *Thank God!*

Major Headly strolled from the tree line. The red glow from a cigar outlined his face. "What are you smiling about, Bishop?"

It wasn't until then that Bishop realized Headly was also smiling.

Headly motioned to the two exhausted soldiers on the ground with heads hung low. "Oh, you think it's over?" Headley laughed a long course laugh. "Hell, son. It hasn't started yet!" He slowly meandered to Bishop and looked him up and down, shaking his head. "You don't look so good." He pointed again at the two soldiers. "These two have asked to be dismissed from any further testing. They're through and heading back to camp for a hot shower, cold beer, and nice dinner." Headly blew out a mouthful of smoke in Bishop's direction and grinned. "Truck has room for one more." He posted his fist on his hips and leaned forward. In a condescending voice, he said, "How about it, Bishop? Come on; you got nothing left. I can see it in your face. You know it, and so do I. Doubt you'll make another mile."

If Headly had been a civilian, Bishop would have taken a swing at him. But he was right about one thing—Bishop didn't have another mile. His body knew he couldn't go any further, but he swore if he was going to fail, it wasn't going to be in front of this bastard. He would walk until he couldn't and just wait for a truck to haul him back to camp. Bishop pulled in a slow, even breath. *He'd failed, couldn't make the cut.* But he didn't allow the disappointment to show, not to Headley.

Bishop released the breath and pushed past Headly without saying a word. The RV cadre issued Bishop more instructions to locate RV seven as he refilled his canteens. Filling the canteens was only for show. Bishop understood he would never drink a drop of the water but wanted Headly to see him doing it. Wanted him to know he wasn't quitting. Didn't want to give him the satisfaction of being right.

The average distance between RVs all day had been between five and ten miles. Bishop figured if he set his mind to it and dug deep into his soul, he might make a half mile before collapsing. After leaving Headly, he marched down the dark and lonely road with only the sounds of crickets and frogs for company. Fatigue as he'd never experienced enveloped him, and his spirit sank. *Making another mile just wasn't going to happen.* Bishop was sick at heart. *Thought I had it in me—just wasn't up to the challenge.* As he rounded the bend, a hundred meters from the last RV, a tall captain he'd never met stepped from the bushes.

"Over here, Ranger," the captain said and motioned with a flashlight.

It took a second for Bishop's numb mind to understand the order and a couple more seconds for his exhausted body to respond. He staggered to the captain. Bishop didn't salute. The effort needed to bring his right hand up might just finish him off.

The captain stared at him a second and, in a monotone voice, said, "You look like shit, Ranger. Drop your ruck. You're finished."

Bishop was even more furious with this officer than he'd been with Major Headly. His fist tightened, and he yelled at the captain. "No, sir! I'm not finished, sir. I have this exercise to complete." Bishop was all raw emotion. Warm tears of anger, fatigue, and humiliation slithered down his cheeks. He wasn't going to let this guy flunk him out. Not now. Not after all he'd endured.

The captain smiled and moved closer, laying a hand on Bishop's shoulder. "Ranger, you don't understand. You've finished the exercise. You've passed."

Bishop's knees sagged. *Might pass out from relief.*

Men appeared from the dark woods and helped Bishop to a waiting deuce and a half. They removed the load of rocks from his shoulders and gently lifted him into the back of the two and a half-ton truck, where a medic carefully removed his boots to determine how much damage he'd done to his feet. Not only had he finished, but he'd also finished first. The sound of a beer can opening caused Bishop to turn. Major Headly grinned and handed him a cold Michelob.

"Had me worrying about ya' at RV six, son. Hoped I hadn't talked you out of it."

Headly held up his hand, and the moonlight glistened off a West Point ring. "Us academy guys gotta stick together—right?"

Bishop's Delta Selection Course weeded out ninety-three percent of the class.

When Bishop landed in Albuquerque a little after six in the

evening, the clear skies and sunshine gave the place a soft sparkle, and the lower humidity rejuvenated him. He'd traveled there before, but like so many places he'd traveled, it was always for training or while on assignment. Bishop kept a mental list of the best places he visited—promising himself he'd return for just a pleasure trip. There was a restlessness in him today—couldn't quite figure it out. By the time he got his bag, rented the car, and made a quick stop by the liquor store, it was after seven before he checked into the Hilton. He got his key, requested a lime and bucket of ice be sent to his room, and waded through the hordes of people in the lobby partying after another day at the balloon festival. Bishop had never attended the festival. Wanted to, but something always got in the way.

Anyone would have loved Bishop's room, with its colorful décor and stylish, Southwestern furniture. A strategically placed balcony afforded a great view of the pool six floors below and the Sandia Mountains in the distance. Bishop hated it.

The ice and lime arrived, and he tipped the man with a five. Just needed to relax and unwind before dinner. Bishop filled a glass with ice, added a one-to-three mixture of Bombay Sapphire Gin and tonic, and a quarter of the lime. He drained it before he got into the shower.

After bathing, he sat on the balcony wearing only a pair of gym shorts and an Under Armor exercise shirt. He nestled deeper into an oversized chair and had another couple of drinks, watching the festive crowds around the pool below. As the sun set, the temperature dropped and a cool breeze chilled him, but he stayed a little longer—it felt good. Finally, he slipped on a pair of khakis and a dark blue polo shirt and went down to dinner. He ate at the Casa Chaco restaurant in the hotel—it tasted bland.

He was in bed by eleven. Lying in the dark, the restlessness lay with him. Most of his assignments concerned some chemical, biological, radiological, or nuclear incident. Most of the time, the locals didn't even know about it before he arrived. This was different. Nuclear weapons had been lost in military plane crashes before but never taken by force inside the US. General Cook and Fuller had been right in their concerns. Whoever took them would want to use one sooner or later. The next few days might be a little busy.

By early Friday morning, Bishop had figured it out. His lousy attitude had nothing to do with the hotel or restaurant—*he* was the problem. He was impatient and edgy. Nothing's as bad as a vaguely defined mission, and this one was as vaguely defined as they come. Bishop understood the concern regarding the missing nukes, but he had no clear instructions. *Liaison with other federal agencies.* What did that even mean? He needed to get out of this room before the walls closed in. He was doubtful the perpetrators would seek him out and surrender while he was laid up in this fancy place.

Bishop consulted his mission briefing packet over morning coffee. He kept the TV off every morning until he finished his first cup. Only then did he feel fortified enough to put up with the nonsense that passed for news nowadays. He dug out the GPS coordinates for the attack on the convoy. He needed to see the place. Go to ground zero. Look at it through the attacker's eyes. That might shake loose some ideas about what happened. Bishop considered his work not unlike that of a police detective. Anytime there was a crime, clues existed in some form. The only thing he had to do was figure out what was and wasn't a clue. He packed, ate breakfast, and left before nine o'clock.

Bishop drove west on I-40 out of Albuquerque and took the Highway Three-North exit. Part of the freeway was still closed until repairs could be completed because of the destructive tanker fire. He switched on the radio to a smooth jazz station. Driving in the desert brought back memories of old family vacations, military training exercises, and covert Delta missions far from any US shore. He always loved deserts, except when insurgents were trying to kill him. During the drive, Bishop played with ideas he could use on the FBI to convince them to involve him in the hunt for the nukes. The Bureau was famous for not being overly generous in sharing jurisdiction with other agencies. He didn't blame them. The old saying about too many cooks in the kitchen popped into his head.

Bishop turned down the gravel road where the convoy had been ambushed. It was in the middle of nowhere. No homes, no businesses, no other vehicle traffic. He drove slowly, with the windows down, examining the road and ditches, looking for anything out of place. Probably a useless exercise—the Bureau's Evidence Response Team had most likely lined up shoulder to shoulder and walked the road twice. If there were anything unusual, they would already have it tagged and bagged by now.

In less than a mile, there were signs of the attack. Burnt foliage along the edge of the road, blacked stains on the sandy gravel where vehicles lost their fluids. And an eerie feeling lingered in the air—a sense of death and mass murder. Bishop parked and looked around. The cloudless sky reached for miles, a light blue hue that painted the desert floor with a glaring brightness. About two miles out, a lone helicopter approached from the west, lazily easing its way in Bishop's direction. He shielded his eyes. Too far to tell if it was police, military, or commercial. He walked up and down the road for about a hundred yards, mentally recreating the kill zone the vehicles were funneled into. The day was turning hot, and he began to sweat. Squatting down, he picked up a handful of gravel, studying the area surrounding the narrow road. He let the scene play out in his mind.

Whoever planned it had training. All the ingress and egress points were covered. Most likely used blocking vehicles. Once the target trucks rolled in, there was no way out of the kill zone. He dropped the gravel and stood, dusting his hands on his pants. A waft of something burnt floated past his nose. The road was deserted and peaceful now. The only sound, a gentle breeze rustling through the scrub trees and kicking up dust devils in the sand. When Bishop glanced up, the chopper he'd seen earlier now hung about a mile off to the east, making slow circles. It was a Blackhawk with two six-foot-long green pods hanging off each side. *Yup, military carrying large area aerial radiation detection equipment.*

He was about halfway back to his SUV when the growl of a vehicle approaching from the rear caused him to turn. A dark police car rolled to a stop behind him. *Oh, great, just what I need.* Bishop stared at the officer behind the wheel.

The officer stared back, speaking into his mic for a moment before putting on his cap and getting out. He was a big man. The golden door emblem read New Mexico Highway Patrol, and the guy looked every inch of what a trooper should be.

The officer meandered up to Bishop and gave him a good looking over. "Having car trouble?"

Bishop gazed at his reflection in the officer's dark glasses. *Don't trust the locals out there.* Since he had no way of knowing what, if anything, the guy knew about the attack—best to play innocent. "No trouble, sir—just looking around."

Bishop flashed his best smile. The trooper did not reciprocate. The name tag on the uniform read FLOWERS. *Pretty big flower.*

Flowers cocked his head a moment and pursed his lips. "You have some ID?" he asked as he dropped his right hand to his side—closer to his pistol.

Okay, time's over for being coy. Bishop handed over his fake military credentials and waited. He had used them often when on assignment in the States due to the Posse Comitatus Act. It stated that neither the Army nor Air Force could execute laws within the United States. The only exception was if nuclear weapons were involved, but the president had yet to authorize this for fear it would be leaked. The only Army unit excluded from Posse Comitatus was the 902 Military Intelligence Group. They were a counterintelligence outfit allowed to carry firearms in a federal agent capacity within the United States. The perfect cover for covert P2OG inquiries within the US.

Flowers studied the identification. He held it up and frowned. "What's this?"

Bishop raked his hair back in place from a gust of wind. It was clear Officer Flowers didn't appear very impressed with Bishop's credentials.

"I'm with the 902nd MI Group—out of Fort Meade." Bishop could deliver that line with no effort—had plenty of practice.

The trooper studied the identification another moment before saying, "Got a driver's license?"

Bishop handed over his Virginia license.

Flowers examined the military identification and license, occasionally gazing at Bishop. After a few seconds of probably comparing the photos, Flowers's head shook. "Hold on a minute." He walked back to his car, looking back over his shoulder once.

Flowers sat in the police cruiser and spoke first on the radio, then on his cell—it took over ten minutes. Bishop crossed his arms and let out a breath, gazing in the distance at the mysterious helicopter hovering only a few hundred yards out. *Well, this explains that.* He reflected on whether it had been a good idea to visit the attack site. This scene was still active. Flowers walked back to him. He wasn't wearing a happy face. He handed Bishop his license and identification.

"Follow me in your car."

"Where are we going?"

"Just do as I say, all right?"

The guy's attitude had taken a turn for the worst.

"Am I under arrest?"

Flowers posted both hands on his hips, and his jaw clenched. "If you were under arrest, we wouldn't be having this conversation—now let's go."

Bishop almost protested but decided against it. The guy had talked to someone on the cell, and that someone now wanted to talk to Bishop. Since he had nothing better to do, he may as well play along. He smiled and nodded.

"Whatever you say, officer."

Still, Bishop's curiosity was aroused. Where were they going, and who wanted to see him so bad he got a police escort?

The trooper followed him in the patrol car as Bishop walked back to the SUV. He was hot. The day continued to heat up in more ways than one. Bishop swung in behind the patrol car, and they headed west on I-40 to the highway patrol station in Santa Rosa. They parked in the rear lot, and Bishop followed Flowers to the back door under the sally port. A patrol vehicle was parked to the side, unloading an intoxicated female prisoner. She wore cut-off shorts, a halter top, and an ankle monitor. Curses flowed from her mouth in a poetic rant toward the arresting officers as her blond ponytail swished from side to side. Flowers waited until the troopers took her in before turning to Bishop. He looked him over once more, and his eyebrows furrowed and then released.

"You packing?"

Figured this would come up. "Yes."

Flowers held out his right hand, and with a slight waving of the fingers, said, "I'll take it until after the meeting."

"Meeting with whom?"

Flowers took a step closer and narrowed his gaze. He pointed at the building. "Mister, my lunch break starts after I walk you through that door." In a menacing voice, he added, "And I'm damn hungry."

Messing with this guy any longer didn't make sense. There was somebody who wanted to see Bishop, and Bishop was ready to see him. Time for the main attraction. He seldom surrendered his weapon, but he figured he didn't have much of a choice in this case. He held Flower's gaze and reached behind his back, under the loose-fitting shirt, and handed over the Sig Sauer .357.

Flowers snatched it from his grip, nodded toward the door, and stepped to the side. "After you."

Walking in, they were behind the public reception area. Voices sounded from the other side of the partition. People asking questions and receiving answers from the desk sergeant. A voice from a hidden police radio monitor announced a patrol unit was pulling over a speeder south of I-40 and gave a description of the vehicle and tag number.

Flowers directed Bishop to the left. As he made the turn, Flowers said, "And make another left."

There was an office. The wall facing the hall consisted of a floor-to-ceiling glass window. The name on the open door read Lt. Adams. The office lights were too bright for the small room. They cast a blinding glare as Bishop entered.

The stranger inside was not in uniform. He wore a light grey business suit, a white shirt, and a shiny blue tie. Never took his eyes off Bishop as Flowers handed over the semi-automatic. The guy accepted the weapon from Flowers, laid it in a desk drawer, and slammed it shut. He thanked Flowers, and the trooper meandered toward the door, giving Bishop one last aggravated look on the way out.

No one spoke for a moment. The suit sat on the edge of the desk, facing Bishop with his arms folded. He was about Bishop's age and build, with brown hair, mustache, and a goatee. The suspicious eyes gave nothing away. Bishop returned the stare. *Just my luck, probably a fed.*

"Take a seat." The man motioned to a chair.

Bishop sat and gazed at the fellow, not uttering a word. Something felt wrong. What had he stumbled into? *Don't trust the locals out there.*

"What were you doing on that road?" the guy asked.

Bishop gazed around the office with a dismissive look. *Two could play this game.* "Well, if you'll tell me who you are, I might just answer."

The man didn't blink, just continued staring. His blank expression broke after a moment, and he grinned. He reached into his jacket and produced his identification. "I'm Special Agent Carpenter—FBI."

Bishop let out an audible sigh. "That's a relief. Thought I'd wandered into a banana republic by the way I've been treated."

Carpenter went back to the deadpan look. "You haven't answered my question."

Bishop leaned back in the chair and crossed his legs. "I think we may be on the same side. I'm with the Defense Department looking for several pieces of lost property—six to be exact."

Carpenter's brow relaxed. "That's what I figured. That's why I requested the officer bring you here." He slid off the desk and extended his hand.

Bishop stood and shook it.

Carpenter shrugged. "Sorry for the third degree, but I needed to hear it from you."

"I understand, not sure if I can be of any assistance, but if you need me, I'm here."

Carpenter walked back to the desk and again sat on the edge. "I wish I had something I needed help with. We've covered the whole area. Searched every inch of the attack site and just completed a concentric circle sweep twenty-five miles in every direction. We're dismantling the roadblocks. The weapons have disappeared."

Something about this story didn't add up. Bishop asked, "What do you think—helicopter took them out?"

Carpenter shook his head and folded his hands in his lap. "Not likely. We had good radar cover on this area at low altitudes the night of the ambush. We've checked the log—nothing. Found a magnetic jamming device on top of the OST scout vehicle—right beside the radio antennas. That jammed their transmissions and left them deaf. We're trying to figure out who put it there and when. The state police are pissed. One of their troopers was murdered during the commission of the crime just to steal his uniform and car. The vehicle was recovered with the dead trooper in the trunk stripped down to his underwear. Probably used the car and uniform as part of the deception to divert the OST convoy.

Bishop nodded. *That explained Flower's attitude.*

The magnetic jamming device and stolen police uniform and car were two pieces of new information to Bishop. The picture started to make a little more sense. Someone with advanced knowledge of the route and cargo had attacked the convoy and staged the tanker truck accident on the freeway as a diversion.

Bishop had yet to come up with a convincing argument on why the FBI should let him on the inside of the investigation. He decided on the straightforward, honest approach. "So how can I help? Since my people have detailed me here, may as well make myself useful. I can assist with coordinating military support, if nothing else."

Carpenter opened the desk and extracted the pistol. He handed it back to Bishop. "I appreciate it, but I have one, two, and three-star generals all chomping at the bit to do exactly that. If you have four stars, I could add you to the collection."

Bishop reholstered his pistol and stared at Carpenter. "Above my pay grade."

"Just stay out of the way. There's nothing we need at present. We're looking for clues that can produce leads. So far, we have very few of either. Sending some of our deployed agents back home. Nothing more to follow up. It's as if the desert just swallowed them up. We'll call if we need anything."

They exchanged business cards, and Bishop said, "My cell's always on."

Carpenter slid the card in his pocket and smiled, "I think we're good for now."

EIGHT

After leaving the office, Bishop sat in his SUV for several minutes in the police parking lot—just thinking. It was a beautiful day with plenty of clean, fresh air and abundant sunshine. Looked like a shift change taking place in the parking lot with state police patrol cars coming in and going out with fresh officers behind the wheel. General Cook's orders were to travel to Albuquerque, liaison with the feds, and let the FBI handle the investigation. The Bureau basically told him to get lost—not as encouraging as he'd hoped.

Bishop grabbed his carry-on from the back seat, rummaged in it for a second, and found a New Mexico state map. He ran his finger to the ambush site off Highway Three. Yeah, pretty much in the middle of nowhere. According to agent Carpenter, the chance of the weapons being removed by air was remote. That meant they were trucked out. But where? Which direction? On what road? Bishop scanned the map again and put himself in the attacker's mind. Where would he covertly transport six nukes? Not north or west, too much activity, too many roads, and people. He let his gaze drift to the east side of the map. Fewer people, but still lots of small towns. People in small towns are curious; they talk about unusual things going on in their communities.

Bishop recalled reading in his briefing packet that the satellite covering the ambush site had been brought down for two hours about the time of the attack. *More than suspicious.* He drug his finger south of I-40 on the map to the least populated area within a two-hour drive of the attack site. Lincoln County stood out like a bright light on a dark night—few towns, fewer people, almost uninhabited. That's where *he* would take something he wanted to hide. Highway Three intersected highway Fifty-Four. The fastest way to Lincoln County.

Departing Santa Rosa, Bishop took Highway 54 South. He'd find a hotel on the way. Besides, on a great day like today, he just looked forward to the scenery and solitude. The drive through the barren high desert reminded him why he liked the Southwest. It had an organic beauty—open rangeland, a mixture of grassy plains, and desert-like scrub. From previous visits in the early spring, he'd witnessed one of nature's miracles. Millions of wildflowers and blooming cacti colored the landscape. He let the driver's window down and rested his elbow on the sill. His mind continued working through the possibilities. Another thing Carpenter said popped into Bishop's mind. *The weapons have disappeared.* By disappeared, he was also probably referring to their radiological signature. It was simple to hide the physical weapons, but their radiological signatures were another thing. The Department of Energy had paired their scientist working NEST and RAPTER with FBI agents. They continued attempting to pick up any kind of rad signature from the stolen weapons. Probably them in the helicopter that spotted him at the ambush site earlier. So that meant the attackers must have had a prearranged location to hide the weapons that wouldn't allow aerial detection. Hiding a nuke took even more expert planning—someone with inside knowledge.

The endless highway was mostly deserted. Bishop drove over ten miles before seeing the first car. A late model, white Cadillac Escalade had pulled to the right shoulder of the road with its emergency flashers blinking. A middle-aged woman stood beside it, looking at the flat tire on the left rear. Her long hair and loose-fitting dress flapped in the stiff breeze. Bishop pulled behind the Cadillac, put on his emergency flashers, and got out. It then became apparent she was a bit older than middle age. She'd had some work done. Kinda busty and tall. Her long golden hair and pink cotton dress blowing in the breeze reminded him of a television commercial for some woman's perfume.

She released an appreciative sigh, "Thank you for stopping. Could you please let me use your phone—I forgot mine at home."

He eyed the tire and looked back at her. "What else is wrong except the flat?"

"That's all."

"How about I just fix it, and you can be on your way."

Her expression took on a sweet mother-like look. "You are *so* kind. Thank you."

Bishop took off his khaki shirt, leaving just his tee-shirt and jeans to get dirty. The woman stood on the roadside slightly behind him and watched with her arms crossed. She eyed him while twisting her hair like a young girl, humming some tune Bishop didn't know. He finished the job in twenty minutes and was startled by her stare. It wasn't at all natural. Her eyes had a strange distant expression. She strolled up while he wiped his hands with a shop rag he'd found in the back of the Cadillac.

"I really appreciate you."

She startled him by put both her hands on his right bicep. They were ice cold.

"I don't even know your name, I'm Minerva McFadden."

Bishop finished wiping his hands and shook hers. "Troy Bishop—glad I could help." He nodded at her car. "I would think that Cadillac has OnStar."

She waved the idea away. "Oh, that thing hasn't worked for months."

She made Bishop a little nervous. Strangers who touched him always did. He had *the feeling*. That sensation he got when things didn't add up. Time to get out of here. "Well, if there's nothing else… "

She moved closer, and a broad smile encased her face before saying, "Would you like to come to a party this weekend?"

Her eyes had a hungry look. Like a used car salesman gets after seeing a clean trade-in roll onto the lot. The strange, wide smile worried him.

She'd caught him off guard, and he stammered, "I'm just passing through. You know, vacation. Maybe do a little hiking."

"Perfect," she exclaimed, "our ranch is near Gallinas Peak. Best hiking in the area. Here's my card—I'll tell the people at the front gate to expect you. Just show them this, come around one o'clock on Saturday."

Bishop reluctantly took the card and stuffed it in his pocket, he'd toss it later. Anything to get rid of her.

She gave him another pleasant smile and lightly touched his arm again with those cold fingers. "You'd fit in just fine at the party. Most of the people are boring—been seeing them for years. But…" She leaned closer and lowered her voice.

Bishop had to fight the urge to back away.

"I think you're an interesting person," she said. "My husband collects interesting people." Without waiting for an answer, she whirled toward her vehicle, let out a giggle, and slid behind the wheel. She pulled onto the highway and was gone before he could get back to his SUV.

Well, that was weird. Bishop rechecked the map. The area she spoke of, Gallinas Peak, was off this highway. He continued south and never saw the Cadillac again. She must have been flying. As he approached the small town of Corona, there were signs for Gallinas Peak. Small town was an understatement. The place was nothing but a few shops, a motel, and a gas station—almost a ghost town. More abandoned buildings than occupied ones. The plethora of railroad tracks and equipment was its most prominent feature. Looked like the rail transfer station there was long ago abandoned. A town used up and forgotten with time in a painted, deserted desert.

Bishop almost turned left on Highway 247. That would take him into the heart of Lincoln County, to a desolate no man's land, but his curiosity got the best of him. Instead, he followed the signs for Gallinas Peak down a gravel road. After about five miles, there was a sprawling ranch on the left. It extended for about a mile from the road into the wood line at the base of the mountain. Over the entrance to the place, a sign read McFadden Ranch. There was a guard shack with a couple of people inside.

Bishop studied the place—looked more like a small town than a ranch. Numerous barns, sheds, and whole neighborhoods of tiny, well-kept homes. The side of the mountain showed signs from a past fire. About halfway from the base, the façade of a huge house tucked into the rock's face looked down on the town. Reminded Bishop of a heavy gun emplacement in the side of a cliff. Weird woman—weird house.

Blackened skeletons of once mighty trees littered the side of the mountain along with new growth pines. Burnt stumps, some twenty feet tall, stood beside downed trees piled in heaps on top of each other—all charred. The place had an eerie quality. Who would live in such a setting?

"Minerva McFadden and her husband, the man who collects interesting people," Bishop said out loud.

An old, tan, doublewide trailer house sat directly across the road from the sprawling ranch entrance. A large tin-covered patio shielded the entrance to the front door. The rust streaks on the tin had caused small holes, sending dozens of tiny rays of light onto the wooden floor and several dozen plants below. Most of the trailer's paint had been sandblasted off from the harsh environment. The trailer looked like it might crumble in another good wind. An ancient, pale green Dodge pickup sat beside it, baking in the New Mexico sun. It had lots of dents and signs someone had once brush painted it in places with a darker shade of green. Bishop pulled into the driveway of the trailer house to turn around.

Bishop followed the gravel road back to Corona and turned right. He needed to make a decision here. Keep going or stop for the night in Corona. Since he didn't have a destination and hadn't eaten lunch, Corona was as good as any to stay. A sign pointed to the right; it read GALLINAS ROAD. Bishop pulled onto the road leading to Gallinas Peak summit to turn around and head back to Corona. He gazed at the late afternoon sky. Still plenty of daylight left. He wanted to get a look at the top of the peak. Might be worth hiking one day. This road looked like the fastest way to the top. It might give him a nice view.

One additional fact Carpenter related still nagged at Bishop. The OST scout vehicle had a magnetic jamming device attached near the roof antennas. Must have been attached before the attack. But when?

How? Had someone in the Office of Secure Transportation broken bad? Or, did the theft of the trooper uniform and patrol car have more to do with it? Still more questions than answers.

Following the park signs, Bishop drove the winding road through heavy forest. The fire had not reached this side of the mountain, and the views were spectacular on the way up. Bright sunlight filtered through the giant Ponderosa Pines, and the sweet smell of clean air welcomed him. The 8,200-feet elevation cooled the afternoon temperatures, and Bishop rolled up the car window and drove another mile and a half before getting to the top.

Parking, he marveled at the view. He walked to the edge of the peak and gazed into the distance. It sat on the fringe of the mountains and plains. The top of the summit had tall, scattered pines slowly swaying in the light breeze. *Absolute quietness.* A fire lookout tower stood with a small, wooden, red house at its base. Bishop gazed at the tower. Had no idea those old things were still in use, but this one appeared well maintained. That would be the place to get a nice view. Better ask permission first. He swiveled his head in all directions, not a soul in sight—not even a car. He ambled to the house and was about to knock when the soft sound of running water from the rear of the home caught his attention. He knocked on the front door anyway, but no one answered. After several knocks, he skirted around the left side of the house and walked toward the back and the sound of running water.

Just as he turned the corner, he stopped cold. The young naked woman stood in the flow of water from the shower nozzle attached to the back wall of the house. She held a bar of soap at her side and didn't seem to notice him.

Uh-oh, wrong time. Bishop quietly backed out of sight around the corner before she saw him. He meandered toward his SUV but stopped halfway. He turned his head back toward the rear of the house and mentally went over what he'd just seen. Something looked wrong —or more to the point—something wasn't right. He shook off the feeling and walked back to his car. As he opened the door, he glanced back at the house again. The *feeling* rushed through him once more. Going back to get another look at the beauty was wrong on several levels, but he had to know, even at the risk of being labeled a creepy guy. He walked back to the corner and peeked around to see if what he remembered was correct.

She stood still as a statue. The woman, frozen in form, hadn't moved an inch since he'd first spied her. He tried figuring it out. Her medium-length black hair wasn't even wet. She held the soap in a tight, white-knuckled grip, rigid as if made of stone as streams of water flowed down her chest, thighs, and legs. Her slender body stood erect, and her eyes looked straight ahead. The cool water caused goosebumps to decorate her smooth, olive skin.

Bishop's boot accidentally bumped the corner of the house. His curiosity almost caused him to step from around the corner, but she must have heard the bump. She slowly turned her head and caught his gaze. She slowly shook her head but didn't speak. Her fearful eyes darted to the lower left, her lips and chin trembled, and her ashen complexion confused him. He followed the downward motion of her eyes to the edge of the concrete pad used as the base for the shower. No more than a foot from her left leg was a giant rattlesnake. Its large head and eyes stayed fixed on her—its tongue whipping in and out, tasting the air. It was coiled and ready to strike. Her brown, teary eyes pleaded for help.

Bishop didn't dare approach any closer. Staying out of sight was his best option. If the snake got spooked, it might go into defensive mode and attack the closest target. He eased back to the corner and ducked behind it while reaching for the pistol in his back waistband. Using the corner as a bench rest, he took careful aim. The woman's eyes widened at seeing the gun. She stood between the snake and him, blocking his direct line of fire. The viper's head weaved slowly to the left and right —mesmerized by the falling shower water splattering on the concrete. When it swerved to its left, it showed itself for a split second. Timing would be everything. Bishop cocked the weapon, took a deep breath, let half out, and waited.

The shot startled the young woman, and she screamed and jumped, dropping the soap. She jerked her head toward the headless snake lying beside her, grabbed the towel hanging from a hook, and darted a few feet in Bishop's direction. She wrapped the towel around her petite body, and a blush rushed up her neck, while trying to cover her nakedness. She stared at Bishop, who'd stepped from around the corner.

A shiver coursed through her. "I hate those things," she whispered.

"Yeah, me, too," he replied and slid the weapon back into the waistband holster.

She glanced again at the snake as if to assure herself it was really dead before stepping back to get a better look at Bishop. From the high cheekbones and skin tone, she had lots of Native American blood. The clear, green eyes gave her the face of a glamour model. She eyed him up and down and smiled.

"Well, since you've seen me naked and saved my life, I should introduce myself. I'm Cora Ballenger." She held the towel tight with one hand and extended the other.

He shook the outstretched hand. "Troy Bishop, nice to meet you."

She glanced back toward the snake one last time, and another visible shiver rushed through her. She turned to Bishop. Her head tilted and nose wrinkled. "You always carry a gun?"

He shrugged and matter-of-factly said, "Most of the time."

The flippant answer made her smile. "Why are you here?"

Since she appeared to like the first, Bishop decided on another flippant answer. "Heard there was a damsel in distress."

A tiny smile cracked her lips. Her eyes glistened sensually, the white teeth set against her light brown skin. Studying her expression, Bishop had no idea what response his silly answer might engender. He didn't realize he was holding his breath until she spoke.

"Well, you were right on time." She took a couple of steps toward the back sliding glass door, keeping the towel tight against her body. Opening it, she turned. "Are you coming in, or just planning to stand there?"

Bishop followed her into the small living room. The house smelled good, something baking. It reminded Bishop, again he'd missed lunch.

"I won't be but a minute." She disappeared into a back room, and the door closed.

In Bishop's line of work, he seldom had what most people consider a typical day, which only proved the point. How the hell did he end up standing in a stranger's house waiting for her to get dressed?

Cora removed the towel and looked at her naked body in the full-length mirror. She raked her black hair away from her face and frowned. How did she end up with a gun-carrying stranger in her living room?

The snake thing had rattled her a lot more than she'd let on. *But she didn't cry.* She vowed to never cry again—showed weakness. She'd played it cool and figured if she invited Bishop inside, that would prove she wasn't afraid of anything—snake or stranger. But Cora was afraid. She was scared of so many things happening around her. Scared of what her future would be. Now, to further complicate her life, this guy strolls up. Her luck with guys was dismal. Didn't want or need another relationship.

She had a plan. A quick grin crossed her lips. She quickly dressed in jeans and a navy turtleneck sweater. She checked her hair and face, decided against anything but some lip gloss, and slipped on a pair of running shoes. Tying them, she couldn't stop thinking about the man in her living room. She'd never been saved before—it felt good. He was handsome and had intense eyes. She liked his eyes. This wasn't like her to invite a stranger into her world, but after what he'd done, what choice did she have? Well, she did have a choice. She'd go out there right now, thank him again, and show him the door. She had her hand on the doorknob when she stopped. But showing him the door wasn't what she wanted. She wanted to get to know him a little better. Could she be that starved for attention that an exciting stranger who made a lucky shot could make her feel this way? The short answer was yes.

Her grandfather always said everything happens for a reason. It might be a good reason or a bad reason, but destiny ruled our lives, according to him. Of course, he was full-blood Apache, not like her. He believed more in the old ways. He expected her for dinner tonight. That could be her excuse with Bishop—how to get rid of him. She had dinner plans, and he had to leave. Yeah, that would work. A distraught feeling coursed through her, a feeling of doubt. She'd just play it by ear with Bishop and see how it went. But she'd keep the dinner excuse in her back pocket, just in case she needed it.

———

Bishop walked around the small living room, examining paintings, photos, and a pine cone collection on the end table. The pictures were of vistas in the area. Sunrises, sunsets, and the desert blooming in spring. They were nice, but something was missing. Something about the shade of colors, brushstroke, and light gave them a lonely closed-end feel. Like the artist was sad, or lonely, or both.

The tiny house's furnishings had pretty much the same look as his hotel room back in Albuquerque. The late afternoon sun filtered through the thin curtains and cast its rays across a well-worn, multicolored, Native American blanket laying over the back of the old sofa, giving it a splash of color. The smell from the recently used fireplace still lingered in the air—a cozy well-lived-in house with lots of memories. The kind of place someone could live comfortably and simply, well away from the troubles of the outside world.

The bedroom door creaked, and she walked out. She flashed a shy grin, rubbed her palms down the legs of her jeans, and strolled to his side.

"These paintings are pretty good. Did you do them?"

She moved closer. "No, my grandfather."

He turned her way, and she unconsciously took a quick step back. Her face held apprehension, and she rubbed her hands on the sides of her jeans again. Probably time for him to leave. Overstaying a visit could lead to trouble. Besides, he was hungry and needed to check into the hotel in Corona.

"I should be moving along." He walked to the front door. Just as he opened it, she stopped him.

"No, wait." She licked her lips and shifted from one foot to the other.

"Yes?" When he looked into her eyes, he thought he saw something. He didn't know what, but she was struggling to make a decision.

She bit her lower lip and blurted out, "Would you join me for dinner? It's almost ready." She stood very still, holding her hands in front like a nervous young child on her first day of school. Her clenched jaw confused him. It was like she wanted him to stay but struggled with the decision she'd made.

Bishop stepped back from the door. He hadn't planned on stopping here and now had a dinner invitation. Something felt wrong about the whole thing. Not wrong, like the way he felt around Minerva McFadden, but still uncomfortable. Cora's anxious, girl-like expression could just be her nature. Introverts had their own way. He had to eat somewhere. Having dinner with a stranger was probably as good as any. At least she was an attractive stranger.

Bishop pushed the door closed. "Love to join you."

Her shoulders relaxed, and a quick smile appeared. She brushed loose hair from her face. "Good, we're going to my grandfather's house; he's grilling. We're bringing the baked beans and potato salad.

Bishop took a step toward her, and she didn't retreat this time. "You're sure it won't be an imposition? Inviting someone for dinner?"

She shook her head. "Not at all—we'd love the company." Her lips flattened, and she lowered her head a moment before looking back up and releasing another quick smile. "Don't get much company around these parts."

Bishop asked, "Can I do anything?"

"Yeah, you can drive us." She strolled into the kitchen and whispered into her cell phone. "Bringing someone to dinner, he's driving me, that okay? Thanks." She took a container of potato salad from the refrigerator and set it on the kitchen counter. After pouring the beans into a sealable dish, she announced she was ready.

The weather had changed since they'd been inside. The wind had picked up with sunset, and the once cool, comfortable breeze was now cold. The tall pines on top of the peak looked like drunken giants swaying in the evening twilight, their sweet scent filling the air. Bishop eased down the gloomy mountain road with the last traces of light struggling through the thick pine needles. Shadows streaked across the road as the trees moved in the wind, giving the place a threatening quality. This would be the darkest place on earth by the time they came back up.

She stared at him, the outline of her face fading in the darkness. "Why did you stop at my house today?" Her voice was just above a whisper, but it seemed to have an urgency. Reminded Bishop of someone who asks a question but didn't want an honest answer.

He shrugged. "To tell the truth, I wanted to climb the fire tower—thought I should ask first."

Her sharp laugh surprised him. She shook her head and covered her mouth with her hand. "I'm sorry—it just seems so improbable, that's all."

"What?"

She paused a beat before answering. "That someone with a gun just happened to stop at the exact time I needed help."

"Everything happens for a reason," he said.

She didn't answer, and he couldn't see her expression due to the darkness but got the feeling he'd accidentally struck a raw nerve. Her silence lasted a little too long. Something still felt wrong here. Probably should have skipped the dinner invitation.

She cleared her throat. "Why do you carry the gun?"

By her tone, he could tell she wanted a serious answer. "I always carry one when I go hiking."

"Never seen you around. Are you new or passing through?"

"On vacation—just passing through."

They drove in silence until he reached the bottom of the mountain.

"Turn left here at the highway," she said.

Bishop drove through the night desert toward Corona. She directed him to turn left on Highway Forty-Two and back onto the gravel road he'd been on earlier. Soon the lights from the sprawling McFadden Ranch appeared on the left. Cora glanced at the ranch and quickly turned her head, looking out the passenger window.

She pointed. "Turn right into the next drive."

Bishop did a double take as he rolled into the same drive he'd used to turn around a couple of hours earlier. The drive leading to the broken-down trailer and old Dodge truck.

———

Newman Smith marched down the brightly lit hall of McFadden's home. He stopped at the entrance to his boss's office. McFadden stood with his back to Smith, facing the vast picture window, looking out at the lights of *his* town in the valley. The town McFadden had built and continued to support with his wealth. For a seventy-year-old, he was in fantastic shape. On a good day, he could pass for sixty. Apprehension coursed through Smith. Knowing a great man was one thing, but when everything you are, or ever hope to be, was made possible by that man…

"You called, Clark?" Smith asked.

McFadden looked over his shoulder. "Come in." He ran a hand across the top of his grey hair as he walked to his executive desk.

"Have they called?" Smith asked.

McFadden took one last look out the window and sat in the leather chair behind his desk, motioning for Newman also to take a seat. A delightful grin spread across McFadden's lips before saying, "Both Monk and Piedmont called. Neither Sandia nor the FBI has a clue. We're in the clear."

Smith released a breath. "Thank God." This had been the only thing on his mind the last few days. Hadn't been able to sleep or eat, waiting on the confirmation.

"I want you to notify General Shaw and Speaker Wilson. They've been on the same pins and needles we all have. Let's not keep 'em waiting, okay?"

"I'll handle it."

McFadden's brow crinkled. "Once we get through the reunion this Saturday, let's button up the ranch. No one in or out. The feds have agents scouring this whole part of the state—especially up north. The reunion will serve as a good cover. After it's over, we'll go dark, and they should have no reason to come near us. After everyone's in place, we'll begin phase two."

Smith had a giddy tingle of relief wash over him, mixed with the exhaustion from lack of sleep and stress. "I still can't believe it."

McFadden smirked and leaned his forearms on the desk. "You remember what I taught you growing up, right?"

Smith remembered and recited it. "Nothing beats having the right people, in the right place, at the right time."

McFadden grinned and stood. "Happy I made an impression. Make the notifications. We're on the threshold of building a new country, Newman."

———

Bishop glanced at Cora. "This is your grandfather's house?"

"Yes." She opened the SUV's door and slid out, grabbing the beans. "Would you carry the potato salad, please?"

The night wasn't as cold in the valley—hardly any wind. A sky full of stars had blossomed as they drove down the mountain. They seemed to stretch to infinity.So close you could reach up and touch them. The complete silence of the clear desert night relaxed Bishop.

As they stepped on the porch, an old man opened the trailer home's door, and the smell of grilled chicken filled the air. Smelled great. Cora kissed him on the cheek and gave him a big hug before introducing Bishop.

"Samuel Turner." He pumped Bishop's hand.

He reminded Bishop of the old Native American actor, Chief Dan George, his expression wise and noble. The old guy looked in his eighties with deep lines drawn into his face from age and sun. The bushy grey eyebrows, dark brown, leathery skin, and a broad welcoming smile put Bishop at ease. He was a few inches shorter than Bishop. The long, gray hair and deep-set, dark eyes gave him an authoritarian air.

The smell of fresh biscuits also permeated the trailer. Bishop's stomach released a low growl, reminding him he'd only had a granola bar and bottle of water for lunch—he was starving. Cora and Samuel organized the food, and Bishop studied the home. The old trailer was spotless but had more knick-knacks than Bishop had ever seen in one place. Every shelf, table, and piece of furniture had more than its share: trinkets, pieces of prettified wood, and colorful rocks.

Looked like a souvenir shop along I-40 exploded. The walls were covered with Samuel's oil on canvas paintings. Many showed Gallinas Peak, but without McFadden's house cut into the side of the mountain. Samuel took a seat and motioned for Bishop to come to the table.

"Mr. Bishop, please sit down."

Cora poured iced tea for everyone, then joined them. Dinner conversation consisted mainly about who Bishop was and what he was doing in such a remote part of New Mexico. He stuck with his cover story and deflected questions about what kind of work he did. Cora never said a word about the snake.

After a long lag in table talk, Bishop said, "That's a pretty big spread across the road."

Samuel nodded and grinned. "Yes."

Since that didn't reignite the conversation, Bishop followed up with, "I've been invited to a party there tomorrow."

Their heads turned toward him. Cora's shoulders tightened, and beads of sweat sprouted on her upper lip before glancing toward Samuel. His dark skin was now pallid. He slowly sat his fork down, wiped his mouth with his napkin, and gave Bishop a quizzical look.

In a low tone, he asked, "Are you friends with the McFadden's?"

Samuel's question, while delivered in a relaxed voice, was laced with fear and curiosity. Somehow, Bishop had screwed up. He wasn't sure how he'd offended them, but he'd waded off into something he didn't understand. He answered honestly.

"No, we're not friends. I fixed a flat for Mrs. McFadden earlier today, and she asked me to come by the ranch for a party."

Bishop turned to Cora. She had stopped eating and refused to meet his stare. She had even stopped breathing and the hand holding the fork shook. Samuel's expression gave nothing away. He nodded again and caught Bishop's gaze.

"You never met either of them before today?" Samuel asked.

"No. Did I say something wrong?" Bishop looked to Cora again, who had recovered a little but still had a concerned expression. "I'm sorry if I offended."

Samuel picked up his fork and took a bite of potato salad. "No, Mr.

Bishop, you've said nothing wrong. The McFadden's just aren't very good neighbors—that's all."

Bishop started not to ask, but he was curious. "Why do you say that?"

"It's a long story." The old man's warm smile returned.

NINE

After dinner, Bishop and Samuel sat on the tin-covered front porch listening to the muted sounds of the night desert while Cora put up the leftovers and finished the dishes. Bishop strolled out to his SUV and retrieved the gin and tonic bottles and mixed drinks for them. Cora declined and fished a half-full bottle of homemade honey wine from the back of Samuel's kitchen cabinet.

Samuel lit his pipe and stared into the distance. A rich, woodsy smell enveloped the porch. Samuel preferred the gin with as little tonic as possible. He and Bishop sat for a long while, sipping the drinks and not saying a word. The chill of the night settled around them and finally forced Bishop back to his SUV to retrieve his jacket. As he strolled back to the porch, he stared at Samuel and his granddaughter, Cora. He had seriously upset them with just the mention of McFadden's name. He was intrigued by Samuel's comment. The *McFadden's just aren't very good neighbors*. It wasn't the comment so much as the fear and doubt Bishop's admission about going to the party engendered in Cora and Samuel. Bishop felt a little foolish. He was in New Mexico searching for stolen nukes, and all he could manage was to stir up an ongoing fight in the neighborhood. He'd just let the matter drop and be on his way tomorrow. Probably expanding his search east made the most sense. At this point, without more information, he was looking for a particular needle in a haystack of needles in any case.

Samuel appeared warm enough with just the pipe and gin. Bishop donned the Carhartt jacket and returned to his chair. The covered porch was dark; Samuel hadn't turned on the outside light. The faint sliver of moonlight illuminated scattered shadows of plants and patio furniture.

Bishop gazed at the canopy of stars. "This is beautiful out here, away from the city."

Samuel nodded but didn't answer. Bishop got the feeling he wanted to say something but was working up to it. The awkward silence continued a little too long. The McFadden Ranch loomed bright and expansive across the road, and Samuel studied it with a sad smirk as he sipped his third gin and tonic. He finally spoke.

"The McFadden's are evil," he said in a tone of conviction.

Bishop wasn't sure how to reply. He didn't want to get back into the thing that gotten him into trouble earlier, so he didn't answer.

Cora walked back out of the trailer with her glass of wine and an old jacket of Samuel's draped over her shoulders. She stood beside him and laid a hand on his shoulder without speaking. He reached back and laid his hand on hers, and a loving smile crossed his lips.

Samuel slowly took a draw from the pipe and settled into his chair a little more. "About forty years ago, I lived on the Mescalero Apache Reservation, south of here." His stare scanned the horizon, and he pointed the pipe in the direction of the reservation. He patted Cora's hand, and she took a seat beside him. He cleared his throat and continued.

"There was a big falling out between factions of the tribe, and over a hundred of us left the reservation. Formed a convoy and headed north." The trace of a grin swept across his mouth. "We called it the great migration," he said. "We believed the tribe had drifted away from the true Apache ways. They were becoming too much like the white man, forgetting the language and traditions and the beliefs that defined us as a separate people. Our group had a more fundamentalist belief. So we left."

"My parents were part of the group," Cora chimed in. She pulled the jacket tighter. "Even though my dad was Anglo, he went with my mother and her people."

Samuel continued. "We came to settle on that land," he pointed again with his pipe toward the massive ranch across the road. "When our group left the tribe, we didn't have much of a plan. Stopped for the night right over there and decided to stay awhile. Everyone agreed just to stop," he sighed, taking another sip. He was quiet for a while, perhaps recalling those days. He cleared his throat again, the emotion swelling. "We lived in tents and pop-up trailers for close to a year. We planted gardens, and a few of us found work with the railroad in Corona."

Bishop understood from his tone the memories were disturbing. His voice cracked several times, and Cora squeezed his shoulder. Seemed like he was leading up to something. Something so painful he hated to think about it. Perhaps it was the gin or their earlier dinner conversation, or a combination of both. "What changed?" Bishop asked.

Samuel looked his way, the glow of the tobacco in the bowl of the pipe highlighting his face. "McFadden, that's what changed. The man who owned the land lived out of state, didn't care if we squatted there or not. He never intended to keep it anyway. Then he sold it to McFadden. We didn't see much of our new landlord for the first few months. Too busy making money and had no time for a bunch of Indians. That was fine with us. We didn't own the land, so every day we stayed was a gift. Finally, he began work on his castle in the mountain—that's what he called it—his house."

Bishop only nodded. The house cut into the side of the peak might be considered a castle. Cora refilled her wine and mixed another drink for Samuel. He took a long swallow. *Yup, the gin had loosened the old man's tongue.* Perhaps a little more than Bishop would have liked. He didn't want to get involved with a neighbor-to-neighbor squabble. An uncomfortable air settled over the trio as the old man kept speaking.

Samuel grunted. "McFadden ignored us for the most part but finally got around to making his pitch. He asked for a meeting, and we all attended. Told us he planned to turn this desert," Samuel spread both hands wide, "into a world-class ranch. Said he intended to stock it with Angus, Brangus, and Beefmaster cattle. He told us he'd need all the help he could get once he was up and running. Wanted to know if we'd be interested in working for him? Said he'd build housing for everyone that wanted to stay and work on the ranch—even promised a school for the kids."

Bishop leaned closer; the story now started to interest him. Samuel again sat silent for a while, and Bishop still had no idea why he thought McFadden evil.

Cora spoke up. "I was born on the ranch—in the clinic McFadden built."

Bishop could wait no longer. "I'm not clear—if he built houses, a school, and a clinic—what's so wrong with that?"

The outline of Samuel's head turned in the pale moonlight. He slurred a little from the liquor. "Because in exchange for those things, he wanted our souls." His voice broke, and he coughed to cover it. Samuel sighed. "He also took something from me I loved the most."

Cora reached over and rubbed his shoulder once again. She said, "McFadden built his ranch and made it clear that anyone wanting to stay and work could live for free with a school and health care, but they must follow his rules."

Samuel let out a tired sigh. "We were fools ever to believe him. Fools to think we could get something so big for so little. He's had a plan for forty years. We were the disposable part of that plan."

Bishop still didn't understand. Everyone who had a boss had rules. Why should this McFadden guy be any different? Samuel said nothing more. There was much more to the story, but the old memories were too hard for him. They sat a while longer, and the silence began to take a toll on everyone's nerves.

Cora stood. "Ready to go?"

"Anytime you are," Bishop answered.

Samuel struggled from the low chair, and Bishop lent him a hand.

"Thanks," Samuel said. "Have a good time at the party tomorrow." His weary voice finished with, "Don't make any deals with McFadden." He nodded, and the smile returned."I'm going to bed."

TEN

It wasn't that late, but the day's drive and big meal worked on Bishop. He yawned on the way back up the mountain to Cora's house. He looked forward to a hot shower and soft bed. He'd check in for updates with General Cook tomorrow before starting his eastward search.

"Tired?" Cora asked.

He turned and smiled. "A little—you?"

"Yes, I've had enough excitement for one day. Where are you staying?"

Bishop hadn't thought that far ahead. The weeks of planning and working out every last detail down to the minute in Beirut had left him not wanting to think any farther ahead than necessary. It was the only way he could decompress after a stressful op like that.

"Hadn't thought about it too much."

She shifted in her seat and turned toward him. "Where did you stay last night?"

"Hilton in Albuquerque."

"Hmm."

Bishop pulling up and parked beside her house. "I saw a hotel in Corona driving in."

"Yeah, there's a couple of places." She pointed at the dashboard of the SUV. "Is your clock correct?"

"Yeah. A few minutes past nine."

"If you drive to Corona, you'll be sleeping in your car. The streets roll up early. Hotel's already closed."

"What?" Bishop was worn out. The thought of driving a couple of hours to find an open motel didn't appeal to him.

Cora paused a moment and said, "You could stay here. On the couch," she quickly added. "No sense driving for hours and spending good money if you don't have to."

Bishop considered the suggestion but quickly dismissed it. "Thanks, but no thanks. I'm back on the road tomorrow."

"Oh. Thought you were going to McFadden's party."

Bishop laughed. "No, I don't go to stranger's parties, especially after what your grandfather told me."

Cora opened the passenger door and looked back his way as she got out. "Couch is still available. Least I can do for a knight in shining armor." A smile cracked the corners of her mouth.

Bishop hesitated. *This was probably a bad idea.* Something was going on here he didn't fully understand or want to be a part of. This girl might have problems that someone in his position couldn't afford to get involved in. An involuntary yawn slipped from his lips, and Cora laughed.

He decided. "You sure?"

She motioned with her head. "C'mon, bring your things."

Bishop grabbed his bag and followed her inside. The tiny house had grown cold and uninviting, but the smell of the baked beans lingered. Bishop dropped his bag in the corner, and she went to the fireplace, started a fire, then strolled into the kitchen.

"Want a nightcap?"

"Whatever you're having will be fine."

Moments later, she appeared with two glasses of white wine. The light from a corner lamp, the warmth and glow of the fireplace, and the smell of dry crackling wood gave the place a cozy, pleasant feel. They sat on opposite ends of the couch and watched the flames play and swirl.

After several minutes, Cora spoke, never taking her gaze from the fire. "If you change your mind and decide to go to the party tomorrow, be careful… Don't let on you know me or Samuel."

Bishop couldn't help but be interested. The fear and apprehension Cora and Samuel felt toward this McFadden guy wasn't close to normal. He had decided not to go to the party, but all the mystery gave him second thoughts. He'd make a final decision after a good night's sleep. "I might go, we'll see."

Cora exhaled. "Watch out for Minerva—a bad spirit possesses her, you know."

Bishop had just taken a sip of wine when Cora's remark caused him to spit it back into the glass. "A what?" He coughed, wiping a few drops from his chin.

"You'll see," she said.

Bishop considered continuing the conversation, but it was getting a little too strange, so he changed the subject. "How did you come about living here, on top of this mountain?"

Cora pulled a cover over her legs and took a sip before answering. "After college, I taught for a while, but that didn't work out—so I applied to the US Forest Service for this job. I'm only up here from May through October. By the end of this month, I'll be back working at the forest service center."

There was hesitation and concern in her voice, and this gave Bishop pause. There was more to that story—lots more. "Seems like a lonely job—up here by yourself—sitting in a lookout tower."

Cora stared into the fire a moment before saying, "I like it," she yawned, drained the glass, and sat it on the end table. "Think I'll turn in."

He stood. "Thanks for the sofa."

She nodded. "I'll bring you out some blankets and a pillow."

Ten minutes later, Bishop lay on the couch looking at the fire. It was dying now, just the hot, red coals left. The room became a little darker each second. He wanted to attend the party at the McFadden's tomorrow out of curiosity more than anything else. Wanted to check out the *man who collects interesting people* and his wife *possessed by a bad spirit*. He'd let headquarters decide. He'd call in tomorrow for any new leads. If there was nothing new, he'd attend the party before expanding his search east. Not much of a plan, but it was all he had. He smiled at a quote from the old Oklahoma oilman, T. Boone Pickens. "I'd rather have an idiot with a plan than a genius without one."

Something caught Bishop's eye—something outside the window. It was pitch black except for the dim moonlight struggling through the tall pines, but he could have sworn he saw a shadow move past the window. He felt for the Sig Sauer on the floor under the sofa. Rising from the couch, he walked to the window and peered out—nothing. He slipped through the dining area wearing only his boxers to the sliding glass door facing the back of the house—nothing. The shadows of tree limbs dancing in the light mountain breeze cast strange outlines on the ground.

Bishop lay back on the sofa, the pistol a little closer this time. He remained very still and listened for at least ten minutes. As the room darkened from the dying embers, his body relaxed, and his eyelids fluttered and became heavy. He fought it for another five minutes but finally gave in and plunged into a deep restless sleep. Dreams of shadow men watching through the windows caused him to toss and turn.

———

FBI Special Agent Daniel Piedmont turned the corner in his car and searched the numbers on the homes. This upscale community of Chevy Chase, Maryland, was one of the more established neighborhoods. One and a half million plus was the price range—lots of older couples and government executives from DC.

Piedmont stopped in front of the two-story colonial with the Boston ivy climbing the walls, almost to the roof. The stately oaks swayed in the breeze, and a few orange and red leaves floated to the ground. The morning was crisp, and the sweet aroma of someone burning wood wormed its way through the community. A few of the ivy's leaves had also started turning color, signaling the end of summer. The northern breeze ruffled Piedmont's short black hair as he exited the car and looked around to see who was watching. At this time, on a Saturday morning, only a middle-aged couple rode past on bicycles, and a yard service crew was finishing up across the street and loading their mowers into a trailer.

Agent Piedmont waited for the lawn service to leave while checking his appearance in the car window's reflection. He tightened the knot in his tie and swept back his hair again, smiling at the image. He leisurely walked up the sidewalk and stopped at the door. Looking back over his shoulder, the bikers were out of sight, and the mowers had moved down the block to another house around the corner. He scanned the exterior walls and windows of the porch for cameras before ringing the doorbell.

The elderly man answering the door wore casual, brown chinos with a forest green short sleeve shirt. His silver hair was combed straight back, and the scent of fresh aftershave wafted past Piedmont's nose. "Agent Piedmont?" the man asked.

"Yes, sir," Piedmont said and displayed his FBI identification.

A satisfied smile crossed the old man's lips before saying, "Come in, I was surprised to hear from the Bureau—didn't know you had a dog in this fight."

Piedmont chanced one last look around the outside before following the senator into the inside. The foyer had high ceilings with a gold-inlay eighteenth-century chandelier overhead. Expensive Persian rugs covered the dark stained wood floors. A fresh paint smell lingered in the air as Piedmont trailed Senator Fillmore down a short hall and took a left into a private study. The sunlight streaming through the open shutters spilled across the desk, leaving bright yellow lines over the piles of papers.

Fillmore asked, "Could I get you a cup of coffee?"

"That's very kind, but no, thank you, sir. I can't stay but a minute."

"Take a seat, and let's see what you have."

Piedmont handed Fillmore the 9"x12" envelope before taking a chair near the desk. Fillmore squinted at the bright sunlight shining through the plantation shutters. Before sitting, he closed the wooden slats, giving the place a shadowy feeling.

Piedmont crossed his legs and smiled—*perfect*. "Sorry about all the cloak and dagger, Senator, but I've been assigned to unofficially leak this information before your hearings on Monday. Didn't want to do it during business hours in the District."

Fillmore nodded while slipping on a pair of half-lens reading glasses. "I appreciate the help and understand your discretion; McFadden's been a slippery one to corner—doesn't leave much of a footprint." Fillmore slid a letter opener in the top of the sealed envelope. "My committee's been looking into his campaign contributions for months. I am finally starting to make some inroads. He could be indicted soon if things break in our favor."

Piedmont casually turned and listened for movement in the house. He leaned forward in the soft leather chair as Fillmore pulled the papers from the envelope. "We're alone, aren't we? I don't want anyone to associate the Bureau or me with coming here today."

Fillmore chuckled and adjusted his reading glasses while studying the papers. "Oh, don't worry about that—domestic help has the day off, and my wife won't be back for another couple of hours. Now explain what this information has to do with McFadden's dealings and how it can be used in my hearings?"

When Piedmont didn't answer, Fillmore looked up, and his eyes fixed on the gun in Piedmont's hand. The first shot hit him in the chest and the last two in the head. Piedmont calmly unscrewed the silencer and removed the papers from Fillmore's lifeless hands. He carefully slipped them back into the envelope and strolled to the mirror outside the study in the hall. He adjusted the knot in his tie again, swept back the short black hair, and gently touched the thin scar on the bridge of his nose. He glanced back into the study at the corpse. Fillmore was just another small-minded fool. The man couldn't see how his ridiculous inquiries might do great harm to a patriot like Clark McFadden. Piedmont would never let that happen. He'd protect Mr. McFadden with his life.

Piedmont scanned the inside of the entryway for cameras, opened the front door, and took a quick look outside. There was no one on the street or sidewalk. He used his handkerchief to wipe the inside and outside doorknobs before calmly meandering to his car. He had just enough time to get back to FBI headquarters before being missed.

———

Cora rose with the sun. She didn't mind getting up early, she liked the cool mornings—more birds singing. Sitting in the fire tower with a hot cup of tea, wrapped in a blanket and warm jacket, was heaven. It was the climb up she hated.

She'd dreamed about Bishop last night—they were making love. This was surprising. She'd not dreamed about a man in years—much less making to love to one. Perhaps it was because she understood theirs would be a short-term affair. No long relationship, no baggage to contend with. He was a traveler just passing through, and she was stuck here, as least as long as Samuel lived. Couldn't leave him, and he'd never leave his place. He had a mission not fulfilled. He wasn't the kind of man to leave something undone.

After her shower, Cora slipped on her robe and cracked open the bedroom door. Bishop lay sleeping and shirtless on the couch with the blanket at his waist, just the top of his blue plaid boxers showing. Sunlight creeping through the curtains outlined several old, puckered scars on his well-toned body. Cora focused on them. *Had he been in an accident, a fight, a war?*

Just then, his eyes popped open, and stared her way.

"Good morning," he said.

How did he know she was there? The door hardly made a sound. "Good morning—sleep okay?"

"Great." He sat up and swung his feet to the floor.

The pistol lay just under the edge of the sofa. She nodded. "You always sleep with that?"

He glanced at the weapon, half-hidden by his hiking boots, and a boyish grin cracked the corners of his mouth. "Didn't know if there were any snakes under the couch."

"Yeah, right. Get some more sleep if you want. I have to go to work."

She ducked back into the bedroom to finish dressing. She removed her robe and eyed her nude body in the full-length mirror. She ran her hands over her breast and down the sides of her hips before turning to check her profile. What would he do if she walked out there right now and lay beside him on the sofa? He'd shown as little interest in her as a man could for an attractive woman. She frowned. *Was she attractive?* Other men had found her desirable, but only one had won her heart. Even he was gone now. Her frown evolved into an ugly scowl as her eyes checked every feature on her face and body. Her hands drifted to her flat stomach, and she sucked in her breath. *Yeah, it wouldn't hurt to lay off a few carbs.*

When Cora left twenty minutes later, Bishop's soft snoring filled the room. She slowly climbed the steps to the tower, keeping a firm grip on the handrails. How would life be in another place with a man like Bishop? *Silly questions for a grown woman to even think about.* But she did think about it. In fact, she dreamed about it. She could only exist here; someplace else, she could start living again. But that was for another time at some unknown date in the future. Until then, she could only dream.

———

FBI Special Agent Sean Carpenter wasn't happy this morning. Not just because it was a Saturday or because he had to break a promise to take his wife to dinner for their tenth wedding anniversary this evening. No, his problems went far beyond that. He sat at his desk in the Albuquerque FBI office, reading reports instead of investigating leads from the stolen nukes case. Fact was, the leads had dried up.

When the FBI set up the Joint Operations Center in the field office, they'd gotten a flurry of calls. Of course, all the calls came in due to the cover story about the theft of government communications equipment from a hijacked tractor-trailer off I-40. Until the government came clean to the public and acknowledged the theft of nukes, there was a limit to future leads. Since the last few calls entailed eyewitnesses to aliens making off with the equipment and traveling at lightning speeds out of the galaxy, Carpenter decided to catch up on the mountain of paper on his desk.

This report was from the Department of Energy concerning the stolen warheads. They were due a refurbishing, and that's why they were in transit to Sandia National Laboratory in Albuquerque.

Carpenter sipped his coffee and studied the report. Being the Weapons of Mass Destruction Coordinator for the Albuquerque office didn't make him an expert, but you didn't have to understand the basic math. Plutonium-239 has a half-life of 24,110 years. Even in a weaponized form, how could the gamma rays and neutrons be shielded from detection? Unless… Carpenter had recently convinced himself the weapons probably hadn't been whisked away but hidden, waiting for the search to die down. And they were hidden within a reasonable distance of the ambush. It was still difficult for him to believe someone had just driven them away from the attack site. But being an avid reader of Sherlock Holmes, Carpenter recalled Holmes saying, "When you have excluded the impossible, whatever remains, however improbable, must be the truth."

Carpenter walked to the full wall map of New Mexico and took another sip of coffee as he examined the area. They had covered the attack site and miles in every direction. They must widen the search area. The resources so far provided by DOE wouldn't be adequate. They were going to need more detection equipment to find the radiological signature—lots more.

Carpenter strolled back toward his desk, sipping the coffee. A thought crossed his mind, and he turned back to the wall map. *Wonder what that guy, Bishop, is doing?*

———

When Bishop awoke the second time, his body was stiff and still craved rest, but he wanted to get up. He peeled a banana, made some coffee, and dressed. He walked out into the cool morning air, munching on the banana. He strolled out the back door around the small house and found an old Moped covered with a blue tarp. He turned the corner and stared at the front window, which looked into the living room. He squatted and examined the soft soil of the flowerbed under the window sill. Bishop ran his hand around the footprints. About a men's size ten. No regular boot or shoe prints, but some kind of smooth-soled footwear. The indentations of the ball of the foot and the heel were the most pronounced. *He'd been right.* Uninvited visitor last night. What kind of peeping Tom travels to the top of a mountain in the middle of the night to look into a lady's window? His mind drifted back to the discussions about the McFadden guy. Why would a multimillionaire care about some girl sitting in a fire tower above his ranch? Made no sense…

Bishop punched in the number for the office, and Colonel Maxwell answered.

"Good morning, Bishop here."

Maxwell said, "Let's go secure."

Bishop stared up at the fire tower before clicking the indented switch on the side of his phone, and a sharp chirp sounded. "Secure."

"So, what's going on?" Maxwell asked. "Fuller called yesterday. General Cook promised him an update before noon."

Bishop scratched the back of his head before saying, "Not much. Got rousted by the Bureau when I visited the attack site. Don't think they want to play with us.

"I could make a call if that might help."

"No, don't do that," Bishop said. "Besides, I think they're looking in the wrong place."

"What?"

"It's a long story. I've expanded the search south—looking for anomalies. Heading east later today. You got anything for me?"

"Nope."

Bishop lowered his voice. "Sir, tell the general I'm picking up signs that indicate one or more insiders might have been involved. He was right; we *can't* trust the locals out here."

There was silence for a moment. Bishop understood what was probably going through Maxwell's mind. Not being able to trust the people you *should trust* puts someone in a position of not asking too many questions for fear you might be talking to the enemy. So far, the only one Bishop had discussed it with was the FBI agent—Carpenter. If you couldn't trust them, who could you trust?

Maxwell let out a breath before saying, "I'll tell General Cook," and disconnected.

The rising sun warmed the summit, but Bishop still grabbed his jacket before climbing the fire tower. With each step, the scenery got better until the entire vista was revealed. As he popped his head into the tower, Cora was reading a book. A dark green US Forest Service jacket shielded her from the wind that seeped in.

"Permission to come aboard?" He climbed inside.

She grinned. "Permission granted."

The magnificent view kept his attention. Hues of the desert's colors —browns and reds mixed with the dark green pines and yellow rays of the sun streaking across the cloudless sky.

"Wow," he whispered.

"Nice, huh?"

"I'll say—you have the best job in New Mexico. And this air." Bishop took in a deep lung full.

"This is the last existing fire tower in the state. Only reason they've kept it is because the current forest superintendent began his career up here thirty years ago. This is the last season I'll be posted here. With all the high-tech fire detection stuff out there, this place will become a museum. If I'm lucky, they'll keep me on to run it."

She put the book aside. "I was about to take a break. Enjoy the view and the air—I'll be right back."

Five minutes later, the house's front door slammed, and Bishop peeped out as Cora walked back up the stairs. She held the tea mug in one hand while keeping a death grip on the railing with the other. Her pace was measured—one careful step at a time, eyes watching her feet. Just before she made it to the top, she noticed him staring, and an embarrassed smile swept across her lips. She hopped into her elevated leather chair and looked his way.

"What?"

"Are you afraid of heights?"

Cora took a sip of hot tea. "No!" She shrugged. "Well, maybe a little." She paused when he gave her a harder look. "Well, maybe a lot."

"So how does someone afraid of heights end up with a job like this?"

She lowered her head and stared at the cup. "McFadden. I was a teacher at his youth academy until a couple of years ago. When I resigned, this was the only job I could find."

Bishop lounged back in the chair, propped his feet on a rail, and said, "Let me see if I've got this straight." He pointed over the edge of the tower. "The McFadden ranch is directly below us, right?"

"Yeah, it extends from the base of the peak to the road where Samuel lives.

"And the McFadden Academy is the school on the ranch you spoke of last night?"

"Uh-huh." She nodded. "It's a good school, but I couldn't stand to see the way the children were being brainwashed—I had to leave."

Bishop got that old feeling. The one that had warned him of trouble so often in the past. *Something was very wrong here.* Her story didn't add up. This McFadden guy appeared to be the source of all her problems, and yet she took a job living and looking at his ranch all day, every day. Why didn't she just leave—move away—find another job?

"I don't get it. Who's brainwashing the children?"

"The other teachers and administrators. It's sort of an idol worship of McFadden thing." Cora's cheeks reddened. "Anyway, I just needed to get out."

Her explanation still didn't add up. "You're kidding, idol worship?"

"Wish I were, but it's the truth."

Bishop wasn't sure what to make of Cora. "So, you didn't want another teaching job?"

Cora stood and walked to the other side of the tower. She leaned back and crossed her arms. "You don't understand. McFadden owns this county. I couldn't get a job picking up trash off the road around here without his approval. The only way I got this job is that it's federal. As powerful as he is, he hasn't got his hooks into all the federal agencies yet."

Her sad eyes gazed at the floor, refusing to meet his stare. Something told Bishop to take her in his arms. He walked to her, and without a word passing between them, she leaned her head on his shoulder and wrapped her arms around his waist. The most emotion she'd showed since the snake incident. He held her and softly stroked her hair, saying nothing.

"I loved teaching so much, and I loved those kids. It kills me to see what's happening to them," she whispered, emotion choking off her words.

They stood there awhile in the embrace—neither saying another word. Cora stepped back, and a flush crept across her cheeks. "Sorry."

She looked like someone who would have liked to cry but refused to show that much emotion.

"That's okay," Bishop said. He strolled back to his chair.

She took her seat. "What time is the party?"

"I think any time after one will be fine." He decided to change the subject.

"Ever noticed someone walking around your house at night?" He took a sip of coffee, watching her reaction.

She stared at the cup in her lap a second. Her brow furrowed, and her lips flattened. Bishop couldn't tell if she was angry or perplexed by the question.

She looked up, and they met eyes. "No, did you see something?"

"Not sure, just a shadow. Could have been a limb blowing in the wind, I suppose." He didn't want to tell her about the footprints, not yet anyway.

She took another quick sip of tea and averted her gaze. "The moon has a way of playing tricks on you this high up—probably just a limb."

From her troubled expression and fearful eyes, she wasn't convinced. The morning wiled by, and they talked of other things and continued enjoying the view. Bishop still debated going to the party. He didn't want to go, but the intrigue surrounding the place and the McFaddens tempted him. He tested the water again. Bishop motioned toward the ranch at the bottom of the mountain. "What's really going on down there?"

Sunglasses now hid Cora's eyes, but she removed them before answering. "After college, I taught for a while at the elementary school —it's part of the academy. When I attended there as a child, I never seemed to notice, but as an adult, I began to realize it's almost a place to worship Clark McFadden like a god. Photos of him everywhere. Quotes from him plastered in the classrooms, library, gym. There's even a life-size statue of him in the academy's courtyard."

Bishop sat his cup on the table and leaned forward. "What?"

"Yeah, just the way the whole thing's organized. McFadden's been running the ranch for two generations—forty-plus years. Only the people he likes remain there. The rest he runs off. That's what Samuel meant last night about taking their souls. He's taken away their freedom to think."

"Is that why you and Samuel aren't there any longer?"

"One of the reasons." She caught his eye. "The other is Samuel thinks McFadden had something to do with my parent's disappearance."

"Why?"

A sad smile shadowed her lips. "Can we not talk about it now? Let's just enjoy the rest of the morning."

Bishop had made his decision. He'd attend the party and see for himself if Cora's and Samuel's suspicions were warranted or just some paranoid delusion. Besides, what else did he have to do? Since Carpenter and Maxwell offered no leads, may as well waste his time at McFadden's as driving to a destination unknown. Didn't matter much. After the party, he'd say his goodbyes and be on his way.

Cora fixed lunch—tuna sandwiches with dill pickles and chips—and they feasted while enjoying the landscape and being serenaded by dozens of birds.

After eating, Bishop said, "I'm going."

"To the party?"

"Yeah, you've piqued my interest."

"You're welcome to use the indoor shower in my bathroom—it has hot water. Or if you want a brisker experience, try the outdoor cold shower—you know where it is."

Bishop stood and headed for the stairs. "Thanks, but I'll stay with the indoor shower." He mumbled, "Cold water my butt. I'll be dammed if I'll ever get into cold water again."

This was a personal thing with Bishop. He'd never liked cold water even as a kid and learned to hate it in the military. He'd tried to avoid it ever since his Special Forces SCUBA training. It seemed like all his instruction was in water cool enough to chill beer—not bathe.

———

Clark McFadden strolled around his front drive. He kept his eyes on the horizon. *Wonder what the authorities are doing now?* Newman Smith followed close by his side. McFadden dropped his gaze to the ranch below. *God, I love this view.* "Everything ready?"

"Ready as we'll ever be," Smith said.

McFadden lit a cigar and drew in a mouthful of smoke. He slowly released it before saying, "Have you checked them this morning?"

"Yes, Clark. All are resting comfortably."

McFadden nodded. He'd instructed Smith to check on the warheads every twelve hours. He pointed to the top of the peak. "Got a report that Cora had a visitor last night."

"Oh, anyone we know?"

McFadden shook his head. "No, and that's what concerns me. Some guy driving a black SUV stayed the night. Got a tag number." McFadden handed a slip of paper to Smith. "Have Karl run it."

"Will do."

McFadden pulled in another round of smoke. "Don't much care for strangers at her house right about now." He looked down at Smith.

"I understand." Smith held up the paper. "I'll get started on this."

As Smith walked away, McFadden again searched the skies. No helicopters meant they hadn't widened the search this far south yet. Having the reunion today was the perfect cover. If anyone cared to conduct an aerial fly-over, they'd find a parking lot filled with cars and dozens of men and women. Not exactly the place one would expect to hide nuclear weapons. He'd have to let the front gate know to keep a lookout for unknown vehicles driving slowly past the ranch. Sooner or later, the feds would have to sweep this area. When they did, he wanted it to appear just as an ordinary ranch tucked up against a national forest in the middle of nowhere. *Nothing to see here—keep on driving.*

———

A half-hour later, after finishing his shower, Bishop again climbed the tower to say goodbye before leaving. He'd packed his bag and loaded it in the SUV. If he didn't screw around, he could be in Roswell before dark. Plenty of hotels and restaurants there. He had mixed emotions about leaving. Cora was a nice girl, but troubled. Best he move on. Whatever problems she and Samuel had with McFadden weren't Bishop's business.

Cora had a telescope rigged inside the tower when he walked in. "I'll be keeping an eye out for you—remember, be careful what you say."

Her look of concern caused him to question why she had this macabre interest in McFadden and if going to the party was a good idea. She was fixated with this guy.

"Okay, thanks for everything. I'm back on the road after the party. Appreciate the couch last night."

She blinked, and her shoulders drooped. "Come back anytime. Don't get all that many knights in shining armor around here." Her eyes had misted, but she smiled.

ELEVEN

When Bishop arrived at the front gate of the McFadden ranch, two neckless Native American men with biceps the size of small melons and wearing light blue Guayabera shirts and khaki pants, met him. He presented the card Minerva had given him the day before. They checked the list on a clipboard and acknowledged he was expected.

The older one pointed to an area to the left, just inside the gate. "Park there—the bus will be here in a minute."

Bishop pulled into a parking space between a Dodge and Volvo. Several dozen vehicles were parked on the blacktop. A few other people waited by their cars; their dress was casual. Bishop hadn't dressed up either—the straw-color Dockers and olive-green polo were the best he had. As he got out of the SUV, he studied the row of homes that lined the road just inside the gate. They were all about the same size in various shades of pastels—greens, oranges, and yellows. All had attractive red tile roofs, and the front yards were tastefully landscaped with desert plants.

Bishop walked toward the other guests waiting for the bus. A heavy-set lady wearing an extra-long dress stood with her husband, fanning herself and grumbling about the "insufferable heat." Bishop strolled up and nodded. The couple looked him over. They were in their 50s and also showed traces of Native American blood. The man's hair had started thinning in front. The lady stopped fanning and dabbed her brow, pushing the wet brown hair from her forehead.

"Another hot one, huh?" Bishop said, adjusting his sunglasses.

"Yeah, summer doesn't want to let go," the man remarked. He smiled. "I'm Karl Dorring—my wife, Janet," he said, nodding toward the woman.

"Troy Bishop." He extended his hand.

Karl's smile evaporated. He hesitantly shook Bishop's hand—his grip was wet and slimy. "Happy to meet you." His lips twisted, and he tilted his head toward Bishop. "How do you know Mr. McFadden?"

Bishop didn't want to go into a long explanation, so he just said, "Friend of Mrs. McFadden."

Karl's eyes pinched. "Oh, I see."

"What about you?" Bishop asked.

The woman quickly spoke up. "Karl's the county sheriff." There was brag in her tone.

"How nice," Bishop remarked.

"Thank God," Karl said, looking over Bishop's shoulder at the white shuttle bus approached. It had picked up several others before making its way to them. The air conditioning was a welcome relief as everyone settled into their seats.

The bus left the parking area and drove down the main road past dozens of homes toward the mountain. As if signaled, the homes' families stood on their front porches, smiling and waving to the bus passengers. A few waved back—most ignored them. The sheriff, Karl, kept eying Bishop with an uncomfortable stare. Bishop had seen that look a dozen times, mostly from people who tried to kill him. *What's his problem?* The bus wove along the gravel road for almost a mile before reaching the base of Gallinas Peak. The haunting landscape loomed high above them; blackened remnants of destroyed trees along the road gave the place a threatening appearance. Everyone in the bus sat in silence as they made their way up the mountain. A couple whispered something to their partners, but none made eye contact with the rest. From their expressions, Bishop got the feeling no one wanted to be there but were compelled to attend. This, and the lack of excited chatter you might expect from guests attending an invitation-only party, set Bishop on edge.

The bus pulled into the half-moon drive in front of the massive house cut into the face of the peak. The home was much larger than it appeared from a distance. But still looked like a wart on an already blemished face. The front was a combination of natural stone and huge glass windows looking out over the ranch and valley below. Everyone filed off the bus, but there was still no enthusiastic talk usually heard by happy guests. Bishop was the last to exit. Something was seriously amiss here, but he looked forward to meeting Clark McFadden. See if he was the son of a bitch Cora described.

The bus slowly pulled away, and Bishop strolled to the front door. Standing to the left of the door with his arms hung unnaturally by his side was the largest, and without a doubt, most fierce man Bishop had ever seen. He appeared to be a full-blooded Apache. The giant stood close to seven feet and weighed between two hundred and fifty to three hundred pounds. The oversized head with deep lines in the granite-like skin and predatory eyes gave him a threating appearance. His hands looked the size of catcher's mitts. The only sign of humanity was the large polished turquoise stone that hung around the bull neck with a piece of rough leather string holding it.

The women made sure their husbands were closest to the giant before walking through the door. The men acknowledged him with a nod. One said, "Hello, Ochoa." The giant did not respond or register any expression. Bishop ignored him and walked in.

The interior of the home surprised Bishop. It was fashionably decorated with western-style furniture and colorful artwork—lots of leather and tones of muted red and beige painted walls. The brightness of the place added to its uniqueness. Bishop had expected an almost cave-like interior. The front windows were the only natural light source, but the clever lighting in the ceiling caused the room to look much brighter and more extensive. It was already almost banquet size. Bishop headed toward the enormous fireplace; the bar was there.

"Gin and tonic, please."

"Coming up, sir."

Bishop sipped his drink and wandered the crowded great room. The conversations were muffled as he passed. A few eyes met his. It seemed as if this was a regular gathering, like the same group did it often. He was the outsider, and everyone knew it. Waiters and waitresses mingled in the crowd—the young women all wore white Mexican summer dresses, and the young men khaki slacks and white Guayabera short sleeved-shirts. They all carried trays of drinks or small sandwiches.

Across the room, Karl, the sheriff, spoke to a guy who was a little taller than Bishop but much older—in his early seventies. He had an athletic build and short, salt-and-pepper hair. Karl leaned in close and whispered something to the older man, and they both stared Bishop's way. *Okay, what's this about?*

"Mr. Bishop." The words whispered from behind caused him to turn. Minerva reached out and touched his bicep with her cold fingers. "I'm so happy you came."

Bishop tried to smile but felt the strangeness of the moment. She wore a strapless pink sundress. Just the proper amount of cleavage showing. She looked younger than yesterday. Her eyes had a new sparkle today, and her voice a silkier texture.

"Hello, Mrs. McFadden."

She grabbed his arm with both hands, too familiar a gesture for someone he hardly knew. "Come, I'll introduce you."

Bishop always liked to gauge the tone of a strange place before meeting anyone—especially one like this with unfamiliar people. Minerva didn't allow him that option. She dragged him across the room to a gathering of men talking—one held the group's attention— the guy in his seventies with the athletic build that Karl had been conferring with. The man glanced their way as they approached, but he continued talking. His voice was soft but authoritative.

"The political situation has become ridiculous. Never in the history of this great nation have citizens been stripped of their rights like in the last year." Karl and the others nodded in agreement. The older man paused, glancing again at Bishop and Minerva.

"Would you excuse me please, gentlemen?" He walked to Minerva, and she extended her hand. He took it with ease.

Minerva nudged closer to the man. "Darling, this is the good Samaritan I told you about. Mr. Bishop, this is Clark, my husband."

The man held out his free hand to Bishop. "Thank you for rescuing my wife yesterday." His smile was thin and forced.

Bishop shook the hand and found the grip a little too tight.

"No, problem—glad I could help."

"My wife tells me you're just passing through." His eyes had a strange inquisitive look.

Bishop realized the game being played but didn't understand the reason. "I'm on vacation—wanted to do a little hiking."

"Are you staying local, Mr. Bishop?" Minerva asked.

Before Bishop could answer, Clark McFadden broke in. "Yes, darling, Mr. Bishop's staying with Cora on the peak."

Minerva cleared her throat and her forehead creased, but she quickly recovered. She smiled and, in a shaky voice, asked, "How is dear Cora?"

McFadden smirked.

Bishop understood the smirk was a challenge.

Bishop grinned. "She's fine and sends her regards."

McFadden's expression soured—a flash of anger in the eyes. "If you'll excuse me. I need to see to my other guests."

Bishop had just confirmed what he'd thought all along. The only way McFadden could have known he stayed at Cora's last night was from a spy. He'd been right, the shadow he saw last night was no limb swaying in the moonlight. The footprints belonged to one of McFadden's people. Bishop glanced at the male waiters. They all wore smooth-sole Moccasins. But why bother spying on Cora? To what end?

As McFadden strolled toward another group of guests, Minerva grimaced and blushed. She retook Bishop's arm and led him to a corner.

"Do forgive Clark; he's been under a lot of pressure putting the reunion together. He's not a very good host today, I'm afraid."

"What reunion is that?" Bishop asked, taking a glance across the room at McFadden.

A confused expression crossed Minerva's face before she tilted her head, giggled, and motioned with her hand. "This is the reunion, here.

Oh, silly me, you've not been to one before." She brushed her hair back and leaned closer, whispering. "Every year, Clark gives a reunion for honored graduates of the McFadden Academy."

Bishop looked around the room at the hundred-plus people. "You mean all these folks are graduates of the school?"

"Well, mostly the men. Many of their wives didn't attend the academy. It's a nationally recognized school. Won every academic excellence award the state and country offers," she said with a prideful tone.

"Is that so?" Bishop took another look around as he sipped his drink. Regardless of the accolades from Minerva, something still felt a little off. There was a missing piece, but Bishop couldn't figure it out. Cora told him McFadden had built the school for children of Apache parents who worked on the ranch. There were all mixed-blood men in the crowd—no full-blood Native Americans except the waiters and waitresses.

"Yes, and all of them have achieved excellence in their careers," Minerva said.

Bishop raised his glass in a mock toast, "Well, I'm honored to be among such a distinguished group." He scanned the room again, looking for McFadden.

She tightened her grip on his arm and pulled him closer. "It's remarkable what Clark's achieved in the past four decades. You see those three talking by the window?" she pointed to a group of middle-aged men in conversation. "The tall one is the county commissioner, the one to his left is our county judge, and the one with his back to us is the congressman for this district."

"They're all graduates?"

"Well, the commissioner and county judge are. The congressman is a guest. Clark almost single-handedly funded his last two campaigns. Clark likes supporting conservative candidates."

"Interesting." Bishop eyed McFadden again on the opposite side of the room. He watched Bishop and Minerva intently while talking to another group of guests. She didn't notice the stare from her husband.

"So, what do the other graduates do? They all can't be in politics," Bishop asked.

"Oh, no, many are in business, and some with the military and government. See the man talking to the woman in the black dress by the bar?"

"Yeah."

"He's a Major in the Air Force, works for the national something or other—has to do with our military spy satellites."

"The National Reconnaissance Office?"

"Yes, that's it," Minerva smiled and playfully tapped his arm, "aren't you the smart one."

"Lucky guess." Bishop continued watching McFadden. He stood beside a short, lanky, gray-haired man with foxlike features. They both looked his way and spoke in quiet conversation.

Minerva continued talking and pointed to a different guy. "The man over by the fireplace, the one in the white shirt and gray slacks," she nodded. "He's with the Air Force, works for Space Command in Colorado, inside a mountain."

Bishop took in a slow breath before asking, "Cheyenne Mountain?"

She waved the question away. "Yes, some Indian name like that."

McFadden's eyes stayed fixed on Bishop as Minerva kept talking.

"Mr. McFadden must have quite a school to have these kinds of successful graduates."

"We're very proud of the school and all the boys who've done so well." She gave an approving motherly look at the group of men in their late thirties and fourties.

McFadden had his cell phone out and began pushing buttons.

Minerva let out a sigh. "Too bad some couldn't make it this year. We're especially proud of one graduate—he's a director of something at Sandia National Laboratory. Couldn't be here today—some emergency. Dear, Monk. Such a nice man and so brilliant."

Bishop hung on her every word. She was utterly oblivious to the significance of the intel she was sharing. Pieces of the puzzle began falling into place, but not the final piece.

At that moment, her cell rang. "Hello."

She looked across the room at McFadden—he was on his cell and glared at her with a hateful expression.

"Yes, I'll be right there." She turned to Bishop with an excited smile. "Oh, please excuse me—be right back."

Bishop was glad she left. Gave him a chance to explore. He strolled around the room toward a hallway. He lingered and casually sipped his drink. The hum of conversation continued as the guests mingled. He'd been there long enough for the novelty of his newness to wear off. He waited his chance. McFadden and Minerva were in a heated conversation in the far corner, and no one appeared to be paying Bishop any mind. When no one was looking, he hurried around the corner into the back hall. It was a long, brightly lit corridor leading to a massive wooden door at the end. Along the length of the twenty-foot passage was a glass display case to the right. He meandered toward it. It was built into the rock wall. The display sat behind thick glass and showed the technique of mining uranium ore by using tiny toy-like buildings, vehicles, and human workers to illustrate the process. It started with an open-cut uranium mine and followed the ore through various methods until it completed its journey as purified yellow cake —milled uranium oxide. The toy dump trucks, digging machinery, and piles of dirt reminded Bishop of a kid's playset. Bishop's mind drifted back to his training. Yellowcake was the first step toward enriched uranium, but it was a long way from being weapons-grade.

Further down the hall, the display continued. Bishop looked back over his shoulder to the hall entrance before proceeding deeper. The process of converting the purified yellowcake from uranium tetrafluoride to uranium hexafluoride was explained through green, yellow, and purple information cards posted inside the glass enclosure. The enrichment process of uranium 235 was depicted. At that point, the display ended. The last items in the case were two glass vials mounted inside Plexiglas containers, one with what appeared to be black uranium fuel pellets. The note below indicated it was low enriched uranium dioxide—"for nuclear reactors (simulate)." Beside it, the other glass vile had several ounces of a coarse, off-white powder. The note below read "highly enriched uranium (simulate)."

The short man with foxlike features that had been talking to McFadden earlier turned the corner and walked toward Bishop. He had his hands in his pockets and showed a half-smile like he knew a secret. His expression changed into something of a scowl before approaching Bishop.

"Do you find it interesting?" the man asked. "I'm Newman Smith, Mr. McFadden's attorney."

The guy didn't offer his hand, and neither did Bishop. Figured they must have lost track of him at the gathering and sent the lawyer to locate him. Bishop motioned toward the display case and nodded.

"Yes, very interesting, but a strange thing found outside of a museum, don't you think?"

Smith stood beside Bishop and again smiled. Smith clasped his hands behind his back, smiled and nodded toward the exhibition case. "Not strange at all considering this is Mr. McFadden's business— uranium mining."

"Is that so?" Bishop took a sip of his drink and studied the man.

Smith's smile vanished, and his eyes narrowed. "Yes, and this is his private corridor leading to his office." In a condescending voice, Newman Smith pointed toward the wooden door at the end of the hall and said, "Off-limits to visitors."

The man had a cunning look as if that was his way of making some implied threat. Uneasiness swept over Bishop. This would be a great time to make excuses and leave. The lawyer must have had the same idea.

Smith faced him. "The bus is waiting to take you back to your car, and I trust you had a pleasant visit. Goodbye."

Before Bishop could answer, around the corner walked two large men dressed in black Guayabera shirts and black slacks. *Party's over.*

Smith reached out and took Bishop's glass. "They'll show you out." He led the way as they walk back down the hall toward the main room. When Bishop's left arm was inches from the display case, his nuclear watch vibrated. Smith didn't notice Bishop push the button on the wristwatch. The face blinked once—dark blue. Smith slowly walked across the main room with Bishop in tow and the two goons close behind.

Bishop stared above the front door at the engraved quote in the stone wall. He'd not noticed it until then. Deeply etched into the rock in old English script were the words: *"Every generation needs a new revolution"- Thomas Jefferson.*

Smith opened the door and stepped aside. Bishop turned back before walking out. Minerva stood across the room beside McFadden —she waved a small, sad goodbye. McFadden just stared, a frown pinned to his lips.

Stepping outside, the hot, dry air greeted Bishop. The bus waited with the motor idling in the driveway where it had dropped him off. Smith closed the door to the house, but not before letting the black shirts out. They guarded the entrance, arms crossed. Bishop fished for his sunglasses. Not the first party he'd been thrown out of. *There was that time with the team in the Nanyang Ward of Singapore.* Turning his back on this bunch while walking to the bus caused an uneasy sensation in his stomach. He looked down at his wristwatch and pushed the bottom button again just to be sure. The face blinked dark blue—U-235, *weapons-grade.*

The doors to the shuttle opened, and Bishop stepped in. It was empty except for the driver and one man—Ochoa. Bishop sat down across from him and ignored the beast. It had been a good decision to leave the pistol in his SUV. Shooting a guy as big as Ochoa would probably just make him mad.

The ride seemed to take forever, with the giant non-human-looking creature staring at him. The man never blinked. Not sure he ever breathed. When the bus arrived at the parking area, Bishop hopped off and walked the short distance to his car. Ochoa stood at the door of the shuttle, watching him until he drove out the front gate. Bishop glanced across the road as he pulled out of the ranch. Samuel sat in the shade of his front porch rocking in the chair, almost hidden among the plants and patio furniture, watching the whole thing.

———

Bishop drove about a mile down the road out of sight of the ranch entrance before pulling over. He reached for his cell phone and considered what had just happened. His watch indicated a source of radioactivity inside the display case. Malfunction or false reading? No one would be stupid and or bold enough to keep a hot radiological source inside their house. Would they? Bishop scrolled through the contact list and dialed his cell. A moment later, the smoky, female voice answered.

"Hello, this is Lesa."

Lesa was P2OG's secret weapon. They'd stolen her three years ago from the CIA. CIA stole her two years before that from NSA. She was the best analyst in the intelligence community. Her databases covered all intel and law enforcement agencies to include Interpol. She had the world of criminals, spies, and terrorists at her fingertips. She was also the smartest and saltiest woman Bishop ever met.

"Why are you at work on Saturday?" he asked.

"Is that you, Bishop? I thought you were still out of country?"

He leaned back in the seat and grinned before saying, "How do you know I'm not?"

"Ha! Don't get cute with me, buster. The phone you're calling from isn't cleared for overseas use—I can read your number on my caller ID."

No fooling her. He again asked, "No really, why are you there? I thought I'd get one of the weekend analysts?"

She released a tired sigh. "Director's orders—he wants the A Team on duty until this New Mexico business is cleared up. Think he wants us to sleep here," she chuckled.

"That's what I'm calling about; I'm in New Mexico."

"Figures," she mumbled.

The sound of her taking a long sip of something filtered through the phone. Probably the hot, spiced tea she was addicted to. Her office smelled like an incense shop.

Bishop adjusted the air conditioner vents before saying, "Do me a work up on Clark McFadden. He carries a Corona, New Mexico address. Older guy—in his seventies."

The sound of sipping was replaced with the clicking of computer keys.

"Sure thing, I'll get right on it. Anything else?"

"Yeah, connect me with Andy. Is he in?"

"Like I said, Bishop. All the A Team's working today."

A couple of seconds later, Andy answered. "What is it, Bishop? Have you broken something again?"

"Shut up and listen. Is there any possible way this crazy nuclear watch you gave me would react to yellow cake, you know, milled uranium oxide, or spent reactor fuel pellets?"

Andy let out an exasperated breath. "No, as I said, you'll only get a reading on uranium if it's highly enriched—as in 85% pure U-235."

"That's what I thought, thanks."

Bishop hung up without bothering to say goodbye. He had to think. How did McFadden get his hands on highly enriched uranium? Better question, why was he so arrogant as to display it in his home? The glass and Plexiglas display cases blocked the Alpha particle decay, so there was no health risk, but it didn't make sense even to have the stuff. Hubris had been the downfall of many a great man. Was this guy so confident that he kept contraband in the form of U-235 on display and tried to conceal it by labeling it as a simulate? Bishop pulled back on the road and headed to Gallinas Peak. He had a couple of questions for Cora. Speaking of Cora, Bishop now felt like a fool. He had considered her a delusional, troubled, paranoid young woman. She's been right all along about McFadden. He was a bad man. Question was —how bad?

TWELVE

Bishop pulled up to Cora's house and took the pistol from the glove box. He tucked it into his back waistband as he walked to the tower steps. He'd just put his foot on the third step when the front door to her house opened—she stood there with two bottles. "Come have a beer and tell me about the party."

He took one and followed her around the house, past the outdoor shower, to the shaded back patio. The afternoon had turned cooler from an approaching cold front, and the light breeze felt good. The tall pines swayed and filled the air with their sweet, clean fragrance—might need a jacket later. She must have read his mind.

"It's always cooler up here, over eighty-five hundred feet," she said before flopping into one of the cushioned chairs and gazed at the endless view. "So, how was it?" She took a long swallow.

From her expression, Bishop got the idea she already knew. He settled back in the other chair. "Afraid things didn't go very well—I was asked to leave."

"Really, why?"

"Let's just say, me and McFadden didn't hit it off. You were right about him."

She drew her legs under her into the oversized chair. "I watched you through my telescope."

"See anything interesting?" He took a swallow of beer.

"They searched your SUV, Troy."

He slowly lowered the bottle and turned her way. "Did they, now?"

"Uh-huh, just before you came out—two of them."

"I locked it before I went in."

"They unlocked it somehow—don't think the alarm went off."

Bishop nodded. *Must have found the pistol.* He propped his feet on a nearby stool and lounged back. This put a whole new twist on the thing. Mrs. McFadden appeared more flightily and a little zany. Hard to imagine her involved in anything sinister. But her husband... "Well, no harm done. Does McFadden usually search his guest's vehicles—seems kinda rude?"

In a voice devoid of emotion, Cora said, "If you're interested in seeing what McFadden *really does*, wait till dark. I'll show you something that'll creep you out."

———

Clark McFadden stalked around his bedroom and gawked at Minerva sitting on the edge of the bed. He wanted to wring her neck. "What in the hell were you thinking? Inviting a stranger to our reunion? Are you crazy?"

Minerva didn't answer but stared at the floor.

McFadden turned back to her. "You know they found a pistol in his car. One like cops carry. Did you know that?"

Minerva looked up and narrowed her eyes. "What are you up to, Clark? Mr. Bishop is no more a cop than you are. Heck, at least half the people in this county carry a gun in their car. Besides, so what if he is a cop on vacation—big deal."

McFadden rushed her. He grabbed her with his vice-like grip around the chin and squeezed her cheeks tight. Pushing his face to within inches to hers, his voice low and threatening, he said, "And what if he's not on vacation? What if he's a spy?" He shook her hard.

"You crazy bitch. You invited him right into our home. You still on your meds?"

A tear squeezed from Minerva's eye and skated down her cheek.

He gave her a hard slap across the face, and she fell on the bed as he turned to leave. He hoped he left a good bruise on her flawless face. The one she spent thousands on every year.

When he got to the door, he turned and pointed at her. "You'd better hope he moves on soon. Accidents happen all the time around these parts." He sneered before saying, "Now, get yourself ready for tonight. Your performance had better be your best."

———

That evening, Cora made taco salad laced with spicy ground beef and shredded New Mexican chilies, cheese, and onions. She and Bishop dined, sitting on the back patio, and watched the sunset. The evening was perfect. The place sounded like an aviary, with dozens of birds singing a strange, enchanting melody. Bishop had caught up on all his missed sleep and was completely relaxed for the first time in weeks. This started to feel like more of a vacation than a P2OG assignment. Around eight o'clock, after darkness set in, a cold wind chilled him. Just before he started to grab a jacket, his cell rang—Colonel Maxwell calling.

Bishop answered, and Maxwell requested he go encrypted.

"Wait one," Bishop said. He excused himself from Cora and walked to his SUV. He sat in the passenger seat and closed the door before flipping the switch on the side of the phone. The cell chirped, indicating secure mode.

"You on to something?" Maxwell asked before Bishop could get a word out.

"No, not really. Why do you ask?"

"Lesa said she was doing a work-up for you on someone out there."

Bishop lowered his voice. "It's more of a hunch, really—nothing firm."

The sound of papers shuffling preceded Maxwell's next comment. "Okay, keep us in the loop if you need something."

"Thanks."

"By the way, how're things with the FBI—are they still not playing nice?"

Bishop massaged the back of his neck and stared at the back of the house. Cora had gathered the dishes and disappeared inside. "The FBI's not interested in having me as a partner, sir. I've left contact information with their case agent out here, but I don't expect to hear back from them. Right now, I'm off the beaten path, running down a lead I stumbled on. Don't think the Bureau's even searching this far south."

There was a pause on the line before Maxwell asked, "Which FBI agent are you working with out there?"

"Guy by the name of Carpenter, out of the Albuquerque office. His card says he's the office WMD Coordinator."

The sound of pen scratching paper drifted over the line. "I'll make a few calls and see if I can grease the skids a little."

"Thanks." Bishop disconnected but wasn't a hundred percent sure he needed the Bureau at this point. He had expanded his search down here, looking for anomalies that could pinpoint the stolen weapons. McFadden was undoubtedly one, but was he *the* one. Was it unheard of that a guy involved in uranium mining all his adult life had a vial of U-235? Sure, it was technically illegal, but a lot of crazy souvenirs got passed around to people in high places. Of course, it also could have been a malfunction in Andy's nuclear watch. Perhaps at least putting the Bureau on notice wasn't a bad idea.

Bishop made his way to the house as Cora was coming out the back sliding patio door.

"Sorry about that," Bishop said. "My people are working today and had a question."

She shot him a look. "Must be important to call on a Saturday evening." Cora checked her watch. "It's almost time."

"Where we going?"

"Back up the tower." She slipped the heavy Forest Service coat on. "Better get a jacket; we'll be up there a while."

"Okay, let me grab a beer first."

Her firm voice surprised him. "No alcoholic beverages allowed in the fire tower."

They stood in the shadow of the house, and the darkness had closed in to the point he couldn't read her features or expression. *Was she serious?* He dropped the thought, picked up his jacket, and followed her up the steps. Her pace was maddeningly slow, one careful step at a time. There was still enough moonlight to easily see the steps, but she wouldn't be rushed. Bishop gazed in the direction of the McFadden Ranch. Someone had built what looked like a colossal bonfire way in the back of the property. Bishop was unsure if it was a real fire or just a cluster of bright lights from his vantage point.

Once at the top, Cora said, "Don't turn on any lights or flashlights; keep it dark." She claimed her usual seat and swung the telescope toward the part of the ranch where Bishop saw the fire. The regular bundle of lights from the residential and communal pavilion areas shined as before, but now there was this additional light from the most remote part of the property. *What was Cora up to?*

From this height, Bishop was now sure it was a large bonfire that glowed in the distance. He squinted to make out what was happening. It was the only distinguishing feature on the black landscape in that part of the ranch. That was the direction Cora aimed the telescope. She adjusted the rear dial then stepped aside.

"Settle in and enjoy the show—it lasts for some time."

Bishop switched chairs and peered through the scope. He made another rear dial adjustment, and the fire in the center of the frame, with some kind of substantial wooden altar with steps off to the side, came into sharp focus. In a half circle facing the fire and altar were a group of perhaps fifty men sitting on the ground cross-legged, wearing Native American clothing. Shirts and pants made of buckskin with brightly colored beads sewn around the sleeves and necks. They sat motionless, as if waiting for something to happen. The red and yellow flames from the fire reflected off their faces, and their serious expressions were puzzling. Cora had a pair of binoculars leaning on the edge of the tower, following the goings-on.

"Okay, so what's the deal?" Bishop asked.

"They do this every year, the Saturday night of the reunion," she answered, never taking her eyes from the binoculars.

"Do what? All I see are a bunch of people sitting by a fire."

"Recognize anyone?" Cora's voice remained calm and patient.

Bishop focused on the individual faces. They were men from the party. The commissioner, the sheriff, the guy from Space Command… "Okay, a little weird," he said, "but what's wrong with former students around a fire?"

"You haven't seen weird yet."

Just before Bishop started to comment how boring this was, McFadden walked from behind the altar, also dressed in leather skins. His arms were outstretched, and he carried a large gourd. McFadden turned and faced the altar, held up the gourd with both hands, and spoke for a few seconds. Bishop would have given anything to hear what he said. McFadden approached each seated man on the ground. He offered the gourd, and they took a small sip. He took the last drink himself and again held the gourd up and spoke. McFadden sat cross-legged at the base of the altar facing the men. He talked for almost twenty minutes. Occasionally, one of the men would nod, but only McFadden spoke. Bishop longed for a parabolic mic with an extended range to listen in. As his patience wore thin, he asked Cora, "Any idea what he's saying?"

Cora sat back. "I talked to one of the guys who attended this cere-mony when I still lived on the ranch. Monk told me—"

"Monk Cole?" Bishop interrupted.

Only the dark outline of Cora's head nodded before asking, "How do you know about Monk?"

"Minerva mentioned him during the party. Said he worked at Sandia National Lab."

"Oh."

"You were saying?"

"Anyway, Monk told me about some nonsense McFadden was spouting concerning returning the Apache to their ancestral homeland. An independent Apache nation within the United States. Monk didn't believe it could ever happen but just went along with the group to be one of the boys."

"Really, where is their native homeland?"

"Arizona, New Mexico, and Texas. McFadden told them he would arrange for the Apache to reclaim all of the state of New Mexico as theirs."

Bishop would have laughed at such a suggestion a couple of days ago, but now… "So, how does he plan to accomplish that?" He didn't mean for the sarcasm to seep into his voice, but it did.

Cora shrugged. "Never said, just that he had contacts and a plan to accomplish it."

Bishop pointed at the bonfire. "And those highly educated men believed him?"

Cora lay the binoculars on the counter. "Remember I told you they all held McFadden in a god-like status. They attended the academy and went through his brainwashing. Yes, of course, they believed him. Everything he's ever promised he's done—all their lives, he's kept his word. No other white man has ever done that. Why wouldn't they believe him?"

Bishop's mind drifted back to World War II, Joseph Goebbels, *The Big Lie*. Tell a big lie often enough and loud enough, and people will start believing anything. "He can't be telling the same story every year over and over," Bishop mumbled.

"He probably does but keep watching. I think at some point he's giving them instructions or a pep talk of some kind."

Bishop pushed his eye against the lens and tried lip-reading but had no talent for it. McFadden spoke and pointed to select members of the group. Sure, this was weird, but no stranger than other things practiced by many guy fraternities .Several came to mind—Skull and Bones, Masons, and Knights of Columbus. "So, is this it?"

Cora again had the binoculars trained on the group. "Wait for it, Troy."

He was about to make another sarcastic remark when two of the men turned and vomited on the ground behind them. Others began wobbling and were steadied by fellows to their left and right. Another turned and threw up.

"What tha…" Bishop glanced at Cora.

The moonlight allowed him to see a shadowed smile spread across her lips. "Told you it got weirder."

Every few minutes, another one or two men vomited until at least half the group had been sick.

"What was in that gourd?" Bishop asked.

"Probably Mescaline—what you're witnessing is a perverted version of the sacred Peyote Ritual. It's part of the ancient Apache religion. McFadden has revived the old ways. There are no practicing Christians left on the ranch anymore; he's made sure of that."

Bishop directed his attention back to the scope just before McFadden stood. He turned to the altar, and the others stood as well, all raising their arms toward it. A blinding flash of light exploded from the altar. Bishop jerked his head back—his night vision gone and his right eye stinging from the flash. Cora sat with the binoculars in her lap.

He rubbed his eye. "You could have warned me that was about to happen."

Cora put the binoculars back up to her face. "Check this out."

Bishop again looked through the scope, but with his other eye, trying to blink away the twinkling stars in his head. McFadden and the other men continued standing with their hands outstretched. Bishop didn't notice her at first until she moved. Minerva now stood at the center of the altar. She must have entered from some hidden door after the flash, when everyone was temporarily blinded. Dressed in an all-white leather robe, her skin painted a white color, she looked like a ghost. Bishop focused on her face. The eyes were dilated, and her head swayed back and forth—drugged. She held out a hand and said something.

McFadden climbed the altar steps. He took her hand, and they turned to the men on the other side of the fire. He spoke for a few seconds.

"Look away," Cora shouted.

Bishop turned his head just in time. The intense flash could be seen without the aid of the scope.

"Okay, it's safe."

Bishop took another look, but both McFadden and Minerva were gone—disappeared. A drummer sat on each side of the altar, slowly tapping out a beat on the ancient leather drums. The group of men began milling around the fire in a circle. Some wobbled, being supported by others. Their mouths moved in a chant-like manner.

"Okay, you've won. That's the weirdest thing I've seen for a while." Bishop sat back in the chair. "What was Minerva supposed to be with all that white makeup?"

"I believe she's representing the mythical character of White Painted Woman, or the first woman—mother to all Apache. It's an old legend. Anyway, she has a bad spirit." Cora slid from her chair. "Show's over. Those fools will stagger around until they pass out or recover from the psychedelic high McFadden's got them on."

They started the walk back down the tower. It became clear to Bishop that McFadden was a man who made up his own rules. Laws prohibiting possession of WMD components and the use of illegal drugs apparently did not apply to him as long as he was on *his* ranch. An unsettling feeling lodged deep in Bishop's gut. This assignment was far from over, and it wasn't going to be a vacation.

After walking back into the house, Cora strolled into the kitchen. "I'll get us some wine if you'll start the fire." The night had a romantic feel about it, and Cora was happy she was spending it with Bishop.

"Will do." Bishop stacked a few small logs in the fireplace on top of some kindling.

She eyed him as she pulled the wine cork. *Why hadn't he made a move on her?* She brushed back her hair with her fingers and allowed her palm to caress her cheek. He's already seen me naked. He must have a girlfriend or fiancé back home. Or even a wife, who knows?

She poured two glasses and strolled back to the sofa. Bishop dusted his hands and joined her, accepting a glass.

"I assume you're staying another night?"

"If that's okay." He took a sip and settled into the couch.

The flames highlighted his face, and the two-day beard growth— gave him a sexy, rugged appearance. "You're welcome to stay as long as you like." There, that was an open invitation. Cora wanted him to do so much more than just spend the night.

Bishop stretched out his legs. "Tell me more about what we just saw."

Cora tasted the wine and paused—formulated her thoughts. *Guy's more interested in McFadden than her.* "From the time the boys start school at the academy, they're being evaluated. I learned this when I taught there. The first four years, they're given IQ, aptitude, and physical agility tests. This fosters a very competitive spirit and sets the tone for the rest of their education. At least that's what I witnessed as a teacher." Cora shifted and leaned back, taking another drink. "They're always being pushed to excel at anything they do, be it academic or athletic. Their after-school activities consist of rough play and sports— that's also encouraged."

Bishop's expression made her feel a little self-conscious.

"Sort of a leave it all on the field attitude, huh?" he asked.

"Yeah, I guess." What was he thinking? She just couldn't read him. She raked her fingers through her hair again and extended her arm along the sofa to within inches of his shoulder. "McFadden has a youth program with his most trusted people acting as leaders. All the boys start as Braves in first grade. They can't wait to join. You'd think they were Cub Scouts in waiting. By the fifth grade, about 25% get promoted to Warriors—best and brightest. In the ninth grade, the top 10% of Warriors get promoted to Scouts. These are the ones who've scored the highest on their exams and show the most promise."

Bishop sipped the wine and stretched his legs out a little more as he sunk deeper into the sofa. A flashback from his years at West Point crossed his mind and caused a smile. "Sounds like a military school?"

"It is—discipline can be brutal. Anyway, the Scouts are the crème de la crème of the students. Once they leave the ranch for college, everything is free—all the financial aid McFadden can offer—sky's the limit. The men you met at the party and around the bonfire are some of the Scouts." There was something that constantly nagged Cora about this crazy child promotion idea. She never fully understood the rationale behind it. She cleared her throat. "Thing is, very few full-blood

Apache ever get promoted to Scout. Mostly the boys with mixed blood. The ones who could pass for dark-complexioned Anglos."

Bishop turned her way. "I thought only full-blood Apache lived on the ranch."

Cora slowly shook her head. "Nope, over the years, McFadden brings in professional cowboys with trained dogs a couple of times a year to help round up, vaccinate, and brand new calves and sell off the older cattle. The cowboys live on the ranch several weeks and stay in the guest housing. All young, good looking guys. By the time they leave, several teenage girls on the ranch are always pregnant. Their sons grow up to be the Scouts." Cora had always thought this bizarre, but saying it out loud for the first time, now chilled her because she too was of mixed blood. "I don't believe it's an accident."

"What?"

"The girls getting pregnant."

"Why?"

Cora struggled on how to phrase this. Her voice dropped to a whisper. "Because… because it happens with such regularity. Not like teen raging hormones, but almost like a planned event everyone knows about but doesn't discuss."

He pursed his lips and asked, "Why's that?"

Cora shrugged. "McFadden talks about how much he loves and respects the Apache and their culture, then does everything he can to dilute the blood of the race."

Bishop had his mouth open to ask the question but held his tongue at the last second. Cora understood what he was thinking. Was *her* father one of those good-looking cowboys? Well, at least he had the decency not to say it.

She grinned. "My father wasn't one of those guys. Believe it or not, he was an architect. Had a degree from the University of Texas."

Bishop nodded. "So, what happens to the rest of the boys? The ones not selected to be scouts?"

"They're offered jobs on the ranch—the warriors get the first choice, then the braves."

"Who were the guys in black shirts who escorted me out today?"

"McFadden's Praetorian Guard—all Warriors. They seldom leave his side."

Bishop stared at the fire, apparently in deep concentration.

Cora exhaled; she was so out of practice on the dating scene. This whole thing seemed awkward and uncomfortable. But she had a plan. A last-ditch attempt to give him one final chance. She stood. "Think I'll turn in—you okay on the sofa another night?" *Please ask to sleep with me…*

He appeared to wake up from his thoughts. "Yeah, I'll be fine."

"Well, good night." She shuffled off to her bedroom and closed the door. She left a small crack and kept her eyes on him. He sat staring into the fire. She was so lonely for someone, anyone, to change the boredom of her everyday existence. Even this curious stranger would suit her, but he appeared not to be interested. Probably for the best. Affairs with passing strangers weren't her style anyway.

———

The man slipped closer to the small red house beside the fire tower. He'd just about caught his breath from the long walk up the mountain road. The cold wind chilled him and made the strong pine scent a little sweeter as the giant trees majestically bent with each gust. He remained behind the biggest one, hidden deep in the darkness, and watched. The inside light of the cottage was still on, and the SUV belonging to the man called Bishop was parked to the side. This was another recon visit, but if the time came to kill Bishop, the man had been promised he'd be the one chosen. A chance to prove himself. A chance to spill enemy blood and maybe be promoted.

The man rubbed his hands together to get a little warmth as he crouched and waiting for just the right time to approach. Through the window, Bishop slowly rose from the couch and walked toward the kitchen, holding an empty glass.

The figure scooted to the edge of the house. Streaks of moonlight filtered through the trees, moving with the pines as they lazily tilted from side to side. Looked like ancient spirits of ancestors returning to their favorite mountain. Complete silence surrounded him as he carefully peered into the window of the living area. There was a fire in the fireplace and something in another glass by the sofa. *Where were they?*

He never heard a sound, not even a twig snapping, before being jerked backward off balance—the breath knocked from him as a stone-hard object slammed into his midsection. A strong arm came around his neck, choking his air off, and the sharp point of something metallic rested against his throat. A soft, haunting voice whispered into his right ear, "Move, and I'll kill you."

He relaxed—there was no use struggling. The guy could kill him anytime he wanted. *Helpless.* The hands of an experienced searcher quickly went through all his pockets and around the waistband as the unyielding chokehold stayed in place.

Again the hot breath near his ear. "You tell McFadden it's not nice to spy on a lady's house. Do you understand?" The tip of the sharp blade, with an experienced flick, lightly pierced his throat just over the jugular. A drop of blood wormed its way down his neck, sending him into a near panic.

With that, he was flung hard to the ground. He rolled twice, jumped up, and turned—nothing. Kneeling, he looked to either side of the house—nothing. *What had just happened?* Was it a dream? He touched the small cut on his neck, and the warm sticky blood coated his fingers—no dream. His pounding heart almost tore a hole in his chest as he ran down the hill. On the way, he glanced back at the house and window. Bishop stood inside, looking out into the darkness as he pulled the window shade down.

THIRTEEN

Bishop woke to the ringing of his cell. He'd slept hard during the night, but his back muscles ached from the lumpy couch. Took a second to orient himself to time and place. He checked his watch, precisely six o'clock. The sweet smell of the fire from last night still lingered in the small, cold house.

He scrambled for his cell and cleared his throat before saying, "Hello."

"Bishop, this is Special Agent Carpenter."

It took Bishop another second to clear his head and remember who Carpenter was. "You're up early, Agent Carpenter."

There was a beat before an aggravated voice said, "Well, I didn't sleep very well last night. You see, when someone from the National Security Advisor's Office calls an FBI Deputy Director, who calls my Special Agent in Charge after eleven o'clock on a Saturday night, and then he calls me, it doesn't make for a restful night's sleep. I would have called you last night but couldn't find your card."

Bishop smiled; Maxwell had wasted no time in "greasing the skids."

"Sorry if I caused you any trouble."

"Yeah, I bet you are. I don't know who you really are or what agency you're actually with, but I'm damn sure it's not the 902nd MI Group. Those guys don't have the juice to get the National Security Advisor on a Saturday night."

Bishop didn't respond—decided just to let the guy vent.

After a moment of silence, Carpenter got down to business. "Are you still in New Mexico?"

"Yes."

"I've been instructed to give you a full briefing before lunch today."

"Where?"

"Think you can find Sandia National Laboratory?"

"I'll try," Bishop quipped. He'd been there twice over the years for advanced training in nuclear and radiological terrorism.

"Okay, there'll be a pass for you at the main gate. Go to the visitor's lobby—I'll meet you there at ten o'clock. I was told to inform you your *Q Clearance* will be passed, so you shouldn't have any problems getting in; just show you I.D at the gate."

"I'll be there."

The line went dead before Bishop could say goodbye. Cora stuck her head out from her bedroom. She was fully dressed and ready for work. "Who was that?"

Bishop stood and gave a long stretch. "Work, I have to go to Albuquerque."

She frowned. "On a Sunday? Are you coming back?" The voice held a slight tone of panic.

Yesterday morning, Bishop would have said no. But lots had changed, and he needed a base close to the action until he figured it out. He smiled. "Who would want to give up such luxurious accommodations?" He glanced down at the wrinkled covers on the sofa.

She flashed a shy grin, and blush colored her cheeks. "I have to go to work. See you when you get back."

———

The drive to Albuquerque relaxed Bishop. A beautiful sunny day with a nice chill still in the air after the little cold front moved through last evening. The sky in the distance showed an ominous dark line on the horizon. Radio said another more significant front was headed their way. Bishop took Highway 42 north to Willard, then Highway 41 to I-40 west. It took just over two hours. During the trip, he couldn't shake the McFadden incident. Lots of things out of place there. That weird house, the reunion of exceptional students, and the meeting around the bonfire. Not to mention restricted nuclear material lying around. All that, coupled with what Cora told him last night, painted a disturbing picture. By the time he arrived in Albuquerque, he still hadn't figured it out. The illegal U-235 was the stumbling block. Everything could be explained away as the actions of an eccentric millionaire except that.

Sandia Lab is located on Kirtland Air Force Base in Albuquerque. It's been around for about sixty years—its original mission was ordnance engineering. Sandia turned the nuclear physics packages built by Los Alamos and Lawrence Livermore National Laboratories into deployable weapons. Since its inception, it's been a leader in energy research, supercomputing, threat verification, and nonproliferation.

Bishop pulled into the Eubank gate entrance, showed his identification to security, and drove inside. They issued him a guest badge and dosimeter at the front desk.

"Be sure to have these clipped to your shirt in plain view at all times," the receptionist instructed.

When he turned around, Carpenter stood behind him. "Follow me," he said without greeting. They walked down a short hall, painted bright white, and took a left. The place should have been almost deserted at ten o'clock on a Sunday morning, but dozens of people marched the halls in open-collar shirts, sweaters, and or lab coats. Most had a stack of papers or an arm full of notebooks. Bishop followed Carpenter into the second door on the left. It was a small meeting or interview room with bare white walls, a desk, and two chairs. *Great room for an interrogation.*

Carpenter took a seat behind the desk, and Bishop sat in the chair on the other side. Carpenter studied him for a moment and opened a notebook. "I was instructed to give you a briefing and cooperate with you in any way you requested." He sucked in a breath and grimaced. I was also instructed not to ask about your employment because I didn't have the clearance. Carpenter's nostrils flared, and his eyes took on a cold, hard look.

"Okay, for starters, this was an inside job. Too many systems with too many backups failed at once for this to just be a coincidence."

Bishop crossed his legs and sat back. "Figured that. What systems?"

Carpenter held up his fist and extended his index finger. "Number one. We determined the radio on the lead OST convey vehicle had been jammed. Someone attached a magnetic device near the antennas, which rendered the vehicle radios inoperable." Carpenter raised a second finger. "What should have taken hours—to gain entrance to the OST transport trailer—took only minutes. Its security measures did not deploy." Carpenter showed three fingers. "The tracking satellite being off station at just the exact time to accommodate the theft looks suspicious." He held up the fourth finger. "And the fact we've been unable to track the things by their GPS signals or radiological signatures indicates tampering."

Carpenter leaned on the desk with his elbows and rubbed his face. He looked exhausted and at his wit's end.

"I assume polygraphs are in order for a lot of government employees, then."

Carpenter gave a weary smile. "Yeah, everybody involved in the testing, loading, transporting, and receiving is getting their time on the box."

"Any good leads?"

"Nothing yet. We've checked out all the local information. I'm waiting for the polygraph guys to crack this thing, hopefully. Afraid that'll have to pass for my briefing. Not much more to tell. Do you have any request or information we can work on from your investigation?"

Bishop stood and meandered to the far wall. He needed to say this in just the right way, because Carpenter looked like he was ready to go ballistic—no need to help him along. Bishop leaned against the wall and crossed his arms again. "I do have one request. I'd like a database search of all federal agencies to determine the personnel who have graduated from the McFadden Academy and are now in military and federal employment."

Carpenter's head shot up. "As in Clark McFadden?"

"Yes."

"Are you nuts? You know who he is?"

"We've met—not a very nice fellow."

Carpenter marched over to him. "Do you also know he's best friends with the Speaker of the House?" Carpenter's neck muscles bulged as he studied Bishop.

"Didn't know that," Bishop replied.

Carpenter threw his hands up and stormed back to the desk. "That's just dandy. The only thing you can recommend is I check on the richest man in New Mexico, whose friends with the Speaker." He dropped into the chair and didn't try to hide his disgust. He stared at the desk and ran his hands through his hair.

Bishop sauntered back to Carpenter and leaned forward, balancing himself with just the fingertips of each hand on the top of the desk. "I thought the Bureau could handle that better than my outfit."

Carpenter stood again, apparently not able to sit still. His stare drilled a hole in Bishop. "Okay, fine, but don't expect fast results. We'll have to contact each agency individually and then confirm it with OPM—it'll take a while." He gawked at Bishop for a few seconds like he expected a reply. When Bishop didn't respond, Carpenter said, "Follow me." He brushed past Bishop on his way to the door.

They walked further down the hall and entered another room. A sign on the door read *Engineering Display.* The place was big, white, and spotless. Tables lined the walls, with mysterious-looking pieces of God knows what scattered like broken children's toys. An antiseptic odor mixed with petrochemicals lingered in the background. A balding, older man in a white lab coat waited, staring at them with his arms behind his back. Guy was barely five feet and didn't weigh a hundred and forty pounds. He stood beside a cut-away model of some type of nuclear weapon. Bishop recognized the common design. On the wall above hung a large color chart showing the individual pieces, each labeled in red ink. The title of the diagram indicated it was a W80 Naval Warhead. Bishop glanced at the tables again. All the individual pieces of the warhead depicted on the chart were laid out on the table with their parts identification labels under them.

"Dr. Heimmer, this is Troy Bishop," Carpenter said.

Bishop nodded and flashed a friendly smile.

Heimer ignored him.

"Go ahead, Dr. Heimmer," Carpenter said.

The older man touched the device and spoke very softly as he recited the briefing he'd obviously given many times.

"The physics package for the W80 warhead is 11.8" in diameter, 31.4" long, and weighs 290 pounds. It has an adjustable explosive yield of between 5 and 150 KT TNT. It utilizes super grade Plutonium which is 93% Pu239 and 7% Pu240.

He then went over, in excruciating detail, the design of the weapon, starting with the pit, or core of nuclear material surrounded by high explosive panels, that were connected by a maze of wires to the fusing mechanism. He explained the detonator and a dozen other weapon features needing to function correctly before critical mass could be achieved. During the briefing, the guy's expression never changed, and he took short quick breaths between each sentence.

After allowing him to drone on for over ten minutes, Bishop couldn't take anymore, so he interrupted. "Excuse me, but why were the weapons being transported to Sandia?"

Dr. Heimmer's head flinched back. He smiled like a patient father. Condescendingly, he said, "Mr. Bishop, the US hasn't developed any nuclear weapons since 1992. Our inventory is in constant need of repair and testing to ensure they'll function properly in case..." He lowered his head and grinned. "Anyway, that's the job of the National Laboratories. Any other questions?"

Bishop didn't like the little guy—*pinhead!* "Yeah," Bishop said. "Which wire do you cut?"

Heimmer's brow creased, and he started to say something, but Bishop spoke first. "Just tell me how to disarm the thing."

Another patient smile from Heimmer. "It's impossible for a layperson to either activate or deactivate these devices. You'd have to be a specially trained nuclear physicist." The way the guy said physicist made it clear he was one.

"Thank you, Doctor," Carpenter said, opening the door for the small man. After he left, Carpenter's expression darkened, and a grimace lined his lips. "About activating and deactivating the weapons. One of the reasons they were sent to Sandia was to install a coded control device—it wasn't installed before the theft. They already have a command disablement system, active protection system, and permissive action link. All these should prevent someone from arming them without proper authorization, but…"

"But what?" Bishop asked.

Carpenter met his stare. "We have to assume the devices may have been tampered with before shipment, rendering all the safety features inoperable."

"So, you might not need a physicist to activate a nuclear firing sequence?"

Carpenter nodded, and his face sagged. "Yeah."

———

McFadden stared across his desk and pondered the problem. His lawyer, Newman Smith, was the recipient of his gaze. McFadden popped a knuckle and took a sip of whiskey. "What do we know so far?"

"Not much, according to Karl, Mr. Bishop rented the car at the Albuquerque Airport a few days ago." Smith flipped the page on the notebook and said, "On the contract, he listed his place of residence as Virginia. Has a Virginia driver's license."

"Think he's government?"

"Could be, or just on vacation as he says."

McFadden popped another knuckle. "Who just happened to show up here at this exact moment?"

"Good point."

McFadden winked and grinned. "I say he disappears."

"That might not be such a good idea, right now, Clark. Do we want a search going on around the ranch? Someone other than Cora must also know he's here, especially if he's government. Drawing attention is…"

McFadden grunted. "Okay, okay, then what do you propose?"

"How about just roughing him up a bit?"

McFadden gave a noncommittal shrug. "All right, run him off, but don't mess him up so bad he can't leave by his own power. Don't want to be seen hauling him away."

Smith got up and removed his glasses. He cleaned them on his shirt. "And if he doesn't run?"

"Then we'll know he's with the government—he'll have to disappear. You still flying to Washington tomorrow?"

"Yes."

Make sure you personally contact each Scout who wasn't at the reunion—no exceptions."

"I'll take care of it."

McFadden stood and looked out his office window. "I want them all out of the district by *H hour*. We'll need everyone we have after that —can't afford to lose a man."

"I understand," Smith said as he rose to leave.

McFadden sat alone, seething over Minerva. Her inviting Bishop to the reunion had caused this problem, and now *he* had to deal with it. After his marriage to Coleen had ended so tragically, McFadden had sworn off marriage for two decades. When he met Minerva at a party in Palm Springs, he'd only considered her another sexual relationship in a long line of such relationships. Beautiful, great body, fantastic screw. He'd decided he needed an heir. Someone to carry on his work. Little did he know that she was unable to have children. But his life's plan couldn't be stopped by something so trivial. He must go on.

He was surprised how much he'd changed since his younger days. In college, his only interest had been girls and liquor. With his multimillionaire dad's money, he could have as much of either as he desired. It wasn't until after school, working for his father, McFadden realized what he most hungered for—power. He'd been good at making deals and discovered the power of what large sums of money could do to influence people and their politics. *Anyone could be bought off with enough money if they thought no one would ever find out.*

He'd married Minerva, a former Miss California, and set about to make all the money possible. Somewhere along the way, his focus on conservative politics began to overshadow all else. He honestly considered himself a patriot, and patriots should always answer their calling and never to anyone else. This country had given him everything a man could ask for, and he wasn't going to sit still for some California or Northeast namby-pamby liberals to screw it all up.

Speaking of screwing up, he'd come close to screwing it all up with his first marriage out of college, but his dad had saved him. Not listening to the old man almost led to Clark's downfall. He'd never made that mistake again. His dad was his hero. The old man taught him about people, and that Vegas trip cleared up his marriage problem.

In 1976 Clark and Coleen rolled up to the newest addition to the Vegas Strip at 3805 South Las Vegas Boulevard in the car his dad had sent to the airport to meet them. It wasn't so hot that spring: clear skies and the temperature pushing ninety. Coleen gazed up at the fourteen-story Marina Hotel, all new and sparkling in the blazing Nevada sunshine. Hardly a year old, it stood as the latest jewel on the south end of the Strip's crown.

Colleen broke into a wide smile as she studied the big blue Marina Hotel Casino sign out front with the marquee below. They were just across from the famous Tropicana.

"This is fantastic," she said before releasing a girlish giggle.

Clark tipped the driver as the bellhop grabbed their bags. "Like it, huh?"

"I'll say. I want to go to the pool."

Clark laughed. "Let's get checked in first."

As they headed to the lobby, Clark was well aware of what was at stake this weekend—their marriage. Coleen was the most beautiful woman he'd ever known. Probably why he'd asked her to marry him so soon after college. She was twenty-two, just a year younger than Clark. Her light red hair sensually flowed across her shoulders. When she took her bra off, the long locks curved around the full ripe breasts, showcasing them in a way that sent Clark's groin pulsating. He'd been with lots of girls in college, but when Coleen wrapped herself around him, his mind went blank. He could live in her sexual embrace forever.

Yeah, Coleen had everything he ever wanted in a wife, except there was one problem. She was a drunk. Clark could live with someone who drank a little too much—hell, so did he sometimes. But Coleen pushed way past the point of *a little too much.* No, she got falling down, stinking drunk. But the worst part was before she went down, she became nasty, real nasty. She'd had problems with her family since she was a teen—*issues,* she'd called them. The resentment turned to hate when she perceived they were jealous of her successes in beauty pageants. She'd won every one she entered. Besides her looks, her singing voice ensured she'd always taken the *most talented* award in every contest. Had more than one record producer after her.

Clark had tried talking her into Alcoholics Anonymous, but she wouldn't even discuss the idea. Couldn't get past the first step. *Admit she was powerless over alcohol—that her life had become unmanageable.* She was slowly becoming a nervous wreck. This trip, he'd have a serious conversation with her, and if she couldn't behave, well, he didn't want to consider that option.

Clark's dad had paid for the weekend getaway in hopes Clark and Coleen might mend a floundering relationship. His dad had always objected to Coleen. Never wanted them to marry in the first place. Of course, Clark had ignored the old man. But Clark had also come to realize things couldn't go on like this. Being around a mean drunk was never fun, but living with one had become intolerable.

Coleen just celebrated her first full year in therapy. Clark couldn't tell it had done her much good. She still carried all the same old baggage from her childhood and insisted that she could handle her drinking. Well, perhaps the therapy might do some good given more time. But time was in short supply. As Clark's dad aged, he wanted Clark to start being the face of the company. That included numerous gatherings, parties, and other social events that Coleen must attend. She always showed up all smiles, looking better than a woman had a right to, and winning favor with everyone. But after a few drinks, things began going to hell. Slurred words, dropped glasses, and trip-ping were the norm. No, something had to change—one way or another.

After getting settled in their room, Coleen stripped off her clothes. Clark watched her drop the bra and slip off the baby blue panties as she picked up her bikini. He strolled to her and plucked the bikini from her grip and tosses it on the bed. He kissed her long and hard, letting his hand drop between her legs. Clark lay her on the bed and caressed her breasts, licking the nipples with short sucks in between. His hand continued playing between her legs. She pushed him back.

"Clark, please, let's get a little sun and a swim first."

He grinned. "Let's do the sun later."

She pouted. "Please. If you wait till tonight, I'll give you a special surprise."

Clark knew what that meant. He would wait for that. "Promise?"

"Promise."

She slipped from underneath him and into the bikini.

She had a figure made for a bikini. Turning heads and bulging eyes of guests followed her to the chaise lounge, where she and Clark parked themselves beside the pool's blue water. Women punched their partners to stop gawking. Clark and Coleen had a swim and ordered drinks from the pool waiter. Coleen only had a couple, which wasn't bad for her. If he could just keep her at a drink an hour, she'd stay sober enough. Right now, she was more interested in having Clark rub her down with lotion. She unlaced the strap holding her top before quickly flopping down on her stomach. The unexpected quick flash of flesh probably caused more than one heart to skip as other men acted like it was no big deal to their wives and girlfriends. Of course, Coleen realized what she was doing—teasing. She so loved to tease, a master of the art.

After a couple of hours of sunning and another drink, they made it back to their room. Coleen staggered a little removing her bikini, and Clark led her to the shower. That's where she liked to spring her surprises. They bathed each other, and she rubbed her hand between his legs.

That mischievous grin showed again. "You like that, Clark?"

He leaned back against the shower wall as the warm water cascaded around them. His loins wanted to explode with pleasure, but he held it.

She dropped to her knees and took him in her mouth while massaging his scrotum. Clark almost passed out from pleasure. He held her head as it went back and forth and round and round. Just before he climaxed, she stopped.

Her face took on a pixie expression. "Now finish it, big man," she stood and leaned against the shower wall lifting a leg and resting her foot against the opposite wall. Clark loved that pose. He pinned her against the wall, slipped his hands under her hips, and lifted her off the shower floor. When he entered her, a squeal of pleasure escaped her throat. She slowly moved up and down, side to side, and round and round. When Clark's climax exploded, he let out a loud groan and pushed deeper, pinning her harder against the wall. A moment later, she let out a moan, and her body trembled while she whimpered in his ear. This was why Clark had to find a way to rehabilitate her. He loved her, but the sex was like a power charge. It cleared his mind and reset his attitude like nothing else. Being sexually dependent on another wasn't something Clark McFadden ever considered. Strangely, he didn't mind with Coleen.

They dressed and went to dinner in the Marina Showroom. Tonight, the hotel showcased *Bare Touch of Vegas*. It was a dinner show. Coleen had the Polynesian chicken, and Clark enjoyed the prime rib. Coleen was charming, and the excitement on her face confirmed she enjoyed the performance. During the show, Coleen had several more drinks in quick succession.

When her head bobbed, Clark whispered, "That's enough."

She shot him a death stare and ordered another and then one on top of that. Probably just to aggravated him, she lit a cigarette, one of the new bad habits she'd picked up recently. Clark detested anyone smoking a cigarette around him. The tobacco of the useless underclass. Men of distinction smoked a fine cigar or pipe, like his dad. Clark especially hated women smoking. He started to pull it out of her mouth but didn't want to make a scene. He seethed with anger at how a perfect evening could go so wrong so fast.

When they arrived back in their room, there was still tension. Clark excused himself to the bathroom for a minute, and by the time he got out, Coleen had ordered a chilled bottle of expensive Champagne. Clark didn't argue as the waiter uncorked the bottle with a *pop* and filled the two glasses. He tipped the man and locked the door. At least she wouldn't be out in public making a spectacle of herself.

But Coleen was just warming up for the finale. She downed a quick glass of bubbly and gawked at Clark as she slipped into her night-gown. In a hateful tone, she said, "Don't you ever embarrass me in public like that again."

"Embarrass you? You were the one doing all the embarrassing." That was so like her. Trying to turn the argument around and make him the bad guy.

She poured another glass and wiggled an index finger at him. "Don't think I don't know what you're up to, you son of a bitch!"

Now Clark was dumbfounded. What in the world was she talking about?

Coleen gulped the wine in one swallow, half dribbling down her chin and chest. "I know your father paid for this trip, and I know why. Well, let me just tell you I know a lot of things." She pounded her chest with a finger and shouted, "Things that could get that old bastard run out of town and you with him. Things the cops would love to know."

Her words were so slurred he had trouble understanding them. His mind flashed back to a few weeks earlier. He'd walked into his office, and she stood by his desk reading the Thompson file. He shouldn't have left something like that just lying around. It outlined what bribes had been paid to whom concerning the new government mineral leases—*a big mistake…*

Clark rushed to her and grabbed both arms. She dropped the empty glass. As he squeezed, he said, "If you ever say a word about that to anyone, not even I can protect you." He gave her a firm shake. "Do you understand?" He walked back to bed and dropped on the mattress and unlaced both shoes.

Coleen just stared at him, still in a fighting mood. Her hands dropped to her sides, making fists as her death glare cut into him. As Clark was halfway finished slipping off his trousers, she said, "We'll just see about that!" She bolted to the door and was in the hall before Clark could get his pants up or off his foot. He ran after her, the trousers trailing, still with one foot caught in them. By the time he made it into the hall, Coleen stood by the elevator frantically pushing the down button.

"Get back in here," he said, advancing toward her.

She half ran, half staggered down the carpeted hall to the fire exit door using the wall for support. She pushed the door open as Clark caught up. He grabbed her arm, and she twisted and staggered into the stairwell. He followed, and the door shut behind them with a loud click. Clark jerked back on her wrist just as she started down the stairs. She spun around, clawing his cheek with her loose hand. *Had to knock some sense into her.* Clark gave her a hard slap across the face and lost his grip on the wrist.

It all seemed to happen in slow motion. Coleen stood on the second step below him. As she sensed herself about to fall backward, her eyes widened, and she reached out with both hands. In a shrill voice, she cried, "Clark!"

Clark realized the danger too late. He grabbed for her, but by then, she was out of reach. She fell and did a backward summersault on the non-forgiving concrete steps. She came to rest in a clump against the wall at the bottom; her neck twisted unnaturally, the dead eyes still open and casting an accusatory stare at him. Time stopped for a moment. Clark couldn't move—or think—or even breathe. He only gazed into the beautiful face with just a trace of blood dripping off her chin from the lip he'd busted.

Had to get help, had to let someone know. Clark raced back to the room and picked up the phone receiver. His finger was an inch from pressing the operator button. At that second, something caught in his brain—no, she was dead. No one could help her or him except one man.

Clark woke the old man up with the words, *"I just killed Coleen!"*

The wise old businessman calmed Clark and got the details. After Clark finished the story, in a disgusting voice, his dad said, "Christ, what a mess."

"What do I do?"

"Who knows about this?"

"Just me."

"No one saw you enter the stairwell?"

"I don't think so."

His father's voice took on that demanding tone. "Think, Clark. Did someone see you or not?"

"No."

"Okay, stay in the room. I'm making a call. Expect a call back in five minutes. He'll know what to do."

Clark's head was spinning. He felt like he'd be sick. "Who, who you calling? Who's 'he'?"

In a calming voice, his dad said, "Tom, of course," and hung up.

McFadden grinned at the memory and took another sip of whiskey as he looked across his ranch below. He turned back to his desk and marked off another day on the calendar. Twenty-four hours closer to *H hour*.

———

The drive back to Cora's gave Bishop time to think. He had to at least consider the possibility. Could McFadden be involved? How could fixing a flat for a stranger on a lonely New Mexican highway turn into this? An old quote from Albert Einstein came to mind. *Coincidence is God's way of remaining anonymous.* Regardless, Bishop had a lead, which was more than that anyone else did. He'd shared his suspicions with Agent Carpenter, but the guy wasn't buying the idea that a man like Clark McFadden, billionaire, and pals with the speaker of the house, could be involved in such a scheme. His arguments against it did make some sense, especially when he said, "What on earth would he have to gain by doing such a thing?"

Bishop glanced into the rearview mirror. A wall of dark clouds followed. It was the time of year when cold fronts and weather systems lined up one after another. By the time one blew through, another was building up strength. He switched on the radio and caught a weather report. The first big front of the season was on his tail, and the rain wasn't far behind. A significant temperature drop was expected during the evening and tonight. If he didn't waste time, he might make Cora's before it caught him.

When he made the turn to Gallinas Peak Road, he rolled down his window—the temperature had dropped 20 degrees since he left. He started the drive up the peak and got about a mile from Cora's when he saw it. A broken down pickup truck blocked the narrow mountain road. The hood was up, and steam billowed from the radiator. He stopped and got out; the man leaning into the engine area seemed not to notice.

"Having trouble?" Bishop asked, walking toward him.

The man raised his head from the hood area and turned. He had a .45 pistol in his hand and pointed it at Bishop. "No, but you are."

From behind the truck, two other men appeared. They both carried baseball bats.

Bishop put his hands in the air. "I think you may be right," he whispered and took a couple of steps back to put a little space between him and the gun. The words of one of his old Delta instructors came back to him. *If you ever find yourself in a fair fight, you've seriously miscalculated.* Bishop's weapon was holstered in the small of his back, as usual. But there was no cover, and trying to draw against someone with the drop on you wasn't smart.

Bishop studied the trio as the two men wielding the bats approached. It was clear from the way they held them they had no training in effectively using them as weapons. These guys were ranch hands, darkly tanned and tough as nails, but not trained fighters. If they planned to shoot him, they would have already done that. Looked like they were instructed just to bounce him around. Of course, beating him senseless and rolling him down the mountain to his death was also a distinct possibility. Either way, he needed to deal with these two goons with the bats first. But Bishop needed a distraction.

The youngest guy approached, tossing the bat from one hand to the other and smirking. Bishop recognized him from last night outside Cora's home. He had a small band-aid on his neck where Bishop had pricked the skin with his knife. As the guy closed the distance on Bishop's left, the older, bigger guy holding the bat with both hands closed in on the right.

Only one chance. Bishop met eyes with the kid with a smirk and teased. "Cut yourself shaving, or are you even old enough to shave, yet?"

The man's sneered vanished, and he released a guttural roar as he tightened his grip on the bat and charged. He swung it hard and fast about waist level. Bishop jumped away and arched his back out. The edge of the bat brushed the front of his shirt.

The guy was off balance for a split second while completing his swing. Bishop lunged for the bat and folding his hands over the kid's hands, locking them tight while shifting to the left and swinging the bat in a high arc. The man followed, doing a complete flip. He hit the ground hard as his wrist snapped. He screamed and rolled away from Bishop.

Bishop turned in time to see the bat from the guy on his right coming straight toward his head. With the bat taken from the first assailant, Bishop ducked and blocked the blow. The dull thud of wood against wood echoed as the bats met, sending shock waves down Bishop's arms. He did a sweeping kick against the man's left knee. The knee cap shifted to the inside of the leg as the guy cried out and collapsed. Bishop quickly moved in behind him as he fell and, using his left arm, applied a chokehold. He twisted the guy around, using him as a shield against the one with the .45 pistol.

Bishop drew his Sig Sauer and had it pointed at the fellow by the truck before anyone realized what happened. "Drop the gun," Bishop said.

The man lowered the gun to his side, let it fall to the ground, and raised his hands.

"Good choice, "Bishop said. He dropped his shield, and the man fell to the ground, still writhing in pain and holding his knee. Bishop kept the guy by the truck covered and approached. "Kick the gun to me."

The guy kicked the gun hard, and it slid to within inches of Bishop's foot.

"Turn around," Bishop ordered.

When he turned, Bishop picked up the gun and threw it into the deep ravine to his left. He struck the man hard in the back of the head with the front of his pistol. The guy grunted and dropped to his knees, grasping his head. Blood oozed between his fingers.

Bishop surveyed his afternoon's work. "You know if you guys keep coming back up here, you're eventually going to make me mad." He opened the driver's door of the truck, cranked the vehicle, and put it in gear, turning the wheel as far as he could to the right before releasing the emergency brake. Because it was already pointed downhill, that was all it needed to start rolling. After about ten feet, the right wheel found the edge of the road. The truck rolled almost sixty yards down the ravine before it found a pine tree large enough to stop it.

Bishop motioned with his pistol. "Okay, you two on your feet and help your friend."

The ones who could still walk put their disabled companion between them, and the trio staggered and hobbled their way down the road. Threatening clouds rolled overhead, and with the heavy tree canopy, it got darker and darker as the smell of rain moved in. Wind whipped the giant pines back and forth as Bishop got back into his SUV. By the time he drove the last mile, torrents of rain blew almost horizontal as he pulled up to Cora's.

He sat for a minute, hoping it might slack up. He wasn't too surprised when it didn't. His windshield wipers were going as fast as they could, and the sudden temperature drop fogged the windows inside the SUV.

McFadden had upped the ante by sending the three idiots after him. What was he afraid of? It was clear they hadn't meant to kill him. No, they wanted to rough him up a little in hopes he'd leave. Made no sense unless McFadden felt threatened. Through the blurred windshield, Bishop detected movement on the tower steps. He hardly recognized Cora slowly making her way down the tower—looked miserable, like a drowned rat. Her Forest Service jacket had no hood, and her short, black hair hung limp around her face and neck. She was soaked but held on to the handrail, taking one slow step at a time. With her gaze and total concentration on the steps, she had not even noticed he'd pulled up to the side of her house.

Just before she got to the bottom, Bishop made a run for it. Cold rain pelted him, and he opened the front door for her just as she rushed in. Her eyes widened when she recognized him, and she must have slipped or lost traction because she began falling forward at the threshold. Bishop quickly grabbed her around the waist and pulled her inside. Her momentum caused her to swing around into his waiting arms. Their faces were inches apart. Her eyes fixed on his. He softly kissed her. She grabbed his face and pulled him closer, their lips bonding tighter.

They continued kissing and undressing without a word, peeling off the other's wet clothes until they stood naked. Cora led him to the bathroom, started the shower, then jumped up, wrapped her legs around his waist, and kissed him hard. They slowly bathed each other in the hot water with a thick, soapy sponge. The drops cascaded over and around them, encasing them in a soapy bubble of passion. They toweled each other dry, and Cora knelt, drying Bishop's lower legs with the towel. She looked up with a childlike expression, and he held out his hands. She took them, and he pulled her to her feet and softly kissed her neck.

He carried her to bed, and they spent the rest of the afternoon making love. Outside, the cold wind lashed the sides of the house, and rain fell in sheets pounding the roof. The thunder rumbled, and lightning flashes through the windows lit up the bedroom walls, but they hardly noticed with their bodies intertwined. An hour later, she nuzzled his cheek and kissed his ear. The room was dark and cold. She slowly ran her hand down his inner thigh and up to his crotch.

"I'm hungry," he said.

"Hungry for me?" she goosed him in the ribs.

He rolled toward her. "Always." And kissed her nose. "But right now, I'm starting the fireplace. I missed lunch. Any leftovers?"

"I have a better idea," she said. She pushed the sheet and heavy blankets aside and slid out of bed, grabbed a robe, and headed for the kitchen.

Bishop found a pair of clean jeans in his bag and a warm, light gray sweater. Before he finished dressing, Cora ran into the bedroom, quickly rubbing her arms and shivering. "I'm freezing—think I'll warm up with another shower—supper's in the oven."

Bishop marched into the living room, threw a few logs in the fireplace, and started the fire. Just as he finished, the ringing sound from his wet pants still lying on the floor caught his attention.

He rummaged through the pockets and found his cell. "Bishop here."

The voice was Lesa's. "I got the information you requested."

Bishop peeked at his watch; yup did it again. Lesa dictated that all the analysts she supervised respond in less than twenty-four hours to a request from the field.

"Do you want to receive the information encrypted?"

"Naw, pass it in the clear."

Lesa's voice sounded faded, probably the storm's interference. "You hear me, okay, Bishop?"

"Sure—go ahead."

"This McFadden guy is a doozy," she laughed. "He was born Clark Augustus McFadden in 1951. His father owned mines and a mining company that furnished the US with about seventy percent of its uranium ore during the '50s and '60s. By the time Clark took over in the late 70s, his dad was New Mexico's first billionaire. When he died, he passed his wealth over to his only child, Clark. He's involved with several political action committees to elect conservative candidates. Also, he's buddies with the Speaker of the House of Representatives."

"I've already figured most of that out."

"Want to go straight to the G&R, then?" she asked.

Bishop grinned. The G&R was always the best. It consisted of known, or strongly suspected, *gossip and rumors*. "Okay," he said.

"Well, for starters, his first wife died under mysterious circumstances in the mid-seventies."

"Really?"

"Yeah, he was questioned, but no charges filed."

"What else?"

"Looks like McFadden ran for county judge back in the late seventies—soundly defeated and never stood for elected office again. There have been several hikers who disappeared in the area of Gallinas Peak and McFadden's ranch. They were never found, and McFadden refused authorities permission to search his property. He supposedly mounted his own search with *his* ranch hands. Also, apparently, there was a large fire in the area of the ranch in 2004. Story is he had something to do with it."

Bishop furrowed his brow. "Why would he want to start the fire?"

"Some believe he wanted to discourage future hikers and folks visiting the national forest from straying onto his land."

"So he burns it down?"

Lisa laughed again. "Hey, he's your problem—not mine. Sounds like some kind of nut. And another thing, his wife Minerva has been treated at least twice for bipolar disorders. Used to be an actress—mostly B movies." Lisa's voice faded a little more before the signal became stronger. "One last thing, but I don't think it's very significant."

The shower turned off in Cora's bathroom.

Lisa took a breath. "McFadden was one of the original thirteen people in 1972 that entered balloons into the first Albuquerque Balloon Festival."

Bishop's eyebrows rose. "Really?"

"Yeah, he's entered and piloted his balloon, *The Spirit of Liberty*, in every festival since, except this year."

"Hold on, isn't this year the fiftieth anniversary of the festival?"

"Yes."

Bishop's gut had that feeling. The one he got upon realizing he'd just discovered something important. He looked back in the direction of Cora's bedroom door and dropped his voice. "Then I find that piece of information the most significant of all."

"Why?" Lesa's puzzled voice asked.

"Because when a man changes a long-held tradition for no apparent reason, it means something."

———

Bishop drew back the curtains and peeked out the window into Cora's front yard. The rain hadn't slacked much, but the skies weren't as dark as before. The best smell he could imagine on a cold, rainy day drifted from the kitchen. Whatever Cora was baking made his mouth water—some kind of pastry or bread. Cora strolled into the kitchen. She wore jeans and a dark blue turtleneck, with her hair in a half-dried short ponytail. She stopped and kissed him.

"Dinner's almost ready."

"Smells good, what is it?"

"My favorite comfort food—chicken pot pie."

Bishop slipped on a pair of warm socks and hiking boots, and Cora poured wine before serving the meal. He cracked the top crust of his pie with his fork and steam rolled out. "There's one thing I don't get," he said.

She looked up. "About what?"

"I can see how McFadden keeps these kids under control at the ranch, but once the scouts leave for college, they're on their own—right?"

Cora shook her head. "Not hardly. Most attend the University of New Mexico for their undergraduate degrees. McFadden keeps homes near the campus for them. He has house counselors to oversee the students. He even has a house for the few girls selected to attend college—that's where I stayed." She looked up and met Bishop's stare, then shrugged. "For those who attend schools for advanced degrees, like MIT, Stanford, and Berkley, McFadden makes special arrangements on a case-by-case basis. He has made considerable contributions to the schools he wants his best and brightest to attend.

Cora must have believed she saw disapproval in Bishop's eyes because she explained. "I had to do it if I wanted an education."

They ate in silence for the next few minutes. Finally, Cora said, "A few girls are allowed to attend college occasionally. They are the teachers at the academy, nurses at the clinic, and other traditionally female jobs which require degrees. At some point, they're matched with a scout as a mate."

She gazed at her plate and moved the food around.

Bishop looked. "Matched? What does that mean?"

"Just what it implies. McFadden's people pick a male and female student in good health that scored high on the IQ test and match them."

Bishop had never heard anything so ridiculous. He didn't question what she said, but it was right out of the Middle Ages if it were true. But there was also a more subtle, sinister aspect to what Cora said. A man who would build his own town, populating it with people utterly loyal to him, might just try and create his own *race*…

Bishop didn't want to ask but did. "Who were you matched with?"

She shrugged again, keeping her eyes on the plate. "It doesn't matter now."

"Why?"

She shot a glance. "He graduated three years ago from college and was commissioned as a new lieutenant in the Army."

"Where's he now?"

She didn't answer at first, just looked at him. Finally, she whispered, "Dead, he lasted three and a half months in Afghanistan before an IED…"

"Sorry."

Cora began clearing dishes to the kitchen sink.

Bishop remained seated. "Were you engaged? You know, before he left."

She stared at him as though the question was strange. A look of realization finally spread over her face. She walked back into the small dining area.

"When I said we were matched, I meant it literally. We were never intended to marry. He would leave, and I would stay and raise our child. That's the way McFadden likes it. He gives ten thousand dollars each to the couple for producing a male child. We were free to marry whom we chose, but not before giving McFadden at least one child."

Bishop's eyes widened. "What?"

"My match was killed before that happened."

Bishop stood and walked to the fireplace. He wanted to believe her, but the story seemed so bizarre he struggled to comprehend it. To think that something like this was going on for so long without anyone spilling the beans was incomprehensible.

She slowly moved to him. "McFadden encourages all Apache to take Anglo mates. As I said, he wants to dilute the race. He's no friend to us." She put her arms around Bishop's waist, and he hugged her. "My mother was full apache, but my father came from an old southern family in Louisiana."

He gently stroked her soft hair. "I'm sorry," he whispered.

"Don't be, it's over now. After Cliff was killed, they decided to match me with another. When I resisted, they pressured me until I finally left. Samuel had already moved out years earlier, so I moved in with him until I got this job with the Forest Service."

He pushed her back slightly. "We need to talk about something."

She grimaced, and her brow pinched. "Is it something bad?"

"It might be."

"I hate spoiling the rest of this evening with bad talk."

"I understand, but you need to know this."

He led her to the sofa and told her about the previous night's prowler and the ambush that afternoon. To his surprise, she seemed to take it all in stride.

"I kinda suspected McFadden has been keeping an eye on me since I left the ranch—that's just his way."

Bishop's cell ringing interrupted his thought.

"This is Bishop."

"Maxwell here; I have a message from General Cook."

"Yes, sir."

"He wants to see you in his office at 10:00 AM the day after tomorrow."

Bishop glanced at Cora. "Is he aware I'm on to something out here?"

"Yes, that's why he wants to see you."

"Do you know what it's about, sir?"

"Yes. See you day after tomorrow."

Maxwell hung up without further explanation. Bishop looked at Cora, and her expression said it all—suspicion.

"Who was that?"

"The office."

Her eyes pinched. "What did you mean, you were on to something?"

He walked nearer to the fireplace. *That was a huge mistake, taking a business call in front of her.* "I'm working on a project out here, that's all."

She strolled beside him. "You carry a gun, you're an expert shot, and you can defend yourself from three attackers. A few nights ago, you told me and Samuel you were a consultant from Washington and on vacation. Now you tell your office you're on to something—explain, please."

Bishop gave his best contrite look. "Well, to be honest, I'm looking for something stolen from the government last week near here."

"Such as?"

"Such as something I can't talk about."

Her lips flattened into white slashes, and she crossed her arms. "So you work for the government?"

"The Defense Department, to be exact." He showed a shy grin.

"Why didn't you just say that Friday night?"

"Because sometimes it's easier to find something when no one knows you're looking for it."

Her expression softened. "So, you're a cop or something?"

He took her into his arms and leaned closer to give her a kiss. Just before their lips met, he whispered, "Yeah, or something."

FOURTEEN

The next day, Bishop got up hours before dawn. He'd explained to Cora the night before that he had to leave for a day or two. He booked himself on the 8:24 AM non-stop to Washington.

She woke as he got out of the shower. "Morning."

"Morning," he replied. "What's the chance Samuel might be awake this early?"

She yawned and stretched. "Probably good. He seems to sleep less and less."

"Think I might stop and say goodbye."

"Go ahead; he'll make you drink some of that wretched piñon nut coffee he loves so much."

———

Carrying his bag to the SUV, Bishop marveled how much the weather had changed in the few days since he'd arrived. The sky had cleared and the rain had stopped, but a cold wind blew and chilled him, even wearing his heaviest jacket. He hoped his leaving would take some heat off Cora—McFadden's people were becoming bolder. Just knowing he'd left might convince them he was no threat. That was the other reason he wanted to stop at Samuel's. He wanted McFadden's ranch hands to see him leaving.

When Bishop pulled in front of Samuel's trailer, the kitchen light was on. Bishop got out of his SUV and walked across the rocks and sand yard toward the trailer. Samuel sat hidden from sight on the dark porch behind chairs and plants. He was bundled in a heavy coat and a thick wool blanket and drinking from a cup.

"Thought that might be you, Mr. Bishop." Samuel rose and held out his hand.

Bishop shook it.

"You're up early," Samuel said, leading him into the trailer. "How about a cup of coffee?"

"Sure."

"Have a seat." Samuel poured Bishop a cup and refilled his own.

"I'm leaving for a couple of days," Bishop said. "Kinda keep an eye on Cora—there have been people sneaking around her house at night."

Samuel handed Bishop the coffee and sipped his cup while his eyes peeked over the top. "McFadden's rats."

"Looks that way," Bishop said before taking his first sip. He suddenly recalled Cora's warning—the stuff *was* nasty. Tasted like dirt brewed to perfection. Bishop related the run-ins he'd had with McFadden's men. "I need you to do me a favor while I'm gone."

"What?"

"I guess you know the ranch pretty well, huh?"

A grim smile traced across the old Indian's face. "Yeah, I helped organize and build it."

"Then draw me a scale map of the place, showing any areas someone could hide something of value."

"How big a something?"

"Three feet or four feet long, weighing about three hundred pounds. There are six of them."

Samuel pursed his lips. "Are they part of the stuff that was stolen off the freeway last week?"

Bishop's eyebrows rose. "You know about that?"

"News said some cargo thieves hijacked a truck carrying government computers—that's all I know."

Bishop nodded. That was the official line put out to cover the big brouhaha surrounding the theft and investigation. "Well, it wasn't exactly computers."

"How are you involved?" Samuel asked.

Bishop swirled the coffee in his cup. "I was sent to locate and recover them."

Samuel grinned. "Knew you were a hunter the first time I laid eyes on you. Don't know if this is important, but the same night the things were stolen—several of McFadden trucks rolled into the ranch about three in the morning, from up north."

Bishop snapped to attention. "You saw them?"

"Yup, sitting on my porch with the light off when they came rolling into the entrance across the road. Wondered what was going on that time of the morning."

"How many?"

"Six or seven of the white one-ton duallies with camper shells."

Bishop calculated the number of vehicles and number of warheads, plus the time necessary to travel from the ambush site to the ranch— yeah, it worked. He glanced at his watch. "I have to hit the road. Thanks for the coffee."

"Like a cup to go?"

Bishop held up his hands. "No, thanks—I'm good. Be careful of McFadden's people while I'm gone."

Samuel followed him to the door. "Mr. Bishop, my granddaughter and I made a pact. Since we both believe McFadden was involved with her mother and father's disappearance, we're going to make McFadden's life as miserable as possible. The law won't help, but with Cora watching him from the peak above and me sitting across the road, we hope to catch him dirty on something."

Bishop turned and stared at the old man. "You may already have."

Samuel and Cora were either the bravest or most foolish pair Bishop had ever met. They had no idea what the stakes or real dangers were.

When Bishop pulled out of Samuel's driveway, the eastern sky had just started showing its first light. The rays of the sun outlined the landscape into colorful earth tone shadows. Orange, yellow, and red hues seemed to rise from the ground in patterns that possessed a magical quality. But Bishop didn't have time to marvel at the scenery—he had a plane to catch. The roads were clear, so he drove fast and got to the Albuquerque airport in record time.

He checked the SUV back in to the rental car agency and had plenty of time to get to the gate before his flight departed. His reservations were for a rear aisle seat—always his preference. Bishop always liked to get to the gate well before boarding. He'd hang back and observe the other people about to board the flight. Each expression, each body movement, every word they spoke told their story. When Bishop found an angry, passive, or overly excited face, he always examined them extra closely. Since 9/11, those were the faces that mattered, those were the faces he needed to remember, those were the faces that could kill you.

There was a long line leading into the plane—everyone in coach was still settling in, moving and storing overhead bags, buckling seat belts, etc. If not for the delay, he might never have noticed Newman Smith lounging in a first-class window seat reading The Wall Street Journal.

Bishop did a second take, but there was no doubt—it was him, weasel face and all. Bishop turned his head away before being recognized and moved past Smith as quickly as the line would allow. When he arrived at his aisle, he dropped his carry-on in the seat and headed for the toilet.

Just before he entered, a flight attendant said, "Sir, you need to take your seat in preparation for takeoff."

Bishop recognized she was one of the hard-core, no-nonsense female flight attendants who kept the airline industry on time and on budget from her stern expression.

He grimaced and touched his midsection. "A bit of a stomach problem, be right out."

In a sharp tone, she said, "Go ahead then but don't be long. We can't push back until you're buckled in."

Bishop shut the toilet door and jerked out his cell. He scrolled down the list and hit *Ghostbusters.*

The gruff male voice answered, "This is Hal."

"Bishop here—how goes it?"

"SOS buddy, how about you?"

"Hal, I've got a live one on the line and need some help."

"Where are you?"

"On a plane about to leave Albuquerque en route to Dulles." Bishop gave Hal all the information about the flight and a good description of Smith.

"You have an authorization number for this op?" Hal asked.

"No, just came up a minute ago. Contact Maxwell. Tell him it's one of the primaries in the inquiry I'm working."

"Enjoy your flight, Bishop; we'll be waiting at Dulles for you guys."

"Thanks, Hal."

The knocking on the door was expected. "Sir, you need to take your seat."

Bishop flushed the toilet, washed his hands, and stepped out. He was confident the purpose of Smith's Washington trip would soon be revealed. Ghostbusters was P2OG's special surveillance unit. Recruited from ex-CIA and FBI personnel, they were the best in the world. They got their nickname from the fact they could keep someone under surveillance and never be observed themselves. No intelligence trade-craft or counter-surveillance route could defeat them.

Bishop sat back in his seat and waited for takeoff. He had planned to nap on the flight, but with Smith on board, he didn't dare. Besides, he had to figure out what Smith was doing on a flight to DC. When the plane touched down at Dulles a little after two, he still hadn't figured it out. Bishop hung back and was the last one off the plane. He carefully made his way to baggage claim and spotted Smith.

Bishop looked around for someone—anyone he recognized. Where were the Ghostbusters? Had something gone wrong? Was there a mix-up? Smith reached for his suitcase and swung it off the belt. He extended the handle and turned toward the nearest door marked TAXIS.

That's it. For some reason, Ghostbusters wasn't there. Bishop would have to do one-person surveillance and hope for the best. Just as he moved from behind the wall in pursuit of Smith, a firm hand fell on his left shoulder.

Hal's gruff voice said, "Relax, Bishop—we've got him."

With that, the big man passed him in the direction of the exit. He spoke into a sleeve mike. "Showtime, boys, he's coming out."

Bishop shook his head. How in the hell had Hal gotten behind him? Bishop took a cab to his townhouse. That evening, he went for a long run and settled in for the night with Chinese takeout. He attempted watching some TV, but he couldn't concentrate on the movie's plot. Too many things running through his head. He needed to get back to New Mexico. He gave up and hit the sack a little after one o'clock. He tossed and turned for an hour before dropping off. His last thoughts turned to Cora and Samuel—were they okay?

————

Newman Smith taxied to the Ritz-Carlton in Foggy Bottom near Georgetown. He made the 3:00 PM check-in and went to his suite. Smith always stayed here when he visited DC—comfortable room, incredible restaurants in the area, and the best bar in the District. A little after six, he strolled into the bar/lounge area, found a quiet corner table, and ordered a Scotch. Moments later, two McFadden Academy graduates joined him. He rose to greet them. "Gentlemen, what will you have?"

The threesome talked for almost half an hour. Smith drained his glass for the second time and asked, "So it's confirmed? The President will be meeting the Secretary of Defense and the Joint Chiefs at the White House at ten that morning?"

The older of the two men nodded. "That's what's on the schedule—I checked before I got off work. If there's a change, I'll let you know. As of now, he's in residence all day."

Smith looked at the younger one. "And the Vice President will be presiding in the Senate that day?"

The man took a sip of beer and glanced around the room before nodding. In a quiet voice, he said, "Yes, she'll have to be there during the appropriations bill vote—it's going to be close. She may have to cast the deciding ballot."

Smith sat back and let the warmth of the liquor soothe him. He always loved it when a plan gelled together with no drama. "Good, make sure you're out of the District at 'H hour.' Mr. McFadden wants you guys available to step into more important positions after that."

The men nodded. The younger one stood, finished his beer, and smiled. He leaned closer to Smith and whispered, "Shouldn't be too hard—everyone else will be dead."

———

Cora readied herself for bed. She pulled the quilt off the floor; there in the corner lay one of Bishop's V-neck tee shirts. She lifted it to her breast and took in his scent. Would he be back? She pulled the shirt over her head and slipped her arms through the openings before turning out the light. *He'll be back.*

———

The following morning, Bishop arrived at General Cook's office a little before ten. Mary buzzed him in before he could open the door with his code.

"How was New Mexico?" She had that sly grin that meant she knew something.

"Cold." He sank into one of the leather chairs and allowed his stare to fall on General Cook's closed office door before looking back at Mary. "What's going on with me being recalled?"

She lowered her voice and leaned over the desk a little in his direction. "Don't know, but the General has Fuller in there."

Bishop frowned. If the National Security Advisor was in Cook's office, it couldn't be good. Fuller never went to other people—they were always summoned to him.

Maxwell stuck his head out of the general's office. "Ah, Bishop, come in."

As Bishop passed Mary's desk, she mouthed, "Good luck."

Cook slumped in a guest chair with a sour expression. Fuller had taken over his seat behind the executive desk. Maxwell started to shut the door just before Fuller spoke.

"Excuse me, colonel Maxwell, but could you give us a moment, please," Fuller said.

Maxwell glanced at Cook. He gave an almost imperceptible nod.

Bishop froze. *Holy shit.* Fuller just kicked Cook's deputy director out.

Maxwell cleared his throat, "Yes, sir."

As Maxwell closed the door, Fuller greeted Bishop. He didn't offer his hand, never did.

"Come in, Colonel Bishop," Fuller motioned to Maxwell's empty chair. "Happy you could join us."

Join us? Like Bishop had a choice. Cook kept the sour expression. There was enough tension in the room to fill a domed stadium.

Bishop took his seat. "Good to see you again, Mr. Fuller."

"We wanted to go over a couple of things about your trip out west," Cook said.

Bishop started to answer, but Fuller interrupted. "Why don't you just tell us everything that's happened since you left DC?"

Cook only nodded in agreement. It was clear *his* boss, Fuller, was running the show. When you don't know what your boss or boss's boss is looking for, it's hard to gauge what elements of the account should be stressed and what can be brushed over.

Bishop related everything as it happened over the last few days. Fuller leaned back and sipped from a Starbucks cup and only stopped him twice for a couple of clarifications. Fuller's intelligent eyes hardly blinked as Bishop continued the story. Occasionally Fuller and Cook exchanged knowing glances but didn't speak.

"So, what are you contending?" Fuller asked, dropping the empty to-go cup in the trash can beside the desk.

"I'm not sure I understand, sir." Bishop said.

Fuller's expression hardened. "Are you accusing this McFadden fellow of being involved in the theft of the weapons?"

Bishop glanced at Cook—his expression gave nothing away. *Time to stake out my ground, for better or worst.* "Yes, sir, I think he's in up to his neck."

Fuller's lips became tight thin lines. "And you say the common denominator appears to be this McFadden Academy?"

"Yes, sir."

"Would you excuse us for a moment, please?" Fuller said.

Bishop rose and walked back to the reception area. He sat beside Maxwell on the leather couch, both staring at Mary.

"What happened?" she asked.

"Beats me," Bishop shrugged. "I'm either getting promoted or terminated—no idea."

His grin signaled he was most likely kidding, but with Fuller, you never really knew—he was a political animal. The best National Security Advisor in years, but still a politician. Maxwell remained silent, probably still seething over being asked to leave. They waited for almost ten minutes before the door opened again. The sound of Cook's voice echoed from inside.

"Thank you for coming by, sir."

Fuller buttoned the top button of his suit coat as he passed, stopping to give a nod to Bishop. "Good work."

"Step back in, Bishop," Cook's voice boomed.

Maxwell didn't move, and Cook ignored him as he closed the door to the office. The General reclaimed his desk chair. Once inside, with the door shut, Bishop asked, "What was that all about?"

Cook readjusted himself in his chair. "It seems Fuller was concerned that we were getting too close to someone with a lot of political juju."

"McFadden?" Bishop asked.

"No, Speaker of the House, Wilson," Cook said.

"I don't get it."

"The Speaker and McFadden are friends. Vacation together, exchange Christmas cards and visit often. In fact, McFadden is buddies with a lot of politicians around this town—big contributor. The only senator who didn't like him was Fillmore from Missouri. Before he was murdered, he was about to open hearings on influence peddling and planned to name McFadden as one of the persons under investigation."

Cook shifted and reached for several pieces of paper off the desk. He studied them for a moment. "Here's the surveillance report from Ghostbusters on Newman Smith." Cook's forehead wrinkled, and he cleared his throat. "Stayed at a Ritz Carlton last night. Two men visited him at the bar before dinner. They talked for a while in a back booth and then left. Ghostbusters tailed them and ran their license numbers. They're both Secret Service agents. One is assigned to the Presidential Protective Division, and the other is detailed to the Vice Presidential Protective Division."

Bishop tensed. Cook had assumed his favorite position—leaning back with his fingers laced across his barrel chest and his cheaters perched on his nose.

"And that's not all," Cook continued. "Another man joined Smith for dinner. Ghostbusters followed him, also. It turns out he's an intern at the Supreme Court."

"This is starting to get interesting." Bishop crossed his legs and got more comfortable.

"You haven't heard the best yet. After dinner, Smith went back to his suite. About nine o'clock, General Curtis Shaw showed up and met with him for around twenty minutes.

Bishop knew that name but couldn't quite place it. "Who is General Shaw?"

"Sorry," Cook said, "he's the commander of Fort Belvoir."

A flutter rushed through Bishop's gut. Fort Belvoir had twice the number of workers as the Pentagon. It was home to ten different major Army commands, nineteen different agencies of the Department of the Army, Army Reserve and National Guard components, and a host of DOD agencies. Like Raven Rock Mountain Complex and Mount Weather, it was one of the designated relocation centers for the Pentagon should the main building be knocked out.

Cook continued, "And last but not least, a little before ten, Speaker of the House Wilson arrived and met with Smith until almost eleven." Cook raised both eyebrows and grimaced.

"Did we get any audio on these guys?" Bishop asked.

"Nope, not enough time to set it up," Cook said.

"Do we still have surveillance on Smith?"

"He caught a flight back to New Mexico this morning," Cook mumbled.

"What's our next move?"

Cook leaned forward with elbows on the desk and clasped his hands together. He studied Bishop before answering. "We wait."

"On what?"

"After listening to your story, Fuller had an idea. When you stepped out of the office just now, he Googled the bio on the Speaker of the House."

"Why?"

"To check his education."

"Don't tell me."

"Yup, another honored graduate of the McFadden Academy. He was in the fifth graduating class."

"What about the two agents, the intern and General Shaw?"

"Same."

"According to Fuller, Speaker Wilson is a bare-knuckle politician. He's a lot nastier than he's portrayed on the news. He loathes the President, and the feeling's mutual." Cook looked at Bishop. "If it's ever discovered we're spying on him, it could bring down this President— especially if we're wrong. If it turns out this was just several alumni getting together for old times, that's one thing, but Fuller doesn't want to make that call. That's why we're waiting. Fuller's going to ask the President for permission to proceed."

"And if permission's granted?"

Cook picked up a plain white envelope and withdrew the one typed page inside. "I've been instructed to read you this verbatim." Cook readjusted his glasses and exhaled. "TOP SECRET//SCI//PEO."

Bishop stiffened. *Good God, PEO—A President's Eyes Only Directive.*

Cook said, "The President of the United States directs you to make a surreptitious entry into the McFadden Ranch located in Socorro County, New Mexico. You will conduct a covert search to determine if there exist on premises any materials capable of being utilized in producing a nuclear device and determining if any nuclear weapons abide on said property. SCI operational protocols will apply."

Cook looked over the top of his glasses with a blank expression. "Do you acknowledge a full and complete understanding of this order, or do you wish me to reread it?"

A lump formed in Bishop's throat. A three-sentence *Presidential Warrant*. Bishop had heard about them but never knew if they really existed. People sometimes whispered about them to their most trusted colleagues in quiet restaurants and wine bars around DC. The kind of memo you never acknowledged to outside people, even if you read it. The thing would probably be filed away in the *President's Book of Secrets* or whatever BS name they gave highly classified Presidential Directives. Future presidents could marvel at the audacity or temerity of those they succeeded.

"I understand, sir." Bishop said.

Cook nodded, and without showing Bishop the order, dropped it into his shredder and flick on the switch. The grinding of the crosscut shredder filled the room. *That was it.* It no longer existed. Fuller had made sure no one was in the office but he and Cook when Fuller released the memo to him. Cook had made sure no one was in the room when he read it to Bishop. And now it was gone. Everyone had complete plausible deniability in the matter. Everybody but one person: Bishop, *The Man in the Arena.*

Bishop wasn't disappointed or bitter toward Cook or Fuller. They were doing their jobs and following the rules outlined by their superiors. The fact Bishop and guys like him were the *point of the spear* wasn't new. Direct action people were always the point. The success of the mission rested in his hands. If he succeeded, there wouldn't be any big celebrations or parades, and if he didn't, the whole mess would quietly be swept under the government rug and never spoken of again.

SCI operational protocols were intel jargon for: *during the mission, the operator will retain no identification or information that identifies himself or that he is involved in a covert operation on behalf of the United States.* In the event of capture or detention, Bishop could not acknowledge acting as an agent of the US Government, nor would the Government acknowledge his employment or seek his release.

"So, when is the President likely to sign it?" Bishop asked.

"Fuller will approach him later today, when he feels the time is right."

Bishop stood. His mind clicked a mile a second with possibilities. "If that's all I'd like to start getting ready."

Cook rose and extended his hand. "Be careful. You can't afford to get caught on this one."

Bishop shook the hand. "Can I ever afford to get caught, General?"

Bishop walked past Mary's desk. Maxwell had disappeared. Just before opening the hall door to depart, Bishop turned back. "Mary, give Andy a call and tell him I'm stopping by to pick up a few things."

She started to dial the number. "He'll want to know what things."

Bishop thought for a second before saying, "A six-pack of trackers and several flies on the wall should do."

He was gone before she could say another word.

———

Bishop arrived at P2OG's offsite a little before noon and went straight to Andy's shop.

"You found them, didn't you, Bishop?" Andy said.

"What?"

Andy gave an exasperated sigh. "The nukes, of course."

Bishop shook his head. "Didn't anyone ever tell you curiosity killed the cat."

"No, I'm not a cat. By the way, did the nuke watch work?"

"Actually, it did."

"Ah-ha! You did find them, then." Andy showed a satisfied expression believing he'd tricked him.

"No, I found a small sample of highly enriched uranium. That's what set the watch off."

"Oh." Andy's joy turned to muted confusion. Finally, he asked, "How did you find highly enriched uranium without finding the weapons?"

"Long story, wish I had the time to explain. Do you have the items I requested?"

"Yeah." Andy retrieved two black plastic cases from under the counter. Bishop figured he must still be mulling over the uranium mystery.

"Sign here." Andy pushed the property receipt toward him.

Bishop scribbled a signature and strode for the door. "See you later, Andy."

"Later," he mumbled. Still scratching his chin.

Bishop headed for home; he had packing to do. By midafternoon he was ready to go, but there was no word from Cook, which meant no word from Fuller, which meant no Presidential approval. Bishop's stomach growled and reminded him he'd skipped lunch again. He threw a pack of Ramen noodles in the microwave and watched the news. By late afternoon he couldn't sit still; he called Mary.

"Anything, yet?"

Her voice sounded scratchy. "No, but I think I'm coming down with a damn cold. Who gets a cold this time of year?"

"Don't know. Is Maxwell there?"

"He and the General are both out."

"Do you know where they went?"

She coughed. "Yeah, the White House."

"Never mind, Mary. Hope you get to feeling better."

———

"… and Bishop said he wanted me to draw it for him," Samuel told Cora.

Cora sat at her kitchen table, facing him. She studied the map he'd brought.

"Did he say why?"

Samuel rubbed his face and rested his chin in his hand. "No—just said he wanted me to do it. Look it over and see if I've missed anything."

She traced the drawing with her finger and glanced at the notes Samuel made in the margins. Everything seemed to be as she remembered. The McFadden Academy, gym, and daycare, the communal laundry, the great outdoor kitchen and covered open-air pavilion, the clinic, garage, barns, corrals, and a dozen other buildings were as she recalled.

"What's this?" She pointed to the base of the mountain—almost directly below McFadden's house.

"That's the cave," Samuel said, "I made a note about it there," he pointed to the lower left-hand margin.

"Never knew there was a cave on the ranch."

"Most people don't. McFadden excavated and expanded it when he built his house. Even built a natural spring-fed pool inside. The entrance is camouflaged, so unless you know where it is, it's hard to find."

Cora pursed her lips. That area was in one of the exclusion zones. Growing up on the ranch, there were three areas you never dared go unless you worked there. The main house, the base of the mountain below the house, and of course, the two heavily wooded fenced acres which surrounded Ochoa's. No parent ever had to worry about their children straying near Ochoa's. There were stories about what happened there—bad sounds at night, like someone screaming. The old tale about mountain lions making those scary, disturbing noises wasn't really believed by folks, but no one asked too many questions about what happened.

Cora looked up. "Everything looks good to me—I'll give it to him when he gets back."

———

General Curtis Shaw sat at his desk and reviewed the file on the relocation exercise. His aid, Major Phillips, waited in front of the desk.

Shaw asked, "Have all of the base units and agencies been notified?"

"Yes, sir."

"Any problems?"

Phillips dipped his head and said, "Well, to be honest, sir, several questioned the necessity for a full base closure so close to the last drill three months ago."

Shaw dropped the file on his desk, and his stare bore in on Phillips.

"This is a special exercise. We've been ordered to do a full secure shut down this year between 0800 and 1200 hours. Tell the crybabies to just suck it up for four hours. I have no time for whiners this year. Understood?"

Phillips came to attention. "Yes, sir—understood."

Shaw eyed Phillips and pointed his index finger. His voice rose with each word. "And Major, I mean a full shut down. All gates locked and guarded. All critical facilities and infrastructure patrolled, and all external communications cut, except through secure channels. Nothing goes in or out unless cleared by this office."

Phillips's back stiffened. "Yes, sir—I'll see to it."

———

Bishop had dozed off with the TV still on when his cell rang. "Bishop, here."

Maxwell's voice seemed strained. "Number one has ordered a go. I repeat, it's a go."

"Thank you, sir."

"And Bishop—he reiterated, don't get caught."

"Happy to know he's thinking about me."

———

FBI Section Chief Benjamin Witcher tried to pick up the pace. He was on the third mile, but today it seemed a more challenging run. The jogging trail near the park behind his house was his getaway—his recharge zone. He had gone to college on an athletic scholarship in track and managed to keep fit throughout his FBI career. All his agents in the Weapons of Mass Destruction Directorate at FBI headquarters knew this trail was where his most important decisions were made. This was where Witcher cleared his mind of all the background noise at headquarters and sorted out the best course of action. The day's stress and job aggravation began melting away after about the first mile or two. This was only his second run this week. He usually did five runs a week. His body and mind craved the relaxation of running on this isolated trail. The theft of the weapons in New Mexico had sent a chill through the law enforcement and intelligence agencies. The FBI's WMD Directorate was at the epicenter. He'd been working sixteen-hour days for the last week and was mentally and physically exhausted.

Witcher glanced at his watch—7:33. The sun had set over forty-five minutes ago, and he was almost at the halfway point. He'd have to pick it up on the way back. He came to the curve where the giant oaks hung over the trail like a tight leaf roof. What little light emanated from the path lights could not penetrate the veil overhead. As he entered the gloom, a cyclist was kneeling beside his bike, making some adjustments to the front wheel. His long blond hair flowed to the top of the backpack, and the heavily muscular legs and shoulders were a sign he did more lifting than biking. Just as Witcher ran past, the fellow spoke to him.

"Good evening, Mr. Witcher."

Witcher slowed his pace and looked back at the man. The fellow continued working on the bike, paying him no mind. The voice was familiar, but he couldn't place him from behind. Besides, he didn't know any man with hair that long, except a couple of undercover FBI types. Witcher stopped and addressed the stranger. "Excuse me, do we know each other?"

The kneeling man stood and glanced over his shoulder down the lonely, dark trail before turning back to Witcher. Even with the low light conditions, it was apparent who he was.

"Piedmont, what the hell are you doing here. And what's with the wig?"

Piedmont didn't answer but stared morosely. "Sorry, Benny."

The silenced pistol spit fire twice. The muffled shots were barely audible. Witcher staggered backward and only then realized he'd been shot. The searing pain in his chest—the sensation of being hit with a bat. His legs gave way, and he fell hard on his backside. Piedmont approached. This had to be a dream. Piedmont was one of his best Supervisory Special Agents. Witcher looked up. "Why?"

Piedmont didn't answer. He leveled the gun and fired again. Witcher felt like he'd been punched hard in the throat. The slight taste of blood he'd noticed from the previous shots was suddenly overshadowed by the flood that poured down his throat and shirt. Witcher couldn't breathe—he grabbed his neck, feeling his life drain between his fingers. He braced with his other hand to keep from falling back. He was nauseous and dizzy, watching Piedmont stretch the pistol to within inches of his head. He tried to cry out but couldn't.

———

Piedmont looked both ways down the trail. There was no one in sight. He rolled the body off the path and down the small hill. The tall summer grass would hide it till tomorrow. He again checked the trail —all clear. He took the liter bottle of water from his pack and washed the blood off the concrete. Climbing back on the bike, he rode to the parking area. It was dark now. No other cars were in the lot. He lifted the bike to the carrier, secured it, got in the car, and drove away. After he left the park and was back on the highway to Manassas, he pulled the blond wig off and smoothed his short black hair.

FIFTEEN

Bishop wanted to leave that night, but it was already too late by the time he got the go-ahead. The direct flights were few, and the connections weren't good—better to wait till tomorrow. Besides, he needed Carpenter's help, and he knew he would be less than enthusiastic about his request. When he called him, Carpenter was much less enthusiastic than Bishop would have figured.

"You have to be shitting me," Carpenter exclaimed.

"You said if I needed something to give you a call—this is what I need."

There was a long silence before Carpenter spoke again.

"So, I guess if I say no, you'll make another call, and I'll get my ass chewed out again. Is that how it works?"

"I'll make another call. What happens after that is anybody's guess."

Carpenter released a tired breath. "Okay, then. I'm in."

"Thanks, buddy."

"Yeah, right."

"Oh, Carpenter. Don't tell anyone in your office what you're working on."

"What's that supposed to mean?"

"Means what I said. I'll explain when I see you."

"You're a pain in the butt, Bishop."

"I know, but you'll get used to me."

The sound of Carpenter slamming the phone down was the last thing Bishop heard before being disconnected.

———

Wednesday morning, Bishop caught the 8:25 flight to Albuquerque. He called Carpenter upon arrival from baggage claim at the Albuquerque airport.

"Hey, you here?" Bishop said into his phone, scanning the lobby before heading for the terminal's front door.

The voice sounded grumpy and inpatient. "I'm here. Where are you?" Carpenter answered.

"Walking out to the taxi area in less than a minute."

"Fine, I'll be there."

Bishop hoisted the duffle bag to his shoulder and marched through the two automatic glass doors. The weather was nice. A cool breeze still chilled the air. Even better—there was no humidity. That's what killed Bishop back in DC. Place was built in a swamp. Even a late afternoon jog turned into a sweat bath. The brilliant New Mexico sunshine forced him to slip on his Oakley's. He waited and watched for Carpenter. Figured he couldn't miss him. Soon, the large FedEx truck rounded the corner and slowed as it approached. The uniformed driver had a disgusted expression. As the truck stopped, Bishop hopped into the passenger area and tossed his bag on the floor.

"This had better not be a joke." Carpenter seethed.

Bishop looked him over. The FedEx shirt tucked into the navy shorts and running shoes almost looked believable. "Didn't know you had such great-looking legs."

Carpenter met Bishop's smile with a smirk. "Okay, where are we going?"

"I'm hungry. Let's find a drive-thru Chipotle. I'll buy."

Carpenter turned. "What?"

"We have a long drive. Let's eat before heading out."

Carpenter rolled his eyes and put the vehicle into gear. Fifteen minutes later, they exited the drive-thru, each with a burrito and drink.

"Corona… what the hell are we going there for?" Carpenter asked.

"That's where the stolen weapons are," Bishop answered in a matter-of-fact tone. He sat on the duffle bag beside Carpenter and munched his burrito.

"Okay, unless you want me to stop right here, you'd better start talking. Just because my headquarters says I have to work with you doesn't mean I have to put up with a bunch of shit."

Bishop held up his hands into a surrender position. "Now, don't go getting crazy on me—I'll tell you what I think, and you can judge for yourself."

Over the next half hour, Bishop explained everything that had happened the previous week, including the information Ghostbusters had uncovered. Carpenter drove and listened without interruption. When Bishop finished, he waited for Carpenter's comments. They were a long time coming as Carpenter's mind processed the information overload Bishop just dropped in his lap.

"So, let's see if I got this straight. McFadden's the one responsible for the ambush and theft. He had his people infiltrate the NRO to blind the spy satellite, the OST to get him into the weapons trailer, and then one or more of the national laboratories to disable the tracking and fail-safe mechanisms?"

Bishop nodded while finishing off his drink.

"Then he just drives the nukes to his ranch and hides them?" Carpenter had that expression Bishop had gotten used to. "Do you know just how stupid that sounds?"

Bishop shrugged. "Yeah, well, sometimes it's just that simple."

"And you have Presidential authority?"

Bishop said. "Yup. If you need written orders—I haven't gotten any. Totally black op. Plausible deniability and all that government super-secret stuff."

Carpenter snapped his head around in time to see Bishop's grin. "So this is an off-the-books operation, huh? You still haven't explained why I'm in this get-up, driving a FedEx truck."

"You're my cover. McFadden believes I'm out of the picture—I want it to stay that way—it'll make my job easier. Besides, you're the only one I trust out here."

Carpenter glanced Bishop's way as he drove. "And why's that?"

Bishop shrugged. "Just say I'm a good judge of character."

Carpenter grunted and kept his eyes on the road. He drove several more miles before speaking again. "And what's your job?"

Bishop stared at Carpenter for a couple of seconds. "Okay, what I'm about to tell you can't be passed on to your superiors."

"Stop!" Carpenter cried, "I can't be keeping secrets from my bosses. I still have too many years to retire."

Bishop smirked. "Never mind, then."

Carpenter drummed his fingers on the steering wheel and remained silent, keeping his eyes straight ahead. After about ten seconds, he said, "Okay, just tell me the least damning thing you intend to do."

"I'm going to violate several state and federal laws within the next twenty-four hours, and you'll be an accessory before the fact."

Carpenter made a face and turned his head back to the road. He had a white-knuckle grip on the steering wheel, and the muscles in his neck bulged. In a quiet voice, just above a whisper, he mumbled, "Now, why did you have to go telling me something like that?"

Carpenter quizzed Bishop on his theory for the rest of the drive and tried to break it down. Bishop defended it and explained away all of Carpenter's doubts. By the time they arrived at Corona, Carpenter was only about halfway convinced.

"There's no way you can prove it without finding the weapons. I can tell you if that's all you have, you're not going to get a judge to sign a search warrant."

Bishop kept his gaze on the landscape before nodding and saying, "Never planned to."

"Planned to what?"

"Get a search warrant. Wouldn't even know how to apply for one."

Carpenter took the right turn on the park road, which led to the peak. "That's where the violating state and federal laws come in, I suppose?"

"Yeah. Look, if I'm right, and McFadden has the things, I believe he might be crazy enough to uncork one. If that could be prevented by a small unauthorized incursion onto his property…"

Carpenter didn't answer but kept his eyes straight ahead on the road. They were just a mile from the top of Gallinas Peak when Bishop handed Carpenter the note.

"What's this?"

"If you don't hear from me by Friday evening at 2200 hours, call this number."

Carpenter glanced at the paper and read the name. "Maxwell?"

"Yeah."

"What do I say when I call?

Bishop's expression turned dark. "Tell him who you are and ask when's the last time he heard from me."

"And?"

"If he hasn't heard from me either by then, I expect you won't ever be hearing from me."

Carpenter's eyes widened.

Bishop shrugged. "McFadden's Ranch is a dangerous place—enemy territory. When you're working an op like that, it's best to have a proof of life factor built in. If neither of you've heard from me, then you'll have to go to plan B—if there is a plan B."

Carpenter reached the peak and slowed as he approached Cora's little, red house. "Are you staying up here with the forest service ranger?" Carpenter asked.

"Yes," Bishop replied. He ducked lower in the truck. "Get me as close as possible to the front door."

"Does the ranger know what you're up to? Can we trust this guy?"

Bishop grabbed his duffel bag. "Well, the ranger's not exactly a guy."

A mischievous grin spread across Carpenter's lips. "You dog. At least it proves you're human. I was starting to wonder."

Bishop didn't answer.

Just before stopping the truck, Carpenter said, "Look, don't get me wrong, but I can't just do something like this without higher authority. I'm just a field agent, and…"

Bishop nodded. "The deputy director who contacted your SAC about working with me. His name was Weaver, right?"

Carpenter's eyes pinched. "Yeah, so?"

"Call him. He's probably already expecting your call. Ask him if he'll take responsibility for you assisting me?"

"Hold on. Are you saying he will authorize it?"

Bishop slowly met eyes with Carpenter. "If he doesn't, just forget the whole thing."

Carpenter folded the note and dropped it into his shirt pocket. "Why do I get the feeling you already know the answer?"

Bishop kept his eyes on Carpenter as the truck came to a stop but released a sly grin. "Because I do." He had ducked low beneath the dash by the door. He looked up at Carpenter. "I want to get in before anyone watching from outside can see me. If you hear back about that request to check on the McFadden Academy graduates, pass it to Maxwell. He'll know what to do." Bishop kneeled on one knee with his head barely peeking over the dash of the truck.

As Carpenter came to a stop, he extended his hand. He had a smile. "I think you're one crazy son of a bitch, but I like you—good luck."

Bishop nodded and grabbed the hand. "Get back to work, or I'll call FedEx to dock your pay." He opened the truck door and ran inside the house.

———

From her perch in the tower, Cora eyed the FedEx truck pull up close beside her house. She wasn't expecting any deliveries—hadn't ordered anything in weeks. She looked at her watch. Oh, well, it was lunch time anyway. She gathered her jacket and hung the carry-all bag over her shoulder. She closed the tower window and took the last swallow of water from her plastic bottle.

On her way down the stairs, Cora wondered again about the delivery. Come to think of it; she'd never had a delivery to the house, always to the station headquarters building. She continued the slow descent as the driver began turning around and started back down the mountain

—he never even got out of the truck. She could have yelled for him to stop, but what was the use? He wouldn't hear her anyway. She strolled to the front door and went inside. Cora dropped the bag and jacket beside the sofa and turned toward the kitchen. There stood Bishop holding a beer.

"Surprise."

Cora jumped back and yelped. Her body shook, and she clenched her eyes and fists. "Don't ever do that again." Then she ran and leaped into his arms. She broke the embrace and pushed him back. "Where did you come from? How did you get here?"

"Special FedEx delivery," Bishop nodded toward the door.

Cora squinted. "Sneaky devil. Another cop trick?"

Bishop's demeanor had changed. He wasn't smiling anymore. "I'm paying a visit to the ranch tomorrow tonight—going to have a look around. All of McFadden's people think I've left for good. I want to keep up that deception. That's why the FedEx."

Cora's jaw dropped. "You're going on the ranch? You're not serious."

"I'm serious."

Now she knew. He was a cop... or something, and he was going after her old nemesis, McFadden. "That reminds me." She turned and reached for the paper on the kitchen table. "Samuel told me to give you this."

Bishop sat the beer down and closely studied the map, and Cora helped herself to his beer.

"I wish you had called," Cora said. "I could have made something special for dinner tonight. Samuel invited me to dinner tomorrow night at his place. Should I cancel?"

"No. Go ahead. We need to keep everything looking as normal as possible."

"You sure?"

"Yeah."

"Troy, I want to go with you tomorrow. I could show you around the place. I know the ranch as well as anyone."

Bishop took her in his arms again and hugged her. "That wouldn't be a good idea. I need someone on the outside to help out if things get crossed up. You're the closest and could get help the fastest—you need to stay here."

She pushed back and pouted but then flashed a quick smile. "Okay, but I want a full report when you get back."

He glanced back to the map. "Have you looked this over?"

"Yup, it's accurate. Say, when do you think you'll be back from your little foray?"

"Not sure," Bishop mumbled, continuing to study the map. His eyes scanned the lower half of the page. His finger outlined the cave and underground pool. "This cave. What's up with it?"

Cora hadn't expected a twinkle in his eyes, but there it was. It was like he'd just discovered something important.

"Don't know," she said. "Didn't even know it existed till Samuel told me. It's in the exclusion zone—that part of the ranch restricted except to a few."

A sudden chill rushed through her. "Troy, you're not looking for stolen government computers, are you?"

———

Minerva McFadden stood at the door to Clark's home office and watched him. He kept his head down, studying the map and pieces of colored paper scattered across his desk. As usual this time of day, he sipped his glass of bourbon, neat. He'd not noticed her yet, which gave her a chance to observe him *in the wild*. He wasn't trying to impress or convince anyone of anything. His relaxed expression was so refreshing for a change—almost like the old Clark. But something was afoot. She didn't understand what, but every time she'd questioned him the last couple of weeks, he'd denied knowing what she was talking about. One thing for sure—it wasn't another woman. The guy never went anywhere anymore. Never left the ranch without her. They'd go on an occasional trip to Albuquerque or Santa Fe for a bit of shopping and dining. They were never gone more than a couple of nights. Clark seemed like a different man when he wasn't at the ranch—more relaxed. Which made little sense. What could possibly be going on at the ranch to cause him stress?

He must have read her thoughts because he raised his head, and they met eyes. "What?"

She casually strolled inside as he folded the map over the pieces of paper and rested his hands on top.

"You need something?" he asked.

Minerva stopped short of the desk and asked, "What's so interesting?" nodding toward the top of his desk.

Clark folded the map and papers a couple of more times and answered. "Just business."

She didn't reply but just kept eying him. "I know what you're up to."

Clark blanched but didn't reply. He slowly sat his glass on the desk and eyed her.

Minerva rested her hands on the back of a chair in front of the desk. "I showed up a little early the other night at the reunion for my performance on the altar. Overheard what you told the rest of them."

Minerva had no idea what he was up to. She *had* shown up early, all painted up for another performance as White Painted Woman. She'd been doing it for years. No actual harm in helping the boys feel like they never lost something important from their childhood. About the only thing of interest she'd overheard was the last of Clark's orders for everyone to keep a very low profile and let him know if any government types showed up asking questions.

A coldness swept over Clark's features as he stood. "What did you hear?"

His hollowed-eyed expression frightened her, and she took a step back. The bluff hadn't worked—she'd struck a nerve. She showed an innocent grin. "Nothing, I really heard nothing."

He rushed her and grabbed her arms, shaking her. He was hurting her arms.

"Damn you, what did you hear?" he shouted.

Dizziness enveloped Minerva. A sick sensation turned her stomach rock hard, and she couldn't speak. Clark's eyes blazed with a fury she'd never seen.

Crying, she dropped to her knees. "Nothing, Clark… I heard nothing. Nothing at all. I was only kidding, only kidding," she sobbed.

He kneeled beside her. A terror she never knew tingled her skin as he spoke.

"Tell me now." He slipped his hands around her neck and squeezed. Even at his age, he was powerful. His grip choked off her answer.

She pulled at his hands, and he eased up.

"Tell the truth."

She gazed into his eyes. "I swear, Clark, I didn't hear a thing. I remember what you've always said about listening in on your private conversations. I was only teasing. I swear."

He rose and looked at her for several moments before returning to his desk. "Might be best if you weren't so nosy. Understand?"

She pulled herself up with the help of a chair. "I'm sorry, Clark. I understand." *He was crazy.* And whatever he had planned was dangerous. She needed to get away.

––––––––

Cora was elated to see Bishop and, to be honest, he was happy to be with her again. They spent time catching up that afternoon and evening, and she made them some eggs and toast with spicy link sausage. He continued studying the map and memorized all the details. He kept coming back to the depiction of the cave and underground pool. He read Samuel's notation in the margin for the fifth time. Being stored underground and underwater were two of the best ways to mask a radiological signature from a nuke. That place would definitely have to be checked.

"What's this?" Bishop pointed to an area in a heavily wooded section of the ranch well away from the main area.

Cora walked back to the table where he sat and leaned over his left shoulder, placing her arm around his neck. Her right hand caressed his chest. "That's Ochoa's place."

"The big ugly guy at the party?"

"Yeah, he's always lived there by himself."

"Think that would be a place McFadden might hide something?"

Her fingers tense along the base of his shoulder. "Maybe more than anyone realizes." She took a deep shuddering breath.

He turned and met her eyes—they were misted. "What's wrong?"

Cora walked to the other side of the table and dropped in the chair. She wiped her eyes with her fingers. "Sorry, it's just that…"

"What?" Bishop leaned closer.

"Remember I told you that residents of the ranch that fell out with McFadden were either run off or disappeared?"

"Yes."

"Well, rumor is, when they disappear, they go to Ochoa's."

"You mean they're being held there as prisoners?"

She shook her head. "No one knows for sure. The only people who are allowed in the place are McFadden and Ochoa. Samuel thinks that's where my folks ended up."

Bishop sat back and considered the information. He also needed to add that area to his list of must-search locations.

———

Cook had been popping Tylenol all afternoon. The headache continued to throb—making his head feel like a bass drum. He massaged his temples and concentrated on the information he'd just received. It was not surprising, but he had hoped for the best and gotten the worst. He looked up when he heard the knock at the door, and Maxwell stuck his head in. Cook waved him into his office.

"I want to put satellite or drone surveillance on that ranch. Which would you recommend?"

Maxwell pursed his lips a moment before saying, "If Bishop's right, what's the chance, someone on the inside, connected to McFadden, will discover the surveillance request?"

Cook opened his eyes and leaned forward, resting his arms on the desk. "That's what I've been wrestling with all day. Can we afford to do it? Is it a risk we can take?"

Maxwell shrugged. "Tough call."

"I don't think we can afford to be blind at this critical time. It's a risk, but we have to take it."

"I agree," Maxwell said. "Under ordinary circumstances, a drone would be best, but the satellite program might be better now."

"I tend to agree. There is one other thing."

"Yes, sir?"

Cook leaned back and laced his fingers across his chest. "Fuller brought it up the other day after realizing Speaker of the House Wilson was a McFadden Academy graduate. I hadn't considered it before then but haven't been able to get it out of my mind since."

Maxwell stood very still; it looked like he stopped breathing.

Cook continued, "Do you realize who the next in the Presidential line of succession is, after the Vice President?"

Maxwell furrowed his brow and looked down for a second. When his head rose, his eyes were wide. "The Speaker of the House. You're not saying…"

Cook stared at him, and a grim smile crossed his lips. "I'm not saying anything, Colonel."

"…but how sure are we that he's gone?" McFadden asked, lounging in his leather executive chair with his feet propped on the desk. He held out his glass for a refill. Newman Smith figured he'd ask this question. He poured the bourbon over the two cubes of ice then refreshed his own.

"The front gate guards saw him leave a couple of days ago—in fact, the same day I traveled to DC. No sign of him at Cora's since he left, but we keep watch until her lights go out each night, anyway."

McFadden used the tip of his finger to outline the lip of the glass as he stared out the window. His lips stretched thin in thought. "Do we know where he went?"

Smith glanced at his boss. "No, he left without warning from Samuel's. We assumed he was heading back to Cora's, but he never came back."

McFadden lifted his gaze to Smith. "Doesn't it seem strange to you that a man who'd bested us in every way decides to just up and leave for no reason?"

"Maybe he figured his luck had run out. I don't believe we should make more out of this than it is—we're overthinking the problem."

McFadden stared out the picture window. He took a slow sip. "Yeah, maybe, but let's keep an eye on Cora. My bet is, if he shows back up, it'll be there."

———

Thad Farrow walked across the mall past the Vietnam War Memorial. Washington, DC weather was still a little warm and sticky, so he slung his suit coat over his shoulder. The short drive from Chantilly, Virginia, gave him a welcome chance to get out of the office for the afternoon. Since the Secretary of Defense appointment as National Reconnaissance Office Director last year, he'd had far too few opportunities to leave his desk—except to attend a meeting somewhere in the District.

He walked up the slight rise and scanned the benches under the trees. General Harry Cook sat near the Korean War Memorial, studying the nineteen stainless steel sculptures of GIs scattered through the grass. Cook had also removed his coat, and a breeze caught the end of his tie, making it flutter. Farrow didn't know Cook very well, but no one else seemed to know him, either. He'd heard stories from the CIA and other DOD types about the organization Cook led and the fact he always got what he wanted.

"Good afternoon, General Cook."

Cook came out of his trance and stood. "Director Farrow, thanks for coming."

They shook hands, and both sat on the bench—the breeze ruffling the leaves overhead.

Cook turned back to the sculptures and cocked his head. "You know we're over sixty years removed from that forgotten war." Cook nodded toward the sculptures. "1950 to 1953, they slugged it out over there in that miserable place."

Farrow sucked in a slow breath. Cook had something on his mind, but Farrow decided to wait and let him bring it up.

"My dad was wounded there." Cook turned to face him. "Got the Bronze Star."

Farrow nodded sympathetically.

Cook crossed his legs and leaned closer. "Thad, I have a real problem on my hands, and I believe you're the only one who might be able to help."

"I'll do what I can."

Cook swung his left arm on the back of the bench. "The National Security Advisor has authorized a domestic operation, and my group has the lead. One of my people is about to make a covert entry into an area in New Mexico, and I need your birds to keep an eye on the place, at least until he's out."

"New Mexico? Would this have anything to do with," he looked around to see if they were alone, "you know what?"

"It has everything to do with it."

"Well then, that's not a problem. Just shoot us a request."

Farrow now couldn't figure what the meeting was all about. He got tasking request for his satellites every day. Why was this one different?

Cook grinned. "Well, to tell the truth, it's a little more complicated than that. " "I can't make this an official request through regular channels."

Farrow faced him. "I don't understand?"

"Thad, we believe several outfits may have been compromised. The sensitive nature of this requires us to skip the usual channels."

"A spy in my shop? Who? Give me a name."

"We believe he's a major in the Air Force—don't have a name."

Farrow considered the information. "Because this is a domestic surveillance mission, that puts it into a touchy category—I'll need some higher authority if no formal request is issued."

Cook reached into his inside coat pocket and withdrew an envelope. He handed it to Farrow.

Farrow read the handwritten instructions on the personal stationery of the Secretary of Defense. Farrow's eyebrows rose about halfway through the document. He stood. "I'll see to it personally, General."

Cook rose and looked again at the sculptures. He turned back to Farrow. "Remember, only you and the officer-operator can know. Make sure he has no history with any place in New Mexico, and patch the real-time images to my office."

"Will do."

They shook hands, and Farrow began the walk back across the mall to the parking lot. The rumors had been correct—Cook always got what he wanted. The old guy had an aura and reputation that caused people to like and trust him automatically. Of course, an authorization letter from the Secretary of Defense also helped. Farrow glanced back in Cook's direction, but he was nowhere in sight. Farrow shook his head and smiled; the general had left him with a real mess.

———

The next day, Cora went to work as usual, and Bishop stayed low and out of sight in the house. He wanted to do the penetration last night, but Cook had insisted he wait till tonight. Cook gave no reason, and Bishop asked for none. After working for the man for so many years, Bishop didn't question what the general said. Every order Cook issued had been carefully thought through. After work, Cora shuffled around the house, picking up a light jacket for the trip to Samuel's. Bishop pulled all the drapes and blinds, making the small house seemed especially gloomy.

"Wish you were going with me." She stopped at the table where he studied Samuel's map.

He looked up. "I'll be okay. Think I might try and grab a nap—it'll probably be a long night."

She planted a quick kiss on his cheek. "I won't be long."

"Hey, when you tell Samuel I'm back, make sure he understands that's privileged info, not to be shared."

"Who would he tell? His only neighbor is McFadden." She flashed a smile before walking out the door. The sound of her motor scooter cranking hardly fazed Bishop's concentration as he memorized every detail of the map.

Bishop figured he'd digested enough information on the McFadden Ranch for one day and put the map aside. He peeked out the front and back windows—nothing, but he still suspected eyes were watching. He strolled to the bedroom and unpacked his gear from the duffle bag. After checking everything, he yawned, kicked his boots off, and lay on the bed. Bishop decided he'd wait a few minutes after midnight before leaving. Cora would need to turn in especially early. If the house were being observed, the watchers would quickly become bored looking at a dark residence. That would be his time.

He must have drifted off without realizing it because the front door suddenly burst open, and he heard the sound of feet running through the house. He rolled to his left, grabbing the pistol off the nightstand, and pointed the gun at the bedroom door as Cora ran inside. Tears streamed down her cheeks.

"He's gone—they've taken him," she screamed.

Bishop rose, dropped the gun on the bed, and Cora rushed into his arms. "What happened?"

"I don't know. There was blood everywhere," she sobbed, "and he's not there."

Cora shook so hard Bishop had to hold her for a few seconds. He gently pushed her to arm's length. "Tell me everything you saw."

They sat on the edge of the bed. Cora wrung her hands and wiped tears from her face as she took deep breaths and composed herself. "When I arrived, there was blood on the front porch and a hole blown through the front door. I went inside, and there was more blood but no sign of Samuel. I found the old double-barrel shotgun on the floor, the one he keeps behind the refrigerator, and two empty shells inside."

"Looks like he didn't go down without a fight," Bishop remarked.

Her eyes were wild with fear, "He's at Ochoa's; I know he is. I'm going after him."

She started to get up, and he pulled her back. "No, you'd never get past the front gate."

"Then you find him, Troy. Bring him back."

Bishop held her close, and the sobbing turned into an all-out cry.

"I'll find him," he said. The search had now also become a rescue mission. *Would I have time to do both?*

<h1 style="text-align:center">SIXTEEN</h1>

The long shadows of evening crept across the closed window blinds. Cora took a pill and was at last sleeping. Bishop turned off all the interior lights except a small night light in the bathroom and readied himself. Every so often, he'd chance a peek out one of the windows, but the blackness of the night revealed nothing about who might be watching.

He filled two canteens with water and did a final equipment check. Samuel's recovery was now part of the mission, but that would have to wait until he finished his search for the nukes.

Bishop stared at Cora before he turned to leave. In the dim light of the room, she laid there, eyes open, staring at him. She didn't move—just looked his way. He kneeled beside the bed and softly brushed the loose hair from her eyes. "Thought you were asleep. You okay?"

She didn't answer but offered a shy grin. She ran her gaze over Bishop's black outfit and face smeared with dark tones of camo paint. "You look like one of those commando guys in the movies." A sudden realization crossed her face as her eyes widened. "That's what you really are, Troy, aren't you?"

"Try and get some rest. I don't know how long I'll be gone. I left a couple of names and numbers on the table. If I'm not back by this time Friday, call and tell them."

She rolled off the bed and hugged him. Her warmth and smell made him want to stay. He could spend the rest of the night in those arms.

"Be careful." Her lips brushed his before the long goodbye kiss. "Bring Samuel back." She lay on the bed and covered herself with the thick comforter, watching him disappear into the dark shadows of the house.

Bishop looked out the back door with the night goggles. Nothing showed through the lens but the green outline of trees. No movement or sound. Staying low as he slowly opened the sliding glass door, he slipped out and knelt behind the woodpile—listening and watching. The soft click of the door lock told him Cora had secured it. The night was cool, and a gentle wind blew across the peak, bringing the sound of some far-off night bird. The swishing movement of the big pines overhead was the only other sound.

Bishop stayed close to the house and crept to the front. He waited for a couple of minutes, then quickly moved toward the edge of the mountain. This was where the tricky stuff started. How to negotiate his way down a steep cliff in the dark sprinkled with rocks and burned-out trees was the question. His troubles began at the outset. Too few footholds. Too many loose stones. After an hour, he'd only climbed down a couple of hundred feet. At this rate, he'd never make it before sunrise. He stopped and rested for a minute, then surveyed the area. There was a clear path to his left. He'd have to go slightly out of his way, but the time he saved might make it worth trying. He swung toward the area and started his descent again. The ravines and rocky outcropping of the terrain continued to slow him, but he made better time on the new route.

About an hour before dawn, Bishop reached his objective—a small ledge, a few hundred feet before the bottom. He was exhausted. He'd climbed up alpine mountains during training with less effort. He walked around the area and studied the shallow depression in the ground about six feet in diameter with some scrub oak surrounding it. He'd seen it from the fire tower a few days earlier and made a mental note. This would be his hide. He unloaded his pack and spread the camouflaged tarp over the depression. After staking down the sides, he moved the rest of his gear into the depression, under the tarp, and slid under a loose edge. A four-inch gap between the ground and tarp offered him a full view of the ranch below. He looked to the east and just made out the first rays of sun streaking through the sky. His perch was about a hundred feet directly above McFadden's house.

To his left, a scream from the area of Ochoa's house broke the early morning's silence. Bishop winced and rolled on his back. He stared up at the beige-colored tarp. To leave this secured position during daylight would be suicide. He'd have to wait until dark before he could move around the ranch. That would be more than twelve long hours from now.

———

Special Agent Carpenter stood in the shower and let the water spray on his face. He'd not slept well again and knew why—Bishop. The fact he'd been in contact with the guy and not informed his supervisors still troubled him. Well, he'd remedy that today. He planned on writing a full report outlining everything he and Bishop had discussed. He'd talk it over with his supervisory special agent and see what he thought. Couldn't keep this quiet any longer. To go out on a limb any further for Bishop wasn't something he wanted to do.

"Breakfast is almost ready," Jean's voice boomed from downstairs.

Carpenter dried off, ran a brush through his hair, and slipped on a pair of dress slacks, shirt, and socks. He grabbed his electric shaver and cleaned off the stubble on the way to breakfast. He left twenty minutes later, thinking about what he'd write as he walked out the door.

Two coffees later at work, Carpenter sat back and reviewed his report. Yup, he'd covered all the critical points. He started to save the report in the H drive on his FBI computer, but the phone call interrupted him.

"Hey, Carpenter, something just came in for you; it's at my desk." It was Peggy's voice, and she sounded more chipper than usual this morning.

"What is it, a puppy?" Carpenter liked Peggy, and they joked constantly.

"Right, a cute, fuzzy puppy with a cold, wet nose and wagging tail," she laughed. "Or perhaps it's an envelope from OPM with an answer to that request you sent them."

Carpenter stood. "I'll be right there, thanks."

He walked through the cubicle maze and took a left. Peggy's cube was always easy to spot. It was the one with the plants by the window. Miniature palms, ivies, and several other things no one could identify lined the top of her cubicle. Peggy was typing with her back turned when he stuck his head around the corner.

"Let's see it," he said.

She jumped and rested her left hand across her chest. "Don't scare me like that."

He winked. "So how would you prefer to be scared?"

"Here," she handed him the yellow envelope.

Carpenter didn't get in a hurry about leaving. He enjoyed looking at Peggy. She was the top intelligence analyst in the division and easy on the eyes. If he were ever going to cheat on Jean, Peggy would be his choice. He slowly opened the envelope, keeping one eye on her. He assumed she knew the effect she had on him and enjoyed the playful exchange as much as he.

He slid the thick stack of papers from the envelope and enjoyed her sexy grin. He smiled and glanced at the report. The smile disappeared as he quickly flipped the pages. There was a tightness in his chest. It was hard to breathe.

Peggy frowned. "What's wrong?"

His eyes darted around while he shoved the report back inside the envelope. "Nothing—nothing's wrong," he stammered. "Has anyone else seen this?"

"No, it came sealed with your name on it, why?"

He tried to look normal. "No reason."

"You sure nothing's wrong—you don't look so good."

"I'm fine, Peggy, fine," he mumbled, walking quickly back to his desk.

He flopped down in his chair and stared at his computer screen. The report he'd just written moments ago stared back. He hit the delete button. The computer asked him if he was sure he wanted to delete the document—*his work had not been saved*. He hit the *yes* button and deleted it. He sat back in his chair and let out a deep exhale. Moving his hand across his forehead, he wiped off a bead of sweat. What should he do?

———

Bishop lay on his stomach and scanned the ranch through the four-inch slit between the tarp and ground with the binoculars. This was a perfect location. The scrub oaks lined the depression he'd staked the camo tarp across, leaving him just enough space to see without being seen. A better recon blind he could not imagine.

Little had happened since he arrived. The ranch hands finally began stirring between seven and eight o'clock, and a few vehicles rolled between the cattle barns. Samuel stayed on his mind. Too much activity to move during the daylight. A wave of exhaustion and fatigue settled on Bishop. He sat the binoculars aside and rolled on his back. He lifted his right hip and removed a rock nestled under it. He knew he needed to sleep, so he closed his eyes and tried to relax.

General Cook knew him better than Bishop knew himself. So that was the reason Cook had insisted he wait over twenty-four hours to execute the penetration. Cook, sly old soldier that he was, had carefully evaluated the climb from the top of the peak—especially in the dark. He probably considered the angle of descent and a dozen other factors before ordering Bishop to do nothing but wait and rest up. It was the right decision.

It had been a while since Bishop had spent any time in a recon hide in enemy territory. September 2001, Bishop was a young officer assigned to a Delta unit in Pakistan providing special ops training to one of their anti-terrorist units. After the World Trade Center and Pentagon attacks, Bishop's team was quickly dispatched to Tora Bora. CIA analyts had been listening in on bin Laden's radio traffic from his mountain redoubt and narrowed his location to a north, south ridge near the Pakistani border. After hooking up with a troop of Mujahideen, Bishop's unit took the lead until reinforcements could arrive. They were again the *tip of the spear*. They needed to stay as close as possible to the transmission location to send back intelligence and assess the best way to assault the target.

Higher-ups nixed a daring Delta plan to perform a night assault on the mountain behind bin Laden's location and take him by surprise. That left them with only one option—a frontal assault right up the throat of the mountain. The plan included Afghan allies taking the lead, with US Special Forces providing back-up. That was the plan, anyway. When the Afghans failed to press the attack with enough enthusiasm, it was too late to change strategies. Bishop's unit, acting as a forward observation post, provided coordinates to aircraft that launched laser-guided bombs and missiles against the cave complex.

When it became clear bin Laden had escaped, Bishop's unit was tasked with capturing or eliminating al Qaeda stragglers. Bishop was grateful to get out of his freezing hole on Tora Bora. The joy lasted exactly six days. He received wounds assaulting an al Qaeda safe house and got a one-way ticket to Walter Reed Hospital—his war was over.

Bishop put Samuel and Tora Bora out of his mind. He'd never get any rest dwelling on them. He thought about a better time and place— scuba diving on the wreck of the Cristobal Colon in Bermuda. Funny, that had been his big plans a week ago. Strange how things took a one- eighty so fast. But when this was over, he was on his way to Bermuda, and a couple of weeks doing what *he* wanted to do—which was not much.

———

Carpenter walked through the door of the men's room at the FBI and was met by Wiggins. He looked at the thick yellow envelope as Carpenter stepped into the accessible stall.

"Going to catch up on some paperwork, Carpenter, or afraid there's not enough toilet paper?" Wiggins laughed on the way out.

Carpenter again removed the thick report from its envelope. He looked over the list of federal employees who were graduates of the McFadden Academy. The top four sheets listed all the names, and the following sheets described the work history of each person, the agency they were employed by, and what position and grade they held.

His supervisory special agent's name, Adams, was at the top of the list. On the third page was his Assistant Special Agent in Charge's name, Nevins. *This is a hell of a thing, trapped in the crapper and surrounded by the enemy.* Carpenter sat on the toilet seat and reviewed each page, then divided them into three groups. The first: federal law enforcement; second: military; and third: everyone else. The law enforcement and military made up 85% of the list. *Oh, shit.*

All the names were mid-level executives in their agencies—the ones who instructions from the decision-makers passed through before execution. Carpenter decided what he had to do but realized that his career would probably be over if he went through with it. Unless, of course, Bishop was right—so much depended on him being right.

———

Bishop awoke sweating. While his tarp shielded him from the sun, it also held in the day's heat. The familiar musty, military smell of a tarp overhead somehow comforted him. He rubbed his eyes and checked his watch—1:36 in the afternoon. Not bad, six good hours of sleep. He squirmed out of his jacket and rolled over, picking up the binoculars again. Still, little movement registered from the ranch below. Like perhaps people were laying low for some reason. Several women laughed and chatted as they cleaned the long wooden dining tables under the covered pavilion after the communal lunch. That reminded Bishop—he was hungry. He dug in his pack for a granola bar and a bag of nuts.

Sipping water and munching on snacks, he continued watching the goings-on below. The sun reached its zenith in the early afternoon, and Bishop's hide heated up to the point he had to do something drastic.

He finally stripped down to just a tee shirt and pants. A dog barked to his right. Bishop rolled over and swung the binoculars toward the sound. The black Rottweiler trotted up the side of the mountain just above McFadden's house, making a beeline for Bishop's blind. Soon a horse and rider came into view, following the dog. Bishop's mind calculated the possibilities. Unlikely he could have been spotted. Was this a regular patrol, or had the dog somehow smelled him? Bishop reached for the pistol and pulled the silencer from his pack.

Bishop screwed on the silencer while keeping his eyes on the man riding the horse. The rider hadn't noticed Bishop's hide and followed the dog up the side of the hill. He couldn't go much further up the incline on the horse. He'd soon have to dismount and lead the animal. That would make it easier—kill both of them before they knew he was there. Bishop could pull the dead rider into the hide with him. He had done that once, in the Middle East, years ago. But the thought of spending the rest of the afternoon and evening with a dead guy as company did not appeal to him—especially in this heat. Even if he managed to drag the guy unobserved into the blind with him, he still had a significant problem—the *horse.*

———

Doctor Monk Cole left the meeting and walked the short distance back to his office at Sandia National Laboratory. Like all the others last week, the conference had to do with the theft of the missing weapons. The government was no closer to recovering them than the day they were stolen, as far as Monk knew. This information he would convey to Newman Smith. His regular reports and those from other former students in federal law enforcement and military helped determine when Mr. McFadden would make the final move. Monk had been given the honor of accompanying the weapon to the target and arming it.

After entering his office, Monk closed the door and dropped his lanky frame into the chair. He laid his glasses on the desk and massaged his eyes with thumb and forefinger. He was tired of waiting and looked forward to the operation finally kicking off.

From the time he was a young boy, Monk had longed to be a scientist. Because of his IQ and grades at the McFadden Academy, he was selected to attend MIT. He received his undergraduate degree in engineering as well as his masters and doctorate. Yes, science was his passion, but he had another. One that was never fulfilled.

When Cora's match, Cliff, was killed in the war, Monk asked McFadden if he could be matched with her. He'd yet to select a girl but always had strong feelings for Cora. She never seemed to notice or care about him, but Cora consumed most of his thoughts—he loved her. The idea she preferred leaving the ranch instead of being matched with him was disappointing and hurtful.

Monk's phone rang, and he slowly lifted the receiver.

"Monk, how's it going?"

It was the laboratory assistant administrator, Charlie Hooper.

"Good Charlie, how about you?"

"As well as can be expected. Say, the FBI has you lined up for a polygraph test tomorrow—how's your schedule looking?"

Cole dropped his head into his free hand and rubbed his face. He knew everyone, including the assistant administrator, was getting tested sooner or later.

"Well, I'm busy as usual. What time do they want me?"

"There's a 10 to 11 slot tomorrow morning—want that one?"

"Sure, put me down."

"Great, consider it done."

Cole hung up and did a deep exhale. McFadden's people had trained him in the methods to beat the box, but he'd secretly never had the confidence in himself to pull it off. Monk did have another plan in mind, just in case he decided to chicken out. He always had a backup plan.

———

Bishop pushed the barrel of the silenced pistol through the slit and aimed. The dog and rider were still fifty yards downhill—much too far for an accurate pistol shot. He'd wait until they were almost on him before making his move. He'd have to go for the rider first. Once he was down, Bishop could deal with the dog on his terms. If he were lucky, the creature would be startled and confused by the rider's fall, and that would give Bishop time to take him out.

The rider's face came into view. He was young—late teens or early twenties. The rifle he had in the saddlebag doomed him. Bishop couldn't afford to let the guy start shooting. One shot would alert the ranch, and they'd be on him. Bishop hated it, but the kid had to die. There was a fallen, burned-out, tree trunk twenty feet in front of Bishop's blind. That would prevent the horse from walking right over him, but the rider would soon see the camo tarp if the dog didn't smell Bishop's scent first. The guy was only twenty-five yards away now. Better get this over with.

Bishop took a deep breath, let half out, and tightened his finger on the trigger. He put the pistol site between the rider's eyes and began a slow squeeze on the trigger. From Bishop's peripheral vision, something moved to his left. The dog saw it too and made a hard right turn. The Rottweiler ran fast and low to the ground, barking several times. Bishop watched the tail of a rabbit duck into a clump of rocks as the dog closed on it.

The rider laughed, said something Bishop assumed was in the Apache language, and turned the horse toward the dog's new course. Bishop released the tension on the trigger and wiped the sweat from his face. *Close—too close.* He lowered the gun to the edge of the hole. He wiped more sweat from his brow with his forearm and continued watching the rider and dog move away along the side of the lower mountain.

———

Special Agent Daniel Piedmont waited in the receptionist's office to be summoned into the director's office in charge of the Domestic Terrorism Division at FBI Headquarters.

The secretary smiled again. "It shouldn't be much longer—the conference call will be ending anytime."

"That's fine, thank you." Piedmont smiled back. He already knew why he'd been summoned. The FBI's WMD Director needed a new section chief to replace Benjamin Witcher. Piedmont still regretted killing the man, but it had to be done. Killing Witcher was the only way to open the section chief slot. Piedmont needed that slot because Witcher had a higher clearance and "need to know" than he. Piedmont would soon be at the heart of everything the FBI was doing in the investigation of the stolen weapons.

The secretary answered the phone. "Yes, sir, I'll tell him." She nodded in Piedmont's direction. "You can go in now."

Piedmont strolled in with the confidence that comes only from prior knowledge. The director stood and extended his hand.

"Thanks for coming by, Dan—take a seat. Because of Ben's death, I need a new section chief." The man's eyebrows pinched, and he grimaced as he said the words, "Ben's death." He shifted in his chair and stared at Piedmont.

"You were his top man; think you could handle his job for a while until a permanent replacement is named?"

Piedmont had the uncontrolled desire to laugh out loud. He wanted to jump on the desk and shout, *Well, sure, you old fool. That's why I killed him. I can't believe he was promoted over me in the first place.* Piedmont didn't say a thing or move a muscle but stared back at the director with a solemn expression, appearing to think about the offer.

Piedmont slowly nodded. "Well, sir, that's a big responsibility … but, yes, I think I can do it." He reached up and touched the small nose scar with his index finger. It had almost become a reflex action of late.

"Great, I'll see you get a clearance upgrade and an updated briefing on the case—welcome aboard."

———

Bishop tried catching an afternoon nap. He'd be up all night in his search for the nukes on the ranch. Long ago in Delta, he'd mastered the art of resting without dropping into a deep sleep. Typically, there were always two operators in a hide if the mission required numerous hours of observation. Impossible for one guy to be highly effective after about twelve hours. Rarely only one operator manned a blind, but it was usually a short-term observation mission when he did. Bishop couldn't sleep. He was bored lying in this steaming hole, smelling his sweat, and waiting. He decided he'd put the time to good use by observing everything going on below at the ranch.

As late afternoon turned into early evening, the shadows began rising and falling in the landscape, giving it an almost magical quality. At the base of Gallinas Peak, the lower part of the ranch had been spared from the fire. Most of the area was laced with silver leaf maples, yellow ash, and ponderosa pines. An occasional piñon pine and a host of junipers gave the air a clean, sweet smell. Sprinkled down the hillside were cactuses and an occasional purple aster. A sound to his right alerted Bishop. A couple of young deer were grazing on what grass there was on the rocky hillside.

The ranch workers were finishing up for the day and putting away the equipment. From one of the barns, a large brown box truck pulled out and drove near the airstrip. Painted on the side, in red, white, and blue were the words *Spirit of America*. That had been the name of McFadden's hot air balloon. The truck driver opened the back doors and crawled inside. Because of the angle, Bishop was unable to see what he was doing. About five minutes later, the guy came out and closed the doors.

Bishop checked his watch—6:17. It was almost sunset, and the cool breeze blowing across the mountain made the hide much more comfortable. Time to check-in. He pulled out his cell and switched to encrypted. He dialed General Cook's number and waited. After several seconds there was a long, loud beep, and the line went dead. He looked at the phone. A call failed message showed on the screen. Bishop had what was referred to in P2OG as a *field phone*. It had a lot of interesting features. Not only could it go encrypted, but if it was operating through a traditional cell tower, it could knock another caller off their call to allow Bishop's to go through.

The nicest thing about this twenty-first-century communication device was its ability to operate as a satellite phone if there was no cell tower to transfer the call. In other words, Bishop could always communicate with headquarters from anywhere in the world. He switched the calling protocol to satellite mode, dialed two additional times, and got the same signal. Never had this happen before. Disgusted, Bishop turned it off and put it back into the pack. He laid back and listened to a coyote in the distance. The soft call of a whippoorwill drifted from somewhere above him. Those were the sounds of the evening turning into night. Those sounds gave comfort and sometimes fear to a mission. Comfort from the prying eyes of day—fear from the unknown dangers of the night. Bishop ate a couple of granola bars and drank half a canteen of water. Then he pulled a smaller pack from the larger one and loaded only the equipment he needed for the night's foray. With any luck, he would be back well before dawn, break camp and climb back to the top of Gallinas Peak without being seen. What would he do if he found Samuel? He was too old to do the climb. The thought troubled Bishop as he low-crawled from his cover toward McFadden's house.

––––––––

Speaker of the House Henry Wilson lounged in his oversized leather chair and tried to concentrate on the papers in his lap. He slowly removed his wire-rimmed glasses and yawned. It was after eight o'clock in Washington, and his staff had long departed. He realized he was wasting his time. Studying these legislative notes for a speech to give to a Congress that would no longer exist in five days seemed silly. He decided to do something he enjoyed.

He struggled to extract his large frame from the chair and walked to the door. After a quick peek down the hall, he closed and locked it. He kneeled before his personal safe, securely bolted to the floor, then typed in the six-digit access code and heard the click as the safe released its lock. He removed the white envelope and fell back into his chair.

The draft copy of this speech was still a work in progress. He could ask for no guidance or assistance in its preparation. This was something he alone must do. He ran his left hand through his thick hair and leaned back, reading his previous words:

"My fellow Americans—I come to you today with the most tragic news. There was a nuclear explosion in our nation's capital moments ago. The extent of the damage and loss of life is not yet known. Efforts to make contact with the President and Vice President have been unsuccessful. While this attack was intentional, at this time, it does not appear to have originated from a foreign power. We must therefore conclude domestic terrorists were involved. I want you and the world to know that the loss of our capital in no way hinders our ability to respond to any external threat or attack.

Acting under the Constitution's authority, I have assumed the office of President until such time as the President or Vice President can be confirmed as living. I am in a safe, undisclosed location under the protection of the US Secret Service. I will act in all matters as the chief executive until relieved as per constitutional mandate. Our military and law enforcement agencies are on the highest alert, and until this can be sorted out, I am declaring martial law. Beginning now, there will be a national dusk to dawn curfew. Anyone traveling during the day must have a photo ID. Anyone violating the curfew will be detained and questioned. I ask you to bear with us during this tragic time in our nation's history. The days ahead will be difficult, but with God's help, we'll get through this together. God bless you all, and may God bless the United States of America."

Wilson smiled—perfect. The youngest president since JFK. He'd deliver the speech next Monday afternoon on live TV from Fort Belvoir.

Because of the small amount of residual light remaining in the west, Bishop crawled on all fours on the rocky slope. Little danger of being spotted at this angle. He stopped and readjusted his night-vision goggles—he'd soon need them. The approach to a target was always the most dangerous. Tripwires, pressure plates, as well as other alarms, cameras, and booby traps lurked to catch the unwary intruder. Bishop eased forward, checking each square foot of ground by softly waving his gloved palm lightly over the rocky soil before placing a hand or knee on the ground. He'd crawled perhaps fifty yards when he heard a voice.

Bishop dropped flat on the dirt and listened. The sharp edge of a baseball size stone punched hard into his rib. Just as he readjusted his position to avoid the rock, he heard the voice again. Quiet chanting of a female's voice drifted above him and to his left. The words were unrecognizable to Bishop, something in soft tones with a lyrical rhythm. Sounded like Apache, but the voice was familiar. He crawled a little farther and through the night goggles recognized Minerva. Her outline was easily discerned in the darkness. The long hair cascading over her shoulders across the well-defined breast. She was seated, cross-legged, with her arms raised toward the west. She had no clothes from the waist up. She chanted almost in a trance-like state, and the haunting sounds sent chills through Bishop.

Nothing was as it appeared in this place. The face McFadden showed the world was that of a successful businessman, strongly conservative, with a sense of national pride. In reality, this joint was about as weird as it got. The party, the meeting of the group at the altar the other night, and now this. Bishop couldn't wait all night for her to leave, so he crawled to his left, giving enough room that she would not hear his movements.

Creeping forward, a deep sense of anxiety and dread fell over Bishop. In Delta, they'd called it the flutter of fear. It usually happened right before the jumping-off portion of the mission. That time when the person began to wonder if they'd done everything necessary to ensure their safety and the safety of the other operators. That time when doubt rolled into the subconscious, and a little flutter wafted through the gut. It wasn't uncommon, but it wasn't always good either. A person in this state of mind sometimes became so cautious they'd make mistakes. Sometimes they'd fail to seize the initiative at a crucial moment. Bishop stopped crawling, lay on the ground, and took a couple of deep breaths to relax before again sliding forward toward his objective. The flutter of fear feeling never left him.

SEVENTEEN

"He's moving, sir," Maxwell said, barging into Cook's office.

Cook had dozed off; the eighteen-hour days were kicking his butt. He was still leaning back in his chair, reading glasses on the bridge of his nose and a lap filled with papers. He looked up. "What?"

"It's Bishop; he's moving toward the house."

Cook cleared the cobwebs from his mind and shifted the papers to his desk. He typed his user name and password into the computer and waited. Soon a dark blue warning banner with the emblem of the National Reconnaissance Office appeared on the screen—the live satellite feed. It went black for a second, and the next picture that appeared showed a dark landscape. Cook squinted and leaned closer to the monitor. The white shadows were infrared images of people taken from the satellite. It was a real-time feed sent directly to his computer. He and Maxwell studied the screen for a moment.

Maxwell pointed to the prone figure on the ground, moving toward the well-lighted structure below. "The NRO identified this guy as Bishop," Maxwell said.

"Who the hell's this?" Cook touched the screen a little to the right of Bishop.

Maxwell stared at the motionless figure near Bishop, who appeared to be seated. He shook his head. "No idea. Looks stationary."

Cook glanced at Maxwell. "Did Bishop check-in before he left the hide?"

Maxwell grimaced. "No."

"Have you tried contacting him?"

"Several times, but the call won't go through, sir."

Cook didn't like this. He knew if Bishop could have checked in, he would have. The unknown figure worried him. Did Bishop see the stationary person? Could it be an ambush?

————

Bishop reached the top of the mountain excavation that held McFadden's house. Being built into the hillside, it would be difficult to access without the possibility of detection—another chance he'd have to take. He turned back and looked at the vague image of Minerva in the distance—the quiet chant continued. Bishop slid feet first down the excavated side of the house, using his hands to slow his descent along the steep slope. A small avalanche of loose rocks slid down the hill ahead of him. He gritted his teeth, spread out his arms on the ground, and came to a halt until the rocks stopped moving. After a moment, he again started his slow drop down the incline. By the time he reached the base, he figured he'd made enough noise to wake the whole county.

Bishop squatted in a shadow of the hill and tried to control his breathing. He wiped away the sweat from his eyes and listened for the approach of unwanted visitors. After a couple of minutes, he crawled toward the light shining out from McFadden's study window. It illuminated the ground to about twenty feet in front of the glass. Bishop shifted the night vision goggles to the top of his forehead and stayed far to the side of the window as he approached on his stomach. He did a quick peek into the room—empty. A bit of luck at last. He rolled to his side and took the small case from his pack. This was one of the cases he'd received from Andy—the flies on the wall.

Bishop opened the case and gazed at what appeared to be six common house flies on a plastic strip. Andy had won an award several years ago for his development of the covert eaves-dropping system. Bishop peeled one of the flies off the sticky surface and closed the case, then rolled back on his stomach and reached to the edge of McFadden's picture window. In the lower-left corner, he stuck the fly and then removed a receiver and earpiece from his pack. He turned on the receiver and listened. Once the fly left its case, it automatically activated. Inside the room, the soft ticking of the wall clock assured Bishop the fly was transmitting.

Someone approached from the rear. Bishop drew himself into the shadows of the cliff and held his breath. He slid his right hand down to the commando knife strapped to his leg. Releasing the catch, he silently drew the dagger into the fighting position, ready to spring out of the darkness. Footsteps drew nearer, and he braced himself for combat.

Minerva rounded the corner, walking on the path to the front door. Bishop had been wrong. She wasn't naked from just the waist up. She was totally naked. Her curvy hips swayed as she slipped a full-length cotton dress over her head as she walked. The momentary effort of putting on the dress caused her not to notice Bishop, only feet to her left. She struck a fine figure, well preserved in face and body. Minerva carried herself in a relaxed, sensual manner. When she reached the front door Bishop quietly released the breath he'd been holding. After the door closed, he scrambled back up the incline toward the top.

Bishop crawled over the top of the house entrance to the other side and waited a minute—listening. Nothing but the sounds of the night. He went to the edge of the incline and slid down as before. He stopped, listened again, and proceeded to attach another fly to the lower right-hand corner of the living room window. He adjusted the frequency, and McFadden's voice echoed through the earpiece.

"Yeah, come on over; I want to get this nailed down tonight. Okay, see you after a while." The sound of a phone receiver returning to its base echoed through the earpiece.

Who was coming? What did they want to nail down? When were

they coming? Bishop didn't have the time to wait. The receiver would pick up a quarter-mile from the transmitting fly. He'd have to go on and hope for the best. He wiped the sweat from his forehead and slipped the goggles back into place. From studying Samuel's map, Bishop recalled the cave lay in a straight line down the mountain from the house. Staying in the shadows, he silently made his way toward it.

After crawling halfway down the rocky incline, the headlights of an SUV lit up the road as it drove up the mountainside road to Bishop's right. He lowered himself to the ground and strained hard to discern who the driver might be. It was too dark, and the vehicle too far away. The SUV parked in front of the house, but Bishop couldn't see who got out from his location. He adjusted the volume of his receiver and waited.

The sound of a door opening and McFadden's voice boomed through the earpiece. "Take a seat, Newman, and let's see what you've got."

So Newman Smith was the late-night visitor. Bishop clicked on the recorder embedded in the receiver.

"Something to drink?" McFadden asked.

"Of course, but this calls for the good stuff," Smith replied.

"You know the good stuff, as you call it, is almost gone?"

"Yeah, but I've always enjoyed that particular year of Napoleonic Brandy. Besides, you have the money to buy as much as you want." The sound of Smith's chuckles filled the room.

McFadden laughed. "If only it were so. This is the next to the last bottle I bought in an auction back in '72. I got the last twelve on the market."

"Is it really part of the collection from Hermann Goering?"

"Yup," McFadden said.

Soon, the clang of glasses rang into Bishop's earpiece.

"Smooth as a babies' behind," McFadden whispered.

"Babies' behind, hell—smooth as a twenty-two-year-old coed's ass, I'd say."

They both laughed, and the sound of chairs sliding across the floor caused Bishop to adjust the volume.

"Okay, tell me all about it," McFadden said.

"Right, the plan is for 'H hour' to be next Monday at ten o'clock in the morning. We've confirmed that both the President and the Vice-President will be within the blast zone—total destruction. Both houses of Congress will be in session, and the Joint Chiefs will be meeting the President in the White House, again both well within the blast zone."

Bishop's gut twisted. *Blast zone?*

"What about the Supremes?" McFadden's voice had a casual air.

Smith coughed. "They'll be in session—also within the zone. They're hearing that big border control and immigration case—it's on their docket."

"Perfect."

The sound of rustling papers broke the short silence before Smith said, "This is where the weapon will be delivered. Cole will adjust the dial-a-yield system to detonate at 100 kilotons. That should take out everything for a radius of approximately one and a half miles. We can also count on almost everyone for a radius of two and a half miles from ground zero to be effectively disabled, if not killed outright."

Bishop stopped breathing. *This wasn't possible—detonating a nuke in downtown Washington, DC—too many safeguards in place for it to ever work.*

"Where is this place?" McFadden asked.

"It's an eight-story parking garage off Constitution Avenue, near the White House. If we park the vehicle containing the weapon on the roof, we'll gain the added benefit of having an air burst factor, which will greatly enhance the damage."

"I like it—send out the orders. It's a go for next Monday," McFadden said.

Bishop laid back and stared at the stary sky, trying to process what he'd just heard. *Good God*, they were going to destroy the Capitol in less than four days. While McFadden and Newman said their good-byes, Bishop dug into his pack. He mumbled a prayer and pulled out his phone again. He punched in Cook's number. He'd subconsciously crossed his fingers waiting for the call to go through. He again heard the long, loud beep, and the line went dead.

A sick feeling rose from the pit of Bishop's stomach. He looked at his watch. Besides the radiological detection feature, it also had a built-in alert option. When activated, it sent a burst transmission once every five seconds to a satellite. This would be forwarded to General Cook and was the signal to send in reinforcements. The ops order for this mission had been very clear. *Do not activate the alert unless and until the weapons were discovered.* Any other information could wait until Bishop contacted them through conventional means. But this was an exigent circumstance—right? Bishop's finger hovered over the alert button, but he paused. No, he'd locate the weapons first and tie the knot tighter. If he didn't, he'd have nothing but a conversation to back up the accusation against a close friend of the Speaker of the House.

Bishop slid the night vision goggles up to his forehead and looked at the clear night sky again. His mission had netted far more significant results, much faster than anyone could have believed. How to get the information back remained the question. Cook never said, but Bishop suspected he'd ordered satellite or drone surveillance of the ranch. It was likely he was being observed this very minute by NRO. He got the idea of going back to basics. Could he send a message using his flashlight and Morse code to the aerial platform circling the ranch? Yes, but that might compromise him locating the weapons if observed by someone below. If someone saw it, Bishop wouldn't have the time to complete his search.

Right now, no one knew Bishop had penetrated ranch security. Could he risk a full search? That would make it almost impossible to locate the nukes. His way was clear. Find the weapons post-haste, send the alert signal, get back to the top of Gallinas Peak, and contact Cook with the details. Bishop would have to search for Samuel later—this came first. He watched Smith's SUV coast back down the mountain road to the ranch below.

Okay, this is it. Bishop pulled the goggles back in place before crawling in the direction of the cave. A few hundred yards from the house, he realized he'd reached the base of the mountain. The elevation had leveled out, and he'd began crawling mostly horizontally instead of vertically. He stopped and took a knee. Craning his neck, he tried to figure out where he was. Bishop closed his eyes, remembering the map Samuel had drawn. The cave entrance should be slightly to his right—hidden by a group of trees.

Bishop crawled another twenty-five yards, and some small trees came into view. Were these the ones? As he got nearer, there were full-grown pine trees on the left and right, with several ten to twelve-foot small Junipers in the middle—all in a curved half-moon pattern. He crawled next to one of the small trees and peeked through to the other side—nothing. The trees formed a half-circle shielding perhaps thirty feet of bare land, then a stone wall in the side of the mountain. Bishop studied the overhanging limbs from the larger trees on each side. Their pine needles interlaced overhead to form a canopy—completely hiding the stone wall area behind them. *Good camo job.* But what were they hiding, a rock face? Bishop slid forward on his stomach.

Crawling to the other side of the small trees, Bishop's left boot made contact with something he didn't like. He froze—dozens of thoughts raced through his head. He glanced back—the boot had bumped something near the base of the small tree. Not a logical place to lay a mine, pressure plate, or any type of alarm. Who would step on it? Bishop slowly wiggled the boot—nothing happened… He released a breath in one long exhale.

Bishop turned around and crawled back to the Juniper. Extending his hand, inches at a time, he moved it back and forth along the dark ground under the tree. When it struck the object his boot had bumped, he outlined it with his fingers. It felt like a piece of wood—a board. He slid his other hand forward above the wood and was surprised. The tree was planted in a giant pot resting on a wooden pallet. The low limbs of the Juniper hid its base. Something extended over the edge of the pot leading into the soil. A small plastic tube—he squeezed it. Yup, an irrigation system of some kind. Bishop low-crawled to the other small trees to the left and right of the first one. All three were the same. The trees and pots weighed hundreds of pounds each, but sitting on the pallets, they could be easily moved with a forklift, opening up the entrance to the cave. Their low-hanging branches hid the fact they weren't planted in the ground.

Speaking of the cave—*where is it?* Bishop eased back toward the empty space—only a solid rock wall. He moved on all fours toward it, gently waving his hands over the dirt, looking for wires or anything protruding from the ground. When he reached the rock wall, he stood

—no chance he'd be spotted with the dense foliage behind and above him. If there were ground sensing radars in use, the wall should shield him from detection. Bishop reached out and placed his hand against the rock. He pushed it, and it gave way to his touch—*it wasn't natural rock.*

It was a canvas curtain of some type painted to resemble the cliff's face, flexible with a heavy-duty zipper in the lower right-hand corner. An aluminum stepladder leaned against it. Using the stepladder, Bishop unzipped the canvas from right to left over the top of the cave entrance. Once the tarp fell, the opening became clear. The interior looked about ten feet across and ten feet high. He pulled the tarp to one side and peeked in—only darkness. Bishop eased through the entrance, and the temperature dropped. His watch began to vibrate. He pushed the button on the side—a blood-red light pulsated around the dial—*plutonium!*

———

General Curtis Shaw got up from his desk and staggered past the sofa to the bar. He needed another drink—he always thought better with alcohol. All his wives had said he was a hopeless drunk. *Bitches.* He always kept his over indulgencing nature a secret from his superiors. He learned that lesson the hard way during his assignment in Korea early in his career. His fellow officers had backed him up when the young female lieutenant made the accusations. *Rotten whore.* It had ended her military career but didn't even tap the brakes on his. Shaw had the good fortune to attend West Point with several classes of cadets who had earned high rank early in their careers. They looked after their old football teammate.

Shaw had been a popular cadet. Few demerits, prominent sportsman on campus, and sharper than average. Even the senior cadets admired him. Shaw quickly spotted the best and brightest ones. He befriended them and kept a steady correspondence through their military careers. When they made rank, they always found a place in their commands for Shaw. His promotions coincided with his pals as both advanced up the chain. Now Shaw sat at the pinnacle of his career—commander of Fort Belvoir. The ideal location to receive his last major promotion.

Shaw chuckled to himself at the simplicity and purity of McFadden's plan. Guy had to be a genius. While the national threat focused on international terrorism, McFadden would quietly drive the bomb into the heart of downtown Washington.

Shaw poured himself another big one and chuckled again. Base personnel driving past his residence probably assumed he was working late on the relocation exercise planned for Monday. The exercise promised to be much more than anyone realized. Once the detonation took place, and all Pentagon brass were dead, the next step would be to pull all surviving senior commanders to Fort Belvoir. It would become the new Pentagon, and he'd be the commander. Being sixteen miles from the detonation put Belvior just outside the blast zone. He dropped into the chair and studied the martial law order he'd drawn up.

After Speaker Wilson's announcement next Monday afternoon, he would officially order Shaw to begin the United States' systematic shutdown. Every border would be sealed, and the military would take control of US air space. All ports of entry would be closed, and every illegal immigrant forcibly detained and deported to their country of origin. Anyone not a US citizen could expect to be hunted down by the police or military.

Shaw's authority would come from the John Warner Defense Authorization Act, which outlined the use of the armed forces in major public emergencies. The Posse Comitatus statutes that limit the military's involvement in law enforcement would be suspended. The government could increase domestic intelligence and surveillance of US citizens. It would restrict the freedom of movement within the United States and grant the authorities the right to isolate large groups of civilians.

Shaw took a long swallow and sat back down. Isolate large groups of civilians or concentration camps? Yeah, that sounded better. A complete suspension of rights would follow, and McFadden could, at last, begin to build back the government he wanted. Shaw would soon be one of the most powerful men in America—Chairman of the Joint Chiefs of Staff.

———

Bishop checked the watch for the third time. The red light on the dial continued flashing. No mistake—he was close now. The darkness of the cave and complete silence gave him the willies. He eased forward in the blackness and thanked God for the night vision goggles. The goggle's green tint gave the cave an eerie, unworldly appearance. Dripping water broke the silence somewhere up ahead. He stayed close to the left wall and discovered the cave made a slight turn to the right.

Bishop guessed he'd walked for seventy to eighty feet when he found the truck. It appeared to be the standard all-white dually pickup with a camper shell used by everyone on the ranch. It sat facing him like a large animal ready to charge. Bishop noticed the license plates— they were Virginia tags.

Could this be the vehicle McFadden intended to use to deliver the bomb? Adrenaline rushed through Bishop. A sound from somewhere deeper in the cave broke the silence—like the snort of an animal. Bishop didn't like the thought of facing a bad dog or other unknown creature in such a dark, confined area. He pulled the silenced pistol and crept forward, using his left hand to brace himself against the dark cave wall. The snort sounded again, just ahead in the dark. Bishop stopped and squatted down, giving the area a complete scan—nothing —just a dead end. There were two more muffled snorts directly in front of him. *What the hell.* The only thing in front of him was the back wall of the cave. The sound of someone snoring floated from behind the wall. Another loud snort rang out, and Bishop smiled. *Sentry sleeping on duty.* Bishop touched the back wall of the cave and again found it only made of canvas. The thing was so well camouflaged you had to touch it to discover it was a fake. He looked for the zipper in the lower right-hand corner and found it.

Bishop slowly unzipped a few inches of the canvas cover and chanced a peek through the hole. The fellow sat in a folding lounge chair with his head sprawled back against a wadded-up coat for a pillow. Every so often, he'd stop snoring and let out a loud snort. Bishop finished unzipping the canvass tarp, eased through the hole, and stood over the sleeping figure. Didn't seem quite sporting to knock a man out without waking him up first. Bishop grabbed the MP-5 submachine gun leaning against the cave wall. He smacked the guy hard against the left side of the head with it, and he tipped over, never uttering a sound.

"So much for this being a sporting event," Bishop mumbled. He rolled the unconscious man to his stomach and secured his hands behind his back. Bishop fashioned a gag from a rag he found on the ground and stuffed it into the man's mouth. With that done, he looked around at the cavernous room. The ceiling was about forty feet high. The room had a circumference of probably 200 feet. Against the left wall was a covering of some kind. It sat flush with the floor, and an overhead crane towered directly above it, with cables and a sling hanging down. Bishop knelt beside it and lifted the cover. It was heavy. Using his knife, Bishop scraped off part of the outside plastic sheath and discovered the lead interior lining. Lead was the perfect shielding agent against radiation. He suspected there had to be a silent alarm somewhere but finding and disabling it might be impossible. Better to attach the trackers, get the hell out and send the signal for reinforcements. By the time they could respond from the far side of the ranch, he'd be long gone.

Bishop trotted to a control panel on the wall and examined it for a moment before pushing a button. The lead pool cover slowly rolled up to one end. He took off the night vision goggles and placed them on the floor before pressing the next button. Bright blue, overhead Halogen lights bathed the cavern and revealed what lay beneath the lead cover. In a small natural spring pool, covered with eight to ten feet of water, were six fat, silver cylinders—*he'd found them.*

Bishop stripped off his gear and threw it against the wall. Digging through his pack, he found the box of trackers. He removed his boots and sat beside the hole, not wanting to think about the cold water temperature. Finally, he dipped his hand into the clear spring-fed pool. *Damn, that's freezing!* He wiggled his fingers a few times and judged it about 65 degrees. He dreaded the thought of diving in, but he had to do it. If they somehow moved the weapons before the feds could respond, the FBI would be back to square one. Tucking the six-pack of trackers into his pocket, he took several deep breaths. On the third one, he dove for the bottom.

Damn, colder than he'd expected. He kicked hard, and his ears popped as he went lower to the sunken weapons. The cold water stung his eyes, and he hurried to attach a nickel-size, magnetic tracker to the rear of each W-80 warhead. With his lungs feeling like they wanted to burst, he pushed off the bottom. When he broke the surface, he grabbed the side of the pool and sucked in several lungs of air before pulling himself from the frigid water. Once out, he reached for his watch to send the alert signal. It suddenly occurred to him it would be useless to try and send it while underground. The satellite couldn't pick up the alert until he got outside—or at least in an area he didn't have a few thousand tons of rock overhead blocking the signal.

Bishop slipped his socks and boots back on and stood, shaking himself like a dog. Even his bones felt cold like the time the team had trained in Norway in winter. He began shivering and dreaded the climb back up the mountain, especially soaking wet and at night. He bent down and grabbed his pack and night goggles off the stone floor. Just as he stood, there was a whoosh sound somewhere behind him. A second later, he thought he'd been stung by a large bee in his upper right back. Bishop reached around and pulled out the dart. He glanced at the man he'd left tied at the cavern entrance. He still lay there—out cold. *What tha—*

Bishop's gaze searched the cavern, but no one was there. He reached for the pistol, still in its holster on the cave floor. Feeling dizzy, he lost his balance and leaned against the wall. He slid down it and grabbed the gun.

Bishop pulled the pistol and pointed it in all directions. He tried acquiring a target, but his vision narrowed as blackness closed in on the edges. He shook his head and blinked several times, trying to focus. The gun in his hand no longer extended, ready to fire. The hand dropped to the cavern floor as if he no longer controlled it. He couldn't even lift it—thing weighed a ton. Using his legs, Bishop tried pushing himself up by using the wall. Perhaps, if he could get up, he could still stand. But his legs wouldn't move. *Can't be happening—I haven't sent the signal yet!*

Bishop tried reaching for his watch, but his hand lay frozen in place on his leg. He stared at it, willing it to move. From the shadows to his left, someone approached. Just before Bishop blacked out, he looked into the smiling, ugly face of Ochoa.

EIGHTEEN

Carpenter sipped his second extra-large coffee in as many hours and watched the eastern sky lighten and outline the Sandia mountain range in Albuquerque. He turned the car radio from the light rock station to the early morning news. Glancing at the passenger seat, he gazed at the envelope he'd received yesterday from OPM. The one detailing all the graduates of the McFadden Academy now in government service. Carpenter took another sip, and acid in the coffee mixed with the nervous acid in his stomach, giving him a queasy feeling. The source of all Carpenter's troubles lay in that seat. Why him? Why did he have to be the one to find out? He'd never run from anything in his personal or professional life, but this scared the hell out of him. This was a career changer—a life changer. No way to avoid it, and that's why he found himself sitting in front of the Special Agent in Charge's house before sun-up.

A vehicle's headlights blinded him in his rear-view mirror as it pulled behind his car. Moments later, the familiar red and blue overhead lights on the car sprang to life. Carpenter glanced in his side mirror as the uniformed officer approached. Carpenter rolled down his window.

"Having car problems this morning, sir?" the uniform asked,

quickly scanning the interior with his flashlight. The patrolman, shining the flashlight in Carpenter's face, looked in his early twenties.

Carpenter winced and held up his FBI credentials. "No, just waiting for someone."

The officer examined his identification and handed it back. "Sorry, we got a call about a suspicious vehicle—had to check it out."

"No problem, have a good morning, officer." Carpenter rolled the window back up as the patrolman strolled back to his car. Carpenter couldn't blame someone for calling. He did look suspicious sitting in an upscale subdivision before sunrise. He again rehearsed the short speech he intended to give to the SAC when he walked out to go to work. He'd explain how he'd been instructed to assist Bishop by an FBI Deputy Director, and acting on those orders, requested the list of McFadden Academy graduates. He'd tell him the only reason he came to see him this morning was that both his immediate supervisors' names appeared on the list. This forced him to jump the chain of command and go directly to the head of the office. It sounded good, but would the boss buy it? Carpenter checked the time—7:16. It wouldn't be long now. The front door of the house opened. The SAC stopped and locked it before heading to his government sedan parked in the driveway.

Carpenter took one last swallow of coffee, grabbed the envelope, and opened his door. Striding toward the house, the cool breeze ruffled his hair. The SAC did not notice him approaching from the street. "Good morning, sir."

The SAC jumped and dropped his Styrofoam cup of coffee on the driveway. It splattered across his shoes and cuffs. He cocked his head and leaned forward.

"Carpenter? What the devil are you doing here this time of the morning?"

Carpenter opened his mouth, and his mind went blank. "Sir, we have to talk," was the only sentence he could manage.

The boss glanced at the bulging envelope, and only his right brow rose as he nodded.

"I see." The SAC motioned to his sedan. "Get in—we'll get a couple of coffees to go."

Carpenter opened the passenger door and slid into the seat beside the man.

The SAC looked at him with a curious expression. "I'll drive—but you have to buy the coffees."

Then his expression turned into a smile, and Carpenter relaxed.

———

The cold splash of water woke Bishop up. He tried opening his eyes, but it hurt too much. His head throbbed, and his front temporal lobe wanted to explode. Slowly he opened one eye and then the other. Searing shards of light slashed at his retinas. He blinked a couple of times, and things came into focus. To his right stood Ochoa holding a large plastic bucket still dripping water. Bishop shook his head. He was looking at the giant through bars of some kind. Bishop touched the steel cage. It looked about 4'x4'x4'. He was crammed into it like a sardine with his chin almost on his knees. The top and bottom were solid steel plates, but the sides were bars.

"Sleep well?"

Bishop shifted his head and caught a glimpse of McFadden as he strolled beside Ochoa.

McFadden grinned. "Thought we might have lost you there for a minute. Ochoa sometimes uses too much tranquilizer in his darts—stuff's made for cattle. Some folks never wake up."

Bishop shifted again, and his stomach turned over. The bile rushed up his throat, and he vomited in his lap. It had a foul medicine smell.

McFadden grinned once more and pushed the cowboy hat back on his head while pulling a cigar from his coat pocket. He studied it for a moment. "That's another problem with cattle tranquilizer—makes most humans sick."

Bishop wiped his mouth with the back of his hand. How had he screwed things up so bad? One minute he'd found the weapons and was on his way out, and next, he sat in this stinking cage wearing his own vomit.

McFadden cupped his hands around the lighter before puffing the cigar. He ran his hand inside his jacket pocket and pulled out all the trackers Bishop had attached to the warheads. McFadden looked at them, and his eyes drifted back to Bishop. "You sure went to a lot of trouble." The cigar smoke made him want to vomit again.

McFadden smiled and took a long draw on the cigar. "Who are you, Mr. Bishop? I thought you might just be a drifter when you fixed the flat for my wife."

Bishop said the first thing that came to mind. "I'm a reporter."

"A reporter? Well, look here, Ochoa, a real reporter." McFadden laughed. His face quickly took on a severe expression. "No, not a reporter." He bounced the trackers in his hand and continued eying Bishop. "You have too much equipment and training. A fed, perhaps?" McFadden's eyebrows rose. "Yes, some kind of federal cop, I'd guess."

Ochoa grunted something, and McFadden nodded. "Wait for me in the truck," he said, motioning behind them.

Ochoa dropped the bucket and traipsed away. Once he got out of earshot, McFadden dropped to a squatted position directly in front of Bishop.

"I'm going to ask you one more time, so think carefully about your answer. Who are you, and why are you on my ranch?"

Bishop licked his parched lips— tasted bitter. "I'm a reporter," he mumbled in a less than convincing voice.

McFadden's eyes flashed anger, but he smiled. "Have it your way, then. Let me tell you what's going to happen next. I have to go out of town for a few days, but while I'm gone, you're going to talk." McFadden smiled. "No, you're going to sing your confession of truth. You'll tell us everything we want to know—understand?" He squinted. "No, of course, you don't. We know how to handle people like you— been doing it for a long time." McFadden stood and showed a victorious grin.

Bishop's thoughts raced back to the stories Cora told about missing hikers and others who'd strayed on the ranch, as well as troublemakers like her parents.

McFadden's mouth twisted before saying, "Bet you're wondering what alerted us to the fact we had a visitor last night? When you rolled back the cover on the cave's pool, it triggered a silent alarm at the guard shack and my office." McFadden spat a piece of loose tobacco off his tongue. "Did you attempt to call anyone about what you found? How'd that work out for you?"

When Bishop didn't answer, McFadden smirked.

"I can already tell you—it didn't." McFadden pointed to the ridge-line behind him to a slender metal pole glistening in the sun.

Bishop had noticed a dozen of them as he lay in his hide—they circled the boundaries of the ranch. Never did figure out what they were.

McFadden spread his arms out and said, "We have an electronic web around this place. Only cell phones with a special chip can operate within its confines. A good friend at Sandia Lab gave me the idea."

Bishop ran his hand down his wrist, feeling for his watch. It wasn't there—no way to send the alert.

McFadden paced back and forth beside the cage, smoking the cigar. He stopped, and his eyes narrowed. "As I said, Ochoa will be doing your interrogation. He's—" McFadden grimaced. "Well, let's just say a bit less delicate than I. His talents are more suited to the middle ages. Let me tell you about him—it's an interesting story." McFadden again squatted down eye-level. "He was born and grew up here on the ranch. He got to four or maybe five before he discovered his talent for torture. Neighbor's pets, rabbits, birds—anything he could trap or catch. It disturbed the community so much some thought we should put him in a state home. Around the sixth or seventh grade, the teachers couldn't deal with him any longer, but I saw promise in the boy."

McFadden flicked cigar ash, and the breeze caught it.

"Why are you telling me this?" Bishop whispered.

McFadden's eyes pinched, and his expression darkened. "Because I want you to know what's in store for you—Mr. Reporter! From an early age, I suspected there was something in Ochoa I could use." McFadden grunted and briefly glanced at the monster. "Man's a vessel without a soul. I set him up in his own house, away from the rest of the community. Since everyone fears him, I use him to control them. He's as loyal as a dog, does anything I tell him. Just have to watch him, sometimes. Used to have him put down sick or injured ranch animals.

Until one day, we found him skinning a steer, still alive. He'd been instructed to put it down the day before but chose to stay up all night tearing one little strip of hide off at a time from the poor creature."

McFadden shrugged. "Man does love his work." A grin shadowed his lips. "He's almost thirty, now. Learning new tricks every day."

Bishop shifted his weight in the cage and said nothing. McFadden reached into the jacket and withdrew a remote control the size of a garage door opener. He tapped a button, and Bishop felt a jolt as the cage began rising. He turned and only then saw the mechanical arm and pulleys attached to the top. McFadden studied the device a moment and made a show of pushing another button—the cage stopped moving but swayed in the breeze. Bishop sat eye-level with McFadden.

"Your only choice is how easy you die, Bishop. Do you die in terrible pain over days, or with a quick bullet in the back of the head? You choose."

"I'm a reporter."

"Okay, tough guy. Ochoa likes his clients softened up a bit, so I'll let you play with Samson and Sheba for a while… Newman Smith will stay at the ranch during my absence. He'll be around to hear your confession—think of him as a priest." McFadden let out a belly laugh and blew smoke directly into Bishop's face.

A sick sensation enveloped Bishop, but also something stronger. His mind drifted back to Major Headley smoking his cigar during Bishop's *long walk* as a candidate for Delta. Headley assuring him he was finished, had nothing left, wouldn't last another mile. Bishop sucked in a long breath. Somehow he was going to live long enough to kill McFadden.

The cage jerked up and swung to Bishop's left. He looked down into the muddy dirt pit. Hanging directly over it, the cage began its slow descent into the hole. Bishop had seen a lot of death and knew the smell. That was the scent that filled his nostrils as the cage moved deeper into the pit. The cage dropped the last few feet and landed hard. Bishop felt like his tailbone was driven into his brain. What was this place? His eyes adjusted to the shadows around him. Bones lay scattered around the edge of the dirt pit, with traces of clothes still attached. Gnaw marks cut into the bone's surface, and six human skulls were visible, half-covered with dirt. An old hiker's pack lay ripped open against the wall, and there were boots and shoes half-buried in the mud.

The death smell almost overwhelmed Bishop. He shifted his gaze to the left and found the source. Samuel lay crumpled against a wall, facing him. Most of his right arm and leg had been eaten away. The old man lay on his side, his long hair matted to his face and his eyes looking straight at Bishop. Another wave of nausea rolled over him.

McFadden's voice fell from above. "I'll ask the boys to fetch Cora. Maybe if you watch her gang-raped, it'll help you recall what you want to tell me."

The booming laugh echoed down the pit, and Bishop's stomach turned again. He scanned the hole. Its base was circular, about the size of half a tennis court. The sides ran at least fifty feet straight up. Several indentions in the wall caught his eye. He could use them to climb up to the old roots that stuck out near the top. But he'd have to get out of this cage first. The smell of Samuel's decomposing body wasn't the only offensive odor. There was another lingering scent—something animal-like and feral.

Bishop moved his head back into the corner of the and gazed up at the top of the cage. Running his hand through the bars, he felt the top. His fingers traced the outline of a motor that could raise or lower the door. How could he get it open?

A mechanical clicking sound echoed nearby. It came from behind a small wooden door dug into the wall of the pit. The wooden door in the side of the pit had snapped ajar a couple of inches. Bishop twisted his feet toward the cage door and gave it a hard kick—nothing. Okay, what could he try next?

A wild, guttural sound drifted from behind the weather-beaten wooden door in the pit's wall. Bishop stared at it a moment before another low, deep, animal growl made his skin prickle and his neck hairs rise. He held his breath and waited for the door to open fully.

————

Maxwell got out of his car in the Pentagon's parking lot and glanced at the sky. The day held no promise for sunshine. The heavy clouds rolled overhead, and the smell of rain hung heavy in the air. He strolled through the lot toward the back entrance. Unlike most other government offices, no one looked forward to Fridays here. Fridays at four o'clock were the time things started to unravel. You would think because it was the Muslim holy day, it would be quieter. From Maxwell's experience, nothing could be further from the truth. Fridays were the days bombs exploded, assassinations were carried out, and intelligence estimates got revised. He passed the checkpoint and took the elevator down. Opening the office door, he noticed Cook's secretary, Mrs. Sweeney, wasn't at the reception desk. He went to his office and logged onto his computer. When he opened his email, the first one was from Cook—the time showed 3:18 this morning. It said, "See me when you come in."

3:18! How long had Cook stayed last night? Maxwell strolled back to the reception area just as Mrs. Sweeney walked in. She carried a to-go cardboard tray with three large coffees.

"Good morning, Colonel."

"Good morning."

She busied herself unloading the coffees on her desk. "Silly me— broke the coffee pot this morning. Had to go to the cafeteria for these, here." She handed him two. Would you take the general his, please?"

"Sure."

Maxwell knocked before opening the door. Cook sat behind his desk, rocked back in the leather executive chair. He raised his head, opening weary eyes, as Maxwell entered.

"General, did you go home?"

Cook sat up and wiped his face with both hands. His eyes were bloodshot and shoulders slumped.

"No, didn't make it."

Maxwell sat the coffee on Cook's desk. Last night, he and the general watched in fascination at the infrared image of Bishop working his way along the base of the mountain. When the image disappeared from the satellite's view, they waited. After an hour with no action, Cook had sent Maxwell home.

"What happened last night?" Maxwell asked, taking a seat.

The general looked like hell. His hair was a mess, uniform disheveled, and the stubble gave the appearance of someone a little down on their luck.

Cook ignored the coffee and swung his chair back to the computer, then typed in a command. The screen came alive. Another command produced a black background. "This is a recording of what happened earlier this morning." Cook glanced at Maxwell. "See what you make of it."

Maxwell leaned on the desk and studied the screen over Cook's shoulder. Bright lights appeared from nowhere at the base of the mountain, and Bishop's infrared heat signature began moving. "Is that the same area Bishop disappeared into last night?"

Cook nodded. "There must be some kind of tunnel leading into the mountain big enough to hide a vehicle."

"Any idea where he is?" Maxwell feared asking the question—afraid of the answer.

The general continued staring at the computer screen, his voice only a whisper, "No."

"Did he send the alert?"

Cook took a deep breath and exhaled. "No."

Maxwell pushed the coffee cup closer to him, but Cook had already started typing again and didn't notice.

"Watch this," Cook said.

The black screen focused on the heat signature of Bishop being driven away from the mountain. It stopped, and both the passenger and driver exited. They went to the rear of the vehicle and drug the motionless figure of Bishop from the back. It fell to the ground.

The two standing figures dragged Bishop to an area beside the truck. They pushed and shoved him into a small space, and the image faded slightly. The two got back into the vehicle and left.

"You think that's Bishop?" Maxwell asked, pointing at the motionless figure.

The general's hollow-eyed expression answered before his words. "Got to be."

"What do we do?"

Cook reached for the coffee and yawned. "I'm not notifying Fuller until we have a confirmation. I want you to go out there."

"To New Mexico?"

"That's right, on the next available flight."

"If that's what you want, sir, but I got the impression Mr. Fuller only wanted Bishop introduced into the operational area."

The general half grinned and took a cautious sip of the steaming brew. "I don't need reminding of the operational guidelines, Colonel."

Maxwell stiffened at the rebuke. "Yes, sir."

Cook glanced back to the motionless figure on the computer screen and grimaced as his brow folded. He turned to Maxwell and asked, "How much is a human asset worth?"

Maxwell shrugged. "Depends on the asset."

Cook slowly nodded and allowed his eyes to drift back to the still image on the screen. "There are less than a dozen men in the world that can do what Bishop can. I don't mean to imply he's better than the hundreds of other men with similar backgrounds, but he's the total package. Kill with stealth; infiltrate an impossible tactical objective, and enough WMD training to teach on a college level. What's someone like that worth?"

From the expression on Cook's face, Maxwell didn't bother answering Cook's rhetorical question.

Cook gazed to some distant point on the opposite wall, and his voice dropped low as he recounted the incident. "Just after we invaded Afghanistan, I got my promotion from Captain to Major. I was hurriedly deployed to theater with my intel group about when the Northern Alliance started their move south. Our orders were to support their intelligence needs.

I'd just transferred out of Special Ops and was anxious to show what a gung ho intel commander I could be." The general shifted and sipped the coffee again before grinning. "Perhaps a little too gung ho." His embarrassed eyes caught Maxwell's. "I decided we needed a closer look at a Taliban troop concentration. I took my executive officer, and we commandeered a helicopter to run us up to the front."

"Didn't take long—we were there before we knew it. We came over a low ridgeline when an explosion near the tail of the chopper made it buck and lose power. Somebody had nailed us. The bird started to lose altitude."

Cook's lips were tight lines as he nodded. "I'll give the pilot credit —he was good. Found a flat piece of earth and nursed that crippled thing to the ground, even managed to land right side up on the road. Rattled us, but everyone walked away—just one problem. A dust cloud appeared on the horizon. We'd found the vanguard of the enemy we'd been looking for—they were headed straight for us."

Cook leaned on the desk with his elbows and held Maxwell's stare. "There were four of us in a disabled, unarmed chopper, and probably"—he shrugged—"three hundred bad guys with heavy weapons moving fast our way. No time to call in an airstrike."

Maxwell frowned, and the thought went through his head, *how did he get out of that one?*

The general continued. "The co-pilot sent out a mayday and squawked on all the emergency frequencies. An AWACS picked up our last position and radioed it in, but there wouldn't be any immediate rescue. No one close enough to the operational area with rescue capabilities." Cook smiled once more and glanced at the screen. "Until a radio transmission from an unknown chopper said it was coming in hot and low. I'm not even sure the AWACS knew where it came from. The voice over the radio told us to be ready for extraction in less than two minutes."

Maxwell sat spellbound by the story. He leaned forward like a kid about to hear a special secret.

"Sure enough, the bird swung over a hill to the east and dropped to within twenty-five feet of the ground, running full throttle. It bristled with weapons. The side gunner peppered the approaching enemy vehicles with a mini-gun and chewed up the lead truck. That caused them to stop and break for cover. The chopper skidded up to us, and we jumped in. It swung around and fired a couple of Hellfire missiles at the enemy column just to make its point, then blew out of there as if the devil had it by the ass." The general lounged back in the chair and interlaced his fingers across his chest as he stared at Maxwell. "That, Colonel, was my introduction to the men of Delta. I found out later that the Delta guys had no instructions to pick us up. They were returning from a highly classified mission and were required to observe radio silence. Their commander, Captain Troy Bishop, elected to disregard his orders."

Cook stood and faced Maxwell. "And that's why you're late for your flight to New Mexico. Sometimes orders have to be ignored. The trick is to know which ones you can get away with." He winked, and a smile returned. "Locate the woman named Cora. Find out what she knows and if she has any way to contact Bishop. Your orders are to bring him home."

———

Bishop tensed as the old wooden door in the side of the dirt pit eased open, and the cougar slunk out. It was big—at least 150 pounds. It kept its eyes on him and circled the cage near the pit's wall. Another sound alerted Bishop, and the second one eased out, eyeing Bishop like a cat does a mouse. It was smaller and younger—*Sampson and Sheba*. Sheba didn't move far from the door. She dropped to the mud floor and casually began grooming herself. Bishop redirected his attention to Sampson. The big cat hissed, baring its teeth, and a haunting look showed in the yellow eyes.

The look wasn't typical. It was the look of a disturbed, abused animal. The white scars on its back and sides bore witness to past cruelties—no doubt another victim of Ochoa's sick mind. Bishop turned in the cage and glanced over his shoulder. Sheba couldn't care less. She licked her paw and wiped her face over and over. Sampson was mad as hell and wanted to get at Bishop. The big cat circled, hissing every so often. He looked for an opening to attack, and Bishop turned in the confined space of the cage, not ever exposing his back to the monster. Finally, Sampson charged. He threw himself at the cage and reached in as far as possible with the bared claws.

Bishop scooted back, and only his right knee felt the sting of the claw. Sampson hissed and circled again, keeping Bishop moving around to meet his front. Sampson jumped and tried another long reach inside the cage. Bishop got lucky this time. He moved to the side as the paw reached inside and avoided the strike. He looked over his shoulder again, and Sheba licked her pelt and continuing grooming—never moving from the spot she first laid down. Sampson would be the problem. Sheba was only the companion cat.

Sampson stopped circling and hissed again—keeping Bishop's full attention focused on him. That's when Sheba struck. Bishop never heard her approach—he felt it. The paw with razor-sharp claws reached over his right shoulder and clamped down, trapping him in place. The other claw reached through the cage just as he twisted and felt his skin tear under the cat's grip. Sampson attacked from the opposite side, striking Bishop's arm with a hard blow. Blood flowed from Bishop's shoulder, knee, and arm. He was surrounded and finally realized the genius behind the cage's construction. *You could not defend yourself.* The cats had long since figured this out from years of experience. One distracted, while the other attacked.

Bishop's breath came in short, quick gasps. He tried watching both cats on each side but quickly understood the futility. Bishop's blood coated the bottom of the cage, and the claws' sting caused him to shiver with pain. Sheba now showed the same disturbed look as Sampson. The earlier behavior had been an act to lull him into a false sense of security. Only the cage kept the cats from killing him outright, but how long could he survive with them taking their shots when they chose?

Both cats sat on opposite sides of the cage and hissed. Which one to turn his back on? As he rotated around the slippery, blood-soaked cage, they always stayed at his six and twelve o'clock. How long would he be able to play their game?

Just then, they attacked at the same time. Their combined reach through the bars proved effective. The skin tore on Bishop's back and arm. He kicked hard, trapping Sheba's paw. She screamed, withdrew it, and limped to the wall—eyes blazing with hate. She readied herself for another attack. Bishop looked behind him at Sampson. He, too, prepared to lunge—feet planted; teeth bared. Bishop swallowed the lump in his throat. This was probably going to hurt.

NINETEEN

Monk Cole unscrewed the cap from the small, one-ounce bottle of diluted, dark liquid and threw it down his throat. Screwing the lid back, he slipped the bottle into his pocket and knocked on the office door.

Just like all employees of Sandia National Laboratory were required to take a random drug test in the event of a suspected unauthorized release of information, some were required to take a special polygraph test. Monk had taken and passed polygraph tests before. They were a fixture around areas where top secret/SCI information was shared. McFadden had trained his guys who held the most sensitive jobs on ways to beat the test. Monk had successfully used those tactics in the past. But today was different. He was nervous so close to *H hour*, and the polygraph would pick up that nervousness.

The FBI man welcomed Monk into the polygraph room with a smile. Agent Scott Mobley shook hands and offered Monk a seat in "the chair." That was the term Sandia scientists referred to when talking about the FBI polygraph. With the five-year top-secret security clearance update, the exam remained the best tool for flushing out foreign intelligence officers and nuclear espionage. Over the years, Monk Cole had almost gotten used to defeating the test.

The FBI maintains satellite offices inside each national laboratory to conduct personnel security investigations. Agents administer the Sandia and Los Alamos polygraphs from the Albuquerque FBI Division.

Monk smiled and nodded at the man. This wasn't the first time he had tested him.

Mobley asked, "How are you doing, Dr. Cole?"

"Okay, I guess."

The agent took a seat and typed something into the laptop connected to the polygraph. Cole knew the drill. Soon he would get to the questions. There were usually only four or five, all having to do with non-authorized disclosure of classified material. The FBI referred to this part as the pre-test. When the actual test started, Cole would be required to answer yes or no when hooked up to the polygraph. The pre-test allowed him to explain something which might appear suspicious or unusual before the actual test began.

Mobley looked at him with a concerned gaze. "You feeling okay, Doc?"

Cole slumped in the chair; his eyes were slits, and his stomach bubbled with the sensation of sickness. "I'm having some stomach problems this morning."

The FBI man frowned. "You know the rules, Doc. Think we should reschedule, or do you feel like going through with it today?"

This is my chance. I must appear willing to take the test. He crossed his legs and interlaced his fingers in his lap. "I'm busy and don't want to reschedule—let's just get this over with."

"All right, if you're sure, we'll start with the pre-test." Mobley consulted his notes and looked up as Cole retched a long stream of vomit on the floor.

"What the…?" The agent grabbed a small metal garbage can and pushed it in front of Cole in time to catch the next stream.

Cole gagged and held his head with both hands, leaning over the can. His shoulders heaved, and another round of vomit sprayed into the can and surrounding floor. Mobley stood over him and handed him his handkerchief. Cole wiped his mouth, cleared his throat, and spit.

"You okay?" the FBI man steadied him with his hands on both shoulders. The concern in his voice genuine.

Cole took a couple of deep breaths and nodded. "I think so."

The agent skipped over the vomit on the floor and sat behind his desk. "I'm sorry, but you know I can't test you in this condition—we'll have to reschedule."

Cole steadied himself and showed what he hoped was a disappointed look. "Sorry for the mess—must be stomach flu."

"Don't worry about it. We can get together sometime in the next week or two. Go home and get some rest."

Cole struggled to his feet and wobbled to the door. "I'll see you later." The sliver of a smile showed as he left the office. He fingered the empty bottle of diluted Ipecac syrup in his pocket. By diluting it, he delayed the effects for a couple of minutes. This little performance gave him the excuse he needed to get out of the lab early and have the weekend off. Checking his watch, Cole saw he had two hours until he met McFadden.

———

McFadden stuffed the shaving kit into the small carry-on before zipping it closed. Newman Smith stood at the bedroom door, leaning against the frame. "What time will you meet up with Monk?"

"A little after one o'clock." McFadden looked at his watch. "You all clear on what to do?"

Smith shifted to the other side of the frame. "Lock the place down and coordinate your arrival in DC with Piedmont."

McFadden took the Walther .380 from the nightstand and dropped it into his pants pocket. "Right, keep us informed about anything you learn from Bishop. He's connected with the government—I know it. I don't think he could have contacted anyone, or else the FBI would be crashing through the front gate by now. I'm having Piedmont look into it from his end."

Smith stood erect. "I'll have Ochoa work him over after Sampson and Sheba get his attention. If he has anything, we'll get it."

McFadden looked up. "Bishop just being here means someone

somewhere suspects something. Be ready for anything on this end." He swung the bag off the bed and stood in front of Smith. "Have a couple of the boys fetch Cora. Bishop might be more likely to talk if he watched Ochoa worked on her."

"Okay, I'll take care of it."

McFadden's eyes widened. "Newman, this is the day we've been waiting for. We're going to take back our country from the assholes who've subverted the Constitution." He put his hand on Smith's shoulder and gave him a little shake. "Don't let me down on this end."

"Don't worry, we'll do our part."

McFadden grinned. "I know you will. Let's have lunch before I have to go."

————

Minerva remained silent as the two men left. Hidden in the closet, she'd been afraid of discovery. What would he have done if he'd found her? She let out a breath and gazed into the empty room. Tears formed in her eyes and a lump formed in her throat at the thought of Ochoa questioning Bishop and Cora. She might have the power to stop it, but that would put her in terrible jeopardy. She didn't know if she could afford to cross Clark, even if he was gone.

————

Carpenter stared at his computer in the Albuquerque FBI office. He didn't feel like working and considered just skipping out and not coming back. But that wasn't what the Special Agent in Charge told him to do. The SAC had listened to his story a few hours ago and examined the list of names. The boss didn't give much away. After their meeting, Carpenter couldn't decide whether the old man believed him or not. Since the FBI SWAT team hadn't arrested him yet, he took this as a good sign.

The SAC instructed him to return to work, say nothing about this to anyone, and stand by until he could look into it. Carpenter wanted to jump out of his skin. He couldn't sit still and had no appetite. His phone rang three times before he bothered picking it up. The caller ID showed a 202 area code—headquarters wanted something.

"This is Carpenter."

A chipper voice followed. "Hi, Daniel Piedmont, Domestic Terrorism Division. You have time to talk for a minute?"

Carpenter's jaw dropped; Daniel Piedmont was one of the FBI names on the list. Carpenter gripped the phone tighter. "Sure, what do you need?"

"I'm the new supervisor heading up the *EMPTY QUIVER* investigation from headquarters, trying to catch up on what's happened," Piedmont said. "Any new developments on your end?"

EMPTY QUIVER was the case title the FBI had assigned to the case. It was a US military euphemistic term that indicated the loss, theft, or seizure of a nuclear weapon. This stuff should only be discussed over a secure line. Before Carpenter could object to talking about it, Piedmont got down to business. "I've been looking over a report that mentions you meeting with someone from military intelligence named Bishop."

Carpenter's stomach flipped, and he lowered his voice while covering the phone with his hand. "Oh, that guy. Yeah, some kind of nut, I expect." Carpenter tried sounding natural, but his anxiety was off the chart.

Piedmont didn't answer at first but then asked, "So, what did you guys do with him? Have you been working together on some lead?"

Carpenter swallowed hard and forced a convincing laugh. "No, we're too busy to fool with the likes of him. He went off on some tangent and said he'd call if he turned up anything."

Another pause on the other end. Did Piedmont believe the lie?

"So have you heard back from him?"

Carpenter unclenched his fist and exhaled. "No, not a word."

"Okay, just wanted to clear this up. Don't have anything else, thanks."

"Sure, anytime." Carpenter dropped the phone back into its cradle and pushed back from the desk. Strangely, he was more relaxed and confident. If Bishop called tonight, everything would be perfect. But what if he didn't?

———

Bishop braced himself against the cage, waiting for the next attacks. The big cats had him surrounded, and his strength would give out soon. No food, water, or sleep, plus the exhaustion of fighting off the deadly pair, would make him easy prey to Ochoa's interrogation.

Laughter drifted down the deep pit. Both cats looked up, and their eyes showed fear. They bolted for the cover of the hole in the side of the pit, and Bishop strained his neck to look up. Ochoa looked over the edge. Bishop readied himself for the torture and interrogation to come. How long could he hold out? There was silence from above, but nothing else happened. He sat in the cage another hour—still nothing.

Sampson and Sheba again slinked out of the hole in the pit's wall, keeping their wary gaze fixed to the rim of the crater. Sampson circled the cage a couple of times and dropped to the ground, watching Bishop with those frightening yellow eyes. The cats always kept him between them. As if to emphasize the point, Sheba strolled to the body of Samuel and began to feed off him. Bishop turned his head in disgust. Long shadows began drifting over the hole. Evening was approaching, and Ochoa would be back soon for his fun.

Bishop waited another hour or so before the cage moved, and the hum of a motor from above drifted into the pit. As it slowly rose from the dirt floor, Bishop understood what he had to do. Before Ochoa could get any information out of him, he had to either kill the man or force Ochoa to kill him.

Bishop looked up to the pit's rim as the cage slowly rose. He couldn't see anything. The last few feet before cresting the top of the hole, Bishop put on his war face. He intended to kill the bastard or die trying.

———

Cora rubbed her eyes with her index finger and thumb. She'd been looking through the telescope all day, hoping to catch a glimpse of Bishop. She found the blind he'd built the day before on the flat area above McFadden's house, but there had been no movement. Was he still in there? She took a swallow of water and ate a few crackers before going back to the telescope. Bishop told her he expected to be back tonight. She hung on to that promise, knowing to think otherwise would drive her insane.

————

General Cook checked his email one last time before logging off. Bishop's IR signature disappeared from satellite view at 4:03 AM Mountain Time. There had been no further indication he was still alive. Cook needed rest—the exhaustion had begun clouding his mind and thoughts. He'd leave things in the hands of the duty officer and be back in early tomorrow. Working on Saturdays made his wife crazy, but often it couldn't be helped. He stood and stretched, grabbed his jacket off the rack, then turned for the door. As his hand touched the handle, the secure phone rang. He swung back and answered it.

The short, clipped voice of Fuller said, "Hello, General."

"Good afternoon, sir."

"How goes the investigation?"

Cook wiped his face with his free hand before answering. "Everything's fine—still waiting," he lied. He had no intention of telling Fuller about his suspicions until Maxwell confirmed if Bishop was still alive.

"I wonder if you could drop by my office tomorrow morning, say, ten o'clock?"

Fuller's voice had that sound Cook didn't like. It oozed with the implication, *I know something you don't.*

"Certainly, be glad to. Mind telling me what it's about?"

Fuller cleared his throat. "We'll be meeting with the director of the FBI. We'll need to explain how his agency's been infiltrated and compromised."

Cook grimaced. Yup, better get a good night's sleep.

————

As the cage rose past the rim of the pit, Minerva's panicked expression showed she had no idea how the remote control worked. Her frantic eyes scanned the remote's buttons as she gnawed her lower lip. The cage stopped with a jerk. She pushed another button, and the cage swung to the right over solid ground. She looked up and smiled before pressing another button; it began to rise once more. More panic swept her expression, and she pushed another button. The cage stopped moving.

"The other button," Bishop shouted.

The cage slowly moved down and came to rest on terra firma. She rushed to him—a look of horror at his bloodied condition. "What has he done to you?"

"Hand me the remote," Bishop whispered, reaching his bloody hand through the bars. She passed it to him, and he sat back in the cage with a sigh. Studying the thing for a moment, he pushed a button, and the cage door slowly rose. Once it locked in place, he rolled onto the ground and released a long breath. Bishop lay on his back for a few seconds and stared at her. She leaned over him and stroked his hair.

"I couldn't let them hurt you anymore, Troy."

He took her hand and squeezed it. "Thanks."

Looking up for the first time outside the cage and pit, he couldn't believe what he saw. The whole skyline was blocked with a gigantic, camouflage net. The thing had to be half as big as a football field. It covered the pit and small log cabin near it, which backed up to the woods. It hung thirty to forty feet above ground level, attached to the lowest limbs of the ancient pine trees. The shading gave the area a tranquil appearance.

He slid the remote into his pocket. Rising, he winced from the pain of the cougar attacks. His eyes met hers. "Where's your husband?"

"Don't worry, he's gone—won't be back for days."

"Where did he go?"

Minerva shrugged. "Don't know, but I heard Newman Smith saying something about Washington—maybe there."

Bishop held out his hand. "Let me use your cell phone."

"Clark took it."

Bishop looked at the small cabin. "Is there a phone in there?"

"That's Ochoa's place—I don't know, doubt it."

He struggled to his feet, and his legs were stiff and weak from his cramped confinement. His shirt and pants were a shredded, bloody mess. Weakness set in as he rested a hand on her shoulder.

She embraced him, trying to take his whole weight. "Oh, Troy, take me with you. Don't leave me here with Clark."

He pushed her to arm's length. "Why do you want to leave?"

Her eyes shifted from side to side in a confused gaze. "Because Clark said he'd have to put me away. Some place people could take care of me." She began to sob and dropped her head on Bishop's shoulder. "Don't let him do that."

Bishop held her. McFadden might have even worse plans for her after the attack on Washington—she would probably disappear like the others. "Okay, you can go with me, but how do we get out of here?"

She looked up and wiped her eyes. "I don't know. Newman closed the ranch after Clark left. The patrols have been tripled, front gate's barricaded, and all phone and internet service cut."

"How did you get here?"

She turned and pointed at a saddled horse tied to a tree. Bishop thought for a second. Getting himself out would be difficult. Taking her with him—impossible. "Okay, go back to your house and meet me behind the cattle pens after dark. I'll have something figured out by then. And whatever you do, don't let anyone see you tonight around the pens."

She nodded and smiled, wiping her face again. "I'll be ready."

She jumped on the horse and rode away. Bishop had to find a working phone or some way to contact Cook. No way could he afford to fall into their hands again. Looking around the area, a sense of foreboding swept over him. A human-size cross stood near the small cabin. Leather straps were bolted to it, and fresh blood covered the ground beneath. Bishop's thoughts raced back to Samuel and the screams he'd heard the night before. He studied the cabin, and something inside him said, *stay clear*. He couldn't explain it, but he knew evil dwelled there.

The door opened to his touch, and the dark, gloomy interior made his skin crawl. The place had a stench, smelled like a combination of spoiled food, human waste, and body odor. Bishop knew he needed a weapon before anything else. Strolling around the cluttered room, his eye fell on the kitchen table. Under a pile of wadded-up paper, he spied the handgrip of a pistol. He slid the Sig Sauer .357 from the pile of trash and checked it. It was the one taken from him while he was unconscious. Thirteen rounds in the magazine and one in the chamber —just the way he liked it. He stuck it into his back waistband.

The place looked like a garbage dump. Empty candy and chip wrappers, soda cans, and popcorn bags littered the floor. No one had cleaned it for months. A two-foot stack of comic books tilted against one wall, and an empty mayonnaise jar on the floor almost tripped him as he made his way through the dark living area. When Bishop's eyes finally adjusted to the low light, he noticed the skulls—there were dozens of them. They lined the wall just below the ceiling on long shelves. He recognized some, but they were from so many different animals he couldn't begin to guess. Each had a decoration. A feather stuck into an eye socket, horns and teeth painted different colors, pieces of colored paper glued to the bone. Everything from mouse to cow hung from the wall. The last few skulls were human, their death grins watching his every move.

Bishop crept into the bedroom and flipped on the light switch. The oversized four-poster bed sat against the far wall. More trash covered every square inch of the nasty floor. Dirty underwear, mud-clad pants, and shoes were scattered everywhere—the room of a teenager who never grew up. A very dangerous teenager. The outline of Ochoa's large frame dented the bare mattress, and the smell of urine permeated the place. The nightstand beside the bed told the story of his sickness. Two stacks of old Polaroid pictures lay side by side. Bishop scanned the first group. Women—some young, some middle-aged, all stripped naked and beaten, waiting to be raped and murdered—hung from the cross outside. Terror in their eyes, some were hysterically weeping and begging for mercy. But there would be no mercy for them.

Bishop thumbed through the second stack—the men. Again, secured to the outside cross and mutilated, their lifeless bodies hung limp. McFadden had to know and approve of everything that had gone on here. The victims in these photos now lay at the bottom of the pit, their remains guarded by Sampson and Sheba.

Bishop dropped the pictures in his pocket. If he managed to get out, perhaps the next of kin could at least be notified. Bishop had seen a case of bottled water in the kitchen, so he headed back there. Three bottles later, his thirst quenched, he drifted into the bathroom.

The place had a fetid odor. How could a human live in such conditions? Piles of musty and moldy wet towels lined the floor. The sink was filthy with dirt and traces of what looked like blood. The leaky faucet dripped a constant beat. Bishop found a halfway clean face cloth folded on a shelf and soaked it in hydrogen peroxide he discovered in the medicine cabinet. He cleaned the wounds the best he could, but they were already infected. He needed a good injection of antibiotics but settled for two azithromycin capsules he also found in the medicine cabinet. The box showed they had expired almost three months ago, but they were better than nothing.

What to eat? In the kitchen, he found a can of peaches and downed them in a few minutes. A plate of fried chicken covered in foil sat in the refrigerator. Bishop hesitated but figured the cooks must have prepared it at the communal kitchen, so he stole a breast and leg. It would be dark soon, and Ochoa probably couldn't wait to start his interrogation. When he came back, what should Bishop do? Kill the monster? Would the shot alert other ranch hands to investigate? Bishop needed to know if Ochoa had a cell phone. His might just work —Cook must be notified. As if on cue, the sound of a four-wheeler broke the silence. Bishop looked out the window at Ochoa, staring at the empty cage.

He bolted for the house just as Bishop slipped behind a stack of cardboard boxes in the corner of the living room. When the door burst open, Bishop held his breath. He had the pistol pointed at the ogre's head and had every tactical advantage. Ochoa stopped at the threshold and switched on the overhead light. The small, mean eyes scanned the room, and he cocked his head up and sniffed the stale air. Did he smell something different? Bishop's thoughts turned to the bedtime story of *Jack and the Beanstalk*. 'Fee-fi-fo-fum, I smell the blood of an Englishman.'

Bishop grinned; yeah, except this time, *Jack has a .357*. Ochoa strolled to the bedroom, stayed a few seconds, and walked back to the living area. He took one last look around before walking out and closing the door. From where Bishop crouched, he couldn't tell if the guy had a cell phone or not. Bishop couldn't allow him to report back that he'd escaped. He crept to the window with the intent of shooting him, but Ochoa was nowhere in sight. Bishop watched for another minute or two, but there was no movement outside around the pit. The sun had set, and with the overhead netting, dark shadows played over the ground in bizarre outlines as a slight breeze blew through the net above. The place had an eerie, haunted appearance.

Bishop cracked the door open and listened. He didn't like what he heard—nothing. Where had the guy gone? What could he be doing? *Hell, I should have shot him while he was inside.* Now Bishop had lost his tactical advantage and had to play Ochoa's game. To stay in and wait or go out and find him became the question. Bishop couldn't take the chance—he had to go. If he didn't make contact with General Cook soon, the Capitol would be nothing but a heap of ashes. Bishop eased the door open and did a quick peek to the right and left. It looked all clear, so he slipped out. He moved in a crouched position down the right side of the cabin. Had to make sure not to get ambushed from behind. Swinging around the side wall, he had his pistol ready, but no sign of Ochoa. Bishop crept back down the left side and checked—nothing.

In the time it took Bishop to move from his hiding place inside to the window, the giant had vanished. Bishop couldn't let him go. If he hoped to make good his escape, he needed to keep it secret. He carefully approached the rear of the house and started down the back. His eyes caught the form of something on the ground in his path. He carefully approached the object and studied it. Under the pine straw and leaves lay a bear trap, sharp teeth locked open, ready to spring. Bishop looked over his shoulder and began backing up. There was absolutely nothing about this situation that was in his favor. He needed to backtrack and find a better location to wait Ochoa out. To continue playing the killer's game was madness. When Bishop reached the corner, a voice from behind said, "Drop it."

It wasn't hurried or threatening but firm. "Drop it, I said, and put your hands up."

Bishop's heart sank as he dropped the gun and turned around, arms high. From the shadows of the woods strolled Ochoa, wearing a ghillie suit and carrying a sawed-off 12-gauge shotgun. Bishop had been outmaneuvered. The guy was invisible in the sniper gear and gloom of the trees and overhead net. Ochoa pulled the netting away from his face, and a smile showed on his lips. He motioned for Bishop to walk back to the front of the cabin. When they got near the door, the hard strike from the gun's metal barrels crashing against the back of Bishop's skull caused flashes of bright light to streak across his vision. Bishop dropped to his knees from the impact.

"Now, stay right where you are," Ochoa said.

Ochoa grunted, and sounds of him removing the bulky camo outfit floated through the air. This gave Bishop a chance to clear his head. When Ochoa finished, the sound of him releasing both the shotgun hammers caused Bishop to turn around. Another smile outlined the ugly face as Ochoa unloaded the gun. He opened the Cabin's front door and tossed the gun and shells on the floor. Closing the door, he locked it. He held up the key before shoving it into his pocket.

"Now, come and get it."

Quick as a flash, Ochoa drew a large hunting knife from a sheath and rushed Bishop. He rolled just as the monster dove and came crashing down where Bishop had been. Bishop's pistol still lay on the ground in the back of the cabin; the problem was getting to it. He'd have to go through Ochoa to get there—no good. Bishop scrambled to his feet and ran for the pit. Ochoa closed the distance much faster than Bishop would have thought. For a big man, he moved with the speed of a cheetah. Bishop was left with a dilemma. Even if he could somehow get a gun, a shot might bring several curious ranch hands. Darkness had set in, and only the outlines of the two men could be seen in the dwindling light. Bishop looked at the killer across the pit from him. He could just make out a toothy smile.

"Have I got to chase you all night?" Ochoa snarled.

Bishop looked down into the pit and then at the giant. This gave him an idea.

"Maybe—how fast can you run?"

Ochoa shifted and moved to his left, and Bishop also moved, still keeping the pit between them. After they had switched sides and Ochoa had his back to the cage, Bishop ran his hand inside his pocket. He pushed a button on the remote. The overhead motor came to life and jerked, moving back toward the pit's opening. The open-mouthed expression from Ochoa as the cage quickly shifted toward him showed it had caught him off guard. As the cage shoved Ochoa closer to the pit, he grabbed the top of it and tried to swing around before it moved over the hole. He wasn't fast enough.

When the cage swung over the cavity in the ground, Ochoa kicked at the sides, trying to regain his footing, but it was too late. Bishop stopped the movement with the push of another button and stepped back. The big man stopped kicking and turned in his direction. Bishop studied the remote for a second, feeling the buttons in the dark.

"This is for Samuel," he said, pressing the button as Ochoa and the cage dropped into the black hole with a crash.

<h1 style="text-align:center">TWENTY</h1>

ishop wasn't out of the woods yet. Taking care of Ochoa didn't get him off the ranch. Walking back to the cabin, he weighed his options. With the place sealed and the patrols tripled, what chance did he have of making it to the main road? If he did manage to slip through the net, he would still be in the middle of nowhere and unable to communicate with Cook. There was only one part of the ranch they wouldn't bother guarding—the steep passage straight up to the top of Gallinas Peak. The water and fried chicken had revived him—he might just make it. Seeing as how he had no choice, it seemed reasonable, but getting back to his hide wasn't going to be easy with the extra patrols.

Bishop kicked the door of the cabin open and grabbed an old pack lying on the floor. He dumped it out and threw in a half dozen bottles of water. He slipped into the Ghillie suit Ochoa had shucked on the ground and buttoned it. It was about two sizes too big.

Bishop needed to buy some time. He knew sooner or later someone would come to check on Ochoa's interrogation. How could he stall them? He trotted to the four-wheeler and found a flashlight in the front basket. Walking to the pit, he shined the light into the dark hole. To Bishop's surprise, Ochoa stood on top of the cage holding on to the cable with one hand and dialing a cell phone with the other—*where did that come from?* Bishop ran back to the four-wheeler and shifted it into neutral. The ten feet to the pit seemed like a mile as he pushed the machine faster toward the edge. It silently toppled into the hole, and a scream sounded from below. Bishop shined the light back into the void. The thing crashed on top of Ochoa, pinning him underneath—he wasn't moving. It had also dislocated the cage door from its up position and slammed it shut. Anyone coming up to the pit would surmise Ochoa must have accidentally ridden off into the hole after dark. They wouldn't be able to tell if the cage was occupied without lifting it.

Bishop really needed that cell phone Ochoa had, but the thought of going back into the hole, searching around in the dark with Sampson and Sheba lurking, wasn't a good one. No, he was wasting time. He took the cage remote from his pocket, crushed it under his boot, and threw the pieces as far as he could into the nearby woods. Bishop retrieved the pistol from the rear of the house and tucked it inside his waistband. Turning back to the trail, he began a slow jog toward his hide-out above McFadden's house. That would be the last place they'd look—that is, until they realized he had escaped.

―――――

Colonel Maxwell pulled up to the small, red house on top of Gallinas Peak and opened the car door. The darkness and outlines of the tall pines lazily swaying in the stiff, cold breeze sent a shiver down his back. *Am I even at the right place?* Maxwell eased open the car door a little farther and listened—nothing but the sound of the wind drifting through the pines. He got out and quietly closed the door as he studied the outline of a window on the small home with light creeping around the edges of the shade.

Maxwell was a little spooked as he kneeled beside the house and gazed into the room. He felt like a dirty voyeur. What little he saw appeared normal enough. A living room with the fireplace burning and a dim lamp sitting on the end table. He stood and strolled to the door but still had a bad feeling all was not as it appeared. His stomach knotted with apprehension when he knocked, rehearsing what he intended to say, but there was no answer to his knock. He'd not expected this. He knocked again, still no response. Tried the doorknob, but it was locked. Taking a knee, he craned his neck against the window once more, searching the interior for movement. Place looked empty. Maxwell walked around the house, stopping at the back door. He tried it—locked tight. Making his way back to the front, he decided what he had to do.

Maxwell went back to the car, rummaged in his bag, and found his lock pick set. He was pretty rusty—it would take time. He had plenty of that. He'd flown out of DC in a storm, arrived in Albuquerque, rented a car, and driven here in total darkness. He'd be damned if he would let a crummy locked door stop him after all that. He'd wait inside for the woman to return and explain everything. Cook wouldn't leave the office until Maxwell reported back.

It took almost ten minutes to get it unlocked—*yeah, I'm rusty all right*. He stuck his head in and called, "Hello—anybody home?" With no answer, he entered and softly closed the door behind him. The place was warm and inviting. He strolled to the fire and rubbed his hands. Where could she be? The bigger question was, when would she be back? Curiosity led him to the kitchen. He opened the refrigerator and glanced inside—he'd missed lunch. He stole a beer and headed back to the living room.

Just as he started to sit down on the couch, from the shadows, a woman's voice said, "If you move, I'll kill you." To confirm that fact, the sound of a big revolver's hammer cocking almost caused Maxwell to pee himself. He froze—half seated, half standing, with a beer in his gun hand. "Shit!" he mumbled.

The young woman moved from the shadows, the large-caliber revolver trained on him. "Who are you, and why are you here?"

Maxwell stood up and raised his hands. "Are you Cora?"

Her head tilted slightly to the side. "Who's asking?"

"My name is Maxwell. I work with Troy Bishop."

She walked to the kitchen table and grabbed a piece of paper off the end. She glanced at it, then said, "Turn around and keep your hands up."

Maxwell complied, feeling like a fool, "I can—"

"Shut up, and don't move. I'd rather just kill you, anyway." Her voice was all business.

Maxwell waited, for what he didn't know. After a moment, his cell phone rang. He still didn't move. The voice behind said, "You'd better answer it."

He slipped the phone from his pocket and said, "Hello," his voice cracking with fear.

"I guess you can put your hands down," the unknown caller repeated a second after the woman behind him said the same thing.

Maxwell turned around, and she held the gun in one hand and her cell in the other. "Troy gave me your number before he left—figured calling it was the best way to confirm if you were the real McCoy."

Maxwell exhaled a long breath, and Cora de-cocked the pistol and laid it on the table.

"You almost scared me to death," he grumbled.

She put her hands on her hips, eying him. "Serves you right for breaking and entering."

"Sorry, I do owe you an apology." He extended his hand.

"You owe me a beer, too," she grinned, shaking his hand, "but I'm glad you're here."

Maxwell stepped back. "Have you heard from Bishop?"

Cora's features darkened. She turned and walked away with her head down. "No, not a word. He told me to call you and some guy named Carpenter if he wasn't back by tonight at ten," she said, again turning around to face him.

Maxwell spun his wrist and checked his watch. "It's 8:44 now. Do you have any way of reaching him?"

"No." Cora walked to the sofa and flopped down. "He left last night." She stared morosely at the fire.

"I'll wait with you if you'll let me," Maxwell said, taking a seat on the opposite end of the sofa.

She hugged herself and nodded. "Thanks."

———

Carpenter sat in his living room with his wife, Jean. She talked about what happened that day with the kids, but he didn't hear a word. All he could think about was the time. Five minutes to ten. Bishop said he'd call by ten if things were okay.

"Are you listening to me?" she asked.

He turned and tried to lie. "Sure." But his expression gave him away.

She crossed her arms and directed her attention back to the television.

———

Bishop guessed his jog at about a ten-minute-mile pace. No part of him didn't ache, sting, or cry out in pain with each step. His energy was almost spent. Climbing to the top of the mountain might only be a fanciful dream he'd never accomplish. In training, he always knew when he was about to hit the wall. That sensation of weakness that coursed through his legs and arms just before he'd collapse. The first signs of it eased through his body as he jogged around the corner of a hill and stared down the endless road.

This part of the ranch backed up to the base of the mountain. No one lived here, and only the sounds of Bishop's boots crunching over the gravel and his breathing broke the absolute silence of the still darkness. Bishop used the lights from McFadden's house in the distance to keep him on track and oriented. Just before rounding another corner, voices sounded up ahead. Bishop stopped and listened. Sounded like two men talking in low tones. The clip clop of horse hooves drummed a constant beat on the dry road. There was no place to hide. Bishop stood in an almost barren stretch of trail. Only an occasional skinny tree or shrub to duck behind. He could have dived into a ditch, but there wasn't even that. He was trapped. The voices became louder, and he knew he had to make a move. Killing the two quickly would be no problem—killing them silently would.

Just before they rounded the corner, Bishop reverted to his basic escape and evasion training—he became the terrain. More specifically, he became a bush. He figured the two hadn't memorized every feature on the ranch, so he squatted beside the road and didn't move. Bishop hardly breathed as the riders approached. If one caught sight of something different or heard an unusual sound, it was all over. Thank God there was no dog this time. Might fool the riders—wouldn't fool a dog. The horsemen rode within five feet of him and never gave him a second look. In the darkness, wearing the Ghillie suit, he looked like he belonged. Just another scrub shrub on the lonely road of the high country.

Once they were out of sight, Bishop began a gradual move up the side of the hill. It would slow his pace, but he wouldn't have to be concerned about meeting any more riders. Before he reached his blind, a shot rang out from somewhere down the mountain. Bishop instantly ducked and froze. Shouts from below and the headlights of several vehicles converged around the cattle pens. *Minerva!*

A group of people milled around the pens, but the shrill voice of a female cursing boomed loudest. Bishop relaxed—she's okay. He scrambled to the blind. After a quick examination, it became apparent McFadden's men hadn't found it. Bishop removed the Ghillie suit, slithered under the tarp, and dug into the bag he'd left. Pulling out the jacket, he slipped it on and ate a granola bar. The trip down the mountain in the dark with night vision equipment had been hard enough. To climb back up with nothing, in his exhausted condition, was probably impossible. He lay back and sipped a bottle of water, working out his route back up. He crawled out of the hide and stared at the looming obstacle before him. Thick, dark clouds moved in, and a cold mist of rain bathed his face. He kicked the Ghillie suit under the blind, took the last sip of water, and turned toward the mountain.

Sometime before dawn, Maxwell noticed Cora was only barely hanging on. Dark half-circles shaded her lower eyes, her head slumped, fighting for all she was worth just to stay awake. He sent her to bed, promising to wake her when he knew something. He didn't want to think about it, but it became apparent Bishop wouldn't be returning. When Cora awoke, he would leave and report his failure back to General Cook. Maxwell re-stoked the fire and continued the vigil for another hour. The weather had changed dramatically. The peaceful, clear night had given way to the rumble of thunder and distant lightning. Cold wind blew in gusts and rattled the tiny house. Sheets of frigid rain slammed sideways, raking the windows and roof. Something woke Maxwell as he dozed on the couch, and he looked at his watch. *6:18.* Better call Cook and tell him the bad news.

"Good morning," she said, walking back into the room, yawning.

Maxwell looked up. "That gust wake you, too?"

Before she could answer, a lightning flash lit up the back patio. Cora screamed at the ghostly figure standing outside the sliding glass door. Maxwell scrambled for his gun just as Bishop pressed his face against the door's glass. Cora rushed to unlock it, and he fell into her waiting arms. She held him without saying a word, a sob crept out of her throat, and she buried her face between his drenched neck and shoulder.

Maxwell rushed to him. "Thank God." Maxwell had seen enough combat, and the sight of dead and injured men did little to affect him, but the sight of Bishop's condition—bleeding, freezing, and soaked with rain—confirmed Cook's earlier statement. *There are very few men like Bishop. The total package.*

Bishop looked up from the embrace. "Call Cook—I found them all in a cave on the ranch. McFadden left with one or more yesterday, heading to Washington."

Maxwell's eyes widened. "I'll make the call—you tell him."

Cora looked from one man to the other. "Found what?"

Bishop must have figured there was little use in keeping secrets from her at this point. "Stolen nuclear weapons," he whispered.

"What?" Her jaw dropped. "Samuel, did you find Samuel?"

Bishop pushed her from him and looked into her eyes. "I'm sorry, he didn't make it."

Cora hung her head and covered her face with her hands. Another sob sounded, followed by an all-out cry.

Maxwell handed the phone to Bishop as Cora helped him into a chair. Five minutes later, after Bishop explained all he knew to Cook, Bishop handed the phone back to Maxwell.

Cora had stopped crying, but the look of terror at listening to Bishop's account of what happened on the ranch, coupled with Samuel's death, appeared to have sent her into shock.

Bishop shook, and his teeth chattered. The cold rain, fatigue, and injuries had taken a severe toll.

"We have to get out of here," Bishop mumbled, his eyes barely open. "They'll come looking for me sooner or later."

Bishop's voice had weakened, and the shaking intensified. Maxwell eyed him, then turned to Cora. "Throw this guy in the shower to warm him up a little, and I'll find him some clean, dry clothes."

Bishop opened his mouth to protest, but Maxwell pointed at him and said, "That's an order. Now, hurry."

Maxwell watched through the open bedroom door as Cora helped Bishop undress. While peeling off his tattered shirt, she said, "What did they do to you?"

Bishop grimaced. "Just a run-in with the local fauna."

After a quick shower, Bishop sat on the bed and, Cora applied Neosporin to the cougar wounds. He'd stopped shaking and had regained some strength from the hot water, but he still looked like hell to Maxwell. As Bishop and Cora walked back into the living room, the sound of car doors slamming outside drew Maxwell to the window. He cracked a blind.

"We've got company!"

Bishop perked up. "How many?"

"Four, and they have plenty of guns."

Bishop slipped on his shirt and reached behind his back, drawing the pistol. "How many coming to the front?"

Maxwell took another look, turned, and faced Bishop. He blanched before saying, "All of them."

"Perfect," Bishop mumbled, opening the back door and walking out.

Maxwell glanced at Cora. "Get behind some cover and take out the first one you can get a shot at as they come in."

Cora had a quizzical gaze. "Where's Bishop going?" she asked while sliding around the corner into the kitchen and grabbing her revolver off the counter.

Maxwell went into the kneeling position and used the corner leading to Cora's bedroom as cover. He braced his pistol hand against the door frame and trained the sights on the front door.

Cora ducked behind the corner leading into the kitchen and pointed the cocked revolver at the door.

Maxwell didn't like this—he was a planning guy. Bishop should have discussed what he intended to do before rushing out. He looked over at Cora, and her fear infected him. His stomach twisted, watching the front doorknob slowly turn one way then the other. Cora glanced his way, and he nodded, trying to reassure her. He leveled the pistol and held his breath just before someone kicked the door open. The big man on the other side stepped in, gun in hand. Maxwell and Cora fired simultaneously—it sounded like one loud cannon blast in the tiny house. The man collapsed, falling backward, and another guy scrambled away from the open door before being hit. Maxwell prepared to fire again but could see no movement. From outside, six quick shots rang out. Cora flinched, and her hands shook, but she cocked the pistol again and waited—keeping her eyes on the open door.

"Don't shoot." Bishop's voice drifted in from outside. He stepped over the body of the man that had fallen in the entryway, kicking the dead guy's pistol lose from his death grip. Bishop eyed them with a cold expression before dropping the half-empty magazine from his pistol and inserting a full one. "Let's get out of here before they send somebody to check on these guys."

They grabbed their jackets and hurried out the front door. Just to the left of the threshold lay a pile of bodies, arms and legs tangled. Each had been shot twice in the head.

Cold wind blew a heavy mist across the top of the mountain. Dark, low clouds and fog hung in puffy layers, still threatening more rain. Maxwell slid behind the steering wheel and Cora beside him. Bishop took the back seat. Maxwell caught a glimpse of Bishop in the rearview mirror. His eyes burned with an intensity that sent a chill through Maxwell.

———

General Cook waited in Fuller's office and accepted the coffee his aide offered. He liked the office—large and airy. It contrasted to his small, stuffy, bunker-type in the Pentagon. But he figured, being a military man, the bunker suited him better.

"He's probably going to go ballistic when you tell him what you've just told me," Fuller quipped, wiping the bottom of his cup with a napkin.

Cook's eyebrows rose. "I thought you would handle the briefing."

Fuller gave the Cheshire cat grin he knew so well. "No, if I do it, it'll sound like we're rubbing salt into the wound—you tell him."

Since Fuller was his boss, Cook had little choice, but he already knew how it would go. He'd start the briefing with the bad news, and Fuller would jump in with the available options and opinions—it never failed.

The phone on the desk buzzed. Fuller answered it and listened for a moment. "Very well, show him in." His gaze shifted to Cook. "He's here."

Seconds later, the office door opened, and Fuller's aid entered, followed by FBI Director William Campbell. Fuller and Cook stood.

"Bill, thanks for coming by. Have you met General Cook?" Fuller asked.

Campbell inspected Cook through suspicious eyes. "No, but I've heard of him."

"Coffee?" Fuller motioned for his aide's attention.

Campbell shook both men's hands and sat. "No, thank you, Mr. Fuller."

Fuller waived the aide out and took his seat. Campbell had been appointed FBI Director three years earlier. Being a federal prosecutor for over twenty years led to a federal judgeship just six years ago. He gave that up to accept the appointment as FBI Director. He carried a small, black, distressed-leather case, which rested on his lap. Campbell looked anxious and shifted in the chair. A brief uncomfortable silence settled in the office. Finally, Campbell unsnapped the clasps on the case and opened it.

"I received this yesterday afternoon from the Special Agent in Charge of our Albuquerque office."

He exhaled and handed Fuller the list Carpenter had acquired days earlier.

"It's disturbing, to say the least," Campbell said. "I'm told one of your men requested one of my agents to compile it."

Fuller slipped on his reading glasses and flipped through the pages. He looked up and handed the list to Cook. "That's correct, Director Campbell. One of General Cook's people had the idea."

Campbell stared at Cook, who continued reviewing the document. Campbell cleared his throat. "There are a significant number of FBI personnel on that list. Are they also suspected of being involved?"

Fuller leaned forward and clasped his hands. "It's beginning to look that way, I'm afraid."

A pained expression creased Campbell's brow. "What proof do we have other than this list?"

Fuller looked at Cook. "General?"

Cook half-turned to face Campbell. "Mr. Director, a few days ago, we made a covert insertion of one of our people into the Clark McFadden Ranch. Earlier this morning, he reported that he'd discovered all the weapons and believes McFadden is en route to Washington with one or more of them. It appears he intends to detonate it near the White House."

Campbell's eyes widened, and he quickly looked at Fuller. "Is this correct?"

Fuller nodded.

Campbell's voice rose. "Exactly when were you going to tell me about this?"

"As the general said," Fuller spoke up, "we just got a confirmation less than two hours ago. I'm having my staff put all the information into a report—you'll have it when you leave. Because of the operational security concerns, we need to discuss how to handle it."

Campbell looked from Cook to Fuller. "We raid the ranch, recover the weapons, and stop the one heading to Washington."

Cook lowered his head slightly and eyed Campbell. "The problem is, we're not sure how they're transporting it or the route they're taking."

Campbell glared at Fuller. "Is the President aware of this?"

"Calm down. Yes, he knows—I spoke to him less than an hour ago. He should be about to board Marine One for an extended weekend at Camp David."

"So, what do you suggest?" Campbell asked.

Cook started to answer, but Fuller cut him off. "We're monitoring anyone coming or going from the ranch by satellite and drone surveillance and attempting to locate McFadden. If we raid the place, someone might tip him off, and he'd go to ground. As long as he believes no one knows, the better our chances are of interdicting him."

Campbell stood, "I'll make sure all the FBI people on the list are kept out of the loop—I'd like a copy of that report now, please."

———

Newman Smith peered out his window at the dreary weather—most unusual for this time of year. He strolled back to the fireplace and warmed himself while finishing his coffee. Why in the hell hadn't Ochoa called? He turned around and stared at the wall clock above the mantle. He redialed Ochoa's cell phone, but it once more went to voice mail. McFadden would check in soon and expect a report on Bishop's interrogation. He'd just have to drive over there himself. Smith hated all interactions with that Neanderthal, Ochoa, but what choice did he have? By the time he got there, the boys should be back with Cora, and he might even have a little fun with her before handing her over to the heathen.

———

Maxwell listened during the drive from Gallinas Peak to Albuquerque as Bishop explained all that happened in detail. Bishop munched leftovers from Cora's refrigerator and drank two Cokes during the story. Poor guy could hardly keep his eyes open, finally drifting off to sleep. He curled up in the back seat and didn't move until the SUV pulled up to the Kirtland Air Force Base gate. Maxwell had called ahead, and they were admitted to the executive reception terminal.

A young Air Force captain met them as they walked in. "Are you Colonel Maxwell?"

"That's correct."

The captain shot a concerned glance at Bishop, whose clothes and hair had not fared well in the back of the car. "We were told to expect your party—this way, please." He led them to a rear officer's lounge, where Carpenter met them. Bishop had called him soon after they'd left Cora's and told him where they were heading.

He ambled over to Bishop, and they shook hands before making introductions.

"I heard our directors had a meeting this morning," Bishop said.

"Yeah, that's what I heard. Looks like I'm still heading up this end of the investigation."

"Thanks for all your help."

Carpenter grinned. "If you hadn't insisted on getting that list, well…"

Bishop must have felt the man's embarrassment because Bishop slapped him on the shoulder. "It's up to the FBI; I'm out of it now and have a plane to catch."

The captain escorted them to the rear of the lounge and through two double glass doors. The high-pitched whining of dual jet engines greeted them as they stepped outside. The sleek, white Gulfstream V sat on the tarmac awaiting their arrival.

Maxwell's head shot up. "How in the devil did Cook arrange this?"

"Your good luck," the captain answered, walking them to the steps. "Several DOE types flew in late last night—it was scheduled to return to Andrews empty today anyway—enjoy your flight, sir."

———

McFadden yawned and stretched, setting his coffee in the truck's cup holder. His body and especially lower back felt the pain from the seven-and-a-half-hour drive in an uncomfortable old truck from his ranch to Oklahoma City yesterday. Monk volunteered to take the first shift driving today. The small convoy of vehicles wove its way east on

I-40 toward Nashville—another 700 miles to DC. Monk looked like he didn't have a care in the world.

"You're chipper today," McFadden said.

A smile traced across Monk's lips. "I feel great."

McFadden's neck was sore because of the cheap motel bed. He massaged it, thinking of how to get some kind of response out of Monk —and he knew just how to do it. "I been thinking, are you positive the feds can't track the device by some satellite or plane while we're driving?"

Monk's serene expression changed to frustration. He didn't answer for a moment, probably considering how to phrase the answer to a question he'd already answered a half dozen times. Finally, he spoke.

"It's like I told you before. They can't track what they can't see. We've disabled the thing's GPS, and the cargo we have packed around the weapon shields the alpha radiation from being detected. The only thing that's detectable is the gamma or neutrons." Monk glanced at him for effect before completing the thought. "But the neutrons and gammas are shielded by the paraffin and borated polyethylene wrap inside the back of the truck."

McFadden grinned and shifted in the seat.

Monk caught sight of the grin and laughed. "Was that a test, or were you just trying to aggravate me?"

McFadden settled back into the seat and winked. "Both." He liked Monk. In fact, Newman and Monk were two of his most trusted people in this whole affair. He'd watched them grow up on the ranch and took a particular interest in both, knowing they had potential far above the others. With talent like this, he couldn't lose. McFadden crossed his arms and pulled the cowboy hat down on his forehead to provide shade from the sun. He readjusted himself for maximum comfort and sighed. "Monk, we're going to put this son of a bitch right on their doorstep, and there's not a damned thing they can do about it."

TWENTY-ONE

Maxwell finished his third coffee of the flight and glanced back at Bishop and Cora. They were curled up together in one of the over-size reclining rear seats. She sat in his lap with her head resting against his chest as he softly snored. The flight steward had draped a light wool blanket over the pair about midflight, and they hadn't moved since. Maxwell ate his lunch between phone calls. General Cook called him a half dozen times, and he'd made at least that many calls of his own. Since the investigation had shifted to the FBI, Cook's last call surprised Maxwell. He listened and a frown formed. "Is he serious?"

"Serious as a heart attack," Cook replied.

Maxwell cleared his throat before making the sarcastic comment. "I'm certain Bishop's going to love that."

Cook only grunted. "Wait until after they've patched him up before telling him."

The pilot announced they were on final, and all passengers should take their seats and buckle up for landing. The steward rousted Cora to her seat and gave her and Bishop a large, fresh cup of coffee.

Bishop sat up and accepted a hot towel from the steward and wiped the sleep from his eyes. From his expression, it was apparent he was in extreme pain from the deep cougar wounds. They touched down at Andrews a little after one o'clock in the afternoon and taxied to a discreet side terminal, used chiefly by members of the intelligence community.

The brilliant sunshine and mild fall temperatures felt good when they exited the aircraft. Two cars and drivers waited for them plane-side, and Maxwell gave a wave of recognition. He directed Cora to have a seat in the first car before motioning for Bishop to join him in the second. Bishop opened the back door, and Trevor Blackwell stuck his head out.

"Back from holiday already?" Trevor asked.

"Some holiday," Bishop grumbled before getting in. As Maxwell took his seat in front, Trevor went to work on Bishop. Trevor was a member of the British military—Special Air Service, to be exact. P2OG and the SAS had an exchange program, and Trevor had been attached to them for five months. His specialty was field medic.

"Heard you had a bit of a scrape—let's have a look," Trevor said, motioning for Bishop to turn around in the seat. "Take off that shirt."

Bishop turned his back, and Trevor carefully assisted him in removing it. He let out a low whistle. "She must have been a wild one. Reminds me of a girl I knew in Hong Kong." Trevor dug in his field medic kit and produced a green plastic bottle. Dabbing from it with sterile gauze, he cleaned the wounds on Bishop's back, chest, and arms, then applied an antibacterial ointment. Trevor used several strips of butterfly surgical tape to close up some of the wider rips. Before Bishop knew it, he had stuck him with a needle.

"A high-octane antibiotic. You have a little infection, but this should knock it out."

Bishop slid his shirt back on and faced him. "Thanks."

"Don't mention it. Here." Trevor held out a white paper bag. "There are antibiotic capsules, ointment, and pain medication. Take as directed." Trevor flashed an embarrassed smile. "There's also a few sleeping aids—you know, for the lady." He smiled again. "Happy to see you back in mostly one piece." Trevor turned to Maxwell and nodded. "That should do it, sir."

"Thanks," Maxwell said.

Trevor got out, and Maxwell eyed Bishop for a moment before speaking.

"Cook wants you to get some rest right now, but he has something else for you tomorrow." There was surprise in Bishop's eyes, and Maxwell continued before he could be interrupted. "It seems Fuller doesn't want to let this go. He thinks since we've carried the water on it so far, it wouldn't be right to let the FBI finish the job without our help." A thin grin crossed Maxwell's lips.

Bishop sat back and sighed. "What does he need me to do?"

Maxwell shifted in the seat. "We're deploying all personnel to assist in intercepting McFadden. Since you and Cora can personally identify the guy, we're putting you in a command center outside of Washington. If we encounter a disguised suspect, they can flash a photo to you for a confirmed identification."

From Bishop's demeanor, it was clear he wasn't happy. Maxwell didn't blame him. Had no reason to be. He'd given so much already, and now being asked to give even more seemed worse than unfair. But Fuller wanted to capture as much credit as he could, and Bishop was the guy in the middle.

Bishop only gave a slow nod. "Okay, but I don't want Cora put in harm's way—she's already been through enough."

"Understood. She'll be with you, and you'll be in a fortified, secure location well away from the Capitol. If, by some chance, he gets past us, you two will at least be out of the blast zone."

"And you?" Bishop asked.

Maxwell shrugged. "Cook requested I take command of the off-site —he'll stay at the Pentagon." He handed Bishop a slip of paper. "Be at this location by nine o'clock tomorrow morning."

Bishop stared at the note. "How do we know he's not already in Washington?"

Maxwell's forehead wrinkled. In a shaky voice, he said, "We don't."

———

Newman Smith looked into the pit at the lifeless body of Ochoa. Sheba and Sampson tore away at his thigh and leg, feasting on their former tormentor. Smith walked around the area and looked for evidence of what might have happened. It seemed clear the fool had accidentally ridden the four-wheeler into the pit, but something about the scene troubled Smith. He went back to the hole and called Bishop's name— only silence. He couldn't tell if he was still in the cage. The door remained closed, so he must be there. The angle of the pit made it impossible to know if the cage contained a body—living or dead.

"Bishop!" Newman called again. No answer. He looked for the remote control to raise the cage, It wasn't anywhere in sight. "Bishop!" he called again louder. Only silence. Newman dialed his cell. "Ochoa's dead. Get someone over here and help me get the cage out of this damned pit." Before hanging up, he had a second thought. "Also, find out what's taking the guys so long at Cora's—I want them back here, now."

McFadden studied the map and talked on his cell. "Yeah, we're making good time. Should be in Nashville this evening. Is everything all set?"

"Everything's ready—I'll meet you at the warehouse," Daniel Piedmont assured him.

"You hear anything from your sources?" When Piedmont didn't immediately answer, McFadden repeated the question.

"I was transferred off the case," Piedmont said.

"What?" McFadden laid the map in the seat and sat up straight.

"I can't talk about it right now—don't exactly know what's going on, but it couldn't come at a worse time."

"I understand." McFadden glanced at Monk. "Keep us informed about any changes."

"Will do—I suggest we go secure from here on."

"You think it could be that bad?"

"Don't know, but no use taking any chances."

McFadden closed the phone and stared at the freeway traffic. His eyes pinched. Something *was* wrong. He couldn't quite put his finger on it. Had they somehow started to suspect Piedmont at the FBI—is that why he'd been relieved from the case? McFadden and Smith had worked out everything to the last detail. Even the long, three-day drive to Washington had been planned to the hour. They'd reasoned a mobile target would be harder to track. That became the rationale for traveling during the day. A group of vehicles moving at night might draw unwanted attention, but a few cars, spaced out over a mile, traveling with the normal freeway traffic flow, wouldn't arouse suspicion. And since no one knew they were coming, no one would be looking for them anyway. McFadden had arranged warehouses on the route to hide the vehicles while they rested in nondescript hotels. Could the cabal's plan have been comprised?

Monk lifted the sunglasses to his forehead and glanced in McFadden's direction. "Everything okay?"

McFadden removed a cigar from his jacket and studied it a moment before lighting it. He'd taken up cigar smoking shortly after Coleen's death. What started as a nervous habit had developed into a love affair. McFadden's humidor at the ranch overflowed with expensive cigars. Some he nurtured for months before enjoying. But still, he never smoked one without a fading thought of Coleen. That incident had kicked off the habit.

Clark had done what his dad had told him that night in Vegas. He had turned off the lights, laid in bed, and waited for the phone call. In less than an hour, the hotel room phone had rung. Clark's heart had skipped as he reached for the receiver.

"Hello."

A non-familiar voice had asked, "Is this Clark McFadden?"

Clark's gut had knotted. "Yes."

"I'm an attorney in Las Vegas, an associate of Tom. Are you okay, do you need anything?"

Clark had relaxed a little. "I'm fine. Where's Tom?"

"In the air right now. Picking him up in less than two hours."

Dizziness had flowed over Clark, and his hand had been so weak it had been a challenge to hold the receiver.

"Here's what I want you to do. Don't return to the stairwell. Clean up the room and remove any signs of a physical quarrel. Put on your pajamas and go to bed. Be sure to turn off the light. If someone discovers the body, make sure to allow the hotel staff to appear to wake you. Say you were asleep and had no knowledge she'd left the room during the night. There was never a fight or any disagreement. Do you understand?"

"Yeah, sure. I understand, but I can't sleep, not in my state."

"Doesn't matter, it'll still relax you. Tomorrow's going to be a long day. Tom and I will be there in a couple of hours. Everything I just said came from Tom's mouth. He'll handle it when he arrives. Think you can remember all that?"

"Yeah."

"Now, take a big swig of some alcoholic drink and swish it around in your mouth like a mouthwash. Want plenty on your breathe for later. After that, hit the sack."

With that, the line had gone dead.

Two hours later, a soft knock had sounded on Clark's door. He had gazed through the peephole at Tom, standing alone in the deserted hall, his head on a swivel. Clark had swung the door open, and Tom had rushed in.

Thomas Arnett was a tall, slim man with predator-like features. Eyes set a little too close, and a Roman nose suitable to sniff out any hint of deceit or treachery decorated the rather ordinary face. He'd worn his dark hair short and closely plastered to his head. He'd looked like a KGB interrogator you see in old black and white B movies. He always insisted everyone call him Tom. He and Clark's dad had attended Pennsylvania State University back in the day, Clark's dad in the College of Earth and Mineral Sciences, and Tom in Law. He was one of those smooth-talking Houston criminal defense attorneys that typically only accepted three of four cases a year to continue living his multi-million-dollar lifestyle. He and Clark's dad were still best friends.

"Has anyone else knocked on your door or called you except my colleague?" he had asked, setting his briefcase on the small table.

"No, no one."

"Good, there's still time." Tom's forehead had creased, and he touched Clark's cheek. "What happened here?"

Clark had touched the raw scratch marks Coleen had made earlier. "We fought."

"Not good. Any marks on her?"

"What?"

"Pay attention." He'd raised his voice. "Any marks on her? Did you choke or strike her?"

"Yes, I slapped her."

"Wonderful, just bloody wonderful," Tom had muttered, walking away, massaging his eyes with thumb and forefinger. "Okay, this complicates things but don't lose heart." He had withdrawn a flask from his inside suit pocket and handed it to Clark. Take a drink."

Clark had held up his hands in surrender. "No, thanks. I'm good."

Tom had unscrewed the top and shoved it into Clark's hand. "It's not for you; it's for the police later."

Clark had taken a long swallow.

"Now, take a shower. Wait until eight o'clock and make sure you're seen in the lobby. Ask the desk clerks if they'd seen or heard from your wife. Go to the restaurant and have breakfast. Inquire if she'd been down this morning. Pretend to be worried—concerned. Return to the room about nine. Wait until ten and go back down and insist on speaking with the manager. Tell him your wife appears to be missing and request the staff do a floor-by-floor search. Say she had too much to drink last night, and you haven't seen her since you both retired. She may have wandered off and be on another floor. You just realized all her clothes were still there, but her nightgown was missing. Be sure to sound confused and concerned for her wellbeing."

Tom had paused, catching his breath. "Then return to your room and brace yourself. They'll find her soon enough. The police will be notified and will interview you. Don't deny the altercation. Say you were both a little drunk. But insist you made up and went to bed at the same time, and when you awoke, she was gone. That's all you know, period. Don't let them pin you down on specifics. They'll have two or three detectives ask the same questions in several different ways to trip you up. Say you had been drinking and can't remember details, talk in generalities, don't get caught in a lie when they compare notes later. Understand?"

Clark had been numb. The only thing he could do was nod.

"Now, take another drink, and repeat it on the hour until she's either found or the flask is empty. You must be able to say you were a little tipsy during the interview."

McFadden had nodded.

Tom had collected his briefcase and walked to the door. "Don't answer any questions. Don't even say hello to the cops until I'm back here. Call your dad. He knows where I'm staying." Tom's expression had softened. "The best they could hope for is second-degree murder or involuntary homicide. I can defend those without a problem. Don't worry, young Clark. Your father won't allow you to spend your formative years in a Nevada prison."

Tom had been right about everything. Within a half-hour of being notified, the hotel's staff had discovered Coleen's body in the stairwell. The police soon showed up, and the interviews started. Clark had kept up the regimen of sipping from the flask every hour. He could tell from the detective's expressions they'd smelled it. They'd interviewed him for only an hour that day with Tom present. The next day, they must have suspected something because they'd asked him to the police station for an additional interview, which had soon turned to an aggressive interrogation. They'd tried the flim-flam of double-teaming and then triple-teaming him in the interrogation room. Through it all, Tom had sat beside him, unflappable. They'd put together a signal. When a detective asked a question Tom didn't want Clark to answer, Tom would twist the diamond pinky ring on his left hand. At that point, Clark would shut up, and Tom would object to the question, cite some obscure Supreme Court ruling or the US Constitution, and advise Clark he was not required to answer. At one point, the lead detective had looked like he would have a coronary. His face had turned so red McFadden had to stifle a laugh.

With no forensic evidence, witnesses, or confession, the medical examiner had no choice but to rule the death a tragic accident, and Clark had walked. But Tom hadn't been through with him just yet. He'd advised Clark and his father it might be best if Clark left the country for a while. Not too far, but outside the borders and far enough away from Vegas that it would prove difficult for detectives to corner him for another interview.

That began Clark's banishment. Ostensibly, he had relocated to Bouck Township in the wilds of Ontario, Canada, to study uranium mining techniques from the engineers at the Denison Mine. Clark's dad owned a substantial interest in the place, and they had been happy to welcome a significant investor's son for an extended visit.

Old Tom had been right, as usual. A month hadn't passed before Vegas detectives notified Clark they wanted to close the case but first needed another *chat*. He had assured them he had no problem sitting back down for a chat. *When would you want to come to Canada?* That took the starch out of their socks a bit. They had hemmed and hawed and said they'd get back to him. A couple of days later, they'd called again and requested he travel to Vegas for the interview. Clark had told them that was impossible, that he was up to his neck in work and couldn't possibly make what would amount to a two or three-day trip for an interview. But Clark had reiterated his desire to cooperate if they would only travel to Canada. When they'd used an implied threat, he'd reminded them of the medical examiner's ruling. They had again said they'd get back to him.

Tom had coached him well, and the detectives had followed the script almost to the letter of what Tom had predicted. And Tom had known another thing. He'd know, with the department's limited investigative travel budget and ever-increasing case load, the Vegas detectives wouldn't leave the case open forever. Within seven months, Tom's Vegas contacts had reported it had been quietly closed. Without fanfare, Clark had slipped back into the country in time for his dad's birthday and the balloon festival.

Clark lit the cigar as he glanced over at Monk, lowering the sun visor to block the afternoon glare. Yeah, that Vegas incident had taught Clark a valuable lesson. He could get away with anything, but only under certain conditions. He needed a place where only he called the shots, made all the rules, and controlled everything. It was at that moment when he was still a young man that the idea of his own ranch, own town, own world began to take shape—a place away from everybody and everything—a place he could populate with whom he wanted. The thought of being an English lord with a colony of serfs somehow appealed to his sense of history. He never realized one day he and the serfs would be strong enough to rise and take back the country from the mealy-mouthed, lily-livered, socialist threatening the American way of life. This was his cause. This was his moment in time. Children reading history a hundred years from now would know the name Clark McFadden.

———

Newman Smith pulled the rain jacket tighter and stood with his hands on his hips, staring at the grinding winch as it lifted the cage from the dirt pit. A ranch hand manipulated the levers of the temporary over-head winch manually from its master control panel. Smith looked up at the dim sunlight streaking through the clouds as the afternoon came to a close. Just then, the cage surfaced, and, as he feared, it was empty. Bishop had escaped. Smith's cell rang just as he peeked into the hole one last time. "What?"

A voice answered. "The boys we sent to Cora's."

"Yes?"

"They're all dead."

Smith opened his mouth but said nothing.

"Did you hear me?" the voice said. "They're all dead, and Cora's gone. Do you want us to start a search for Bishop?"

"No." Smith released a tired breath. "He's gone, too."

———

McFadden hung up the phone and gazed at Monk Cole.

"Bishop's escaped."

Monk's ashen expression caused him to explain further. "Ochoa's dead, and so are four warriors we sent to Cora's."

"But, how?"

McFadden dialed his cell. "I don't know. I knew there was some-thing about him—he sure as hell wasn't a reporter." Before Monk could respond, McFadden's call went through. He spoke into the phone. "You guys drop back; we're taking the lead." He hung up and surveyed the map again. "Assuming he's a fed, he may have figured out certain parts of the plan—we can't take that chance."

Monk's troubled eyes met his. "If he knows about the plan, then he knows we're involved."

McFadden gave a nod of acknowledgment. "We have to figure it that way." He glanced at the map and then back to the freeway. "We'll take the exit twenty miles up ahead," he pointed at the map.

"We're not going to Nashville?"

"Nope, they'll be looking for us to be on a freeway. We're getting off up here. We'll get lost in the back roads and take an indirect route. They'll never find us the way I'm going."

Monk remained silent until the exit. As he turned off the freeway, the realization must have hit him. "We'll be wanted men—we'll never be able to return home."

McFadden shot him a glance. "Do you have anything or anybody you want to return to?"

Monk showed a sheepish look. "No, I guess not."

"Don't worry; I have a plan to get us out of the US after this is over if it doesn't go as planned—I still have a few million in an offshore bank."

Monk took a deep breath. "So, we're going through with it?"

McFadden placed his left hand on Monk's shoulder. "We're doing what must be done. Nothing in this country will change unless someone steps up and takes control. We might have to view it from afar, but at least we'll know we started the ball rolling."

"But if they're expecting us—"

McFadden sneered. "They're not expecting what I'm planning." He redialed his cell. "Okay, guys—we're going secure—pass it on."

Months ago, each McFadden Academy graduate attending a university was instructed to purchase six pay-as-you-go cellphones from their local big box store and send them to Newman Smith at a post office box in Albuquerque. McFadden and his most trusted staff now had dozens of burner phones. After activating their phones, they exchanged numbers through snail mail—no electronic records. The prepaid mobile phones could not be traced back to them, nor could they be tracked by the authorities. Once someone went secure, they destroyed their regular phone.

McFadden powered off his phone, removing the battery and SIM card. He rolled down the passenger window and dropped everything on the freeway to be destroyed by the wheels of other vehicles.

————

Cook glanced at Maxwell as he dragged himself into Cook's office and collapsed in one of the chairs. Cook stood at a large wall map of the United States and kept talking on the phone. He acknowledged Maxwell with a curt nod before going back to his conversation.

"Okay, thanks—let me know," Cook said. He took another look at Maxwell. The guy's shoulders slumped, and the rings under the puffy eyes screamed lack of sleep.

"Rough night, huh?"

Maxwell mumbled, "I've had better."

Cook dropped in his chair and rocked back. "Good news—looks like we just about have him."

Maxwell's droopy eyes came alive. "They've got McFadden?"

"No, not yet," Cook said, "but they know about where he is and where he's going—so it's just a matter of time. NSA's been pinging his cell phone and triangulating his calls through cell towers. He's just east of Oklahoma City. We've been listening in on his phone conversations. He's still on I-40 heading east. In fact, he just told someone he expected to be in Nashville this evening."

"That's great. So are we still doing a full deployment tomorrow?"

Cook considered the question. "Yeah, let's plan on it unless the FBI scoops him up tonight."

————

The long shadows of evening cast eerie patterns over Tennessee State Highway 22 South. The traffic had thinned, and everyone needed their headlights. There were fewer homes and businesses the further they drove into the country. Monk sipped the orange juice he'd gotten from the last gas station stop and tried to read McFadden's thoughts. McFadden finally broke the silence.

"We've still got some long driving ahead, Monk. Let me know if you need me to spell you."

"I'm good for now, but where are we going if not to Nashville?"

McFadden let the passenger window down a couple of inches before lighting the cigar. "Andrews," he said, between puffs.

Monk's head snapped. "We're taking this to Joint Base Andrews?"

McFadden looked at him for a moment with a confused and surprised expression, then let out a booming laugh and slapped the seat. "Hadn't thought of that—no, we're going to Andrews, North Carolina."

"Never heard of it."

"Good, maybe the feds haven't either. It's a little town in the middle of the Smokey Mountains."

"What's there?"

"A safe place to rest and hide out for a night."

McFadden's quick smile returned. The ash glow from his cigar gave his face a demonic look.

———

Speaker Henry Wilson paced the floor of his townhouse in Georgetown and spoke softly into the phone. "Why are we going secure communications?" He had already switched to the burner phone and tossed his old one into the roaring fireplace.

———

General Curtis Shaw dried his hair and stood naked under the bathroom heat lamp. It aggravated him to be interrupted in the middle of his shower. "You know as much as I do," he said to Henry Wilson. "Piedmont called earlier and said we were going secure. I assume McFadden had a good reason. Anyway, it's good operational security —don't worry about it."

"But, what's the reason?"

Shaw frowned and tossed the wet towel to the floor. The last thing they needed right now was this crazy bastard coming unglued. "Just relax. I'm sure everything's fine. He's probably just being over-cautious, but we don't want to take any chances, okay?"

"If you say so," Wilson sighed.

———

FBI Director Campbell quietly closed the conference room door and stepped into the hall. His aide nervously wrung his hands and stood at attention.

"This had better be important to drag me out of a national security briefing," Campbell grumbled.

"It is, sir," the aide replied. "We've lost him—McFadden, that is."

Campbell leaned back against the dark wood-paneled wall and ran his hand slowly down his face. He still had the same headache since his meeting with Fuller and Cook that morning. He'd hardly eaten a thing, and the constant inflow of coffee and bad intel about the McFadden affair had made him jittery.

"What happened?"

"We were tracking him fine earlier—even picking up phone conversations through NSA. We'd just started to zero in with two drones this afternoon when the signal went dead."

"Dead?"

"Yes, sir. We attempted to do a manual override activation and power up, but no luck. We're getting nothing but dead air from his phone."

"Did the DOE aircraft get a rad fix on him?"

"No, sir—it's flying at 500 feet along the I-40 corridor, but nothing's reading hot from the freeway."

Campbell pursed his lips and let out a long exhale. "Okay, thanks. Find him. Epand the search area, look for side roads and alternate routes, put every drone available between him and Washington." This wasn't information he wanted to take back into the meeting. As he reached for the door handle, he glanced at his hand. It shook, and he'd subconsciously crossed his fingers.

Daniel Piedmont made the left turn and only glanced at the road ahead. His focus remained on the headlights behind him. He'd just confirmed it—he was being followed. In his second FBI assignment, he'd worked in the elite Mobile Surveillance Team. He'd received training from former intelligence officers and veteran FBI agents about how to observe without being observed. That's what MST did—they spied on foreign intelligence officers, terrorists, and master criminals.

Since being trained by the best—he knew all their secrets. After talking to McFadden, he decided he'd test the water to determine if he'd fallen under suspicion or if it was just silly paranoia. The easiest way to do it would be to leave home and see who followed. A Saturday night out in Washington, DC would be what they'd expect from a single guy. He packed a small rucksack with everything he'd need for the operation, just in case he couldn't come back home. After leaving his apartment, he drove to a small Italian restaurant a couple of miles down the road and ate his fill of lasagna and garlic bread. He sat sipping the last of his wine, studying the other customers.

Who had come in after him? Where did they sit? Any sign of weapons or radio bulges under their clothes? He asked for the check, paid it, and headed down the dark back hall leading to the restrooms. If he was under surveillance, there would be someone outside and someone inside. He decided to try an old trick he heard about from a Soviet defector.

The restroom was empty except for one guy at the urinal as Piedmont walked to the toilet stall. He stepped inside, sat on the commode, and locked the door. Now he waited. He planned to make the agents nervous and force someone to come looking for him. If he stayed in the restroom for an abnormal amount of time, they'd have to eventually go and check—if only to make sure he hadn't slipped out the back unnoticed. The trick could backfire if they decided to force the toilet door, but he figured they were under orders not to tip him off to the surveillance.

Several patrons came in while he sat locked inside the toilet. Piedmont peeked through the crack between the stall's wall and door at each pair of shoes and pants that entered, then put them to memory. He waited a full fifteen minutes before coming out in a fast walk. The trick worked. From the corner of his eye, he saw the young woman look his way and quickly draw the attention of her older male partner by putting a hand on his sleeve. When the man's head turned, Piedmont glanced the other way so as not to meet eyes with the guy. He did, however, see the dark green pants and chocolate brown shoes the fellow wore. He'd been the last one to enter the restroom before Piedmont departed.

Piedmont had to lose the surveillance, but how? They'd have planned for every contingency. He didn't believe they realized he'd discovered them—so that played in his favor. He drove aimlessly around the District for a while, thinking. The only way to shake them would be to go to a location they hadn't anticipated or planned out in advance, then depart by another exit before they could set up to properly surveil the place. The Regency Hotel seemed to offer several advantages. He allowed the valets to park his car and drifted inside. He knew the area well. He'd conducted a security survey of the hotel a couple of years ago for a VIP, and the knowledge he'd gained about the hotel layout stuck with him.

Piedmont proceeded to the back stairs and went down before anyone at the front desk noticed. He rushed to the lower ballroom level, which stood dark and empty. He ducked inside and ran in the shadows to the rear hallway. It, too, was deserted. If there weren't banquet customers to serve, the back area leading to the kitchen annex remained deserted. Piedmont raced down the hall past the folded and stacked tables. Around the corner, he found the exit door.

During banquets, the cooks and waiters all congregate outside that door to smoke. They knew if they opened the door, an alarm would sound, so they'd bribed the hotel engineer with chocolate cheesecake to deactivate it for them. Piedmont held his breath. Had it been reactivated? He touched the handle and listened for footsteps in the long hall—there were none. "Here goes nothing," he whispered.

The door popped open with only a clicking sound into the chilly night. Piedmont looked outside, up the short flight of stairs that led to the street behind the hotel. Shrubs hid the area from the garage and back parking lot. Piedmont peeked over the lowest bush. The sound of squealing tires caused him to jump and duck lower as a sedan made the turn going much faster than usual.

"They drive nicer cars than when I worked there," he mumbled.

Once the vehicle sped past, he ducked low against the building's shadows until he'd made it to the freeway service road underpass sixty yards from the hotel. He crouched there a moment, thinking. He couldn't go home or to any other familiar place for that matter—he had to keep moving. He slung the rucksack over a shoulder and followed the dirt path, always staying in the shadows. Piedmont walked a couple of blocks along the dark fence line which guarded the service road, then ducked under a loose section of wire and hailed a cab.

"Union Station, please."

"Fine," the cabbie said.

"Say, how late does the New York Amtrak run on weekends?"

The cabbie looked at him in the mirror and flicked something off the top of the dash before answering. "The last one leaves for New York at ten."

Piedmont checked his watch. "I might just make it."

He gave the driver a generous smile and a tip larger than the fare when he got out.

"Thanks for getting me here on time," he said before heading into the train terminal.

Yeah, that guy would remember him for sure—and the fact he was heading for New York. He strolled through the terminal and out the side exit door—the one with no cameras guarding it. He turned left and walked down the sidewalk toward the shadows before disappearing again into the night.

TWENTY-TWO

At exactly 11:57 PM, the three vehicles rolled through a sleeping Andrews, NC, and turned right on the park road into the Nantahala National Forest. The heavy tree canopy over the road blocked out the moonlight. McFadden directed Monk up the mountain road, and the sound of rushing water filled the air from the open truck windows. The dim shimmer of the fast-moving river over half-submerged rocks to Monk's right and the dark forest to his left had a dizzying effect.

"Take the next left," McFadden ordered.

Monk slowed and leaned forward in the seat, looking for the entrance—there was none. "Where?"

"Right here." McFadden motioned to the hidden drive in the middle of the curve.

Monk squinted—if it hadn't been pointed out, he probably wouldn't have seen it. Anyone coming up or down the mountain is so focused on driving the switchback, they'd hardly notice it, tucked into the curve. He shifted into a lower gear before making the turn. The other two vehicles followed him up the steep incline. After about thirty yards, they came to a metal gate with a combination lock. McFadden jumped out and shined a small light while spinning the dial. He swung the gate open and waved the other vehicles through before relocking it and returning to Monk's truck.

McFadden nodded and pointed straight ahead. "Just keep following the road up." When they went around the bend, there was the outline of a large log cabin nestled in a three-acre clearing on the left.

"Swing around to the back," McFadden said.

Monk followed the gravel road around the house to the mammoth, rustic barn standing thirty feet tall.

"We'll put the vehicles in here for the night," McFadden said before sliding out of the truck and opening the double wooden doors.

Monk pulled in, followed by the other trucks. McFadden made a point of greeting each man who climbed out of the trucks. They shook off their fatigue and squared their shoulders.

"We're almost there, boys," McFadden said, slapping several of their backs in his good-old-boy fashion. "One more night on the road, and that's it." He eyed them and set his jaw. "I need one man awake and patrolling all night—you guys figure up a shift rotation."

They marched toward the cabin, and Monk took a deep breath of the clean mountain air. The fall temperature at this elevation chilled him. Filtered moonlight outlined McFadden's shadow as he led the way to the cabin. To Monk, the shadow made McFadden look ten feet tall.

———

The dark-clad motorcycle rider whose features were hidden by a helmet and face shield pulled up to the warehouse in South Richmond, Virginia. The place looked deserted. Only the engine sounds from the vehicles crossing the James River Bridge broke the silence. He input the four-digit code in the keypad by the metal door. Behind the door, a clicking noise sounded before the door rose. The rider goosed the cycle inside and parked, then removed the helmet and sat it on the seat. Piedmont looked and listened—still nothing but the sound of traffic from I-95, a quarter mile away.

The truck was still there, just as he'd left it two weeks ago. He closed the overhead door before switching on the unit's six fluorescent lights. The refrigerator in the corner had some funky-smelling liquid draining onto the concrete floor, but the beer inside was still cold. He popped the top on one and walked around the truck to get the feeling back into his legs. Piedmont checked the air in all the truck's tires, then the oil and coolant—everything looked okay.

Piedmont crawled into the driver's seat and sat the beer on the dash. He tried cranking it—the truck started with no hesitation. He let it run a minute and turned it off. Piedmont checked his watch—1:38 Sunday morning. He pulled the blankets and pillow from the plastic bag in the floorboard and turned off the overhead lights. Downing the last swallow of beer, he made himself as comfortable as possible on the truck's seat and closed his eyes. Sleep did not come quickly—his mind still re-ran the night's events. Piedmont walked for over two hours to get to the private garage where he stored the cycle. Always staying to the side streets, he'd more than once had to fend off hookers and panhandlers. He changed into the leathers and stowed his backpack behind him. It felt good to get out of town. Seeing Washington disappear in his side mirrors caused a bit of sadness. Piedmont knew he'd never see it again—not like this, anyway. After Monday, the landscape would be changed forever.

The 100-mile ride to Richmond had excited and renewed him. Piedmont loved riding the motorcycle at night and didn't even mind the freeway traffic. McFadden and the others would arrive tomorrow, and the last stage of the plan could be put into motion.

Just before drifting off to sleep, Piedmont reflected on his life. He'd never been one of Mr. McFadden's wonder boys. Didn't have the legal brain of Newman Smith, or the science brain of Monk Cole. But Piedmont had something no one of their intellect could ever have—ruthlessness. He'd shown this at the McFadden Academy in how he'd played sports and interacted with the other students. Except for Ochoa, who everyone realized was insane, Piedmont was the most feared kid at the ranch during his school days. That's the reason Mr. McFadden had groomed him for a federal law enforcement job with the FBI. That's the reason he'd been entrusted with killing the state trooper, Senator Fillmore, and even his boss, Witcher. And that was probably the reason he'd been selected for the final phase of the plan. A small smile crossed his lips as he dropped into a deep, restful sleep.

———

Bishop held Cora most of the night. Her petite body occasionally jerked from bad dreams, and she mumbled softly in her disturbed sleep. More than once, she sobbed, and he'd held her tighter, caressing her back and shoulders. When he rolled over to the gray light of dawn, her side of the bed was cold and empty. He raised his head and peeked toward the window. Cora sat in a chair, looking into the woods behind his condo. She appeared so still, she could have been sleeping, but her eyes were open. The blanket from the closet covered her shoulders and encased her like a long woolen dress. She stared impassively at something, or perhaps nothing, watching the sunrise. The pose was that of a Native American princess—dignified, defiant, and beautiful. Bishop rolled to his side, and the pain from the cougar attack on his shoulder and back made him wince. He propped himself on one elbow.

"Good morning."

She turned and smiled. "Morning."

"You're up early," he said, readjusting to a more comfortable position.

"Yeah—you, too."

She'd lost everything: Samuel, her job, her house—her way of life. Bishop recalled something from an instructor at West Point: *Not everyone's sacrifice is equal, nor are their rewards the same.* He'd been right. She'd sacrificed everything but kept her life.

She stood, stretched, and yawned; the blanket dropping to the floor. "So, what do we have to do today?"

Bishop rolled across the bed and took her in his arms. "We have an easy day—no heavy lifting. General Cook wants us to drive to some kind of command facility the FBI's set up. We'll hang out and maybe look at some photos if the cops stop anyone that looks like McFadden or one of his cronies."

She touched the bag of clothes on the floor she'd bought on the way to Bishop's place yesterday. "Okay, I'm going to take a shower." Cora gave him a quick kiss—half missing his lips. "You start the coffee."

Cora ducked into the bathroom and pushed the door half-closed. Bishop slipped on a sweatshirt and stretched. From the bathroom, she asked, "Hey, will you buy me lunch anywhere I want?"

Bishop yawned. "Sure, name the place."

"I don't know any places in—where did you say we were going?"

"Richmond," he replied.

———

"Richmond," McFadden said. "That's our last stop before delivering the package to Washington. It's about thirteen hours from here, the route I intend to take. That route should keep us off the main roads and most freeways, staying on back roads and out of sight."

Monk hadn't slept that great and slowly sipped the coffee, holding the mug with both hands to warm himself. McFadden got up and poked the fireplace again. The oak wood had a pleasant, relaxing fragrance, and Monk scooted the rocking chair closer. "I didn't realize you had a place like this tucked away up here in the mountains?"

McFadden flashed a half-grin. "Nobody knows this place is here but a few foreign business associates. It's held in the name of a shell company that can't be traced back to me. I use it for meetings when there are people involved who shouldn't be seen at the ranch."

Monk stared up at the ceiling and the vast interior timber-beam construction. "That's the only time you use it?"

"Yup, I'd much rather be in New Mexico—that's home."

Monk started to ask something but hesitated.

"What?" McFadden said, with a quizzical look.

Monk squinted and leaned forward in the chair. "Do you think we have a chance at pulling this off—I mean, if they know we're coming—"

"Stop, Monk." McFadden held up a hand—palm out. "Just stop right there." He ambled over to him. "This is the single most important act a group of patriots has done since the founding of the republic. The people who want to destroy this great country have the voice of freedom almost choked off, but we're going to release that grip."

McFadden walked back and forth in front of the cabin's fireplace—his expression contorted into something Monk hardly recognized. "Don't you understand we have the power to save a nation—the greatest nation on earth?" McFadden's voice rose so much he was almost yelling. In the past, when he'd showed this kind of emotion, it had inspired Monk. Now it scared him. McFadden pointed at him like an evangelist working a congregation.

"Don't falter on me, boy—stay true to the cause." Froth and spittle formed at the corners of his mouth. McFadden wiped the back of his hand across it. He must have realized he'd overdone it a bit because he quickly calmed down, and his lips thinned with grim satisfaction.

A wave of queasiness passed over Monk.

"It's time for a new beginning—a new country, and we can make it happen—a once-in-a-lifetime chance," McFadden whispered. "Are you with me, Monk?"

In a voice he hardly recognized as his own, Monk answered, "Yes, sir, all the way."

———

"… and I'm tired of excuses—I want every agent somewhere between here and McFadden's last known location. Is that clear?"

The Assistant FBI Directors gave their full attention to Director Campbell. He felt like hell. His usual well-tailored suit had taken on a dingy appearance. The once crisp, starched, white shirt was wrinkled and hung limply from his sagging shoulders. Campbell's disheveled hair and hollow eyes gave the look of a man much older.

Director Campbell glanced at his aide. "For the benefit of those who don't know the latest, Ed will fill you in."

Ed Bradberry stood and cleared his throat. "After we learned about the conspiracy, we began electronic intercepts on all their phones and computers. At least a dozen of them have stopped communication via those devices. We also began 24/7 surveillance on the group. One of them," Bradberry said, shifting some papers on the table until finding the right one, "Monk Cole, was believed to be home sick. He's a nuclear physicist working at Sandia and Los Alamos. We made a surreptitious entry at his residence yesterday—he's gone."

Director Campbell tapped the table with his index finger to draw their attention. "This Cole guy worked on the stolen shipment of weapons. He knows all the disabling codes necessary to allow him to set one off. If he's with McFadden, and McFadden has a weapon—he's got everything he needs to light off a nuke."

Bradberry looked down then quickly back at the other men around the table and cleared his throat again. "That's correct, sir."

The total silence in the room seemed strange as each man probably considered their worst fears were now realized. A mad man with a stolen nuclear weapon, and the means to use it, was closing in on the Capitol.

Campbell walked to the credenza. He poured a half glass of water and swallowed two white capsules in one gulp. "Tell 'em the rest, Ed."

Bradberry laid the papers back on the table, and a blush covered his cheeks as he leaned both fists on the table. "It appears we've also lost another suspect—FBI Special Agent Daniel Piedmont. He gave MST the slip last night and hasn't been seen since. We have a security camera video of him walking through the front door of Union Station around ten o'clock, but we don't know where he is now. He may have traveled to New York—still trying to confirm that."

Bradberry looked at the Director, who had sat back down. "Sir, every vehicle registered to McFadden, or anyone associated with the ranch, is on our watch list. If they're spotted—they'll be stopped. Since Piedmont knows he's under surveillance, there's little use in continuing to keep this under wraps."

Campbell stared back and exhaled. "You're right—put out an APB on the whole lot. Let's start picking them up, and let's hit that damn ranch before the other nukes disappear."

Bradberry nodded and took his seat.

Campbell stood. "One last thing, ladies and gentlemen. We may have an ace up our sleeve. The major roads around the National Capital Area are ringed with rad detectors for a 100 miles radius. Anything that passes through one, no matter how well it's shielded—

we'll know about." Campbell shoved both hands in his pockets. "The only problem at that point will be we'll have less than two hours to intercept and neutralize them."

He looked at the men and women. "It's up to us to find them before it comes to that. Don't force me to shut down all vehicular traffic into DC." His eyes again narrowed. "Now, if you'll excuse me, I have to clean up and advise the President about evacuating the Congress and Supreme Court."

———

A Mine Resistant Ambush Protected fighting vehicle, otherwise known as an MRAP, is made to survive IED attacks and ambushes in war zones. The FBI started receiving surplus MRAPs as the war in Iraq began winding down—their SWAT teams loved them.

Special Agent Sean Carpenter leaned against his and tried relaxing. The growl of the diesel engine from the last of the Bradley Infantry Fighting Vehicles being backed off the eighteen-wheeler trailer finally died away. The Bradleys were also heavily armored but had firepower the MRAPs didn't.

The FBI's Hostage Rescue Team Leader, Rick Ure, tapped Carpenter on the shoulder. He jumped and turned.

"You okay?" Rick asked.

Carpenter wasn't okay, but he'd be damned if he let anyone know. While he'd been an Army captain in 2003 during the invasion phase of Operation Iraqi Freedom—he'd been kept out of the fighting in his role as C.O. of a transportation unit behind the lines. Carpenter never fired a shot, got shot at, or even saw a dead body. Fellow soldiers were guarding the only Iraqis he'd seen after they'd surrendered. This might just be his baptism by fire.

"Sure—I'm fine. We about ready to go?"

Rick whirled his hand in a circle in the air, signaling to vehicles up and down the line. "Yeah, let's saddle up."

Carpenter eyed the road that led to the entrance to McFadden's ranch. No through traffic had passed since they'd arrived almost an hour ago. New Mexico State Police vehicles had blocked both ends of the county road. Carpenter surveyed the vehicles in their invasion force. There were three Bradleys, seven MRAPs, half a dozen vehicles from DOD, the same number from DOE, ambulances, state police SWAT vehicles, FBI Evidence Response Team trucks, and several others at the end he couldn't identify.

Holy crap, it looks like a small army. Diesel fumes hung heavy in the air as each vehicle idled, waiting for their passengers to load. Carpenter climbed into the back of the sandy-colored MRAP and moved forward. The driver and Rick were discussing something. The driver held a map and pointed at an area along the fence line leading up to the main entrance to the ranch. Carpenter squatted behind them as the heavily armed SWAT team loaded up on metal benches inside the MRAP behind him.

According to Bishop's report, they could expect strong resistance from a well-trained, well-equipped, and highly motivated group of defenders. Bishop had stressed all precautions for the safety of law enforcement officers should be employed, and extreme firepower should be available to engage heavily fortified defensive positions. Carpenter had to wonder if they'd overdone it a bit. Nothing this big had been assembled since the raid on the Mount Carmel Compound in Waco in 1993. The press had a field day over that. Building this assault force had already engendered wild speculation from the media over what was going on. A false rumor was leaked. Something about a big raid on a major drug kingpin's ranch—very hush-hush. The press ran with it. That should keep them chasing their tails until this thing concluded.

Rick had devised the strategy for the assault. Two areas were the principal targets. The first—the cave at the base of the mountain, containing the stolen nukes. A Bradley would escort an MRAP with DOD and DOE render-safe personnel to the cave. Their mission— locate and begin to recover the remaining weapons.

Another Bradley would escort a second MRAP to the front door of McFadden's house. Their job was to arrest anyone they found inside. The last Bradley would run interference for him and Rick in their MRAP—they were the command and control vehicle. The rest of the armored vehicles would provide cover and backup to anyone that needed it. Most of the occupants were FBI SWAT personnel recruited from various offices around the country to assist in the assault. Surprisingly, Rick was the only HRT guy on the ground. His men would land or rappel from two Blackhawk helicopters at the cave entrance and secure it before the render-safe team arrived.

Carpenter wiped sweat from his hands as the last agent climbed in. Carpenter took a deep breath and gave the agent behind him a nod. Three of the four looked at him. They were in full tactical gear, assault rifles at the ready. The fourth one held a small silver cross in his fingers. His eyes were closed while his lips whispered a silent prayer. He opened his eyes, kissed the cross, and stuffed it between his shirt and ballistic vest.

Someone bumped Carpenter's right knee.

"Put your helmet on and let's do a radio check," Rick said.

Carpenter took the black combat helmet with the built-in radio and mike from a hook and adjusted it on his head.

"… 6, 7, 8, 9, 10. Did you copy that?" Rick spoke into his helmet mike.

Before Carpenter could answer, the armored beast gave a jerk and pulled onto the center of the road directly behind the already moving Bradley. Carpenter steadied himself from the jolt and nodded back. Even with the noise-insulating material, the MRAP sounded like riding under the hood of a Mack truck. The claustrophobic, hot environment gave Carpenter the willies. He couldn't afford to show just how frightened he was. The fear of the unknown was always much worse than the experience. His hands shook, so he kept his either bracing himself or holding something so no one would notice.

Rick looked back and yelled over the noise. "Use your mike—press the button on the handset to talk, and release to listen."

Carpenter found the cigarette pack-size handset on the wire and pressed the button. "Can you hear me?"

Rick nodded and gave a thumb up. They were only half a mile from the ranch entrance. Carpenter opened the top hatch and poked his head up, looking around. The cool breeze felt good, and he took a couple of deep breaths to calm down. The ranch had sealed itself off from the world a couple of days ago. No one had arrived or departed since then. Carpenter prayed this would not turn out to be another Ruby Ridge. The Director had ordered the maximum fire-power Bishop recommended to overrun any defenders quickly and secure the nukes. God forbid they were already wired for remote detonation. This section of New Mexico would be blown off the map and him with it. Carpenter scratched his arms. It felt like ants crawling around under his skin, looking for a way out. *Got to settle down.* He took a swallow of water from his bottle, and one of the SWAT guys in the back stared at his shaking hand. Carpenter quickly turned away and faced the front.

They were up to about thirty miles an hour now, and Carpenter could just make out the guard shack at the front gate through the MRAP's windshield. It looked abandoned—no doubt they'd been tipped off. This operation had been too big and too loud to keep secret. The ranch entrance was blocked by a big dump truck parked crosswise across the road between the fence and guard shack.

Closing on the main gate, one Bradley and two MRAPS sped past Carpenter and Rick's MRAP. The Bradley escorting them made a hard turn into the front yard of a mobile home directly across the road from the entrance—Samuel's old place. The driver of Carpenter's MRAP also pulled into the front yard behind the waiting Bradley.

"Better button up," Rick said.

Carpenter ducked inside, closing the top hatch. Night satellite images of three men loading something inside the truck blocking the entrance gave them cause for concern.

"Bradley escort—this is the commander—fire when ready," Rick said.

"Bradley escort copies, fire when ready—roger, sir," came the reply.

Carpenter wasn't prepared for the Bradley's 25 mm chain gun—he jumped as the cannon sent 200 rounds per minute of high-explosive incendiary shells chewing into the abandoned truck. Every fifth round was a tracer. Looked like a laser saber slicing through the vehicle. After about fifteen to twenty seconds, the truck exploded into a bright orange flash and a cloud of rolling sand. The explosion's concussion rocked the MRAP, and everything in the vehicle rattled. Carpenter's silent prayer was interrupted by Rick's comments.

"Son of a bitch, there must have been fifty pounds of explosives in that damn thing," Rick said.

The Bradley slowly approached, its turret swiveling left and right, trying to acquire another threat. Only a tiny part of the truck's frame remained—a twisted and unrecognizable piece of scrap metal. The explosion had demolished the flimsy guard shack—there was no trace of it. The Bradley stopped, its gun turret again traversing from side to side. After a moment, it eased up to the edge of the truck's frame and pushed it to the right. Its armored tracks bit into the road as the old remains of the truck pivoted and slid to one side. The Bradley advanced through the opening, and the MRAP fell in behind. There was a slight dip as they drove through the crater caused by the blast.

Carpenter looked to his right and left. The other armored vehicles formed a skirmish line and rolled over the barbed wire fence guarding the ranch toward their objectives.

As Carpenter's MRAP eased farther down the main road into the compound, it appeared abandoned. Only Carpenter and their escort Bradley followed the main road into the settlement. The rest of the vehicles did flanking actions, closing in on their targets deeper inside the ranch. Row after row of neatly kept houses stood on each side of the road with no sign of life.

Carpenter had briefed everyone about the women and children on the ranch, but none showed themselves. An eerie feeling tingled up Carpenter's spine as they drove past the deserted homes. He studied the faces of the SWAT team members in the rear—they probably had the same feeling. The musky odor of men's sweat and fear wafted through the stuffy, hot vehicle. Carpenter wiped his brow and took another drink of water—where had everybody gone? Aerial recon had observed no sign of evacuations. After what Bishop said, it appeared unlikely the residents were cowering inside while government types were overrunning their compound.

Looking through the MRAP's front window, he saw two Black-hawks hovering over the cave entrance on the lower side of the moun-tain up ahead. One moved to the left and began to descend. Carpenter squinted at the Blackhawk's assault team waiting in the open doors for landing. Once they secured the nukes, every other thing would fall neatly into place.

A trail of smoke streaked from the trees below the Blackhawk, and the helicopter erupted into a ball of flame—falling from the sky— bodies tumbling out.

"Blackhawk one—RPGs in the trees!" Rick screamed into the mike.

The second chopper banked to its left just before another rocket streaked by—missing it by a few feet. It continued its turn and increased power until it broke clear of the kill zone.

Carpenter held his breath as the front tire on an MRAP to their right exploded an,d at the same time, an RPG detonated against the explosive reactive armor of their escort Bradley. The Bradley rotated its turret to the right, and its machine gun opened up into a group of shrubs, shredding them. As the dust cleared, two bodies lay where the shrub once stood.

Rick yelled, "We're in a shit storm."

At that point, Carpenter's training finally kicked in and calmness passed through him. He spotted several FBI men staggering from the burning and disabled MRAP to their right—some helping the others.

He yelled at the four guys in the back of their vehicle, "Agents need help over there," and pointed to the right.

Without a word, the men cracked the back hatch and scrambled into the fray. Their exit began drawing automatic weapons fire. A dozen dull pings peppered the MRAP's side.

Rick's voice boomed over the radio. "All vehicles—balls to the wall to your targets—we have to break through."

Carpenter's MRAP increased speed to break out of the ambush. Something moved to Carpenter's left. A bulldozer came into view from around the corner of a barn, its blade raised to hide the driver. It stopped, and the blade lowered a bit. On the hood sat a man with an RPG pointed at them. Carpenter slapped the driver on the shoulder and screamed, "Look out," just as the weapon fired.

———

General Cook leaned forward in his chair, staring at his computer monitor. The live satellite feed of the attack on the ranch played in living color into his Pentagon office. He picked up the phone and dialed a number—Bishop answered.

"How are things going down there in Richmond?" Cook asked.

"Good, got here a few hours ago—not much happening right now. Except for a bunch of FBI supervisors crowded around a TV in a corner office."

"Yeah, they're hitting the ranch. I'm watching it on satellite—looks like FBI's catching hell."

Bishop grunted. "Thanks, I'll tell Cora."

————

McFadden walked out of the truck stop restroom north of Ashville, North Carolina, just as his burner phone rang.

"They're attacking the ranch," Smith yelled into his ear.

McFadden stopped and went back inside the restroom. "Who?"

"Hell if I know—looks like the army. They have choppers and armored vehicles closing in right now."

McFadden stared into the bathroom mirror at his reflection. He'd aged a decade since this started.

"Clark," Smith said, "did you hear me—they're closing in."

"Yes, I heard."

"I'm heading for the emergency tunnel—good luck," Smith said, just before the line went dead.

McFadden walked outside. The rest of the men were finishing up refueling the trucks and opening their drinks and snacks. He reboarded the truck Monk drove. A hollow emptiness caused weakness in his limbs. *Bishop!*

There was no turning back, now. McFadden wanted to tell Monk, but he'd been acting so skittish lately, he decided against it. The three vehicles cranked up and headed north into Virginia. Now the plans would have to change again.

————

Speaker of the House Henry Wilson sat in his study and read the New York Times. He loved Sundays—especially this one. Tomorrow at this time, he would be President of the United States. He couldn't suppress a small grin.

His wife was still at church, and after his early lunch, he lounged at his desk with a glass of Kentucky bourbon on the rocks. The doorbell rang, but Wilson allowed the housekeeper to get it. After a minute, the door to his study opened and Sue stuck her head inside the door. Out of the corner of Wilson's eye, he glimpsed a tall man wearing sunglasses, dressed in a dark suit, walking past his outside study window toward the back patio door. Wilson stood to get a better look at the trespasser. He had his hand on the phone to call the police when Sue stuck her head back inside.

"Excuse me, sir," the housekeeper said, "but you have a visitor."

Wilson didn't understand the strained expression on her face. A second later, the President pushed past her and entered.

TWENTY-THREE

Carpenter never knew if it was training, skill, or just dumb, stupid luck. But when he warned the driver of the threat from the RPG, the guy did the right thing. He stomped hard on the brake sending everyone lunging forward. Carpenter barely managed to catch himself before being thrown into the driving compartment with Rick. One thing about the MRAP—it could stop on a dime.

The RPG whooshed past the front windshield, trailing smoke and sparks, missing the hood by inches. Carpenter's jaw clenched so tight it ached. The dozer began backing up toward the cover of the barn just as the MRAP driver hit the gas, throwing Carpenter backward into the passenger area.

Rick's voice yelled into the radio, "Bradley—get that damn thing."

Carpenter regained his footing in time to look back through the front windshield. The Bradley commander was already on it. He'd swung the Bradley on its tracks and charged the dozer—chasing it behind the barn.

"Let's get out of here—don't wait on him," Rick shouted to the MRAP driver.

Carpenter fought to get back on his feet and hung on as they raced down the road, zigging and zagging to avoid another ambush, toward the base of the mountain and the stolen nukes. To their rear, the Bradley's chain gun opened up and then an explosion sounded. Carpenter looked back, and a ball of flame and black smoke rose from behind the barn. He held his breath to see which vehicle emerged. Seconds seemed like minutes before the Bradley swung from the other side of the barn and pivoted back toward them.

"How does it look back there?" Rick asked.

Carpenter counted at least two other MRAPs hit—one burning with small arms ammo cooking off inside. He didn't see any survivors. "We need help—our flanks are exposed."

Rick spoke into the mike, "Send in the reinforcements—now!"

Carpenter again swung his head to the rear. The only help could come from the New Mexico State Police SWAT teams deployed back at the fence line. They couldn't wait for them, but at least now they had their rear protected—he hoped. The Bradley caught up with them, and they raced toward the base of Gallinas Peak. The RPG attack had ended, but automatic weapons fire still pinged the armored skin of their MRAP.

The surviving Blackhawk swung in wide circles, and its side machine gunner punished the trees where the RPG had taken down the other chopper. Leaves, shredded, fell to the ground like green snow. The dust cloud from the impact of the rounds completely distorted any sign of the defenders. Carpenter's escort Bradley, plus another, added to the melee by ripping through the trees with their chain guns and finishing the job.

The Blackhawk landed, and the surviving HRT assault team assumed covered positions on the ground.

As the chopper took off, Rick yelled, "Okay—go for it."

Both Bradleys lowered their back ramps, and their SWAT teams scrambled toward the cave entrance. The Hostage Rescue Team from the Blackhawk also charged, making it a three-pronged attack. The teams gave each other cover fire, leapfrogging to the demolished trees, and began crawling through the broken limbs and bodies.

The first group entered the cave, then the second before the shooting began again. Several muffled explosions sounded from deep inside.

A voice, breathing hard, echoed over the radio with a southern drawl. "Objective secure—send up the render-safe folks."

Rick showed another thumbs up. "They've got this—let's check out the house."

Their MRAP took the road up the steep incline and parked at the entrance to McFadden's home. Scattered shooting still sounded from the ranch below as the few last-ditch defenders held out until the end. A Bradley and two MRAPs were already at the house, their assault teams somewhere inside the home. Carpenter and Rick kept low and ran to the entrance where a three-man FBI SWAT cover team huddled.

"What's happening?" Rick asked.

The one closest to him answered, "Nothing, yet. They made entry about ten minutes ago—still waiting for them to clear the place."

Rick grinned as a voice came over the radio. "House secure." Moments later, members of the entry team began filing out, and Rick and Carpenter ran in.

"Anybody in there?" Carpenter asked.

The assault team leader raised his protective goggles to the top of his helmet. "Just one upstairs—doc's with them."

Carpenter and Rick ran up the granite staircase and advanced down the dark hallway. Rick had holstered his pistol but kept his hand on the Glock's grip. He and Carpenter found the SWAT medic leaning over the body in the master bedroom.

The medic looked at him and shook his head. The body remained hidden under the covers except for the shoulders, neck, and face. The woman had been attractive, with long flowing blond hair that spread over the pillow. She looked in her late fifties, but the clear, smooth complexion could have been that of a forty-year-old. Her mouth hung slightly open, and the eyes were draped in a half-closed position.

Carpenter and Rick walked to the bed as the medic said, "Dead— she took something, but it'll take an autopsy to figure it out." He held up an unlabeled vial with the residue of a transparent liquid. A few white crystals remained in the bottom and stuck to the sides. He replaced the red cap and dropped it into a clear plastic evidence bag before handing it to Carpenter.

Carpenter recognized the woman's face from their earlier briefings—Minerva McFadden. He slipped off his helmet and ran his hand through his sweaty hair. He looked at the vial. "Get the Evidence Response Team in here once the ranch is secure—until then—seal the house and post a guard."

Walking back down the hall, Carpenter couldn't understand why the ranch residents had put up such a ferocious fight. There was no way to win—they were doomed from the start. But they were from Apache heritage. The same stubbornness and independence showed by generations of their people who refused to submit. The same bravery to fight when the odds were against them, and there was no chance of victory.

———

Fuller was proud he had advised the President to do this. The President entered Speaker of the House Wilson's study, FBI Director Campbell followed, and Fuller brought up the rear. After Fuller suggested it, the President, knowing it was their last chance to avert the holocaust, signed on without question. The surprise visit, with no red lights or sirens, set the stage for the confrontation. One thing the President had insisted on—he would be the only one to conduct the interview. He knew better than anyone that a bigger political heavyweight could only take on a political heavyweight like the Speaker of the House.

The shock on Wilson's face at seeing the chief executive unannounced, in his home, on a Sunday afternoon was priceless. The bastard's jaw dropped, and he stammered to find the right words before finally saying, "Mr. President." It sounded more like a question than a greeting.

The President stopped a few feet from him and, in a fatherly voice, asked, "Henry, what have you done?"

Wilson quickly recovered his composure. "Done? What do you mean?" He tried to smile, but it came across as a guilty smirk. His eyes quickly shifted back and forth between the three men.

"Have a seat." The President motioned to a couple of chairs in the corner by a picture window.

Wilson asked, "What's going on? I—"

"Don't talk, Henry—listen," The President said, taking a chair.

Fuller stood to one side of the closed door and the FBI Director the other. Wilson cut his gaze to them and quickly back to the President. The President's first job out of law school had been a state prosecutor. Wilson stroked the underside of his chin with the back of his hand—it was wet with sweat.

The President leaned forward in his chair, resting his elbows on his knees, and made eye contact with the man. "I'm not going to insult you by making accusations we can't substantiate." He looked over at Director Campbell. "But we can substantiate a lot. You intend to kill me—don't you? Me and my whole family."

Wilson fidgeted in the chair, and his expression darkened. He ran his index finger under his lip and wiped more sweat.

The President continued, "And after the Vice President and I were dead—who would be next in line, Henry—you?" The President's eyebrows rose, and he allowed a grin to shadow his lips. "But to kill us would also require taking down Congress too—wouldn't it? All your friends and colleagues. And to accomplish it, you were ready to destroy the US capital—thousands dead. Is that right, Henry?"

The man's hardcore resolve finally crumbled. His breathing became shallow, and the color drained from the florid face. His head bowed, and he no longer made eye contact.

The President sat back, interlaced his fingers in his lap, and went on. "We know all about your association with McFadden. We know he stole the weapons, and we know he plans to carry out the attack tomorrow. I'm here to ask for your help to stop him. His plan has failed. Moments ago, we assaulted his ranch and recovered five of the nukes. McFadden has the sixth—right? He's en route to Washington —right?"

Wilson raised his head and nodded. He looked back down and whispered, "He said we could save the country."

Wilson's words were only a mumble and sounded like he was speaking to himself.

The President stood. "How does he plan to deliver it, Henry?"

The man buried his face into his shaking hands. "By truck—tomorrow morning."

"Which road will he take into Washington?"

Wilson looked up, his cheeks streaked with tears. "I don't know."

The President glanced at Director Campbell. "You have anything, Bill?"

Campbell walked to Wilson's chair and put his hand on the man's back, "Describe the truck."

Wilson turned toward him and shook his head. "I swear I don't know. We never discussed it."

Campbell took a knee, putting himself eye-level with Wilson. "I know you're in contact with McFadden. How are you communicating?"

Wilson looked at the three men in the room and, for the first time, seemed to realize the thing was finally over. He reached for the phone attached to his belt and unsnapped it from its holder. With a defeated grimace, he handed it to the FBI Director.

———

Bishop watched as Cora slept. She lay curled up in an oversized chair in a backroom of the FBI joint operations center in Richmond. He strolled toward the FBI guys watching the big screen TV in the next room. They were management types with a glass front separating them from the joint operations center personnel. The group sat silent and transfixed, hardly breathing, in front of the 52-inch screen. Probably the same satellite feed Cook had.

One of them noticed him staring. He motioned Bishop to join them in the conference room. Bishop walked in and took an extra chair. The TV image showed a wide shot of the base of the mountain. Groups of heavily armed men in tactical gear mingled around as ambulances loaded people on stretchers. Someone at the table picked up a remote, and the picture panned and zoomed to the base of the cave Bishop knew so well. A line of bodies lay under a large blue tarp to the right.

In the lower-left corner of the frame, Carpenter was talking to another man.

Bishop grinned. Well, as least he'd made it through. "Any word on casualties?" Bishop asked.

The agent who'd invited him in shook his head. "Not an exact count, yet. We lost part of HRT in a chopper crash, and several MRAPs were hit—looks pretty bad."

Bishop returned to the main room, but his mind was troubled. He shouldn't have been thinking this way, but he believed he'd been left out. He'd done his job, but he didn't feel good about it. He could have done more. Besides, McFadden was still on the loose, and he remained the real threat. Bishop was wasting time in this place. He needed to get back into the game, but he wasn't going anywhere if Cook had any say about it.

Cora woke as he approached. She stretched and yawned. "I'm hungry—what's for lunch?"

Bishop wasn't going to fight providence. If he had to be here, then he'd make the best of it. He reached down and stroked her hair. "I told you I'd take you anywhere you wanted."

She looked back with a mischievous grin. "Do you like Chinese?"

———

Since they'd crossed into Virginia from North Carolina, McFadden had kept them on two-lane back roads, which never seemed to go in a straight line for more than a few miles. He could have halved their driving time by staying on a major road, but the danger of detection would be too great. Besides, this way, they would arrive in Richmond just after dark. That's when he needed to be there. Monk had hardly spoken the whole day—what he was thinking?

When the burner phone rang, it startled McFadden. Monk looked at him with a curious expression. McFadden glanced at the incoming number before answering—it was Henry Wilson's.

"McFadden here. What do you want?"

"Mr. McFadden, this is FBI Director William Campbell. What I want is for you to pull over your vehicle and tell me where you are. If you will do that—just pull over and wait—I'll guarantee your safety. We're going to stop you one way or the other. I'm giving you the chance to surrender, and nobody gets hurt. We're picking up the rest of your people right now, and your ranch is under our control. Stop this madness, and no one else has to be harmed. Do you understand?"

McFadden couldn't speak—he felt numb. The whole thing had collapsed. Henry had passed over, and who knew how many others. McFadden could stop now and be done with it, but he wouldn't be defeated. This had been his life's work—to change the corrupt system from the center out. He may not succeed in doing that now, but he still had the winning ace up his sleeve, and he intended to use it. He closed the phone without answering the question.

Monk turned. "Who was that?"

McFadden wasn't sure if the government could now track his phone after the conversation, but he decided not to take any chances. He casually turned it off, then unsnapped the back and removed the battery and SIM card. He shrugged. "Piedmont, he said it might be a good idea to disable the phone until I wanted to use it." McFadden couldn't tell if Monk believed him, but at least he didn't challenge the idea.

"Is Piedmont already there?"

"Yeah, got in early this morning—guess he couldn't wait." McFadden shot Monk a quick, reassuring grin, and Monk returned it. That's a good sign, McFadden thought. He'd been worried about Monk—at last, now he seemed to be coming around. He'd have to be careful what he said from now on. Couldn't take a chance on losing him at this critical time.

———

Director Campbell put down the phone and asked, "Did you get it?"

The man seated with the headset turned a dial on the console. "No sir, not enough time."

"Damn!"

"I didn't get a location, but I've segregated the signal and got an ESN."

"A what?"

"An ESN—electronic serial number." The tech quickly changed screens as the FBI Director, and several others looked on. "We can track him from the phone's ESN now."

Everybody leaned in closer, watching the man type in the code request to the FCC program. He hit enter, gave a long exhale, and sat back in the chair. The computer studied the request a moment before a message popped up on the screen—NO SIGNAL BEARING. The tech stared at it, perplexed for a moment, before typing in the ESN again and hitting enter. Again, the same answer—NO SIGNAL BEARING.

"What does that mean?" Campbell asked.

The tech shook his head and stared up at the director. "It means, sir, that the phone has been destroyed, or the battery's been removed. It's no longer transmitting an ESN."

———

"There's not enough capacity in all the hospital burn units in the entire country to handle the number of thermal radiation casualties we'd suffer if the thing detonated in Washington," Fuller said. He leaned back in his desk chair and watched Cook's reaction.

The general's lips stretched tight. "Hopefully, we'll never have to find out. What's the latest?"

Fuller gave up trying to impress him with facts he didn't seem to care about. He leaned forward and shuffled through some papers. "After we visited with the Speaker, the Secret Service whisked the President away to a relocation facility in Virginia. His family will remain at Camp David for now. As of..." Fuller squinted at the paper before grabbing his glasses. "1400 hours, the Capitol has been declared secure of any hidden nuclear weapons."

Cook's brow crinkled. "Says who?"

"DOE's Nuclear Emergency Search Teams—NEST."

The general stood. "Have they installed the temporary mobile rad monitors?"

Fuller also stood. "Yes, fifty miles out. Plus, there are the permanent ones a hundred miles in all directions."

"What about Congress?"

Fuller picked up his coffee cup before realizing it was empty and set it back down.

"They and their families are being quietly relocated, as well as the Supreme Court."

Cook walked toward the door. "Wonder how long it'll be before the press gets wind of that?"

"Not long enough. Thanks for coming by, General—good luck."

Cook turned. "When are you evacuating, Mr. Fuller?"

Fuller shot a glance at the floor. "I'm not. I'll be in the White House Situation Room."

"Thought the President might need you at his undisclosed location."

Fuller shrugged and showed a rare smile. "Well, with everybody else getting out of town—I figured somebody should stick around to mind the kitchen."

———

Just as he had sunk his last putt on the eighteenth hole, General Curtis Shaw's phone vibrated. He excused himself from his three golfing partners and walked across the green, out of earshot.

"Curtis, did you get out?" Smith's excited voice screeched from the phone.

"Get out of what?"

"McFadden didn't call you? You don't know?"

Shaw looked back at the other men and grew aggravated. He let his voice rise a little. "What in the hell are you babbling about, Newman?"

"The police have overrun the ranch."

Shaw's breath caught. "When?"

"About three hours ago—I can't believe he didn't call—you have to get out."

Shaw strolled further from his friends. A weakness in his legs and knees made it difficult to walk. A rock-hard lump grew in his gut like the one he'd experienced in combat. "Just settle down, Newman. Now's not the time to panic."

Smith's voice rose. "Seems like a pretty good time to me! I've told you the reason I called. Run for it while you have time."

"Where are you, Newman?"

"In the tunnel. As soon as things settle down, I'll start making my way south. Good luck, Curtis."

The line went dead, and Shaw slowly meandered back to his golf partners as they finished their putts. They were deciding whether to drink at the club or go to a favorite bar in town. The vote was for the bar in the city as Shaw jumped aboard the cart. He'd been on the course for four hours and had seen or heard nothing unusual. If the feds knew about his involvement, wouldn't they have arrested him already? His partner parked the cart behind the last one in line and bounded out to retrieve his clubs. Shaw sat there a moment and observed everything and everybody—all seemed normal. Club members strolled past, and groundskeepers went about their business. The warm Virginia afternoon showed no sign of threat or danger.

"Coming?" his partner asked, hefting his bag onto his shoulder.

Shaw came out of his trance. "I'll be along directly. Need to hit the john."

"Okay, but the last one there buys the first round—you know the rules."

Shaw's mind ran a mile a second as the man walked away. Shaw did a complete three-sixty turn when exiting the cart, trying to catch the eye of anyone watching him. No one gave him a second look. His mind kept racing. If they knew about him, then they had to be here, but where were they? At his home, on the base? He couldn't force his mind to clear enough to concentrate. Perhaps they didn't know about him—yet. Maybe he still had time to make a clean getaway. He did another quick turn, but no one paid him any attention.

Okay, he was safe for now, but he couldn't waste any time. He walked the long way around to the parking lot but stopped at the corner of the building. What if they were watching his car? Waiting for him to return. He stood in a side area of the club that backed up to the trees. He decided not to take any chances. He'd leave his bag leaning up against the building and just walk through the woods. In less than a hundred yards, he'd find a convenience store and strip mall. He could have a cab meet him and disappear.

Wait, leaving the golf bag by the building might draw suspicion. Shaw looked around and spotted a men's room behind him. *Maybe dump it there.* He took another long look into the parking lot and then slowly backed down the sidewalk to the men's room. Shaw peeked inside; it was empty. Stepping through the door, he slid the bag off his shoulder and stepped to the urinal. Just as he finished, the sound of a flushing toilet echoed from a stall to his left.

No! Shaw would have to wait until the guy departed, or he couldn't leave the bag without drawing attention. The man exited the stall, still cinching his belt. He strolled to the sink and turned on the water. Shaw zipped up, flushed, and eyed the stranger. He was an older fellow, mid-fifties, graying temples, wearing a Rolex and traditional golf attire.

"Have a good game?" The stranger asked, grabbing a couple of paper towels.

Shaw's hands shook, turning the faucet handle. "Yes, and you?"

The man leaned toward the mirror and raked his fingers through the thick salt and pepper hair. "Any day out of the office and away from the old lady is a good one."

Shaw relaxed a little. "You a member? Don't recall seeing you around."

The man stepped back from the sink and adjusted his pants. "Just a guest—thinking about joining."

"Who's your sponsor?"

"Phil Billings, we're old pals—he's been trying to get me to join for a while."

Shaw dried off his hands as the man headed toward the door. Shaw had met Billings—scratch golfer—owned his own window company.

"So, how's Billing's electronics company doing these days?"

The stranger frowned. "Electronics company? Must be a different Billings. Phil's into windows."

Shaw breathed a final sigh of relief as the man pushed the door to leave. "Hope you enjoyed yourself today—it's a good club."

The man looked back over his shoulder. "It's okay, but the wait's too long for me."

"Wait on what?" Shaw asked.

The fellow stopped before exiting and turned back toward Shaw. A large black automatic pistol now pointed at his chest. "Waiting on your sorry ass to finish that round of golf. FBI, you're under arrest, General."

TWENTY-FOUR

The setting sun hung low in the sky like a lush, ripe orange as the three vehicles drove north on I-95. McFadden hadn't said a word for over two hours—just stared straight ahead. Monk figured he must be thinking about something, but what? McFadden didn't share any more information than he had to. Finally, he spoke.

"How much farther?"

Monk checked the GPS. "Forty-six miles to Richmond."

McFadden glanced at the sun for a moment. "Slow down. I want it to be almost dark before we arrive."

Monk tapped the brakes and reset the cruise control. It appeared McFadden wanted to tell him something but might be thinking it over.

Five minutes later, McFadden twisted in the seat. "How long will it take to arm the weapon?"

"You mean to make it ready to fire?"

"Yup."

"Less than an hour, but we shouldn't do that until just before we're ready to deploy it."

"We're delivering it tonight."

Monk's head snapped in McFadden's direction. "But I thought we were doing it tomorrow."

McFadden's lips thinned. "I know, that's what everyone thinks, and that's why we're going tonight."

———

Bishop shook hands with the FBI supervisor in charge of the joint operations center. What time do you need us back tomorrow?"

The man gave him an exhausted stare and shrugged. "We're open all night. But I think we can manage without you until six tomorrow morning. You're staying in Richmond?"

"We have a room at the Marriott downtown. I gave the duty agent the contact information, and I'll keep my cell on."

"Great—have a good evening."

Bishop walked to the exit, where Cora waited. "We're good until six tomorrow. Let's get cleaned up and have dinner."

She touched her stomach. "Ugh, I'm still full from lunch." She moved close to him, sensually licking her lips. "I have a better idea." Her eyes glistened with excitement.

"Just the kind of appetizer I like," he whispered.

———

Piedmont's phone rang three times before he answered it. The number displayed belonged to Monk Cole, not McFadden. Did this mean something? "Hello."

"Daniel, is that you?" The voice was Monk's all right.

"Yeah, how far out are you guys—is everything okay?"

"Everything's fine; we should be there in about fifteen minutes."

Piedmont checked his watch. "Okay, I'll be ready." Piedmont disconnected and cleared everything away from the entrance to allow all the vehicles room to drive in. He raised the overhead door just as the three-vehicle convoy made the turn off Ruffin Road into the warehouse complex in South Richmond. Piedmont stood at the door and flashed the flashlight three times to guide them. He stepped aside as the King Ranch Super Duty pickup came pulling through; the box truck followed with Monk and McFadden; and bringing up the rear came a white GMC dually. Piedmont took a quick look outside, scanning the empty parking lot before closing the door. Just as he'd hoped—Sunday night at 6:45—the place was deserted.

McFadden jumped from the truck and greeted him with a bear hug. "How are you, Daniel?"

"Good, sir," he whispered. "Think you should know that I was under surveillance by the Bureau before I left Washington, but everything's ready for tomorrow."

McFadden broke the embrace and whispered back. "Don't say anything about that to the rest—anyway, plans have changed—we're going tonight."

Piedmont's brow furrowed. "Tonight?"

McFadden touched his shoulder. "It'll be okay. I'll explain later."

"Whatever you say, sir."

The four warriors from the other trucks strolled toward them, with Monk following. After greetings all around, McFadden again pulled Piedmont aside.

"Can you help Monk ready the weapon?"

"Sure—right now?"

McFadden nodded. "Right now." He turned to the warriors. "Boys, I want you to keep watch outside. Stay out of sight, but don't let anyone sneak up on us."

Piedmont found Monk squatted behind the box truck holding a laptop and a small, silver toolbox. Piedmont leaned against the vehicle. "Isn't this the old truck he stores the hot air balloon in at the ranch?"

Monk stood and grinned. "Yeah, slapped on a different color paint and a new sign. Now we're a tile company."

Piedmont read the name. Arizona Floor and Tile. "Clever."

Monk pushed off the truck. "Okay, we're only opening one door of the truck. We have to get inside and close it behind us quickly—no screwing around—ten seconds from start to finish."

"What's the hurry?" Piedmont asked.

"I'll explain once we're inside. Ready?" Monk handed him the computer and tool case. "Hold these until I get in."

Monk removed the lock and twisted the handle until the left door broke loose. He slung it open, bounded inside, and accepted the case and computer from Piedmont as he scrambled into the back of the truck. Monk quickly pulled on an interior strap and closed the door tightly in place. Darkness enveloped the area before Monk switched on an overhead light.

About five feet from where they stood sat boxes of tiles, stacked four feet high, strapped to the floor.

Monk turned on another switch, and two small fans blew a soft, warm breeze through the back of the stuffy truck. "It's not much, but the best we have. Get as comfortable as you can. It's going to get hot. Help me with these straps."

Piedmont scanned the interior—it had an unfamiliar smell, like something sour. The whole thing, even the doors, was lined from top to bottom and on all sides with a thick, white, plastic material. He reached out and raked his fingers across the surface—it was rough. "What's this?"

Monk looked up. "Borated polyethylene shielding. It's to prevent the gamma rays and neutrons from being detected. Just like this tile. That's why we have to keep the back door closed."

Piedmont loosened the straps on the boxes of tiles. "So the tile's just a decoy?"

"Of sorts, but it also shields gamma rays from detection. You need a high-density material for shielding—floor and roof tiles absorb the rays. Let's move these boxes to the side," Monk said, easing the first forty-pound box to the floor.

Piedmont helped. In the center of the stack sat a dull silver-colored cylinder. Piedmont touched it. It had a strange feel—coated with something. He scratched it and found wax under his nail.

Monk grinned. "Paraffin, also used for shielding. I advised Mr. McFadden to give them a wax bath before transporting."

Piedmont stood and removed his outer shirt, using it to wipe sweat from his face. "So what are we going to do?"

Monk opened the tool case and removed a small knife-like object. "Hold the flashlight on the spot I'm scratching."

Piedmont shined the light as Monk squatted and removed the wax from a quarter-size area on the back of the weapon. Once done, he scraped inside the area until the corner of a piece of tape came into view. Monk retrieved a pair of oversize tweezers from the tool kit and used them to pull a round piece of gold-colored tape off. He held it up for Piedmont to examine. "Teflon."

Piedmont leaned forward and examined the area where the tape had been removed. There was a silver hexagon nut recessed in a shallow hole. Monk retrieved a large Allen wrench from the case and attached an oversized black metal handle. He stuck it into the hole, braced himself, and let out a loud groan, using both hands to turn it counterclockwise. Once it broke loose, he spun the handle until the quarter-inch bolt dropped out on the floor of the truck. Piedmont shined the flashlight into the hole. There was a USB port. Monk wiped sweat from his brow and reached for the computer. He turned it on and sat back, giving a long exhale. He reached into his bag and threw a water bottle to Piedmont before opening his own. "Two-minute break," he said, taking a long swallow.

Piedmont took a drink and splashed a handful on his face. "So, what's next?"

Monk checked his computer. "I'll explain as we go. The rear area of the weapon contains the arming and fuzzing system. The main thermonuclear element is located in the smaller nose section."

"Are we in any danger… you know, from radiation?"

"Nope, this is the same warhead used in Tomahawk Cruise missiles on submarines. Made from super-grade plutonium. It has a strong alpha, weak gamma, and medium neutron nuclear signature. Safe to store and live in the area of sailors and naval aviators."

Piedmont looked at Monk with a blank expression. "Which means?"

Monk finished his water and threw the empty plastic bottle to the truck's front over the boxes of tiles. "Which means it's safe to be around until the time of detonation. Come on—let's finish this up."

"How much damage can this thing do?" Piedmont asked, watching Monk plug a wire from his computer into the weapon's USB port.

Monk typed several keystrokes before answering. "This is a W-80 warhead. It has a variable yield function that allows us to set it from 5 to 150 kilotons." He looked up. "We're setting this one for 150."

"What kind of damage will 150 kilotons do?"

Monk continued typing and glanced at Piedmont. He set his computer aside and leaned his back against the truck, resting his arms on his knees. "It'll be devastating. Everybody within a mile radius will vaporize at ground zero—every structure totally destroyed—no survivors. The gamma radiation blast will leave shadows of people on any concrete or stone wall that's behind them." Monk took a drink of water. "The fireball will reach temperatures of over 580,000 degrees. People who happen to be looking in the direction of the blast at the time of detonation will be permanently blinded—their retinas seared. The fallout from radioactive dirt and debris will kill thousands days after the explosion."

Piedmont sat mute, unable to formulate a response.

"Okay?" Monk raised his eyebrows and again picked up his laptop. "You know everyone thinks nuclear weapons are like you see in the movies—lots of moving parts and timers—bullshit. They're complicated, but the act of detonation is quite simple. Getting through all the safeguards is the trick. Like this category D permissive action link," he said, pointing to the computer screen.

Piedmont slid to Monk's side as he typed. "Can you get through it?"

Monk nodded. "I work on and test these things—watch this." He typed a seven-digit number/letter code and hit enter. The screen began flashing red with bold black letters that read: PERMISSIVE ACTION LINK DISABLED.

Piedmont moved in closer. "Is that it?"

"Just one more safeguard, and it's the tricky one. It's an environmental sensing device."

"What's that?"

"It's to prevent the accidental detonation of the warhead unless it's properly delivered to the target."

Piedmont wiped his mouth and squinted at the computer screen. "What does that mean?"

Monk interlaced his fingers and popped his knuckles. "It's a sensor which detects external effects that should be occurring during delivery —like time in free fall, acceleration curves, temperature, air pressures."

Monk blew a long breath. "Yeah, get this wrong, and the thing could self-destruct on us."

Piedmont's eyes widened, and he pushed back several feet away. "Self-destruct?" He stood and walked to the other side of the truck, crossing his arms.

"Don't worry—I've done this a thousand times." Monk laughed. He typed in the code and waited. Quickly he typed something again, his mouth dropped, and his eyes bugged. "No! They couldn't have changed it!"

Piedmont flattened himself against the truck and yelled, "Changed what?"

Monk quickly stood and turned the computer toward him. The background flashed red with bold black letters reading: ENVIRON-MENTAL SENSING DEVICE DISABLED.

Piedmont's wide eyes scanned back and forth from Monk's smile to the computer screen.

Several tense seconds passed before Monk allowed himself the pleasure of a chuckle. "Can't believe they changed the ingredients in a Whataburger."

Anger flashed in Piedmont's face. "You're an asshole, Monk."

Monk grinned, powered off the computer, and closed it before unplugging the USB. He left the cord attached to the port in the rear of the weapon and plugged in a small black box, which he taped to the top of the warhead. Looking at Piedmont, he winked. "A router. Now I can control the fusing and firing sequence remotely."

Five minutes later, McFadden called the Warriors back inside, and Piedmont pulled the tarp off the black GMC 3500 heavy-duty pickup. Someone let out a *wow* sound as they walked around it. The new wax job, courtesy of Piedmont, made the thing sparkle in the warehouse's bright light. The whole rear was encased in a large utility box that stood level with the cab.

McFadden circled the machine and admired the Washington Metro Police Bomb logo beautifully stenciled on the sides. The red and blue grill lights looked ready to speed him through any obstacle. "This is a fine Job, Daniel."

Piedmont beamed with pleasure at the compliment. "Thank you, sir. Look at this." He stepped to the rear and undid the latches. The doors opened to each side and revealed an extendable ramp. Straps were already in place to hold the warhead.

McFadden smiled. "Let's get this bitch loaded."

Piedmont backed the pickup to the rear of the box truck. He scanned the truck's rear compartment with his flashlight. It was three inches thick with borated foam and lined with another three inches of ceramic tiles—just as Monk had ordered. That should shield the bomb from radiation detection monitors while en route to Washington.

The six men lifted the 300-pound warhead from the rear of the box truck, slid it onto the waiting ramp of the pickup, and tightened the nylon straps. Piedmont pushed it into the interior of the compartment and quickly shut the doors as McFadden looked on.

———

"So, what are you hungry for?" Cora asked.

Bishop had dozed off after some of the best sex he could remember. He barely opened his eyes to see her standing nude in front of the bathroom mirror toweling her hair. "Let's just order in," he groaned and stretched.

"No way, cowboy—we're going out." She ran to the bed and jumped on him. "If I didn't know better, I'd say you were getting lazy." She touched an old, puckered scar on his right arm near the tricep, outlining it with her finger, and stared at the wounds from the mountain lions. "You have a pretty face, but your body has a lot of miles on it. Where'd you get all these scars?"

"Accident-prone." He yawned and pulled at the covers.

She wrinkled her forehead, and her smile disappeared, all pretense stripped away as she lay beside him and cuddled closer. "No, really."

"I used to be a soldier. Not anymore."

"I thought you were with the FBI or CIA or something."

Bishop pulled the covers tighter. "It doesn't matter—all on the same team."

She considered his answer for a few seconds before the mischievous grin returned. "Well, you can't do anything on an empty stomach. Come on, let's get dressed—I'm hungry now." She ran her warm hand under the covers and stroked his inner thigh. "Unless that is, you're ready for a third round—your choice."

He chuckled. "How about dinner and then a third round?"

———

"I need one man to stay here," McFadden said to the Warriors, touching the hood of the replica police bomb-squad truck, "and the rest outside on guard. Monk, you and Daniel come with me." He led the way to a back area of the warehouse. "I want to give it a couple of hours before we head out. How about a bite to eat? I'd like a big steak."

Piedmont spoke up. "You think it's safe to be seen in public?"

McFadden grinned. "I've never been to this town—doubt anyone knows me around these parts. Besides, this might be our last meal together."

An hour later, McFadden drained his second scotch as Piedmont and Monk finished their salads and hot bread. McFadden felt the need to stimulate the conversation. He looked around the dining room and smiled. "I haven't been to a Morton's Steakhouse in a long time— forgot how good they were." Monk had hardly said a word, and this troubled McFadden—what was he thinking? McFadden couldn't suppress his apprehension.

"Boys, there's been a little change of plans." McFadden leaned closer to the pair. "That's why I wanted to talk to you privately." He pushed the remains of his salad aside, and his hard stare pinned them. "Our operation's been blown. The feds know about all of us and our involvement. Earlier today, they hit the ranch—Newman called and said they were charging through the gate."

Monk dropped his fork. "When did you find this out?"

"On the way here."

Before Monk could protest, McFadden held up his hand. "I didn't tell you on purpose. I didn't want it to distract you from your work at the warehouse. Besides, there was nothing we could do about it, and too many people around that didn't need to know."

Monk sat back and stared at him. "You didn't trust me—"

McFadden looked at him with a fatherly expression. "Monk, you, Newman, and Daniel are the people I trust the most. Newman has gone to ground—may even be in custody. I'm not counting on the rest for any help."

The waiter arrived with the sizzling beef plates and served them. After he left, no one spoke for a few minutes, each with his thoughts while only picking at the meal.

Finally, McFadden continued. "They know we're coming." He reached into his inner coat pocket and withdrew two fat white envelopes. Sliding them across the table to the men, his expression carried an air of finality. "There's passports and driver's licenses in false names. Also, there are several thousand dollars cash and offshore account numbers and passwords. You'll have all you need to live the rest of your lives comfortably."

Piedmont grabbed his and slipped it into his jacket pocket.

Monk just stared at the lone envelope—not moving. He must have figured it out. "So, you're taking the bomb in by yourself?"

McFadden nodded without comment, trying to give the appearance of normalcy.

"No, sir. I won't let you," Piedmont exclaimed.

McFadden glanced his way. "Daniel, we did what we had to do to change this country. There's only one more step. If it's not done, then the whole thing will have been in vain. I'm too old to go on the run—too tired. You guys have contributed to my life's dream. You'll continue to pay the price for that dream long after I'm gone."

Monk's voice sounded calm and reasonable as he asked, "How will you do it?"

McFadden searched his eyes for a moment before answering. "I'm going to finish this steak, have another scotch, put on one of those cop uniforms, and drive the damn thing as close as they'll let me before detonating it. Who knows—in a marked police vehicle, I might even be able to bluff my way close to the White House."

———

"It seems impossible, with all the satellites, drones, and other technologies, we can't find someone traveling from New Mexico to Washington with a nuclear bomb," Director Campbell lamented into the phone.

Fuller had called him for an update and now wished he hadn't—the guy sounded mentally and physically exhausted. "I agree, Mr. Director. McFadden's had his share of good luck, but our time will come."

A humorless chuckle was the director's response. "Time is the one thing we're short on right now. The roadblocks go up at 10 PM. A public service announcement will follow, informing everyone DC is shut down due to a terrorist threat, and we'll officially go to code red."

"Thanks, Bill, and good luck," Fuller said.

———

"… and I'm just not sure. Guess I'll go back to the park service—see if my old job is still there," Cora said. "After I get things squared away, perhaps next year, might move somewhere else. Still have Samuel's arrangements to make." Her eyes misted and head bowed.

Bishop sat back as she stared into the half-empty wine glass. He reached across the table for her hand and squeezed it.

She raised her head, and their eyes met. "So what about you—what will you do?"

He shrugged. "Depends on what happens tomorrow."

The waitress interrupted with the food, and they put the future aside and enjoyed perhaps their last Italian meal. The small talk that followed was about anything but what was really on their minds. It seemed surreal to Bishop. They were only hours away from possibly losing the Capitol, and the only thing he could do was have dinner.

A half-hour later, in the parking lot, Bishop opened Cora's door, and she slid into his Black Ford Expedition. As he sat down, she raked her hand through his hair, giving him a sensual kiss.

"You don't owe me a thing, Troy. I'll be okay after all this is over—however it turns out."

She must have read his mind. Bishop had just been thinking about how she'd adjust once she got home. "I bet you won't have to decide right away. Perhaps we could slip off together somewhere for a week or two and think about it."

Just before kissing him again, she whispered, "I'd like that."

———

"Pull in here and fill up," McFadden said, pointing to a gas station. For those he left guarding the warehouse, McFadden had made little in the way of provisions for their escape. Leaving them with a truck full of gas, some money, and time to get out of the city was about the best he could do. They'd have to take their chances on the road.

Piedmont parked, and Monk said, "I'll do it." He swung the passenger's door open and slammed it hard upon exiting. He'd hardly spoken during dinner.

Piedmont turned to McFadden, who lounged in the back seat. "What's the matter with him?"

"He's hurt and a little disappointed, I expect," McFadden said.

Piedmont snorted. "Ingrate."

Monk finished filling the tank and crawled back into the passenger seat. Piedmont dropped the truck in gear and started rolling almost before Monk shut the door.

TWENTY-FIVE

Bishop and Cora sat in his SUV at the intersection, waiting for the light. Cora leaned forward in her seat and stared at something before gripping his hand. He turned, and she flashed a surprised look. The color in her face had drained, and her lower lip shook.

"What's wrong?" he asked.

Her expression contorted into something Bishop had never seen. "I think I know that man."

"What man?"

She pointed. "The one driving that pickup that just pulled out of the gas station."

Bishop turned his head toward the departing truck. "The King Cab? Who is he?"

"He looks like Daniel Piedmont. He was about four grades ahead of me at the Academy. I haven't seen him in years—if that's even actually him."

The light changed, and Bishop pressed hard on the gas to catch up to the truck, entering the freeway ramp to I-95 South. "Was there someone else in the truck with him?" he asked.

Cora's mouth twisted before saying, "I think so, but I couldn't tell for sure."

Bishop followed the truck as it picked up speed but left several cars between them. "So, where does this guy live—what does he do?"

She stared at the truck and took a few seconds to answer. In a shaky voice, she said, "He's with the government—the FBI, I think."

Bishop's heart rate increased. Chance and coincidence may have favored him again. The question was, should he call in reinforcements. "How certain are you that's the same guy? I don't want to alert everyone unless we're sure."

She bit her lower and grimaced, "Maybe 50-50. Maybe a little less, I don't know—only got a glimpse—just a profile."

The truck signaled a right turn and moved one lane over, but Bishop stayed where he was—using the other traffic as cover. They were about halfway across the James River Bridge. A beautiful full moon sparkled like a rare jewel off the water's silvery surface.

Bishop said, "We'll see where they go before we sound any alarm."

Once across the bridge, the truck gave another right turn signal before taking the Ruffin Road exit. Bishop held back and allowed several cars to pass, then followed. He coasted to the exit as the truck took another right on Ruffin Road. It turned into a warehouse complex. Bishop held back and slowly coasted to the East side of the first building in the complex, parking the Ford in the shadows, and switched off the lights and ignition. He opened the door, stepped out in the darkness, and said, "Wait here—I'll be right back."

Bishop reached the edge of the building as the truck he'd been following pulled into the far warehouse on the end. The interior lights illuminated the shadow of a man just inside the door. Once inside, the overhead door closed. Bishop didn't have much to go on, just a hunch, and a hunch wasn't good enough.

Bishop needed good, reliable information before throwing an FBI SWAT team into the mix. A false alert might cause them to miss McFadden driving through town. Bishop quietly slipped around the side of the building to his truck and Cora.

"I couldn't see much, but something screwy is going on. Might be just a drug ring or cargo theft operation—"

"Or McFadden?" Cora asked in a voice just above a whisper.

Bishop nodded. "Yeah, or McFadden."

Bishop reached into the armrest compartment and extracted two extra Sig Sauer pistol magazines. "I'm going to get a closer look. If I'm not back in fifteen minutes, get out of here and call the FBI."

A look of doubt crossed her lips. "Don't be too long." Cora glanced into the darkness before meeting eyes with him. "I don't like this place."

"Be back before you know I've left."

———

Monk typed in the router code and made the final adjustments to the laptop computer that would detonate the bomb while McFadden struggled with the stolen police uniform. He regretted having too much waistline to snap the front of the trousers, but his belt buckle would hide that. The uniform had been cut to fit Monk, and even being in great shape for his age, McFadden needed another inch or two in the waist. Of course, he had no intention of getting out or stopping the truck for very long. McFadden buckled the Sam Brown belt around his midsection, adjusted the gun and holster, and approached Monk. "About done?"

"Yeah." Monk swung the laptop toward him. "I've changed the code and did away with the timed detonation option. To explode the device, press and hold the power button for three seconds." Monk pointed to the button with his index finger. "Once the computer begins its power-up sequence, it'll send the remote signal, and the thing will blow."

An expression of regret lined Monk's face as he explained this. McFadden was touched. He put a steady hand on Monk's shoulder and gave it a firm squeeze. "It'll be okay, you'll see. This has been my party from the beginning. It's only right I'm the guest of honor."

A tear squeezed from Monk's eye and slithered down his cheek. He lowered his head. "I know, sir. Just wish I could—"

McFadden squeezed the shoulder again. "I'd better get going."

The lights on the fifty-foot utility pole at the far end of each row of warehouses made the area too bright for Bishop to approach from the front. Being a commando at heart, he liked the darkness. That's why he opted for the rear of the building. He kept close to the metal wall and crept over weeds, discarded cardboard boxes, and bottles. Only the traffic sounds from I-95 and an occasional night bird call broke the silence behind the building. Bishop's phone vibrated. It was Cook calling. "Hello," Bishop whispered.

Over the phone, Cook shouted at someone. "I don't give a damn what the excuse is. I'm going to bite off a piece of somebody's butt over this!"

"Hello, General Cook."

The yelling stopped, and Cook's voice settled back to the relaxed tone he kept with Bishop. "Bishop, we just got the word. About two hours ago, a DOE monitor picked up a rad signature that matches the stolen isotope. Sorry for the delay, but we just found out ourselves."

Blood drained from Bishop's limbs, and a weakness enveloped him. He looked toward the end of the warehouse fifty yards away. "General, where's the monitor?"

"Oh, sorry, it's south of Richmond—don't know where they could be by now, but the bomb was traveling up I-95 near DC. Roadblocks are up around the capital, feds are scrambling, and everybody's running around Washington like their hair's on fire."

Bishop didn't answer. His mind considered all the options.

"Are you still there?" Cook asked.

Bishop's eyes sharpened as they became more accustomed to the darkness. "Yes, sir. I'm following up a lead—let you know how it turns out." He disconnected.

There was movement near the end of the warehouse. Bishop squatted and remained still. The silhouette of someone stared into the darkness directly at him. Did the guy have night vision gear? After a moment, the figure swung back toward the light and around the corner. Bishop should go back and call for help, but he had to know for sure. Sending everyone on a false alert right now might cause them to miss the real threat. Crawling now, he made his way to the last ware-house on the end. They were constructed of corrugated steel sheets secured by metal screws. A laser-like beam of light shot out into the darkness from a screw hole missing its screw. Bishop stopped and listened before standing up and peering through the tiny opening.

The first image that came into focus was Clark McFadden, dressed in a dark blue police uniform, talking to a tall, skinny guy with glasses. They were staring at a laptop computer. Bishop couldn't hear their conversation. Because of the slight angle of the hole, he couldn't see the whole interior, but that didn't matter—he'd seen enough. He quickly trotted back toward his truck. On the way, he fished the cell from his pocket and called the FBI's Joint Operations Center.

"This is the JOC—Special Agent Rusty Griffin," the voice answered.

"Agent Griffin, this is Troy Bishop with DOD. I know where McFadden is. Get a team together and meet me at the Ruffin Road exit off I-95 South."

The short silence that followed made Bishop believe he'd lost the signal just before the agent asked, "Is this a joke?"

Bishop rolled his eyes and pulled the phone away from his ear. "No," he almost shouted. "I'm Troy Bishop, DOD; check the roster. Me and a Native American woman were there for ten hours today. I need help, now!"

"Okay, hold on a second," the voice said.

Bishop reached the end of the warehouses and ran to the Ford Expedition tucked into the shadows under a tree. As he drew nearer, there was no sign of Cora. *Must be hiding.* He opened the SUV's door. It was empty. Several spots of blood dotted the light-colored leather seat. Bishop's heart stopped. He ran back to the edge of the warehouses and looked down the row. In the dim glow of the front utility lights, the tall, bulky figure knocked on the door of the last one. As the door raised, Bishop couldn't miss what the man had slung over his shoulder —Cora, and she wasn't moving.

Crap. Bishop had forgotten he still had the phone to his ear when the FBI agent came back on the line. "Okay, sir—your identity's been confirmed. We're en route to your location. Will you meet us?"

Bishop winced. A SWAT attack on the warehouse would probably end badly, and with Cora inside, he had little reason to believe she'd survive. He'd put her in this position and left her alone—he'd be damned if he'd let her get hurt.

He described the warehouse complex to the agent, identifying the last one on the end as the target. "Sorry, scooter, can't meet you. Plans have changed. Get here as fast as you can—I've got something to do first." He hung up without waiting for a reply. He didn't want to compromise the recovery mission, but he couldn't allow Cora to be harmed. His plan was a poor one, but it was simple. Sometimes simple is best. Besides, what choice did he have? What he needed right now was a good old fashioned distraction.

———

Monk stared at Cora lying on the cold concrete warehouse floor and felt sorry for her.

Where did you find her?" McFadden asked, looking at the outside guard.

"Sitting inside an SUV parked at the other end of the warehouse complex."

"Was she alone?" Piedmont asked while kneeling in front of Cora and splashing water on her face. She started coming around.

"Yeah—nobody else in the area."

"One thing's for sure," McFadden spoke up. "She runs with Bishop. Wherever she is, he can't be far behind—we need to go, now!"

"Hold on a second—I'll get her to talk." Piedmont started lightly slapping Cora's cheeks to wake her fully. The earlier blow in the truck had just stunned her, causing a bloody nose. As he increased the strength of the slaps, Cora started waking.

Piedmont smiled and struck her until Monk had had enough. He grabbed Piedmont's hand in mid-strike and pushed him backward. "If you touch her again, I'll kill you!"

Clearly, from everyone's expressions, this wasn't what they'd expected from Monk. He didn't care. He loved Cora—he'd always loved her. He'd long ago been promised her by McFadden, but she'd loved another. He didn't blame her for not wanting to marry him. He was probably old enough to be her father.

Piedmont jumped up and screamed, "What the hell's a matter with you?"

"Let it go, Daniel," McFadden said, giving Monk a disappointed stare. "I want to be out of here in one minute. Let's start—"

The crash and shrieking sound of metal in distress made everyone jump and turn toward the commotion. The colossal overhead door collapsed off its rollers and now sat atop a large black vehicle backing directly toward them. Everyone froze until the back of the vehicle slammed into the front of the replica police truck.

Piedmont acted first, drawing his pistol and leveling it toward the driver's door of the vehicle. He fired three quick shots, shattering the driver's side window.

———

Bishop rolled out the passenger door of the SUV before it stopped. Someone appeared to his right just as he stood. He didn't bother wasting time trying to identify if it was a friend or foe. Everyone in here was foe except Cora, and she was out cold. Bishop spun and fired twice, and the figure cried out before dropping. Other shots rang out inside the warehouse, and the whistling of bullets a little too close. Bishop dropped to the concrete floor and looked under his vehicle. There were several sets of legs and feet. Picking one, he fired, and another cry bellowed out as the tall skinny guy with glasses he'd seen earlier dropped to the floor, clasping his wounds and screaming in pain.

McFadden's voice boomed. "Dan—get in!"

A truck started in the warehouse. Bishop looked to his right as the two warriors made the turn toward him with their pistols ready to fire. He shot them both twice. Bishop dropped the half-empty magazine from the Sig and quickly slammed in a fresh one.

Squealing tires and the smell of burning rubber filled his nostrils. The police truck backed full speed toward the rear of the warehouse. It plowed through the back wall into the dark, grassy area behind the building. Bishop didn't know how many guys were left. He rose and dashed to the back of the Expedition and peeked around the side. On the floor lay the guy whose legs he shot out from under him—still writhing in pain.

Bishop never heard the next one's approach until it was too late. Five quick shots from behind startled him. The last found its mark, clipping his lower right arm. Pushing off the vehicle, he spun and dove to the floor—releasing a hail of bullets in the direction of the shots. One caught the shooter in the right eye. He slumped to the floor without a sound.

Bishop crawled to the back of his vehicle and stood. He walked to the one on the floor still holding his legs in the fetal position, pointing the Sig Sauer at his head.

"No! He can't hurt us, now!" Cora cried. She slipped from behind a large wooden crate she'd used for cover.

Monk Cole looked first at Bishop and then turned to Cora. With tears in his eyes, he mouthed the word, *"Sorry."* His head dropped, and he lay back on the floor.

"Let's get out of here." Bishop grabbed Cora's arm and got her into his SUV. He slammed it into drive, and they charged out of the building, with the noise of the disconnected overhead door sliding off sounded like nails on a chalkboard. He raced to the end of the warehouse complex as McFadden's truck turned on the entry ramp of I-95, heading north toward Washington.

"Got him," Bishop said. He hit the cell's speed dial, and the JOC answered. "This is Bishop—forget about coming to the warehouses—close the north side of the bridge."

"What?"

He tried staying calm and spoke clearly, but the emotion welled up inside him, "Close the I-95 Bridge over the James River on the north end to all traffic leading to Washington," he shouted. "McFadden's in a black police truck with the bomb. Do you understand?"

"Yes, I'll make the call," the voice answered.

Bishop raced up the entrance ramp at eighty miles per hour, blowing past a Honda Civic like it was standing still. Blood dripped off his elbow into his lap from the wound.

Cora touched his arm and grimaced. "You're hurt. What are you going to do?" she asked.

"Try and keep them in sight long enough for reinforcements to arrive. If they just get the bridge closed in time, everything should be fine." *Everything should be fine!* As soon as Bishop said those words, he felt like an idiot. McFadden still had a nuke and a plan to explode it. If he couldn't make it to Washington, would Richmond become the target? *A city of over a quarter-million people?* The bomb truck was somewhere ahead of them now, lost in a sea of taillights passing over the I-95 Bridge. Bishop punched the accelerator to the floorboard. He couldn't allow McFadden to get off.

———

McFadden weaved the truck through traffic, resisting the impulse to use the lights and siren.

"That son-of-a-bitch. That's twice he's interfered!"

Piedmont sat in the passenger seat and hung on.

McFadden increased his speed with a determination to push this to the end. "It's not over yet, Dan."

The I-95 James River Bridge in Richmond is six lanes wide, 4,185 feet long, and 96 feet at its maximum height. McFadden found the first signs of trouble when he was halfway across. Traffic started slowing. Brake lights glowed as far as the eye could see up ahead. The vehicle directly in front of McFadden slammed on its brakes, causing McFadden to swing the wheel to the right to avoid a collision as he stomped on his brakes. This caused him to cut off an eighteen-wheeler, which hit his rear bumper. As his vehicle spun into the next lane, he tried pushing hard for the brake, but his foot found the accelerator instead. The massive vehicle lunged forward as McFadden fought for control, launching him over the top of a small BMW convertible in the far-right lane. Brakes screamed as they locked up, and horns blared. Traffic had come to a complete standstill.

———

"There's a wreck up ahead." Cora pointed to the right lane as Bishop rolled to a stop.

Bishop craned his head, trying to get a better look. "How far?"

"Maybe fifty yards or so."

Bishop opened the driver's door. This was the best chance to end it here and now before McFadden detonated the bomb. "Slide behind the wheel. If traffic starts moving again, pick me up."

Cora was sitting on the passenger window ledge, straining to see. "Oh, shit! It's McFadden's truck that's crashed. It's dangling over the side of the bridge."

Bishop's eyes widened. "What?" Before she could answer, he ran toward the line of cars separating them from the crash. His breath came in short, shallow pants, and his hands shook with anticipation of the fight to come. He held the pistol tight in his right hand, with blood dripping off the tip of the barrel from his arm wound. Several people had exited their cars—curious about the hold-up. They stood on their tiptoes, looking for an explanation as to the traffic jam. Bishop pushed them hard as he passed, yelling for them to get back inside. A stream of what sounded like curses followed him as he ran toward the crash.

———

Piedmont raised his head and touched his brow, wincing at the pain from the deep gash. Blood cascaded into his eyes. He tried shaking his head to clear his thoughts and turned to McFadden. He lay slumped over the steering wheel, groaning—blood seeped from his mouth and cut lower lip. Piedmont braced himself as the vehicle see-sawed—*what the hell!* He stared out the front windshield. They were no longer on solid ground. The view from the front was the dark waters of the James River, illuminated by a big, full moon. He glanced to the right. The bomb truck teetered on the one-foot-wide concrete ledge of the bridge. The hood and cab were entirely off the bridge, suspended over the river below. The only thing keeping them from toppling over was the weight of the heavy bomb in the rear.

He shook McFadden. "Sir, stay right here—I'm going to get you out." Piedmont opened the passenger door and stepped onto the truck's running board. He had to get to the other side. He wiped blood from his face with the back of his hand. When he looked up, someone was running through the traffic, directly toward him—*Bishop*. Piedmont ducked back inside the truck for cover, which increased the see-saw motion. He leaned out of the cab and fired several wild shots. Bishop dove for the hood of a nearby sedan and slid across it to the cover of another vehicle as Piedmont's bullets ricocheted around him.

Piedmont still couldn't see well. He wiped his face with the sleeve of his shirt, but it didn't help much. Bishop wove between cars, getting closer. Piedmont fired another two shots just as a man got out of his car. The top of the man's head exploded, and he dropped to the pavement.

Bishop stopped and rested his arms over the top of a Ford sedan for support and unleashed seven rounds toward the cab of the truck.

Piedmont had just braced himself for firing another salvo in Bishop's direction when four bullets tore into his chest and lower jaw. He slumped, and his grip on the door frame loosened. But, instead of falling back into the cab, Piedmont used the last of his strength to slowly lower himself gently into the seat beside McFadden. He couldn't breathe; blood poured down his throat, suffocating him. He struggled to recover, but he was too weak. He released his grip on the frame and rolled his head just as McFadden's hand reached for the laptop computer. A final smile crossed Piedmont's lips. The old man would finish it.

————

The whole thing looked like a disaster movie to Bishop. People either screaming and running away or just sitting behind the wheel, frozen into inaction. The smart ones were hightailing it. Bishop held the pistol in a two-hand grip, keeping it trained on the cab door as he approached the truck from the rear. His damaged arm shook with pain, but pain wasn't a stranger to Bishop—*I am Delta*. He knew he'd hit Piedmont, but was he down for the count? Bishop stood on top of a nearby car's hood, waiting for a target to appear from the passenger door. The bomb truck's rear wheels hovered over the top of a silver

BMW convertible. Long brown hair covered in blood hid the face of the crushed driver.

It wasn't until Bishop focused on the truck's door that he discovered the limp leg hanging out. Since it wasn't moving, Bishop decided to take a peek. He jumped to the bridge's small concrete ledge, eying the truck's cab. Part of the ledge had crumbled away, and the rest was cracked and heavily damaged. He laid a hand on the bomb truck to steady himself on the narrow ledge and swung his right foot to catch the edge of the truck's running board.

He needed his right hand to hold on, so he slid the pistol to its holster. His hand, still slippery with blood from his wound, made him fumble the gun, and it dropped into the dark river below. *Damn!* He eased both feet on the running board and gazed toward the open door of the truck. Weapon or no weapon, he still had to stop McFadden.

There was no sound, and the leg hanging out still hadn't moved, so Bishop didn't feel too threatened. When he got closer to the open door, the truck suddenly tilted down toward the river. His extra weight up front had caused the shift. The sound of more concrete crumbling from behind caused him to freeze, looking again at the cold water below. He hung on and prayed it wouldn't topple over. The truck's tilt made him slide down the running board closer to the front cab. He took a quick look inside. Piedmont lay sprawled on his back—his chest covered in red, with his head resting near McFadden's lap.

McFadden struggled with a laptop computer—trying to open the top. Blood poured from his mouth and covered his shirt and hands.

Bishop did a double take. *McFadden was sitting in a truck, about to drop to certain death, with a dead man beside him, and he was trying to open a computer?* At that moment, the top of the laptop swung up, and McFadden spotted Bishop watching. He shot a demonic grin before reaching for the power button.

"No!" Bishop screamed, and dove for the interior of the cab, with the sound of breaking concrete echoing from behind. He grabbed for the computer McFadden held just as the grinding noise of the truck pivoting down and the sickening sound of metal against breaking concrete followed. Bishop lay on his back in the floorboard beside Piedmont and fought McFadden for control of the laptop. McFadden pulled a knife from somewhere and reached down to slash Bishop just as the truck released from its perch.

Their eyes met the second they were airborne. Each read the other's thoughts—we're going to die together.

Because the truck was so heavy in the rear, it didn't tumble the way one might expect. Instead of doing a half-flip and landing on its top, it managed a complete flip before hitting the water sixty-two feet below. Bishop launched off the floorboard with such force he hit the interior roof with his chest and head. The impact knocked his breath out and rang his bell, but he was still conscious. With the passenger door open, cold water gushed into the cab. Bishop managed one quick breath before the dark water enveloped him. Amazingly, the truck's interior lights still shined. McFadden sat lifelessly. His eyes were open, the mouth set in a twisted grin.

Bishop squinted through the murky water, looking for the computer—had to find it. Had McFadden managed in the final seconds to activate the nuke's firing sequence? The truck bumped as it settled to the bottom of the river. *How deep are we?* Bishop's ears popped and chest tightened as he waved his hands back and forth across the floorboard, hoping to feel the laptop. His vision was limited by darkness and the cloudy green water surrounding him. He didn't have much air left and still had to swim to the surface. *Where is it?* At that moment, darkness became daylight. The interior of the truck lit up like the Fourth of July. Bishop understood. The wobbling motion of a searchlight mounted on a helicopter lit the truck's interior like a spotlight.

The small silver outline of the computer shined from the floorboard under McFadden's legs. Just as Bishop reached for it, McFadden's dead hands came to life and grabbed it.

TWENTY-SIX

Cora couldn't help herself. Once the shooting started, she sprinted toward the accident. She didn't know why. There wasn't anything she could do, but she couldn't just sit and wait. She slid to a stop as Bishop jumped on the truck's running board. Steadying her hand on the side of the bridge, she caught her breath as he approached the cab of the bomb truck.

Keeping him in sight, she eased closer as sirens blared in the distance. The lights of two helicopters heading her way gave hope of rescue. Cora waved her arms at the approaching aircraft. It was over—thank God. At that instance, Bishop screamed, "No!"

Cora cut her gaze back to the bomb truck just as it tilted down toward the river. She rushed toward it. The crumbling concrete and grinding metal signaled the end. She screamed, and her legs weakened as the thing slid over the side. A helicopter hovered, and six men dressed in black, wearing helmets and goggles, rappelled to the bridge. The second chopper swung over the river, its searchlight sweeping the dark water.

Cora rushed to the spot where the truck rolled off. Air bubbles rose to the surface. She stopped breathing, watching the water. Time must have also stopped. She didn't know if it had been a minute or five minutes before she snapped her head back as a strange object rose out of the water. It looked like a slim, silver box of some kind. Because she was looking straight down, it took her a moment to realize a hand was holding the box. When Bishop's head and shoulders broke the surface, she put her palm over her mouth. Tears filled her eyes, and her lips quivered. It was no use—she was going to cry.

TWENTY-SEVEN

Bishop relaxed on the chaise lounge and chewed the last small cubes of ice from his gin and tonic. He buttoned the top button on the cotton pullover sweater against the cool breeze coming off the water. He never tired of this place. Growing up as a military brat, he'd spent his high school years here in Bermuda. His dad had been in charge of the intelligence group at the US Air Naval Base. Of all the places he'd lived outside the US, this felt the most like home. The sights, smells, and familiar sounds lulled him into a contented stupor. This late in the season, most tourists were already gone. The roads were less crowed, and restaurants were easier to access.

The lights from Hamilton sparkled like bright jewels across the dark harbor, and a faint whiff of oleander mixed with hibiscus drifted in the wind. This is where he'd wanted to be for the last month.

The last two weeks of debriefings, reports, and meetings had made Bishop even more restless—he needed to get away for a while. Tree frogs croaked somewhere in the darkness before the deep growl of the diesel engine of the last ferry pulling away from the Salt Kettle Wharf drowned them out.

In the final struggle between him and McFadden in the submerged bomb truck, Bishop had snatched the computer from McFadden's death grip and pushed his way out of the flooded cab—leaving the old man still struggling to wedge himself free from behind the steering wheel. The nuke was recovered that night. McFadden and the truck were brought up from his watery grave the next day. The only loose end was Newman Smith. The sneaky little weasel had somehow evaded capture. No one knew where he'd gone. Everyone figured he'd slipped the police net and was probably outside the country by now. Bishop couldn't care less.

Bishop never heard the stealthy, silent footsteps cross the soft, damp grass behind him. He didn't see the shadow approaching with the object in its hand before it was too late. He jumped, and it came as a complete surprise as Cora swung a fresh gin and tonic over his shoulder—the fastest drink refill in history.

"You're becoming a first-rate bartender," he said, pulling her into the chair beside him. She smelled good, like the first day they'd met on Gallinas Peak.

She rested her head on his shoulder and cuddled closer. "While I was inside, your cell rang—I answered it."

Bishop tensed. "Oh, yeah?"

She looked up. "Maxwell called. They nabbed Smith trying to cross into Mexico earlier today."

Bishop didn't answer, just sipped the drink and stared into the distance before setting the glass on the table beside his chair.

She ran her warm hand under his sweater and massaged his chest, and he pulled her closer. "Maxwell said the White House ceremony went well—everyone got medals and commendations—Carpenter is the hero of the day. The President asked about you, and General Cook lied. Said you were still on medical leave."

He pulled her still closer still and nibbled her earlobe. "Good," he whispered.

"Maxwell said Cook's still a little pissed you didn't make it."

Bishop remained silent. It was useless attending those things. He had more awards, medals, and commendations than he knew what to do with, all done in secret. Because of Delta's and P2OG's classified missions, it wasn't possible to have public ceremonies, which Bishop would have hated even more. More often than not, Cook gave him a verbal "well done" and slipped the new award paperwork discreetly into Bishop's top-secret personnel folder as Bishop looked on. Besides, Fuller, politician that he was, didn't need any extra people to diminish his presence, probably front and center for all photos and press briefings. The only criticism as to Bishop's conduct during the operation came from Andy in the lab. He was still upset Bishop had again lost a precious, expensive toy—the nuclear watch.

Cora wrapped her arms around his middle under the sweater and hugged him. In a voice laced with playful sarcasm, she asked, "So, today you snubbed the president, refused recognition for saving the capital, and aggravated your boss. What are your plans for tomorrow?"

Bishop remained silent for another moment, his stare fixed on the harbor and vast ocean beyond. "I think maybe tomorrow I'll dive the wreck of the Cristobal Colon."

If you enjoyed this story and would like to read more:

- Leave a review on your favorite book site
- Tell a friend about the book and Larry Enmon
- Ask your local library to put Larry Enmon's work on the shelf
- Recommend Fawkes Press books to your local bookstore

Great readers make great books possible!

ACKNOWLEDGMENTS

I wish to thank my beta readers for taking the time to peruse the original manuscript. Daryle McGinnis, Robert Sawyer, and Sam Simon, you were spot on as usual. Your recommendations and suggestions for improving the story were much appreciated.

And other thanks to my editor, Twyla Beth Lambert, for her efforts in making a good story even better.

Thank you, DFW Writer's Workshop members, for the hours of helpful critiques you provided. I very much appreciate my proofers, Mary Culver, Terri Lacher, Ann Barnhart, and Brian Tracey, for catching all those pesky typos the rest of us missed.

And, as always, Jodi Thompson and Fawkes Press, for believing in the book and seeing it through to publishing.